The Resistance of Anna and Magdalena

The Resistance of Anna and Magdalena

CHRISTOPHER WARD

The Minos Press

Published by The Minos Press, Cambridge, England, 2024

www.minospress.co.uk

Copyright © 2024 Christopher Ward

All rights reserved

ISBN: 978-1-7396322-1-2

For my beloved Isabelle Ruth

The main characters

The young women

    Annie (Anna-Elisa Schneider), an eighteen-year-old lycéenne

    Maddie (Magdalena Grandidier de Vernay), Annie's blood sister, also an eighteen-year-old lycéenne

    Verónica, Spanish refugee, cousin of Maddie and also an eighteen-year-old lycéenne

The young men

    Maurice, also Maddie's cousin, a slightly dodgy art dealer

    Eric, Maddie's brother, pilot in the French Air Force

    Franck, Annie's brother, conscript in the French army

The other main characters

    Julius Schneider, Prof at the prestigious Collège de France, famous economist, father of Franck, Annie and Pauli

    Pauli, six-year-old brother of Annie, bane of her life

    Otto von Sternberg, German officer, censor

    The Old Bat, Prune Face, concierge in the Schneiders' building

PART ONE: THE FALL OF FRANCE
JUNE 1940

The Three Young Men: Eric, Maurice, Franck

Eric

Eric, pilot in the French Air Force, tries to escape the German advance

That fat *con* Dupuy is just standing there like a stuffed capon. Eric pulls back the canopy and leans out of the cockpit.

'*Emmène, Dupuy! Eloigne*! Chocks away, you *putain de salaud*!'

Dupuy does not take this well. He turns his back and waddles his bulk away towards the hangar. His shoulders are drooping, have been ever since early morning when the news came through.

The news that the Old Codger, the Marshall Pétain, had thrown in the towel, capitulated to the Boche without condition. Lay down your arms, get on your knees and kiss their arse.

'*Tu lèches leur cul, ils chient sur toi,*' Eric had said. War service roughened your language. *You lick their arse and they shit all over you.*

Well not over him. Never over him.

Eric clambers out of the cockpit onto that beautiful elliptical wing. It's a piece of art all by itself, this wing, although Eric knows full well that it was cribbed from RJ Mitchell's design for the English Spitfire.

The thing is, Eric knows the Boche are after this plane, it's the prototype Potez 230, the nippy little hope of the French Air Force. They say it can outfly the ME109 (athough this is sadly untrue, the Messerschmidt, Eric knows, can do 400 mph at height against the Potez's 350 max). They say it can outshoot the Focke-Wulf (again untrue, the Potez has just a single cannon, no match for the *four* big ones on the

Focke-Wulf). But still the Boche are after the specs of the Potez. Eric knows for a fact that they particularly want the integral wing torsion box. It's an intriguing techy marvel.

So that is why, now the Hun has marched into Paris, Eric took the little Potez and flew away. After all, Villacoublay, where he had been test-flying it, was almost on the outskirts of Paris.

Eric has made it without incident about as far as you can go and still be in France. He has flown the little silver kite almost to the tip of Brittany. He has landed at a civil aerodrome just outside Morlaix.

But Brittany is hardly a safe haven. Dupuy arrived yesterday in the tender with tales of woe, bringing with him all the design drawings and what spare parts he had been able to cram into the truck. The two-hundred-mile journey took him four days, the roads clogged with craven civilian refugees fleeing Paris. The army, of course, was nowhere to be seen. They had followed the government's example and simply run away.

But even if the government has fled, Eric considers that there is still a war on. Didn't that stern, what's his name, that Colonel de Gaulle broadcast the other night – *Resist, French men and women, resist!*

So Eric has considered his options. At top flying speed, the little Potez might just be able to outfly whatever the Hun has to offer locally, provided he gets a good start over them. And with a range of a couple of hundred miles, he could perhaps get over to, say, Cornwall.

So that's the plan. Last evening, he got Dupuy to make a bonfire of all the design docs and he himself has knocked the spares about such that the Boche will be able to make nothing whatever of them. All that is required now is for that *salaud* Dupuy to yank away the fucking chocks.

Well, Dupuy is over by the hangar now and he has an obstreperous set to his shoulders. He hasn't said anything but he is plainly not going to cooperate, not now the Old Codger has wagged the white flag.

So needs must. Eric jumps down from the curve of the wing onto the tarmac, where he tugs at the chock ropes. The chocks come away and the plane wobbles a little, almost starts to run forward. Eric hauls himself back up onto the wing and hops into the cabin. He pulls the canopy over tight and revs the engine. Thank God it's the big Hispano-Suiza V12 version, nearly 700 horsepower and incredibly much more reliable than the feeble affair they put on the old version. That geriatric old Potez 190 was total *bidon*. The engine would cut out without notice and its wings were so slim you'd be lucky to get a glide back to the aerodrome.

Eric taxis the plane onto the runway. He looks back towards the hangar where Dupuy is now skulking. He doesn't turn on the radio. Anyway, the conning tower is empty, the entire staff of the aerodrome decamped in the night.

The Hispano-Suiza engine is turning over with a reliably throaty sound to it. He checks all the instruments, twice. Good to go.

Only thing is, the fuel gauge, which shows half empty. Dupuy had said that was all there was. Probably the rest had already gone onto the black market.

Or maybe that little *pute* was lying. The Hun should give him a medal for his war effort.

So with a hope and a prayer, Eric checks the wind sock and yanks himself up to peer over the engine cowling at the runway. Which is clear, except for a black cat about fifty yards ahead. The cat is carefully washing its paws.

Eric draws back the throttle and waits. He looks back

towards the hangar where he can see Dupuy on the telephone. Eric reckons he is probably not calling home.

He gives it a minute more and then hauls himself up again and looks over the cowling down the runway. The cat has completed its *toilette*. It is strolling into the rough grass beside the runway. Time to go.

He checks everything again, then clamps on the earphones, tightens his belt and opens the throttle full. The noise is incredible, the Hispano-Suiza roaring like a pride of enraged lions. Despite the earphones, the racket still splits his ears.

He takes off to the south. When he's up and away, he swings the crate around to head north west which is where his chart tells him Cornwall lies. There's a headwind now but he lives in hope.

The sky is the azure of the Breton early summer, deepening to ultramarine where the land meets the sea. The noonday sun shines on the little plane. The silver wings sparkle. Eric climbs to two thousand feet, keeping the throttle open to full power. He needs speed and height to avoid patrols but he needs to stay low enough while over land so as not to give too much notice of his presence.

He doesn't see the ME110, the twin-engine *Destroyer*, that is flying back from a surveillance visit to Concarneau. It has been checking that the French fleet is skiving in port as was promised to Hitler by that superannuated old mummy, the octogenarian Pétain. It is just bad luck that the big, slow Messerschmidt should be above and behind him, in one of the blind spots of the little Potez, and that the ME110 should be descending and gathering speed. It is this which allows its pilot to take a fairly accurate bead on Eric and to fire off both his cannon with a fair hope of a hit.

Eric hears nothing above the din of the engine and the

wind rushing by but he feels a slight loss of control. He looks along the smooth and gleaming wings, first to port, all clear, and then to starboard. Which is where he sees that something has ripped at the trailing edge flap. Just a nick but the Potez begins to wobble alarmingly.

Maurice

Maurice watches the Germans entering Paris

I saw that evil, Maurice writes in his diary that night. I saw it entering Paris. I saw the funereal pomp of the dark tanks rattling slowly and solemnly over the cobbled roadway. I saw the Panzer soldiers standing with ceremonial stiffness in the turrets of their tanks, wooden and unsmiling. It was a fantastic act to celebrate their triumph, *riding in triumph through Paris.*

Paris tried to hide her eyes. The shutters of the windows were closed, all of them, in the hope that it was not true. The sun blazed on the empty streets.

But each tank, each truck bore the great symbol of their triumph – the burning red flags with the white circle and the black spider in the middle. Indolently they passed us, indolently those flags flapped in the hot breeze.

I leaned against a doorway and wept.

Franck

Franck was called up into the French army and was captured on the River Meuse when the German Panzer corps burst out of the Ardennes Forest.

Franck is writing to his sister Annie from a Stalag somewhere in Silesia. Annie has asked him in her first letter to him about how he was captured.

Dearest Anna, *la plus belle soeur du monde*,
How are you and how is everything with Papa and Pauli? How is dear Maddie and the lovely Verónica? What news on Eric? How is the Old Bat? Have you been to Mamma's grave? Put some flowers from me – I think of her every day, every hour.

You ask how I was captured. It's almost too dreary to speak of. After all I was just one among the five million who marched away without a thought. Three times, you remember, three times we were called up in '39, and then it was almost a year of *la guerre morte* before we saw any action. And when it came it was a squib. One minute we were sitting tight in our blockhouse along the Meuse drinking wine and eating a good cheese and bread, the next the lieutenant looked out through the slit and there were the Boches driving their tanks onto rafts and floating them across the river. They were a couple of hundred metres away, well within shooting range. We grabbed our rifles but the lieutenant held up his hand.

'It seems we have lost,' he said. 'Why get ourselves killed for nothing?'

Anyway, we tried to raise the captain on the radio but he and everyone else at staff had piked off in the night, so we tied a white handkerchief onto the barrel of Didier's rifle, shoved it out of the slit and wagged it about. At first the

Boches were too busy loading the tanks. They didn't even look our way. Then one of them saw us and raised his hand in a sort of salute. Almost affectionate it looked, almost comradely.

We saw him going over to tell his officer but the officer just glanced at us and then turned away. He evidently told the mec who had seen us to get back to work as the bloke went across on the next raft and we didn't see him again. Eventually – and it took about two hours, during which we were really and truly shitting ourselves (darling, excuse my English) – the whole troop and a couple of dozen tanks were across. Only then did the officer, an *oberleutnant*, come over with a corporal and a couple of ORs. We thought that we were for it. That they would probably just lob a grenade into our pill box and have done with it. We would have done just that, if it had been the other way around.

But no, the corporal peered in at us and called out *Raus!* So we all filed out, feeling relieved but pretty sheepish and not at all valorous.

The *oberleutnant* was a very smart young man and he spoke good French. He told us to pile our arms in a heap.

'Sadly,' he said, 'I cannot take you as prisoners right now as I am pretty tied up, with the invasion and everything.'

But he got his corporal to dish out certificates saying we were now officially PoWs, and we were supposed to head to some camp where they would check us in.

By then, some more Panzers were rolling down the road.

'*Bon courage,*' the lieutenant said. They strode off and went back to getting the tanks across and pretty smart work they made of it.

Well, we had no idea what to do. Our lieutenant told us to wait a few minutes while he went to check. And did he come back? Not likely! Gillevic the Breton went off to find him. After a few minutes Gillevic came back and said he'd seen the lieutenant. He was nicking a bicycle from a farm up the road. Gillevic called out to him but the bastard just got on the bike and pedalled off for dear life.

We started wandering off in groups of twos and threes. We had no idea about this camp, where it was or anything. So with some others I went into town. And who should we see outside the bistro drinking wine but our bloody lieutenant. When he spotted us, he jumped up and legged it.

So we went to the bistro ourselves. We'd just been paid and were flush. We ordered a round.

Pretty soon we fell to cursing, not the Boches but the bloody French. Everybody grumbled *We've been sold, that pute Pétain, that pute Laval, all the forking putes who landed us in this merde.* It was all conspiracy, all betrayal.

We bought round after round and drank like fish and we were all shouting at the same time. The radio was on loud in the bistro and the news came through that the Old Gaffer had set up in Vichy and the deputies were meeting in the casino. The casino! That raised a good laugh. But then the socialists came on, and we were mainly socialists, we heard our own Spinasse. 'We must break with the illusions of the past. We believed in individual liberty, in man's independence. This was in anticipation of a future beyond our reach…'

We all shed tears when we heard this and spat in the mud. And then, the announcer said, Laval 'thanked the speakers in a few words full of emotion'.

Our words, too, were few. Oh là là, said Gillevic. The rest of us were stupefied and speechless.

And then the Boche trucks rolled into town, full of grinning soldiers, and it was all up with us. A couple of elderly Fritzes were detailed to see us to the camp.

So you see, ma belle, that we shall not bare our arms and show our scars and say what deeds we did that day. *Come off it*, as our English cousins would say.

It is all so banal, so dreadfully banal.

Darling, write to me something beautiful. You see how coarse I have become, a regular *poilu*. My life is coarse and I am coarse in it. Write me something that will give me hope that all is not lost forever and that one day we shall be again as we were before. Write to me about yourself and about Maddie and the pouting little Verónica. Perhaps you will tell me that you three played the Brahms trio, so that I may have a picture of you, Verónica's slim silver fingers on the keyboard, and Maddie's bare shining arms moving in the warm light of evening, and you, my little Anschli, you my princess and my love.

I long for you and your letters.

Je t'embrasse.

Franck

PART TWO: PARIS 1941
The three young women: Annie, Maddie, Verónica

1

The drum rolls and we girls troop out through the broad stone portal of the Lycée Condorcet into the courtyard. It's supposed to be spring, *Paris in the spring, my dear*. I can just smell it wafting in the air, the first scent of sap pushing up somewhere, against the odds. But not here. Within these high dead walls, it's sunless and bloody cold.

I see it's Maddie who's banging on the drum, Maddie my blood sister. I'd forgotten they made her drum monitor this term. It was either that or kick her out.

She's doing her stuff, beating as hard as she can on the old kettle drum. It's bringing a nice flush to her usual pale watery look. Then a wicked gust of wind scours the dark yard and her flaming hair flies out behind her. She's got her untamed look on.

We crowd into the yard and start to form up. It's the first day of the spring term and we are all chafing. Here we are again, back in our sky-blue *tabliers*, with our names stitched across our bosoms. We are waiting, as always, just waiting for so much, waiting for everything. Like just now we are waiting for the sun to climb above the stone walls of this old dump.

The forming up is utter chaos and takes forever, hundreds and hundreds of us, all jostling into lines and rows. Typical! We top girls, we seventeen- and eighteen-year-olds who are in *première*, shuffle thankfully to the back. We shove the little ones to the front where they'll be under the full glare of the basilisk eye of Mlle Bazin, our headmistress.

We get our backs right up against the north wall. From here we face the noble elevation of the south side with its arcades and arches. And above there is the bright horizon of the roof where the sun will rise. Eventually.

Now I turn and crane my neck and look above me. Already, high up on the blank north wall at my back, there is a bar of sunshine stroking the grey stone, coaxing it into life.

Out front, in the danger zone, a couple of new kids are wandering about uncertainly. They're juniors, barely more than tykes, about two feet tall. If the monitors catch them out of line, they'll be for it.

But help is at hand in the shape of Verónica who, late as ever, saunters out of the portal, insouciant as the Infanta of Castile. Her pinafore is rumpled. From here it even looks a bit grubby but she wears it like a robe of state, shoulders back, head erect. Her hair is in her Maenad mode, her bright black tresses flying out and furling over her shoulders like thick hanks of yarn. She's more pale and skinny looking than ever. Her clothes are literally hanging off her.

She looks around and frowns, muttering something to herself, then meanders forward and takes the two little kids by the hand and shows them where they can get in with the other littleys in their year. Then, still dawdling, still frowning, she heads towards me at where I've wedged myself into the back row right up against the wall.

'*Hola querida!*' she says. Hallo, my dear.

I hug her and kiss her. She's always been slim as a wand but now she's just bone.

'Get in here,' I say. making space for her between me and Natalie Tardieu. She pushes in. Her shoulder bone digs into me.

'Leave some space for Maddie,' I say.

Verónica pushes Natalie Tardieu up a bit so there'll be space. Natalie shoves her back but for all her slight look, Verónica is as tough as a polecat and Natalie gives way, scowling all over her fat face.

The drum rolls on and la Bazin appears with her band of grim spinsters. They line up before us on the low dais against the grey south wall. Their expressions are bleak and fixed, like you see in old sepia tint photographs. At a sign from la Bazin, Maddie stops rolling, puts down the drum and strides over to us.

'Budge up, Annie dearest,' she says. I try to give her a hug but she holds me away by my shoulders and bends down and kisses me full on the mouth. She smells of lily of the valley and her lips are as soft as satin. She gives Verónica the *bises* and pushes in on the other side of me.

'When did you get back?' I whisper this because la Bazin's eyes and ears are swivelling. The action is about to begin.

I haven't seen Maddie once these Easter holidays. She's been at one of their other houses, the one at Dinard, I think, the one that's right there on the beach, naturally.

La Bazin now makes a sort of conjuring motion with her manly hand and the singing starts up, so Maddie just mouths her answer which looks like *Yesterday*.

Je suis là, Maréchal…, we sing. *I'm here, Marshall…*

Maddie, Magdalena Grandidier de Vernay. She leans into me. I can feel her warmth.

It's a family that's pure creaky Old France, one thousand per cent fusty Old High Catholic. They're wicked Closet Monarchists and Anti-Republicans through and through, the very acme of the Two Hundred Families who have had their hand on the neck of France – and in the till – since the days of Pepin le Bref. Of course they are all big supporters of The Marshall, *le Maréchal Pétain.*

So quite how Maddie comes to be such a nihilist is a puzzle to us all. Just now she's leaning harder into me, pushing me just for the hell of it or the love of it or something. I pass it on to Verónica who shoves up against Natalie Tardieu. That plump wet lets out a squeal and shoves her back.

Je suis là, Maréchal...

Maddie tires of pushing and starts to sing the hymn in an affected corncrake voice. I don't even try. I open and close my mouth like a gasping halibut and raise my eyes to where they say Heaven used to be. Far above the sheer walls of the inner courtyard of the Lycée Condorcet I can see a square of blue, the fair blue sky of early spring.

As always, all the girls are making a massive effort to sing out of tune. Not because we're Gaullists or terrorist-sympathisers or anything like that or even anti-Pétain but because we're teenage girls, just bloody-minded. Our din even drowns out the powerful tenor of la Bazin and her squad of female bass-baritones.

Before the Fall, we used to hoist the Tricolor and sing the Marseillaise but they've put a stop to all that. Now we just have Maddie on drums and this stupid stupid song.

Je suis là, Maréchal...

For what? For why? *Le vieux, le Maréchal, the Old Gentleman,* the mec who's already cancelled off all that previous stuff about liberty, equality and fraternity and so on and so forth, which was probably crap and certainly I never bought the Revolution, all that blood and off with his head, but at least it sounded somehow more hopeful than the slogans they're pushing now, the *Fatherland, Duty, Family,* which seems somehow more limiting, at least for the half of us who happen not to be men.

So where was Heaven exactly, before the Fall? I peer and

peer into the blue. At last I see one bird which flies diagonally across the azure square, heading out.

As we get into the fourth verse of *Je suis là*, Verónica decides to rev it up a bit. She bores easily. She starts a descant in her sweet soprano voice. La Bazin turns a sour eye on her but there's nothing much she can do in the middle of the song. Anyway, Verónica's decorative variations have a rather nice effect on the plodding melody.

Maddie prods me hard in the ribs.

'Pouf, what?'

She leans over and breathes in my ear

'That's her!'

'Who?'

'The New Woman!'

'Who's that?'

Maddie puffs out through her lips.

'The Beaver, you idiot.'

My eye searches along the line of beaks who are stacked up on the dais belting out *Je suis là, Maréchal...* And there she is, the New Woman, the Beaver. I'd sort of forgotten about her

It is actually not all that hard to pick her out from the dowdy line-up as she is the only one under eighty-five. She has to be that short plump one, the youngish one with the untidy hair and the quite pretty face, or *jolie laide* at least. The only one that's not singing *Je suis là* with craven gusto. She's got a red angora sweater on and a really tight skirt that's clings unfashionably to her hips. She's sporting a long skein of blue beads that comes right down her front. On her head sits an orange turban, these are all the rage now that women can't afford their *coiffeur*. She's definitely Bohemian, a real Boho. Yes, this must be the Beaver.

Maddie nudges me again to pass it on, so I put my mouth

up to Verónica's ear.

'That's Mlle de Beauvoir. Our new philo beak.'

Verónica looks towards the dais, The Beaver is not hard to pick out.

'That one? She looks a real goer, anyway.'

'You'd know,' I whisper, unfairly, and Verónica kicks me quite hard on my calf. It is unfair, because she's only had sex once and that was with a *poilu* she met on the train. He was on his way to the front and they did it there and then, in the railway carriage, between Bordeaux and Angers. She didn't like to turn him down. Of course she comes in for a fair share of friendly flak but she doesn't mind that much. On this, as on most things, she doesn't really give a damn.

So this is the Beaver then! During the holidays, Maddie sent me a postcard all about her, written in her aristo scrawl – and yes it was posh Dinard where she'd been because that was where the postcard was of, posh girls on an endless beach. When I at last deciphered her handwriting, I understood that M. Kahn our philo teacher had got the sack for being Jewish, and that this Beaver was being drafted in. Handily, she comes complete with her nickname, Beauvoir, Beaver…

'What do you think it was?' Maddie breathes hot into my ear.

'Hard to tell just from the look of her.'

In the postcard, Maddie had written *Miss Beaver expelled from last school for corrupting a minor. Details are lacking. I am agog.*

Anyway at this point, *Je suis là* finally ends or more accurately fades away. Verónica's last high note is left ringing in our ears. Mme Bazin steps forward, adjusts her pince-nez and barks out 'Welcome, girls, to the new term'. She then dismisses the assembly. Except us. *Première to stay behind.*

***

'I'm freezing,' Verónica says 'and I'm starving. I think I'm going to faint.'

She leans back against the grubby wall of the courtyard and puts her hands on her super-flat stomach. Actually, it's more concave than flat. In general, she looks like death warmed up. As la Bazin approaches us with strides of nearly military length, Verónica calls out,

'Please Miss, may I be excused?'

'No, Hidalgo, you may not' is Mlle Bazin's idea of a kindly reply. 'And have the courtesy to stand up straight and shoulders back when I am speaking to you.'

Verónica pouts and makes the effort. She straightens up, swaying slightly. She's always been a skinny little thing but now she has a definitely wasted look. It's a bit the same for me. I'm becoming a waif. You wouldn't know me now for the sturdy tomboy of two years back.

We're all J3's of course – *Adolescent Females* – so in theory we get enough on the ration to at least stay alive. But then I give loads of my stuff to my kid brother Pauli who is always ravenous, and even to Paco, my dead Mama's old dog who would eat the furniture if I didn't give him some of my meagre meat ration. Verónica must be giving food away to someone too. I suspect the wicked Dad.

I whisper to her

'Are you OK?'

'Nope,' she says. 'Things are a bit tight *chez nous* just now…'

Anna-Elisa Schneider, Verónica Hidalgo, taisez-vous!

Mlle Bazin barks at us and we shut up. Then she starts to address us. She's been a teacher so long that she has no way of talking other than as if she's doing a public address. Her pince-nez are clipped tight above the large lobes of her fleshy nose. Her grey hair is scraped back into a severe chignon. It all cries out spinster, schoolmistress, *dried up old virgin*. Shudder.

She says,

'Only yesterday, girls, I have had the news. The very best of news.'

Unexcited, we wait.

'Yes, girls, indeed the best of news. I learned that soon we will be privileged to receive here amongst us the Head of State…'

She pauses. There is a small gasp from down the line. I think it's that toady Natalie Tardieu. Someone claps but no one joins in and it quickly peters out.

'Yes, girls, our dear Maréchal has asked to see examples of excellence in education in the new France, in the France of the National Revolution. Particularly the education of girls, our future wives and mothers. And our governors have proposed our school, the Lycée Condorcet. This is such a privilege. We must prepare well, very well.'

Verónica grabs hold of my arm and clings on. She stoops. She looks like sick.

'Miss, please…' I appeal to la Bazin but she ignores me. She is saying,

'…so you will form a choir to sing a hymn in honour of the Marshall who has sacrificed himself to the redemption of defeated France…'

I am actually holding Verónica up right now. I look round her at Natalie Tardieu on her other side for help but Natalie has on her face the look of a saint in rapture and pays me no attention. I turn to Maddie but she is glaring at la Bazin. She shouts out,

'Marshall Pétain as our perfect sacrifice! Like Christ, you mean?'

With Maddie you have to know she is a hot Catholic, and fierce with it.

La Bazin hesitates, her granite lips part slightly. But she is not here to debate Christology. She whips a folded paper from the pocket of her skirt.

'Now, girls,' she says, 'here is the hymn you are to sing. It is a new one, specially composed.'

> ...Maréchal, Maréchal,
> Envoy from God
> To save beloved France
> O you whose age
> Matches in its nobility
> The youthfulness of Joan of Arc

'Jesus Christ!' says Maddie loudly. She shakes her head violently and her flaming hair swirls across her shoulders. There is a dab of colour in her pure white cheeks.

'And you, Magdalena, you are from the best of families and so you will be required to lead the group.'

Verónica actually slumps against me now. Fortunately, although I may be on the short side, I am definitely strong and this girl is so very light and slender. She looks at me with her bright mouse eyes and makes a mouth like she wants to throw up. With this diversion I don't follow la Bazin's abrupt *paso doble* turn.

'...three thousand bastards...'

I prick up my ears. We're thirty or so in *Première* and we're all listening now.

The three thousand bastards turn out to be last month's tally of new-borns who are the fruit of Franco-German couplings.

'...I will not hear of any girl from this school consorting

with a German,' says la Bazin. 'Do not even speak to a German, unless it is essential. And should any girl...'

Sadly, her only penalty is expulsion, and who cares about that? Most of us would clap our hands.

Maddie whispers in my ear,

'Fat chance, anyway. I haven't had a period for months.'

'Nor me,' I say.

'Nor me,' whispers Verónica and slides to the ground in a dead faint.

'*Qu'elle mange de la brioche!*' Maddie is imperious. 'Brioche and coffee...'

So off we set, walking Verónica between us, arm in arm. The girl not only looks pale like sick, she *is* sick. At least, she tries, bending over and dry retching while we hold her up. We half-drag her out through the sacred north entrance of the school where only teachers may go in and out. The old porter Chupin gives us a leery look. He's supposed to stop us but Maddie has plenty of dirt on him and he looks the other way.

Half carrying Verónica, we lurch our way down the rue de l'Odéon to the Café des Artisans. This dive is totally out of bounds but Maddie has clout here and sometimes brings us after school. Now she enters like a queen regnant. Monsieur Gaston, the old grey beard who runs it, dashes out from the back and shakes her hand with a good deal of grinning through a large gap in his teeth and mouthing welcomes in his thick Normandy accent. He is one of a myriad old de Vernay retainers, lodged in an outer filament of the vast web of patronage the de Vernays have spun across France. Maddie is incensed by such feudalism and also exploits it without shame, like now.

'M. Gaston, brioche, coffee, piping hot, if you please.'

We sit Verónica down and M. Gaston brings thick slices of brioche and conserves and a pot of coffee, real coffee. Maddie doesn't say thank you. She just asks for water. Where on earth the old man has found the sugar and the butter to make the brioche and where oh where the real coffee can have come from – these are deep questions which I don't ask. We just fall on the brioche and gulp down the coffee which is truly hot and heavenly, like a food and a drug all in one. Verónica crams brioche into her mouth with both hands and gulps down water and coffee by turns. I rub her arms and pinch her cheeks and little by little she begins to look almost human.

'So!' says Maddie.

'So?'

'So here's the plan. We learn the song and Verónica does the descant. Then we shoot the Old Gaffer.'

We get back to school half way through Greek. Mlle Georgette looks stern and wants to report us. Georgie is our used up old Classics teacher whose heyday was a hundred years ago when she published her *Grammar of the Ionic Dialect* and was the toast of the *Faculté des Lettres*. However, Maddie tells her we were on an errand for la Bazin to prepare for the visit of the Marshall.

As Georgie is afraid of Maddie she just flicks her hand at the empty desks at the back and carries on with her lesson which is a page from Book VI of Herodotus. A man called Hippokleides gets tight at his own wedding, and does a turn, standing on his head on the top table and bicycling his legs. His father-in-law says 'Hippokleides, you have danced away your marriage'.

Normally I love this random stuff. The Greeks have a bit of life about them and Herodotus tells the most fantastic yarns. They're like the *faits divers* in the newspaper. The mother who had twins, one black and one white, the two-headed calf, that sort of thing. But how can I pay attention today, after what Maddie just said? She's crazy! So I am completely unready when suddenly there is Mlle Georgette looming over me and pouncing.

'Anna-Elisa Schneider, kindly translate. *Ou phrontis Hippokleidei*. What does Hippokleides reply to his father-in-law?'

I recoil. Georgie reeks of old woman, dried up sap. I know she's picking on me because she's afraid to get at Maddie. I'm fair game, brown little foreigner.

'Err.' We're supposed to have read all of Book VI over the holidays. Georgie gives me a rap on the knuckles with her ruler, tyrannical crone that she is. It really hurts and I think *Maybe we should shoot her instead*!

She turns away and bears her narrow spinster's bottom in its thick plaid skirtings up towards her desk.

'I am waiting, Schneider, I am waiting.'

But while her back is turned, Maddie passes me a slip of paper. I call out,

'*Ou phrontis Hippokleidei*... Hippokleides doesn't care.'

While we are pondering the real meaning of this subversive story, the bell rings and Mlle Georgette dismisses us.

And now for Philo. Now for the Beaver.

We throng into the philo room but she is not there. She has been there, quite recently, it seems because there is the lingering smell of filthy gaspers, and we see an opened packet of cheap *Boyards* ciggies lying on the desk.

I plump down and Maddie gets the desk behind me. I turn back to her and say in a low voice,

'So what does it mean 'corrupting minors'?'

Maddie has some information about this.

'*Une sale bonne femme qui court après les petites filles,*' she says. A dirty old woman running after young girls.

'Erk.'

'I met a girl in Dinard who was taught by the Beaver at her last school. Apparently she goes for *fruit vert, absolument fruit vert*, unripe fruit.'

'What does that mean?'

Maddie does a *moue* and lifts her eyes to the heavens. Despite being a Catholic virgin, she is super-knowledgeable about sex.

'Wake up, little one. This girl Bianca said the Beaver finds virgin girls mysterious. She has a *keen taste for their bodies*.'

'You've got to be making this up.'

Maddie laughs.

'Nope. Just reporting what Bianca said.'

'Good God! Is that why Beaver was thrown out?'

'Probably. Bianca said she grooms the chosen one and then betrays her.'

Maddie makes her eyes go huge in mock terror and she flicks her flaming mop to the other shoulder.

Sadly this exciting conversation is cut short because the door opens and in comes the wicked Beaver herself.

She walks in, smoking. Now that's against regs. She takes a long puff and throws the gasper on the floor where she stamps on it. Then she walks to the front of the teacher's desk, leans her bottom against it and hoists herself up. Once up, she sits looking at us, swinging her calves back and forth. The calves are on the plump side. She twirls the long skein of blue beads she is sporting. After a couple of twirls she drops the end of the skein down into her lap.

She stares at us, at each of us in turn, so we stare back at her. Her face is quite round. Her cheekbones are high, she looks almost Asiatic. She wears heavy make-up and her lips are red with rouge. She has blue eyes so bright they look amost luminous. She uses these amazing headlamps to look us over. She regards us for a minute, and we regard her.

'Sorry I'm late,' she says at last in a rather grating voice.

This really is a first, a teacher apologizing to us for lateness.

'Yes,' she goes on, 'I had to sign up, forms and that. I even had to sign to say I'm not a Jew.'

'And did you?' Maddie calls out. This is also definitely against regs, you put your hand up. But the Beaver doesn't seem to mind.

'I did. I'm not a Jew. So I signed.'

'Pah!' Maddie exclaims.

'Yes... Grandidier de Vernay...' – here she is reading Maddie's name off the front of her *tablier* – '...Hmm, that's quite a handle... what's your given name?'

Maddie says her name, grudgingly, like she's losing power or something.

'Well, Magdalena, your point?'

'You've taken a Jew's job? M. Kahn was Jewish. He got kicked out.'

'So?'

Maddie wags her head from side to side. We all keep quiet, wanting this to go somewhere. But where?

At last Maddie answers.

'So.'

And the Beaver laughs. It is so unexpected that some of the girls laugh too. But not Maddie.

The Beaver closes her eyes. There is a pause, as silent a pause as a class of schoolgirls can manage. The Beaver just goes on sitting on her desk with her eyes closed and we are left wondering. It's like confronting a dog you don't know.

Will she bite or will she wag her tail?

After a couple of minutes like this, which is almost soothing, she slides off the desk and starts pacing up and down. She picks up a piece of chalk from the ledge beneath the blackboard and tosses it up and down, catching it neatly each time. At last she turns to us and says,

'We can only save ourselves and barely that. I cannot save M. Kahn.'

We all know Maddie will reply. She is too steeped in Catholic stuff on personal responsibility and love your neighbour as yourself. Never will she let that pass. She doesn't.

'You profit from his loss.'

'I do. So do you. You get me to teach you.'

Again the Beaver does a sort of laugh but this time nobody laughs with her. Not that we loved M. Kahn, he wasn't the lovable type but we sense this is not a laughing matter. She paces a bit more. She tosses up the chalk a couple more times and then she lets it fall on the floor where it breaks.

'It was my choice,' she says, 'my authentic choice.'

'And you're not ashamed?'

Good God! Can you actually ask a teacher that?

The Beaver paces again and it is a full minute before she faces us.

'It was my choice. I am responsible for the consequences of my action.'

Maddie is silent. Mlle de Beauvoir clambers back onto the desk and perches there again. She folds one leg across the other and looks around the room.

'Listen. These days we are faced with choices every minute of every day. We are forced literally to think for our lives. And don't say you are constrained. You are always free to choose…'

Maddie puts up her hand, all polite now. I don't think she knows where this is going any more than I do but she's the persevering type.

The Beaver recognizes her. She turns her head slightly as though to listen more carefully.

'Are you sure?' Maddie asks.

'That we are always free to choose? *Pouf*, of course! Nothing is given, *il n'y a pas de fatalité*. We are condemned to be free. And so we can make free choices, and then we are responsible for the consequences. That is the moral point – because all our choices are moral – and the most moral choice is the one with the best consequences.'

'So,' Maddie says, and this time she does not put up her hand, 'suppose I decide that when the Maréchal comes here to the school, the best choice is to kill him because I think otherwise he will go on to do a lot of harm – and that killing him will inspire a million freedom-loving French men and women to believe they can again one day be free...'

'Oh mon Dieu!' The Beaver claps her hands and jumps down from her desk. She starts to pace up and down in front of us. She bumps into the table, she seems a clumsy woman.

'Oh mon Dieu, what a thought! What a thought!'

She continues to pace, saying nothing for a minute. Is this a keynote of her style, pacing and silence? She turns her back on us and looks up at the map of the world which hangs on the wall by the door. This map shows *L'Empire Française* in all its extent and glory. Mlle stretches her arm up and puts her finger on France. From the back, her plump little figure is quite straight up and down. It lacks curves.

She moves her finger across the Empire, tapping one by one on all the colonies, starting with that vast swathe of Africa, from Cap Bon to the hot wet forests of the Congo. Then she taps on Madagascar and the Comoro Islands. Then the finger moves on to Indo-China. From there it moves to touch, but only lightly, on the points of light in the Pacific and the Caribbean.

At last she turns back to us and says,

'Magdalena, make your choices. Make sure they are your own authentic choices. And remember *the blood of others.*'

The bell rings and we all start to move in our benches and put our books away.

Maddie pokes me from behind. I lean back and she mutters in my ear to come round to hers tonight, and then she turns to Verónica who is beside her and tells her to come too.

'Ma and Pa are out at some do. We can play the Schubert. And then we can get smashed. And then we can talk about killing the Old Gaffer.'

'Don't be ridiculous,' I say. 'Anyway, how can I come round on a school night, I've got the shopping to do and dinner to see to and Pauli to put down and Papa to be cared for and the Euripides to prepare for tomorrow and, oh yes, I need some sleep!'

'I'll bell you later,' she says.

I laugh. Our phone's been off for months.

'I'll send you a *pneu*,' she says.

'Alright, send me a *pneu.*'

We go on to my best lesson, English. I am always top in weekly marks in English. English is my mother's tongue. In fact, Mlle Villehardouin, our English beak, is not unafraid of me. Today, she will struggle once again to convince us that *Paradise Lost* is not a sex poem.

2

Well, it seems old Ma Villehardouin has given up on Milton this term although we were just getting to the fruity part. She starts us instead on *King Lear*. I half listen because Shakespeare is great but my mind is on what's next in my crowded, rubbish life.

The second the bell goes, I throw my books into my *cartable* and rush out to collect Pauli. I still arrive late, as always. He's at the *école primaire*, it's a mile from the *lycée* down the rue Claude Bernard and they finish earlier than us. Pauli is sitting on the low stone wall in front of the school, kicking his heels back against the stones.

'*Fais pas ça*,' I say by way of hallo. Doesn't he know that I just spent an entire year's clothing coupons on the new buckle-over sandals he's wearing? These sandals were the latest craze for a while and impossible to get hold of, so all the kids who count for anything had them. So Pauli had to have them.

Actually it turned out it was just a phase, he wanted to join the cool ones and buckle-over sandals were the entry price. Not that it did him any good. By the time we eventually got the sandals, the moving finger of cool had passed on to something so unobtainable that only God's elect could get their hands on it – the Aertex shirt, and this meant real Aertex shirts which disappeared from the shops the minute the Occupation began and now they cost a mint on the black market. So Pauli remains uncool. He just retreats and gets into even more unattractive behaviour. Like now. I'm telling him off but he just pouts at me and goes on kicking.

'*Fais pas ça.*'
'Speak English,' he says.
'What?'

I see that he is holding an envelope in his grubby paw, so I ask for it. It is addressed to Papa and is clearly from Pauli's teacher. I open it. After all, I'm in *loco parentis* most of the time. It is indeed from his form mistress and it asks Papa to look in and talk to her about Pauli. Well, as Papa is never in one million years going to tear his mighty mind away from his papers and his teaching to care one jot about the upbringing of the late lamb he and Mum had in a pathetic attempt to 'save their marriage' – good God, don't they know *anything* about marriage psychology? – I decide that I might as well go right in and get it over with. Pauli protests but doesn't really have any choice but to trot along behind me.

Mlle Fleurette Dupin is at the easel, writing up in chalk tomorrow's lessons. She is at first sight quite a severe-looking body, but I know from all the previous times Pauli has been carpeted that Fleurette's severe aspect is largely because of the granny specs and because she spends all day posing as a disciplinarian in front of a mob of entitled little tykes who would as soon pee on her as learn their ABC.

Up close Fleurette looks actually quite young and not unattractive in a willowy kind of way. She has the most beautiful auburn hair and pale grey eyes which her specs amplify. As this must be at least Pauli's twentieth carpeting, we are actually getting to know each other quite well. She greets me with an earnest sigh and flutters her long dark lashes at me.

'Yes, Fleurette?'

But she wants to be a bit formal. She shakes my hand,

calls me Mademoiselle, and asks me to sit down. She despatches Pauli to his desk, which I notice is right at the back. When I was in primary school, the back row was the Rubbish Dump where the kids just sat all day and did raffia.

I perch on a desk in the front row and she sits down behind her own table and leans forward.

'*Il réfuse!*' she says.

'Refuses what?'

She coughs and adjusts her specs.

'He refuses to speak French.'

'What?'

'For a week now, he refuses to speak in French.'

'What does he speak then?'

'Well, nothing much. He doesn't really say anything. But when he does speak, he speaks in English. Which of course he must know well…'

'Yes, sure.' Our defunct Mama being English.

Fleurette pushes her specs back up her nose with her forefinger and smiles nervously. This softens her look.

'Any idea what's behind all this?'

She shrugs her shoulders.

'We all have our little problems these days. But I thought if you would have a word…'

'Well, I can always try. But isn't it quite good for the other kids, I mean, having another language?'

Fleurette blows a little air from the corner of her thin lips. She has the faintest fuzz above her upper lip, very pale and fine. It's the first time I've noticed it. It makes me think of Lisa in *War & Peace* and I sigh, thinking of romantic death.

'God, no,' she says. 'Not English anyway.'

She comes out from behind her desk. I stand up too, so she is close to me. I can feel the warmth of her slim straight body and I can smell the faint scent that comes off her, mingled chalk and garlic. Up close she looks even younger, her skin is smooth and unlined. The palest freckles dot her cheeks. She seems scarcely older than me.

'I have no tenure,' she says quickly. 'I'm hanging by a thread. Just a jobbing teacher until the men return. And I really need the money. There's Maman and Mémé and my three kid brothers to feed.'

What this has to do with me or Pauli is not clear at first. But then Fleurette says that the ministry is weeding out *'negative elements'*, by which they mean communists, socialists, Gaullists. She mutters,

'If you speak English nowadays, you are compromised.'

We go home by way of the Luxembourg Gardens. It's a long way round but we do it almost every day. Pauli asks for it and I know exactly why. Mama's shade walks in these gardens. She used to bring us here all the time.

Yesterday's spring storm has shaken free the almond blossom, covering the ground in pink petals. Pauli starts scuffling up the gravel on the path. I offer to buy him a drink at the kiosk. He says yes, but goes on scuffling.

'Fais pas ça,' I say.

'Speak English,' he says. So I say in English just what Ma would have said.

'Pick your feet up or I'll smack your botty for you.'

He stops scuffling up the gravel and puts his hand in mine. The sun comes out from behind a cloud of ravishing silvery whiteness.

'Look at that cloud,' I say, 'look.'

He studies it for a moment.

'Looks like a poo,' he says. 'Poopy cloud.'

Shall I go mad? Is this seriously my life, talking with Pauli?

At the kiosk there is a queue a mile long. All the tables are full, old dotards, young mothers with their brats, a few idling students from the Sorbonne and some speccy types, probably from the School of Mines or the Pharmacy College. Alright for them, nothing to do but lounge in cafes and read stuff all day. At last we get to the head of the queue.

'Red or green,' the old server in the kiosk asks.

'Red,' says Pauli, like he always does.

Red drink. It doesn't taste of red. It doesn't taste of anything except the ersatz sugar they put in it. Pauli is fatally addicted.

There is still no table free. An old man signals to us, pointing to the chair beside him. I am so fearful of old men waving, they are always super-irritating and have bad habits – or worse. But it is the only seat, so I take it and pull Pauli onto my lap. He consents and guzzles at his drink. The old mec reads his book which by way of surreptitious craning I see is *Persian Letters*. Old Montesquieu writing about women's subjection. In the end of course the girls in the harem win out. But what they have to go through first!

The oldster hasn't got to that bit. He's in the middle. He really is extremely old and corrugated and his hands are covered in hideous liver spots but he is perfectly dressed in a pale linen suit and a starched white shirt. Courteously, he leaves us completely to ourselves.

This is the best I could hope for. To be left alone is the best heaven right now. But of course Pauli spills his drink. It goes on my *tablier*. I know he did it deliberately.

'You little besom,' I say in English, just as Mama used to. Noticing, the old man says nothing but offers me an exquisitely clean white handkerchief. I say No, thank you, and mop at my front with the napkin we got with the red drink.

We set off home. There is a wet red patch on my *tablier*

right in the middle at the top of my legs. I hold my *cartable* in front of the wet patch. Pauli scuffs alongside. Now he has worked the maximum havoc he is a happier child. He holds the side of my *tablier* in his paw and from time to time gives a little skip.

The thing is, he's a mummy-conscious kid without a mummy. That's probably why speaking in the tongue and tones of our sainted mother is his way of getting by.

I seize the chance and tell him Fleurette is sad when he speaks English because she doesn't understand it and it makes her feel bad. Pauli, who deep in his childish heart loves Fleurette, falls silent. But he is a very stubborn child indeed. Who knows where he will come out on this one?

Once we get into the Ave Desormeaux and have to walk on the cobbles, he perks up again. He starts stepping carefully, pacing himself so that his right foot lands on every third cobble. These are the lucky ones.

Home. Our high-ceilinged unfashionable old flat is on the third floor. It looks alright from the street, it's got one of those flashy Haussmann façades. But inside it's falling apart. The roof leaks like crazy and all the window frames are rotting. It's freezing in winter and boiling in summer and the damp seeps in all year round, whatever the weather.

We skulk past the Old Bat's door and run up the stairs. I take them two at a time but Pauli still beats me to our door. He turns, panting, leaning back against the door with a look of cheeky triumph.

'Alright,' I say, 'you win. Again.'

I open the door and reach round to turn on the light switch but of course nothing happens. I remember now that yesterday the bulb in Papa's study went and I took the one out of the hall to replace it. I must remember to take the broken one to school tomorrow. I can switch it for one of the nice 60 watt ones they have in the lats.

The only meagre light in the hall comes through the transom above the front door. It's just enough for us to grope our way in. In the gloom Paco can be vaguely detected, largely because he is half white and you can reconstitute the black parts if you know the general shape of a collie dog, which we do, all too well. The white tip of Paco's tail wafts from side to side like one of Maddie's thurible things and a doggy aroma comes up to meet us. Little by little, my eyes adjust to the gloom. There is the fuzzy muzzle and the liquid pleading eyes looking up at me as though I am some sort of bountiful Diana. Paco is already yawning in anticipation of his supper. His tail begins thwacking like a punkah.

But what supper would that be?

Pauli dashes up to Paco, drops to his knees and buries his face in the dog's fur.

I am afraid that Paco, who was Mama's dog, is a bit of a Mummy icon for Pauli.

'Let me take him today,' he says, and he grabs the lead and clips it on to Paco's collar. Paco capers round Pauli in an ecstasy. I open the front door and Paco tugs Pauli out. I say,

'Don't go for too long now. I'll make supper.'

They don't look back. They are too busy tumbling headlong down the stairs.

I head for the kitchen, which at least has a window. I stumble against Pauli's antique Tri-ang trike, the one our English granny gave my big brother Franck years ago. I inherited it and now Pauli has it. He has left it right in the middle of the corridor. I lift it with my left foot and launch it. It clatters up against the door of Papa's study. I put my ear to the door and hear Papa's animal grunt.

I call out *Bonsoir* to him but he doesn't reply. No doubt as usual, his head is resting in some higher plane where you may grunt irritably but you don't say *Hallo* or *How was school?* Or even *How are you today, my beloved daughter?*

In the kitchen the mangle is still standing in the middle of the floor. Next to it, the old green galvanized iron tub is filled with the sodden blankets which I washed last night in a fatal access of enthusiasm. I haul the mangle to one side and shove it up against the wall and ram the green tub underneath it. This leaves just about enough room for me to get to the kitchen cupboard. I open the doors and run my eyes over our supplies which are sadly low. There is a pound of dry pasta and a jar of challenging 'desiccated vegetables' – shrivelled peas, beige carrots, onion chips that look like cardboard. From experience I know they taste of cardboard too and Pauli has often confirmed this to me. There are two apples, slightly wrinkled, a small piece of dried up Comté cheese, and one egg.

By the time Pauli and Paco get back, the supper is ready. I set the table in the dining room. It's getting late and the low red sun of this April evening is poking its rays through the rotting casement. The old rosewood table that came from Papa's big place in Vienna is lit up red and gold.

I knock on the door of Papa's study and say in my most dutiful voice *A table, Papa*. He grunts and says *Ich komme gleich*, which usually means he will take the time required to finish writing his sentence or paragraph or chapter or perhaps even a whole book, and then he'll come. Yet today he comes into the dining room almost straight away and he is carrying a bottle of his precious Nuits St Georges, the 1921 *millésime*. We must be celebrating something.

He embraces me, briefly, hands to my shoulders and double *bises*, and he pats young Pauli on the head and then settles himself down at the table. He seems unusually cheerful. He uncorks the wine and pours himself a large glass.

Like me, Papa is dark, and a little on the short side but he is big-built with broad shoulders and a big chest. He has the kind of large head people usually call 'leonine' and this look is helped along by his masses of thick unruly black hair, although these days the black is streaked with grey.

This big head of his has plainly been built to hold a lot of stuff as he is a massive brain-box. And then within this lion-like set up is Papa's face, which is surprisingly delicate, small nose, pale lips, black eyes, and a fantastically wrinkled brow.

Papa, of course, cultivates this lion-like character. He thinks it makes all his pronouncements sound weighty. Maybe this is true some of the time. But now he is sitting down at table he seems to shrink. He really slumps, and he is getting quite round-shouldered. No, Papa's posture is not so good.

Pauli gets the egg of course, mashed up Viennese-style in a cup, and Papa and I have a vegetarian pasta with a sprinkling of grated cheese on top. It's actually not that bad. I tossed it in a smidgen of olive oil and a pinch of salt. Amazingly the desiccated vegetables have somehow recovered a bit of their natural colour. They look almost, *almost*, like the real thing.

It was going to be apples for dessert but I thought better of it. Tomorrow night, we'll have apple fritters.

What a good little housekeeper I am!

Papa doesn't talk during dinner, except a bit to himself. There's the odd muttered fragment, in French, or a bit in

German (Papa hails from Austria, old Imperial Austria). Usually he is thinking about his work, because he thinks all the time and what else could he be thinking about. I imagine he thinks even while he is asleep.

If you were watching us, a family at dinner, you'd say Papa was gauche and curmudgeonly, and probably a bit neglectful towards us, his children. And yes, you could say that, but you could also say that this is not all the story. Because he is, after all, our Papa, and we are condemned to love him, sort of, Pauli and I. Especially because Mama is gone, and now our big brother Franck is gone. And when he comes down from his heights, when he actually looks at us and talks to us, he does resemble a version of a dear beloved Papa and we purr, just like kittens.

And I'd add, though you might not have noticed, that Papa is in charge of our destiny. Or so he thinks.

Now he eats a little of the pasta and then starts pushing it round his plate. He is not thinking about food, at all, and anyway I suspect he has had a good meat lunch at the Collège de France where the 24 professorial elect no doubt sit in state between the hours of twelve noon and three in the afternoon and gorge off *filet mignon* while blathering on. With this in mind I ease his plate away from him and give it to Pauli who wolfs down the pasta straight away. He leaves the desiccated vegetables.

Papa reaches for his glass and drinks off his wine.

'What are we celebrating, Papa?'

He looks surprised. Unexpectedly he says,

'Would you like some wine, *liebchen Anschli*?'

Liebchen Anschli, my darling little Anna! I purr.

'What about me?' Pauli says at once, in English, so Papa pours half a glass for me and a finger for Pauli and motions to me to top Pauli's glass up with water. Then Papa says *A toast to me!*

He's keen on toasts. They're usually about some academic thing, Lévy-Strauss's latest book or Professor Carcopino's breakthrough at the School of Rome. Or (very occasionally) Pauli being called to his headmistress for getting his long tots to come out right. Or (once only) me getting an alpha beta in Greek verses.

The sun has sunk almost to the line of the rooftops and is shining right on Papa's face. He shields his eyes with his huge hand and raises his glass. In the light of the setting sun, his hand is the colour of roses. The black hairs on it stand out.

We clink and Pauli cries out *Cheers!* which is always his favourite bit.

'But why the toast?' I ask.

Papa puts down his glass. He puts his hand to his throat and adjusts his necktie. Then he says, very deliberate and ponderous,

'Today I have been appointed Chief Economic Adviser to the French government.'

Mon dieu! For a moment I can't think what government that might be, and then I remember *Le Vieux Maréchal* and that lot down in Vichy.

'And I have been admitted to being *Chevalier de la...*'

'Er, Papa...' I butt in. And stop.

I mean is this such a good thing really? It sounds, well, a bit collabo.

'Cheers!' Pauli cries again.

So we drink. The wine is good, thick and strong. I hold up my glass to the big candle which burns in the centre of the table and it glows like a ruby. We drain our glasses.

Papa replenishes his own glass but not mine.

***

It is late and Pauli's little rhythms are following the sun, sinking fast.

'*Vas dodo,*' I say, '*fais pipi et vas dodo.*'

He pouts and says crossly,

'Speak English.'

I look at Papa. We should discuss what Fleurette said to me at Pauli's school.

But Papa is floating off into one of his vague states.

Pauli sits at the table scowling. His arms are crossed. He's a stubborn little tyke. I know what he wants. He wants me to say what Mama used to say – *Go and be excused* and *Climb the wooden hill.* But that would be just too ridiculous. 'Be excused' for *faire pipi*, indeed! It is just too English. And we live in a flat, for God's sake, we don't even have any wooden hill to climb.

Pauli clings to these Mummy-sayings like he clings to his eternal soul. Since Mama died two years back and his little life changed forever, he clings to all these ways. He's trying to prove something to himself. He wants to be just that same little boy his mummy used to say these things to. And then he wants a big good night kiss.

Well, I'm not his mummy and I'm not going to say those things.

I compromise. I say in English,

'*Pauli, go and get ready for bed, there's a good boy, and then I'll come and read you a story.*'

He is reluctant, I can see that, but he accepts this. He gets down from his chair and goes and kisses Papa on either cheek, French-style. He also kisses Paco on his frowsty head.

What Paco thinks about this is quite clear as he gives a faint wag of his tail but keeps his eye on the main idea which is spelled Leftovers. But Leftovers these days are largely a conceptual thing, something remembered from before the Fall. And even dogs, even those as deserving as Paco, must sadly share in the consequences of the Fall.

However, tonight I have hidden a little of my pasta in my napkin and I now slip this to him. He bolts it all in two gulps. Then I put down the plate with Papa's remaining vegetables on it. Paco is so hungry that he even wolfs down these sad vegetables.

Papa doesn't notice any of this. But then he doesn't notice much below the level of a Great Idea anyway.

Tucked up in bed, Pauli looks briefly like a sleepy angel. I read to him from his *Boy's Own Annual 1937*. His English cousin Edward gave it to him. The story which Pauli asks for is his very best favourite. I must have read it to him a million times and counting. It is about a boy at one of those frightening boarding schools where the English like to park their children from infancy onwards. This boy is called Simpson and he is a weed, I mean a real weed, spindly and pasty-faced with binocular-strength spectacles that are always getting trodden on accidentally on purpose by the other boys. Anyway, to cut a long story short, this Simpson decides to practice cross-country running. He sneaks out of his dormitory each night and runs ten miles round the village, although how he does this in the dark is not explained. And then on the day of the big race they all set off and the crowd jeer at skinny Simpson and then all the boys disappear into the copse and when they come out, there is the weed ahead of the pack and racing to the finish line. He breasts the tape and the applause is deafening. The story is called *Simpson The Dark Horse*.

Actually, tonight I am spared some of this prig's tale. By

the time we approach the dénouement, Pauli is away in the land of Nod. I tuck him up, blow out his candle and leave the room.

As I pass through the hall there is a knock at the door. It is The Old Bat in person, our concierge Mme Lafarge. She is panting from the strain of coming up two flights, or at least she is pretending to pant. She thrusts an envelope at me in a slightly more bad-tempered way than usual.

'It's a *pneu*', she says, 'just arrived for you, Miss.'

She explains at some length how this late delivery has woken her from her hard-earned rest, and that she has a headache you could paint and her famous ankle's on the blink again and so on and so forth for the time it takes me to find five sous in the drawer of the hall table and give it to her and then she stumps off with an ordinary gait, her famous ankle healed for now.

The *pneu* which has just shot across Paris, sped by compressed air through the pneumatic tubes beneath the pavement, is actually addressed to me. This is a first. Never before have I received a *pneu*. In fact, it is the first time one has ever been delivered to our house. Our mail is always for Papa, stuff from the Collège de France or, these days, from the government. But Papa's mail is slow and heavy communications which could never ever come by *pneu*.

I open the little blue envelope. It is from Maddie. Can I come round tonight for Schubert and grog and *the matter we discussed*?

Pouf! Of course I can't! I've Papa's nightcap to make and anyway it's probably already nine o'clock. And she lives miles away, in the Seizième, and even if the metro is still open I'd probably get stuck in one of those hold-ups where you sit in the dark in a tunnel for two hours and keep touching yourself to make sure you're not actually fully dead yet, or someone else is touching you and you have to slap him off.

Anyway, I don't feel like making music on a school night. Or getting tight. And as for the other thing with the *Maréchal*, it is just so ridiculous.

I can't even refuse Maddie's invite. The phone is off, of course and it's too late to send a return *pneu*, the Poste is well closed by now. So I leave it.

But at least this is confirmation that my blood sister is thinking of me, which is pretty much of a comfort.

In the kitchen I mix up some milk powder and hot up Papa's milky drink. He'll pop a couple of tots of cognac in, I know. He's never told me about this little practice but I can smell the brandy when I wash up the mug the next morning.

When I go into his study, Papa is at his big desk. The electricity's back on and two strong lamps shine down on the papers he's working at. In the light and shade he peers at me like a sleepy god. He is wearing his important black specs which give him a very weighty look indeed. I watch his face and see the movement as his mind comes down from the narcotic heights of his thoughts to the level where ordinary things are, like me and his milky nightcap and the prospect of two large tots.

I know this so well, this descent from Olympus to the mortal plain, from his divine ordering of the world to dealing with us and the rest of mankind as we actually are.

Mama used to keep him well in line. She could get him to actually play his part in the family. When we were little, back in Vienna, and he was working on his first big book, she would lock up his study on Sundays and force him to be a father. He would then take me and my big brother Franck to the Stadtpark or the Volksgarten, or to the zoo. I remember exciting Sundays like that. He would ask *Where shall we go?* and we would chorus *The Zoo!*, and we would go to Schönbrunn and make faces at the spitting cobra until it splatted at the glass, pure venom and we would scream with delight.

Now he looks up at me. The light shows up the deep crevices in his face. These lines that run at a slight slant down from beside his nose past his mouth almost to his chin, and the crinkly horizontal ones that corrugate his brow. He passes his big hand back through his thick mane of hair.

'You look just like a Prof,' I say and he nods but he doesn't smile. There is a pause during which he seems to realize that he should say something to me, as fathers may do to daughters from time to time.

'How was school, *ma belle*?'

This should be alright as a routine father-daughter question, if a bit of a yawn. But with Papa it's actually a minefield. This is because Papa has some quite specific plans for me and they are definitely his plans, not mine. He wants me to get a top Philo Bac so I can go to the Sorbonne and study philosophy.

Why he has decided on this particular destiny for me is a deep question. Basically he believes that once he has personally resolved the economic problem of Europe, philosophy will be required to sort out the secondary problem of how we should live aright.

To help him solve the European economic problem, Papa intends that my big brother Franck should follow him into economics, tying up any loose ends in that branch of human happiness. Then I will follow on and study philosophy to resolve that subsidiary question of how we should all live together happily once the economic problem has been solved.

You see my problem?

As I say, these are Papa's plans, not mine. Whatever it is that steers me into my life's activity, it will not be Papa's plans. And anyway, my deepest desires lie elsewhere, quite elsewhere.

Nor is my dear brother Franck all that keen on the destiny Papa has been crafting for him. He said so clearly, very emphatically, among so much else that last dreadful night before he left for the front.

And during these last long months, all the time that Franck has been a PoW, Papa has refused even to hear his name. What happened between them on that night I don't really know. There was shouting and shouting. Now even Pauli is slapped if he dares to speak his brother's name.

I do my bit to remember Franck and keep the notion alive that we are a sort of family, or once were. But it's a struggle. I send Franck food parcels when I can, which is rare enough, and I know they don't get through. He writes to Pauli and me. But between him and Papa, nothing, absolutely nothing.

So, with all that, you will understand that Papa enquiring about my school day is not such a simple question. But I must reply.

'We have a new Philo teacher,' I volunteer at last. 'She is called Mlle de Beauvoir.'

Annoyingly, really really annoyingly, Papa has actually heard of Mlle de Beauvoir.

'Second in her class at the Sorbonne,' he says. 'Top notch thesis on… Spinoza, wasn't it?'

I shrug. I'm trying to remember who Spinoza is. I think we did him or her last year.

'Yes, second in her Promotion,' he goes on. But no shame

in that, because she was second to that clever fellow, the one who wrote the book about sea-sickness.'

He means M. Sartre, of course, who wrote my favourite book, *La Nausée*, which is definitely not about sea-sickness. As I want to actually add something to this conversation rather than just be lectured at, I say

'She got kicked out of her last school for corrupting the young.'

'Did she indeed? Well, that's not necessarily a bad thing for a philosopher. Look at Socrates. He drank hemlock for just that same offence.'

Papa laughs. He always laughs at his own cleverness. It's almost the only thing he does laugh at.

'So what corrupting thing did Mlle de Beauvoir teach you today, *chérie*? Here, here, sit down and tell me.'

So I sit down on the tattered chair in front of his desk and struggle through a short recap of the Maddie-Beauvoir dialogues whilst tugging at a bit of leather that's come loose on the side of the chair. There is a brass stud and I wind the leather round it. Mercifully, while I am doing this, Papa's attention wanders. He forgets his question, like he forgets a lot these days and he says

'Fine, fine, my darling. Now, time for your beauty sleep. I really must get on. I have a big speech coming up.'

Errr, Papa... at such a time as this, is a big speech really such a good idea? I think this but I don't say it. I just tell him to drink his milk while it's still hot. He promises, so I kiss the top of his head through his mop of hair and go to leave the room. I glance back from the door, and there he is, already soaring back up towards Olympus. He is also reaching for the little key to the cupboard where he keeps his cognac.

***

I'm worn out so I just shove the dirty dishes in the dirty sink. I quit the disgusting mess that is the kitchen. I turn my face away from the mangle and the sodden blankets and leave the scene. I briefly consider doing my prep. This is to prepare the first hundred lines of the *Trojan Women* and read Act One of *Lear* but honestly I can't face it. I am tired tired tired.

I go to my room. I look at the photograph on the wall, Franck and me in the garden at Evreux, in the old days when Mama kept a cottage there. I remember that day as if a Flemish master had painted it, the brilliant colours and the jewelled lawn of spring. In the photo we are in the sketchy shade of the great chestnut, the leaves are barely out. It was May but the poppies were already springing up in the long grass. We had been inside playing the Mendelssohn and the Andante from the Brahms, the fourth sonata.

I can hardly bear to look at that photograph. It is as though there was a life and now it is cancelled off.

At the time of the Cataclysm, Franck was missing. There came the anxiety of waiting to be told. Franck always said it was the old people who should fight wars. They're the ones who decide on war, he always said, they're the ones who do well out of war.

So I prayed, *let that chance bullet strike them, the old people. Leave me Franck and his brilliant life, leave all that promise of what he could do and be.*

Now I open my top drawer and reach in to the back beneath my few feminine nothings and I take out Franck's latest letter.

    Darling Schwester,
    You write, how am I? Well, do not expect me to be the same. We are all quite changed. You will see, <u>when we come back</u>.

It seems a dozen years since I saw you. Will you even know me? I have become quite gaunt and old, as though I have exchanged my youthful life for someone else's, some little old man's.

You know what I miss most here, apart from you? It is our music. There is an old bar piano here and on Saturday I get two hours 'off' and can play it. I played the Andante Con Moto from the Appassionata the other day, and thought of you the way the air ends with that perfect cadence on the tonic chord.

And guess who is here? Well, you can't, of course, but it's Messiaen, Olivier Messiaen, the composer. He came in just last week on a new trainload, mostly French transferred from somewhere else. God knows why they keep shunting us around. Anyway, I was slopping out in the San and all the new guys were herded in and told to strip off to be 'inspected'. This one mec made a weird sight with his odd-shaped body and huge thick glasses. One of the guards was trying to take a sort of school satchel away from him and he was fighting like a cat. In the end, the officer intervened and was about to beat the fellow – but the guy showed him what was in the bag and the officer took a peek and seemed to nod and let him keep it.

A couple of days later, I was next to the guy in the kitchens, we were both on spud-bashing and I asked him about it. That's when he told me he was Messiaen. He said when the mec saw what he had in his satchel – it was little pocket scores of the Brandenburg concertos and the Lyric Suite of Berg and some other stuff – he just said *Very good*. So it seems that the Boche is not completely degraded. He still remembers that the musical tradition of his country is above all others.

But, Annie, here is something serious just for you. There is something <u>you must not do</u> – and that is, do not kiss a boy before I return. They are all pimpled youths in short trousers who have done no service and who anyway know nothing worth knowing. Play your music and await the return of the heroes of Troy.

There are in fact a couple of decent chaps here that I might introduce you to.

Je t'embrasse.

Franck

Papa

The brandy was good. He poured three tots into a glass. Tonight he would drink it neat. He would pour the milk away later. The girl meant well, but she could scarcely understand.

Understand, for example, how it all began. How the monster was conceived at Versailles at the end of the Great War, after Germany surrendered, confidently expecting reconciliation and a just peace. It was then that Clemenceau had hoodwinked Woodrow Wilson and imposed his Carthaginian Peace. *Germania delenda est, Germany must be destroyed*, he might as well have said.

Stripping Germany of the coalfields of the Saar and of Silesia. Denying Germany access to three quarters of the iron ore on which her industry depended.

Demanding that Germany pay the entire cost of the War, pay for 'all damage done by land, by sea and from the air'.

Putting millions of Germans under the rule of toy republics and hostile nationalist regimes, under Lithuania, Latvia, Czechoslovakia, Poland.

He had seen for himself the costs. As a young economist, he had gone as an expert witness for the Reparations Commission to assess the damages. He had been in those regions of France devastated beyond description, beyond even imagination.

From Bazentin to Miraumont they had walked ten miles and as far as the eye could see, to the horizon, nothing was left. Not one stone stood upon another but all that had been houses or cow byres was scattered rubble.

When they reached Miraumont, they sought the old source of the Ancre Stream, but there was nothing. A new topography had formed. Vast craters such as meteors had once made at another time and cleared the world of life. Trenches were sunken chasms, a whole arterial system clogged with mud and metal. Everywhere barbed wire was wildly rioting, mimicking the natural thorns and briars which that spent, abused land could not now produce.

Even the natural colour of the landscape was changed. In place of the old palette of browns and greens, the earth was a strange grey as though ash had fallen everywhere.

Qu'ils paient! their guide had said. They must pay! He was a peasant of the place. *Ils paieront*, said M. Theunis, their Belgian colleague. And so they shall!

Not so, Keynes had said. *Prudent generosity is the stance of the victor*. But M. Theunis shook his head and their peasant guide spat on the barren soil.

3

Maurice throws his arms around me and starts to kiss me. I mean, to really kiss me. Although first he has to lift me up to his height. He must be a good foot taller than me.

His lips feel rough and dry and he smells of cigarettes and wine. I close my eyes and try to drift away but this is hard because there are not only the lips and the manly scents, his face is quite bristly too. Anyway, it goes on like this for quite a time. I hear the soldiers moving off but Maurice doesn't stop at once. In fact he goes on kissing me and starts that thing with his tongue. I can scarcely breathe. I just give myself over to it and wonder what comes next.

Nothing much it seems. It goes on for a while and I gulp in air in the shortish breaks. I swivel my eyes and I am looking into the window of the bookshop which before was the English bookshop where Ma used to buy her Aldous Huxleys but which is now full of The Conqueror's Books. I contemplate the titles in heavy Gothic type, and then suddenly I give a start. My eye has spotted one book which has a familiar cover.

At this point Maurice stops kissing me and lets me down.

'Lost interest?' he asks, all sarcastic. 'Didn't I do it right?'

How should I know? I suppose he did but I don't say so. Anyway, shouldn't *he* know? I mean he's twenty-eight or something, plenty of time to learn how to kiss a girl I'd have thought

'Look! Look there, that book.'

He looks bored but glances in the window.

'There, that one! Look, it's Papa's book. There's his name. *Handel und Wachstum in einer europäischer Zollunion.* Trade and Growth in a European Customs Union.'

It's then that I see, reflected in the window, the little sports car. It has followed us.

To understand how all that happened then and before and after, you just have to know that Maddie was never going to accept the occupation of her country with any conventional response, and certainly not with the dull indignation most people showed.

Maddie is fire, she is spirit.

So, of course, it was all Maddie's fault.

What happened at the bookshop and after was hatched the night before, round at Maddie's. She had sent another *pneu* and I went round to hers, which is quite a mission just getting there. It's not just that I take my chances on the metro at night with all the old *tarés* in their gabardine macs and people staring at my violin case like it was a small artillery piece or something. Not only that but hers is a daunting place. Actually, it's meant to daunt, starting off with the twin gas-fired *flambeaux* at the gates, then the ponderous front door that's studded with brass bits so it looks like chain mail and could probably withstand light howitzer fire. Then once you penetrate there are the two stinking wolfhounds called Tristan and Yseult who lie stretched out across the marble hall reeking of meat and farting massively like victors after battle. Their hairy coats glow in the light of the crystal chandeliers that blaze with enough watts to light up the entire *arrondissement*.

And that's just the entrance hall. Maddie takes my hand and leads me up the staircase. We pass massed emblems of Empire hung on the high walls, selections from the heaps of pillage Maddie's Pa brought from overseas, courtesy of France's *mission civilisatrice*. Because the Pa, M. Grandidier de Vernay, was for some years Governor General of Madagascar and he brought home loot enough to fill this and several other of his houses.

There are portraits of the old Merina kings and queens who were overthrown when they failed to accept *la mission civilisatrice* in the generous spirit that was intended. There is rude King Andranopoimerina who stands half naked before his simple palace, which is really just a grass hut. Next to him is his boy, King Radama, who has clearly already fallen under the civilizing influence – he is dressed like a French hussar. Then, got up like the Empress Eugenie, is the wicked Queen Ranavolona, who hurled the Christians from her own Tarpeian rock and generally tried to fend off the dead hand of Empire. But to no avail. Just as the Prussians scythed down the French cuirassiers, so the French cuirassiers made short work of Queen Ranavolona's humble levies.

On the landing are other spoils brought home by the hero – the swords of the Malagasy kings, the crowns of the queens, and a small wooden box, small enough to be a cigarette box which Maddie says is the chief idol of the ancient Malagasy – *Ikelimalaza*, it's called, *Small but Powerful*. I can't resist opening the little box, I always do. Inside, there's some coloured ribbon, a length of garter elastic, and fragments of spice wood. Just that and nothing else. Sadly, *Ikelimalaza* did nothing against the triumphant conqueror.

'Come along,' says Maddie, impatient. She is in her imperative voice and pulls me by the hand into the vast room which is her sitting room. It's actually the 'children's' sitting room, but as Maddie's only sibling Eric flew up into the blue on Armistice Day in his spanking new plane and hasn't been heard from since, she has this palace to herself.

I am late, delayed and grimy from the metro. Two others are there already.

There's dear Verónica, waif-like and even paler than usual. She looks very bony but also chic in a sleeveless silk top and long pants. She is sitting away by herself on what looks like a milking stool, hugging her knees and resting her head on her forearm. Her glossy black hair is loose, tumbling down over her arm. The stool is so low that these gorgeous locks almost touch the floor. How intense she looks! I go to her and she raises her head and one languid arm and greets me with a gentle handshake. I duck down and give her an awkward triple *bise*. She smiles momentarily, flashing her brilliantly white teeth which have that lucky gap at the front and stick out a charming fraction. That's why we sometimes call her Mouse.

And next to her, lounging on a large shabby sofa covered in chintz, is Cousin Maurice, cousin to them both.

'Why is he here?' I ask as rudely as I dare. 'What's he play?'

'Oh darling, you didn't really think we were going to play tonight did you? Tonight of all nights?'

'Well, actually, yes,' I say, holding up my battered violin case. 'Actually yes. I've even looked out the Schubert like you said.' I wave the score at her.

'Sorree,' she says and gives me a hug. I scowl and look over her shoulder at Cousin Maurice. My heart races up.

For Maurice is the boy I love, the boy I think I love, although he doesn't know it. Actually, he doesn't even know me, which is a quite weird fact. The truth is I only saw Maurice once in my life before. It was at the birthday party of my brother two years ago when Franck was twenty-one and I was a slip. This Maurice kissed me then, quite by chance – it was a party game and that was his forfeit. He screwed up his face but that didn't spoil it. I am sure that he has quite forgotten it.

Maddie is doing some cod introduction, such as 'Maurice, my cousin on my mother's side. He's... what is it, Maurice? An art dealer, is it...?'

But I am thrilled. Nothing has changed. He is beautiful. He is no doubt the most beautiful boy I have ever seen. He was beautiful, two years ago, and he still is. He is tall and pale. His eyes are bright and also maybe wicked. They shine on me now with, I'm pretty sure, intelligence and irony or something like that. He stands up and bows.

He obviously has quite forgotten me but he looks me in the eye and says Hallo and then darts in and busses me on either cheek. I feel rough bristle and smell the oil he has on his hair and the reek of gaspers and sweat. He stands back and looks at me, so I look at him.

'You look familiar,' he says.

He is very slender, but his shoulders are immensely broad, so that his body seems to taper. He is tall – and he is perfect. I want him for my collection! I love him, I really do!

So of course Maddie does her best to spoil this moment when perhaps I could have settled easily down next to Maurice and said something nice or funny about his white shirt which is so white it gives him colour despite his pallor, perhaps touched the sleeve to compliment him on such fine stuff while I looked at the V of his pale perfect throat at the open neck.

But no, Maddie is such a virgin and she starts up just as if she were old Bazin, that is if Bazin were of the righteous Left and not the wrinkled *Ancien Régimiste* she actually is.

***

Really, it is all Maddie's fault. And Maurice's too, of course. The thing about last night was how Maddie kept returning to her Main Idea which is so ridiculous you'd laugh if you weren't crying.

She has already wormed out of la Bazin the date that Maréchal Pétain is to come. She says that we will sing the hymn and while he is gazing seraph-like into his destiny in the heavens she will step forward and shoot him dead with one shot through the heart. Nothing, it seems, could be simpler. My role will be just to procure the gun. Verónica's role will be to faint away on the day so that there is a diversion during which she, Maddie, will make her get away.

Maurice mutters 'Too many cowboy films at the Berlitz'.

He seems to have a knack of getting to the heart of the matter which is almost female.

'What's Pétain coming to Paris for anyway, apart from looking at fruity young lycéennes, I mean?'

'Oh, Mau, haven't you heard? Herr Hitler is graciously sending us back some Napoleonic body parts.'

'Haven't we got enough already?'

'It's not big Napoleon. It's his boy, the King of Rome. Apparently we got most of him back in Louis Philippe's time. He's in Les Invalides. But the Austrians kept his heart and guts.'

'Whatever for?'

Maddie gets up and fetches a newspaper. *Old Habsburg custom… the heart is in the Herzgruft, the Habsburg heart crypt… in Vienna… tum tum tum… Napoleon II, King of Rome… called by the Austrians the Prince of Reichstadt… heart in Urn 42… viscera in Urn 76…*

'Weird,' Verónica says.

'Anyway…' says Maddie, 'Pétain's coming up for this

schemozzle. He'll be coming to our school. So then we can shoot him.'

I, knowing Maddie, knowing my blood sister, know that she is serious about this and I start to really fret my mind to work out how to stop her.

The problem is her being such a Catholic, such a virgin. Steeped in notions of sin and virtue and theatrical gestures of martyrdom, all that futile stuff.

How she took on a lifetime commitment to such life-denying things is beyond me. The only explanation is just that these were, simply, the ideas that got to her first.

Verónica meanwhile sits quite still. She is perching awkwardly on that stool. Now I look at it, I see it looks like it came from some Malagasy milking shed. No doubt it forms a rich vein of legend in Maddie's family lore, *SEM Le Gouverneur yesterday visited a model dairy farm where his elegant spouse consented to watch the ready fingers of several comely young Malagasy milkmaids drawing rich streams of milk from contented cows of an improved race that has recently been introduced from the Motherland…* Or some such. All, I mean all, of the vast kit Maddie's Aged Parents have brought back has these references of dominance and the civilizing mission and know-it-all and *il n'y a que…* of *all they have to do is be more like us* (more intelligent, more hard-working, more, well, more French).

Maddie says again and again to Verónica that she should sit in one of the several easy chairs that are ranged comfortably about the room but the girl scowls at her and sits on the stool like a sullen Pythia, hugging to herself her freight of acquired unhappiness and immigrant misery.

Maddie spreads her hands towards us. I say she must be off her head.

***

Maurice says 'You mentioned gin.'

Maddie hasn't but she doesn't mind. She opens a tall thin cupboard which I guess is in a 'Louis' style, although whether XI or XII or XV or XVIII I have no idea. Inside are many bottles. She takes a bottle and shows it to us, like a sommelier. *London gin.*

'Nice touch, Maddie dearest,' Maurice says, 'Seat of our heroic Resistance.'

'How much?'

'*Faire le plein,*' he says.

I take a big splash too.

'*Et avec ça?*' Maurice asks. Maddie shrugs and turns away. She doesn't do Indian tonic water.

So we drink it neat. It is quite disgusting.

Maddie approaches Verónica.

'*Et pour toi, chérie?*'

Verónica adjusts her sullen look towards something a little more accommodating. She nods her lovely head just slightly. Maddie pours her a huge measure.

While we are dulling our senses with this fantastic firewater, Maddie starts on some speech again, something like *Those who should have defended the ideals of our Republic are dancing in Vichy with its assassins. And dancing with a light heart.*

Which is fine but I am not listening. I am looking at Maurice and wondering if I dare to touch him.

'We must act,' she says, '*according to the dictates of our conscience and pay no heed to the Vichy fascists.*' She says, '*By our own behaviour we can transform the situation.*'

Why, oh why, Maddie? Where do you get such notions? Plainly she is mad. I have an infinite love for this crazy girl.

But not right now because I want to put my hand on Maurice's, which lies seductively close to mine. However, there is Maddie boding large, turning to me and seeking my opinion.

I have no opinion. My father has confiscated my soul. My mother has filled my head with nonsense.

'So, sweetie?' she says in her most coaxing voice. What can I say to my dear blood sister's risible idea? I just say no.

'No what?'

'No, I will not *procure the gun.*'

Maddie touches my hand on a certain spot, just below the knuckle of the forefinger. This is to remind me that an age ago, in our far-off childhood, in our twelve-year-old crush on each other, girl-children, we left the beach and lay in the long grass below the spinney, almost naked and completely unashamed, her long pale body pressed against my browner flesh. We exchanged blood and swore that we would from that day forth be sisters and be of a single heart.

She puts her finger on the tiny, almost imperceptible nick where my sluggish blood oozed out, and so I must touch the much bigger scar at the base of her first finger where she slashed at it with a breadknife and her blue blood spurted out excitingly.

That summer I felt true happiness. Our love gave purpose and justification to every last thing. Even when the weather turned, there was somehow joy with Maddie in rain and darkened skies, just as there was in sun and sparkling sea.

And yet I shake my head.

She says then she will do it herself, she will find a gun. After all, her country place is stuffed with the heads of beasts that have been gunned down over endless bloody years of killing. I know they despatch the wounded creatures with a pistol shot to the head. Maddie has done it herself, at her ritual blooding for the chase (which she says she loathed – but did she? These posh girls have a yen for blood, I think). Anyway, I'm quite sure she can get hold of a handgun of some kind.

I rethink. Quickly I change tactic, and say yes I will get the gun. That way, I think I will have some handle on what is going down. I can hold things up, let the obstacles accumulate. As my old English grandmother used to say, *It is amazing how many problems go away if you do absolutely nothing about them.*

This is dishonest of me, of course, and no doubt Maddie knows it because she looks hard into my eyes with her practiced stare. Her eyes turn to marble.

The real question is, how come Maddie is saturated with such innocence? I mean, how has she lived in this world these last years and never noticed how crammed full it is of difficulties in the way of doing the right thing?

It was somewhere around this point that Maurice raised his hand – his beautiful hand, with the long slim fingers and perfectly pared nails. He raises this hand to the level of his shoulder as if asking to speak, and it works because we all stare at him.

'I think your idea is absurd,' he says.

Maddie flushes and looks cross. She drains the huge gin she has poured herself.

'Why so?'

'Because even if you have a gun, he will be protected by a hundred fascist thugs. Because if by a million to one chance you succeed, you will be lined up and shot, a thousand innocent hostages will be killed, all your relatives will be rounded up and deported, several of your houses will be razed to the ground…'

Maddie looks furious, then deflated. Maddie and Maurice and I start to argue madly. Only Verónica sits sad and silent, hugging her knees.

She is such a pretty, snaky, sumptuous thing but ruined, almost it seems sometimes beyond repair.

Yet she is the only one who knows anything about all this, by which I mean resistance and fighting and the pains of war.

Maddie withdraws and regroups. She upends the gin bottle into our waiting glasses.

'So!' she says, clapping her hands together. The resemblance to our headmistress, la Bazin, is chilling.

'So,' she says, 'let's put the Old Gaffer on one side for now. What about we blow up the German bookshop? You know, the one that used to be WH Smith, the one where they chucked away all the English books and stuffed it full of Nazi texts. Let's blow up those Nazi texts.'

Maurice laughs out loud, an unpleasant, scornful laugh. Maddie bridles, hunching up her shoulders. I can see she wants to hit him.

'The problem is not there,' he says. 'Once ideas are out, they're out. You can't stifle them by blowing up a bookshop.'

'So where is the problem then, Maurice?' She is getting seriously angry and wants to challenge him.

'Well, my dear, it's not ideas that are ruining us. It's forty-two divisions and a hundred regiments of Panzer tanks. What do we do against that?'

Maddie is saying now 'Our motive is not to defeat the Occupation. Our motive is to show that *people without fear exist*.' Maurice groans.

We all start nodding glumly. I am now afraid for her, as

if I see already the mark of the condemned on her, my unreal Maddie with her grand fate.

Suddenly I recall a painting I saw in Rome when Maman took us, back in '36. It was a Judith having a go at hacking off Holofernes' head, and there's a helper, holding the mec down. It's a struggle, though. The thick neck resists and the Holofernes is flailing about for dear life. Is this what Maddie actually has in mind?

Again I feel that surge of love for her.

Just now, though, she looks so down it seems like she is going to call the meeting off. But then she speaks up again.

'Blowing up a bookshop is not much, true, but it would be something, like a symbolic act. The Boche are slaves to symbols, they'd get the point. And our people would see something, they'd have hope. They'd see we're not all cowards and *peignes cul*, arse lickers.'

'They'd certainly see that you were dead,' Maurice says. 'And not just you either, but the fifty hostages they'd shoot for every German who got killed.'

Maddie gestures impatiently. Maurice presses the point.

'Maddie darling, how free is dead? Dead isn't anything. They kill you, then they kill another hundred. You spill the blood of others and what do you achieve? Not freedom, anyway.'

The blood of others. That again.

'So, then, Maurice,' Maddie says savagely, almost shouting, 'at the end of the War, how will we hold up our heads?'

'If we're dead, we shan't be holding anything up. And anyway, the war is so over. Didn't the Old Gaffer sign an armistice and then shake hands with Herr Hitler at Montoire. Didn't the Old Gaffer say the path ahead is the path of peace and collaboration? They've won. Get over it. Get on with your life.'

Maddie clenches her fist, glaring at Maurice. She looks like she is going to kill *him*.

As for me, I glug down my gin. It tastes foul but I stick with it and I am beginning to get quite tight, which is great. My thought, for what's it's worth, is that the three of them – the three cousins – they have nothing to lose. Maddie, and I suppose Maurice too, they are protected by their family's class and power and they can indulge in these fancies. And Verónica, our little lustrous refugee *hidalga*, even though her Dad's a wicked anarchist proscribed by Franco, she's still a cousin too, of a sort on her mother's side, and so presumably protected. Anyway, she has nothing much to lose in Nazi France.

Me, I have Papa and Pauli to care for and a regular, ordered, although crap life which I just need to get through as best I can and if I do and we come out somehow alright and alive I might just have some choices left like having lovers (starting with Maurice), becoming a world-famous writer, having six luminous children and dying full of years and happiness, surrounded by those who love me best and who will carry my spirit on for ever and ever into the farthest future. In this, my possible life, being shot and getting dead doesn't, to be honest, really fit.

'What good would it do?' I mutter to myself and then I realize that Maurice is not engaging any more with Maddie but is sitting up closer to me and watching me. He puts his hand on mine. His touch is dry and light, like a caress.

'What good indeed?' he says. 'How would it help? There are no good choices right now but at least as long as you're not dead you've got a chance. Dead is nothing. And another hundred dead with you? I don't get it. Live and have your choices later I say.'

As this is exactly my own thought I nod and he pats my hand and turns to call out to Maddie who is looking desolate.

'Dear Maddie,' he says. She shakes her head, not wishing to listen to him.

'Something happens,' he says, 'the Boche invade, we tell ourselves it's our fault, our responsibility. We somehow willed it, let it happen. We say like Diogenes *we must do something*.'

And he tells the old story of Diogenes who lived in a barrel at Corinth and when the Corinthians went to war and were sharpening their swords and polishing their greaves, Diogenes just rolled his barrel up and down the hill. Asked what the hell he thought he was doing, he says 'With everyone else busy preparing for war, I felt I had to do *something*.'

'Very funny, I don't think,' Maddie said. She is more sad than annoyed now. Maurice is smooth and kind. His voice lulls me. I want to say how much I agree with him but I don't dare. Meanwhile Maddie rallies, looking fierce again, and says,

'Germany has gone. Italy has gone. Austria has gone. Czechoslovakia has gone. Poland has gone...'

'Spain has gone.' Verónica says it in an undertone but Maddie hears her and gives her a grateful little smile.

'Yes, Spain has gone... and Hungary has gone, Ukraine has gone, Norway has gone, Denmark has gone...'

'Yeah, yeah,' says Maurice in English. This doesn't quite deflate Maddie. She finishes with a confident flourish.

'We must save France at least.'

Maurice mutters under his breath that resistance is a

publicity stunt. Maddie then strides over and now she really does hit him, a slap across his face.

And then they set to. Maurice wrestles Maddie onto the sofa so she is lying half across me and he gives her a couple of slaps on the face, not hard, but her cheeks turn red. She lifts her head and bites his hand. Then they start laughing and Maddie says *Pax*, and Maurice says *Pax*.

Maddie gets another bottle out of the thin Louis cupboard and dishes out more gins so that we all get pretty plastered which is nice and we bat all these grand ideas around like *philosophes* and Maurice tells such funny stories, so we end up as a sort of group, although we have agreed absolutely nothing whatever.

Maddie's meeting is failing at its own pace. Wonderfully boozed up, I gaze at Maurice and begin to feel a rare thing below my waist, a feeling that attaches itself not to memories or images but for the first time in my life to a real live man. Plastered as I am, my body rages towards him.

Verónica just sits looking cross. At length she says,

'I thought we were going to fucking fight these fascists.'

And I say,

'I have to go. The metro is so crap these days, always held up, always stopping for no reason. I don't want to spend the night in a tunnel in the dark with some pervert's hand up my skirt.'

'This is so ridiculous!' Maddie shouts. 'Two hours and absolutely nothing has been decided. *Nothing.* Just talk with no result at all.'

Then unexpectedly, Maurice says,

'Alright, *Mädchen*, let's have a go.'

'How so?'

'Pair off, why not? *La petite Annie* here can come with me

and we will do some brave brave thing that will really put the Boche's noses out of joint. And you and Miss Mouse can go off and do your worst.'

'Such as?' Maddie is truculent.

'Search me. Tear down Boche posters, or something…'

'Oh no!' Maddie cries, clearly angry that her hopes of early martyrdom have come to this.

'Well, fishing rods, then,' Maurice says silkily. 'I'm sure your daddy's got a few. Crossed fishing rods hoisted up somewhere like on the Hotel de Ville.'

This is the new craze, two crossed fishing rods put up in a public place – *deux gaules*, for De Gaulle.

Maddie gets into a real bate then and shouts at Maurice for a bit but we are all tired and drunk and in the end Verónica speaks up and says *D'ac*, and Maddie just throws herself down on a sofa looking worn out.

At last she gives in and settles for Maurice's silly idea, which although crap is at least something to do. *Alright,* she says, *alright, just as a start.*

So we agree on it for tomorrow. Maddie will go with Verónica and do the fishing rods. I will go with Maurice. But what will we do? Maurice is a tease, he's not letting on. *That's another deeper question*, he says.

So maybe we are going to blow up the German bookshop after all.

4

And so it is that next evening I am clambering up the filthy steps of the Palais Royal metro like Eurydice escaping Pluto's clutches. The leaving train booms up behind me like the voice of hell.

But there is my Orpheus, my beautiful Maurice, waiting for me at the top. Behind him is a street lamp that backlights him so that he stands out in black. The light makes a saintly radiance around his head. It is so wrong I almost laugh.

He gives me a brotherly sort of duty kiss on either cheek and I get today's variant of the manly whiff, the sweat and smokes, and I feel the roughness of his lips. He smiles quickly and gives me what might at a pinch be an admiring look. My empty stomach aches and gurgles. I gave all my supper to Paco.

Maurice is wearing kit that looks sensationally unsuitable. It's a smart fawn-coloured tussore suit and, just like last night, he's got on a brilliantly white shirt, unbuttoned far enough for me to admire once more his smooth pale chest. He's wearing snappy brown brogues and these are polished to a fantastic lustre. Only the knapsack slung over his shoulder is a tad out of keeping with his look.

'What have you got in there?' I ask. For sure it is not explosives or a hand grenade.

He slips back the cover of the knapsack so I can see. There's a screwdriver, a chisel, a not very large tin of paint, and two brand new paint brushes.

God, this is so ridiculous I can't believe he is taking it seriously. But then he rubs the back of my neck. It feels affectionate, so what do I care? He takes my hand.

'Let's look like lovers, *ma petite*,' he says and slips his arm around my waist. 'That way we won't be bothered.'

Fine with me.

We set off down the Avenue Foch, arm in arm. The street lights are off but the moon is up, full and low, so we have no problem seeing. No one is about. There is one Boche car parked on the opposite side of the road. It's a *traction avant* that they must have commandeered, there's a Maltese cross painted on the side.

'That one?' I ask. I am kind of assuming now that we are out to scratch V for Victory on cars or daub it on walls and I want to get it over with.

He shakes his head. His arm around my waist is making the going a bit awkward, he is so much taller than me. As we turn into the Avenue Gallieni, he slips his arm away and takes my hand instead. This street is also pretty much deserted. There are just two lovers, real ones, embracing in a doorway. They look nice. We trot on and reach the Ave Meyerbeer.

'Here? There's no one about.'

But he shakes his head again and on we walk. I am actually fine. I'm happy holding his hand, though in a terrified sort of way. His is so dry and mine is so very damp. My heart is thudding.

At last, when I am almost tired of walking, we come into the rue Charlemagne and he lets go of my hand.

'Here's good,' he says. 'No Boche cars to scratch but we can do a paint job.'

'Charlemagne's alright.' I reply. 'Charlemagne's good.'

It's not an omen but Charlemagne's one of Papa's heroes. 'Ah, yes, the great unifier, the great European,' he always says. He's like a Pavlov dog, you say something that slots into one of the three thousand things that sit inside his mighty head and – woof woof – out it comes *The great unifier, the great European.* Or whatever.

Maurice mutters *Come on then*. I think we are both glad we are at last going to get on with it.

We go carefully as it is pretty dark in this street. The moon doesn't penetrate to the ground here but lights up the sharp angles of the mansards high above. The tiles glisten like the scales of a silver fish. Maurice holds my elbow and steers me into an alley where there is a faint light coming from a ground floor window.

'Good,' he breathes in my ear. I can feel the warmth off his body. 'Two ways out. Rue de Rivoli at the other end. Let's do it.'

The alley is long. I see a car passing on the rue de Rivoli, very small and far away.

Maurice unslings the knapsack, puts it on the ground and gets out the tin of paint. He jemmies it open with the screwdriver and pulls out the two brushes.

'One for you, one for me. You do the down stroke on the right, I'll do the upstroke. Then we scarper.'

I hold the brush, waiting. It's dripping paint so I hold it well away from me.

'You first,' he says. 'Just slap it on.'

'No, you.'

'Oh get on with it.'

We nip back into the rue Charlemagne and I'm just about to slap the paint onto the wall of the first house when Maurice hisses *Not this one. The next one.* So we creep along a few yards and there is an identical Hausmann façade and this time Maurice says *Alright, just do it.*

I hold the brush out, my arm full length, and sweep it down the wall. Maurice stoops and sticks his brush on the bottom of my stroke and does the upstroke.

We stand back to review our work, like artists. As it is as near pitch black as can be in the hollow of the street we can't really see anything much until suddenly a car swings round the corner and its headlights illuminate the dripping red V for Victory that we have just emblazoned on the wall.

The car stops twenty yards off. It is a little open-topped sports car. We are caught in its headlights. For a moment we are like those rabbits that are too stupid to work out the signals of danger. We stand frozen and then Maurice grabs my hand and we bolt, dashing into the alley, abandoning the knapsack and the paint and brushes on the *trottoir*.

We grope our way along the alley. In the darkness I stumble over a doorstep and fall down. *Good God, woman,* Maurice says. He grabs my hand and tugs me up. We stumble on along the alley towards the bright lights of the rue de Rivoli.

At the corner I pull away from him and bend down. My skirt is torn. There's blood coming from my knee.

'Christ!' Maurice says and grabs me by the arm, jerking me upright. 'Make like lovers, *nigaude!*'

He puts his arm around my waist again.

'And stop bloody crying.'

So I stop. He pulls out a silk handkerchief and has a quick dab at my face, then gives me the handkerchief. I blow my nose on it.

'*Putain d'enfer!*' he says. He grabs the handkerchief and stuffs it in his pocket.

We stroll awkwardly on beneath the arcade, past the shops. Maybe we look like quarrelling lovers.

And then there is Number 248. It's Mama's dear old WH Smith. *But what have they done to it?*

It is ablaze with light. The two great lanterns which hang out front are blazing. The windows are brilliantly lit. I feel I haven't seen so much light since the Catastrophe. And in the window, front and centre, it's not the Graham Greenes and the Aldous Huxleys Mama used to pore over, or the Evelyn Waughs or even Winnie-the-Pooh that she bought once and laughed about with her girlfriends in the tearoom upstairs over milk-and-a-dash and a digestive biscuit.

In the centre, amid the books, there is a fire of red and white and a dirty great black spider crawling. I quickly turn my head away. I can't stand it.

But Maurice seizes me and pulls me into the doorway. He says *Embrace me, you little cunt* and puts his arms right around me and lifts me up and kisses me full on the lips. I wriggle my head back and say *What?* He mutters *Boche patrol* and he angles his head and plants his lips back onto mine, more firmly than before. My eyes are open, I see his are closed. My eyes rove, past the swastika banners to the street and I hear the clop clop of the patrol and a squad of a dozen Boche soldiers clatters past in tight formation.

They pass but Maurice goes on kissing me and I am thinking just of Ma's coming here, all those hours choosing her new English novel and taking me upstairs and ordering me a milky tea and Welsh Rarebit. She would have died to see it now. *Frontbuchhandlung* it's called, and there's a huge sign in scary Gothic script that makes it look like a funeral parlour. And that black spider, that giant swastika flag, red and black and white, crawling in the window.

At that moment I see Papa's book. And almost in the same moment I see the little sports car, reflected in the window.

And then, *Parp parp parp*.

***

'A Renault Viva,' Maurice says.

In the car is a mec, a Boche, and not an ordinary one either, it's no simple Fritz but a decked-out officer type. He is lolling in his seat, easy in his world. His left arm hangs carelessly over the door.

'Oh, Christ!' Maurice says, looking up and down the street.

'Rue Cambon!' I cry, tugging at his hand. There's an alley there I know, next to Chanel's shop, another of Mama's places.

But it's too late, we can't run now. That tight little patrol is still just up the street. They've stood down for some reason, they're smoking and looking in a shop window.

I know what the penalty is for what we just did. Even for such a stupid trivial utterly pointless thing. It's fifteen years hard labour and your whole family deported.

We are at this mec's mercy. But what is his big idea? He has certainly got our attention, all of it. We look over at him but he just goes on sitting there in his cool roadster. He moves his arm lazily against the door. Then he sits up straight and hits the horn again. He beckons to us. So over we must go.

Unexpectedly, he says *Hop in*. He is talking to Maurice. His French is perfect.

'Erm...' Maurice says and waves his hand vaguely towards me.

'What about the girl?'

The girl! Not girlfriend. Not *mon amour*. Just a girl.

'She can sit on your lap, my friend.'

The Renault Viva is very pretty, pale blue with white leather seats and a dashboard of polished mahogany inlaid with rosewood. I know from my brother Franck that this is a top romantic car. The engine is ticking over huskily. I see there is a dicky seat but the mec is apparently not for opening it out for me.

Just do it, Maurice murmurs to me, not very friendly.

The German guy leans across and opens the passenger door and Maurice gets in. He plumps down in the seat, and then I follow him. I scramble about and manage to avoid sitting on the gear stick. I squeeze onto Maurice's lap. The German mec seems to find this quite amusing, at least he has a Krauty grin on his outsized face.

'Otto,' the Boche says, giving us a judicious look.

'Maurice,' says Maurice.

'And the kid? Your girlfriend?'

'No!' Maurice says, firmly.

The Otto nods, pursing his lips.

'So! Just necking then?'

'This is Anna-Elisa,' Maurice says in a neutral sort of tone. Otto nods again,

'I want to show you something,' he says. He revs the car up. It makes some bronchial noises and the two men turn their heads and listen in a concentrated way, as though the noise is passing them some special message.

'Vivastella Grand Sport,' Maurice says.

'*Oh ja*,' the German says, looking at Maurice. 'She's an ACX2.'

Maurice whistles.

"35?'

'*Richtig.*'

The German lets the clutch up and down a couple of times. There are some grinding sounds.

'You guys really need to work on the gearbox of this thing,' he says to Maurice, 'she hates going into first. But after that she's a real little goer.'

'The Matra's better,' Maurice says.

'Must try that one.'

The car jerks away and we proceed quite noisily down the rue de Rivoli and into the Champs Elysées. Otto takes all the corners at quite a speed, parp parping away.

We slow fractionally to take the next corner which is a sharper one. The Otto shoves away at the gear stick and the thing makes a noise like a thousand cats.

'*Scheisse*,' he says, 'no bloody synchromesh.'

'Nah,' says Maurice, shifting in his seat so that my wounded knee gets rammed up against the dashboard. It has stopped bleeding but there's a hideous trail of dried blood down my calf. I try and turn it away from the Kraut.

'Nah,' Maurice goes on, completely careless of me, 'these nippy little Renaults all have the sliding mesh crash boxes. You just have to get the speeds right.'

'Typical,' says the Otto. 'Porsche are working on a brilliant split ring synch…'

This gear box ding-dong between the males is interrupted because the car is stuttering and Otto is jabbing at the clutch and jerking the gear lever back and forth. All this proves fruitless and we judder to a halt.

'Damn! Stalled! Err… Maurice, if I may… would you mind…'

'Off!,' Maurice says to me, giving me a shove up with his thighs. I can't get the door open so I have to clamber out over it, clutching at my skirt to keep it down. I think of my English cousin Vanessa telling me she was taught at her boarding school how to get out of a sports car elegantly. That course is not available at the Lycée Condorcet but I still manage somehow to struggle out.

I stand on the pavement whilst Maurice goes on sitting for a couple of minutes chatting about the mechanics with his new Boche chum. Grrrr.

Eventually he jumps out, lopes forward and puts his arm under the car. After some fiddling about which leaves the arm of his beautiful suit a bit oily, he comes up with a crank handle.

He gives the engine a few energetic turns, Otto juggles with the controls, the engine coughs and eventually starts. Maurice jumps back in and pulls me onto his lap – and we're off again. We swing onto the bridge heading for the Left Bank. Otto and Maurice go on swapping notes about brake horsepower and bickering about whether the single overhead camshaft on the Mercedes six-cylinder job was better than the double version on the English Sunbeam 3 litre.

This is fine by me. It seems we are off the hook for that stupid V-daubing prank. Sitting on Maurice is not so comfortable and I am quite angry with him. But then it is quite thrilling to sit on the lap of a beautiful boy and career through Paris and over the Seine on a spring night in this lovely open-topped car. I haven't actually been in a car since Papa lent his heavy old Panhard to a family of Belgian refugees in the Flight from Paris and they never brought it back.

'So look there, my dears,' Otto says and waves his hand. We have arrived at the Palais Bourbon.

It's the *Chambre des Députés* – or the ex-*Chambre des Députés*, the conceptual *Chambre des Députés* since the *députés* all piked off to the Vichy Casino in '40 and dissolved themselves in Vichy water. The actual Palais, this ex-institution of France, is now some sort of branch of the Kommandantur, Boche HQ, managing France or Jews or something.

Otto stops the car. This is a risky move in my view but he is clearly a risk-taker. The engine stutters a bit but decides to keep going. Otto points and says,

'Look, look, children!'

He wants us to look at the Palais but I don't want to. It always has some stupid slogan on it, ever since they took it over – *Deutschland siegt an allen fronten* [Germany wins on all fronts] – is the usual one. How humiliating is that! That's why I never ever look at it, and I don't now. I look away, I actually look at this Otto character. I try to work out what he's up to.

Because to be honest, up to this moment, I've never really met the Occupier, except once or twice when we Frenchies have been en masse queueing up for coupons or something and there's been a bit of bother and then it's just been some run down old Boche grandpa with a rifle who's sent for, and he shouts out *Do this*! Or *Over there*! Or, most often, *Don't do that*! (which would be just about everything I want to do). But usually this constant ticking off and the endless *formular ausfuellen*-ing is laid off onto our guys anyway, our prefects and gendarmes and petty bureaucrats who crowd forward like poodles to lick the Boche's arse.

You almost never meet a real Boche unless you particularly want to. But I would never go there. That's for *sales putes*.

So I look at the Otto in a very truculent way and he looks back at me. His over-large face, which is of a standard issue 'finely chiselled' German type, gives nothing away, except a sort of ironical smile that is just detectable in the mouth part of the chiselling, but this hint of humour is not available in any other part of his physog. I am actually searching for a sign that might confirm our common humanity or something like that but the evidence is so far pretty slim.

He looks at me with this big, too perfect face. The brows hang over his passionless grey eyes.

'Mademoiselle... Anna-Elisa... look please, look and learn.' He nods towards the Palais Bourbon, so of course I now have to look and there is the *winning on all fronts* monstrosity and above it, newly in place, is the most gigantic V.

Duh duh duh derr, Otto says, doing the Beethoven's Fifth thing.

'That's one of ours,' he says.

By now he's only addressing me. Maurice, the worm, has managed to get his face hidden from the Kraut and he is taking no part in this dialogue. Or monologue, because now the Otto seems intent on preaching at me.

'So, Anna-Elisa,' he says in an uncle-like, faux-benign kind of way, 'you are young, but these days the young must learn fast. You must learn to live in the world as it is and not as you would like it to be. Not risking all your future on painting up stupid V signs on somebody's nice house when we have this lovely big one right here.'

I snort, or try to. At this point, the engine dies. Otto wags his head.

'Anna, Anna, England and Colonel de Gaulle do not have a monopoly on V signs.'

This is getting too personal. I look away.

'Anyway, my dear, in your precious England, a V sign really means *Fuck you*.'

Bloody Maurice doesn't utter a peep. I feel his shoulder move slightly. I think he is laughing.

'And in your own dear old *patrie*, V is for Vichy. So this big offensive V is really our concession to French *amour propre*.'

I wriggle round so that my back is turned on Otto and on the big V.

This brings Maurice's face into Otto's line of view.

'Fancy a drink?' Otto says, and Maurice at once says 'Yes.'

So that's decided then without any reference to me. Maurice simply says to me *Budge out again* and I have to hop onto the pavement so that he can get out and crank up the Renault Viva once more. I am happy to see he gets even more oily crap on his nice tussore suit, this time on the trousers.

We speed off. Otto does some very fast driving into the Treizième.

And something comes over me. The night is still warm and the speed and the wind in my hair are exciting. We have a near miss on one straight stretch and Otto does a couple of what he calls handbrake turns which Maurice very much admires. The two of them have a high old time.

And I find myself thinking that actually there are worse things than riding along like this, even if there is a Boche at the wheel.

We stop outside a building in the rue de Nice. It's got a brassy sign up, blue neon lights. *The Scheherazade Bar and Night Club*. I have never been to a bar, or for that matter to a night club, but I quickly conclude that the Scheherazade is not in the top echelons. A grubby lantern hangs over the entrance. The door is painted scarlet. A couple of doubtful looking young women lean against the wall outside, smoking and flicking their ash into the gutter.

'What do you think?' Otto asks, and I see him looking at me in a whimsical sort of way.

'Erm... looks dirty.'

'Oh yes,' he says and gets out of the car. Maurice says 'Budge up' and starts to stand up himself, so that I have to slither off his lap.

Inside the Scheherazade Bar and Night Club, it is incredibly dark and hot. There is a band playing jazz somewhere in the gloom. Otto leads on and we stumble our way down some steps. A mec in a waiter's dickey has a word in Otto's ear and gets us seated at a low table. The banquette I sit on feels hot and damp. It's covered in plastic. The damp comes through my skirt. The low table has several dirty glasses on it, one of them with lipstick staining the rim. Otto waves his hand and a waitress comes and clears away the glasses. She soon comes back with a bottle of champagne.

Little by little my eyes adjust to the gloom. The Scheherazade is bigger than it looked at first sight. There's a score of tables set around a dance floor. At each table there are one or two young women sitting. Their lips are red and their eyes are black. A few Boches in uniform, not officers, are drinking beer, some of them together with each other, others sitting apart with girls. One girl is sitting by herself. Through all the murk she looks very beautiful. Her complexion is not the white of chalk or alabaster like the others but the palest brown, like *café au lait*. Her eyes are huge. She has long black hair that falls to her bare shoulders. The band is on a low dais in the corner. They stop playing and start to drink beer.

'You want to dance with her?' Otto asks Maurice. He waves his hand, indicating the pretty girl. Maurice shakes his head.

'Good. And you?' He is addressing me. 'You like the *métisse*?' I shake my head vigorously.

Otto pours out the champagne, half a glass for me.

'So you see, Anna-Elisa,' Otto says, 'that painting up V signs or putting up fishing rods or tearing down or putting up posters, these are childish things. They will not change anything, except that you will provoke the Occupier. *Nacht und nebel.'*

I look blank. Otto looks at me, a look of pity I judge. He says,

'My dear, *Nacht und nebel,* night and fog. It's from the Fuehrer's beloved *Rheingold.'*

I look blanker. He leans across and whispers in my ear,

'The Fuehrer says that efficient and enduring intimidation can only be achieved through measures by which the relatives of the criminals *do not know the fate of the criminal.'*

He sips at his champagne, watching me. How is it he knows *all* our dodges, even the *deux gaules*?

'Fruitless,' Otto says, 'fruitless, stupid waste. Pissing in the ocean. That V you painted, whatever you mean by it, nothing but nothing will be accomplished. The *haut bourgeois* living in that house will have the trouble of getting it scrubbed off in the morning, and the only benefit will be the twelve sous the workman earns.'

'I want to go home,' I say. The two men ignore me.

A German NCO is now sitting with the pretty *métisse,* touching her shoulder. The band starts to play again and a woman comes on, bare arms and low cut dress. She sings that Charles Trenet song, *La Romance de Paris.* Other Germans get up with the girls they have been sitting with and they go onto the floor and start to dance.

Ils s'aimaient depuis deux jours à peine

This is such rubbish. Tonight I was committing an act of Resistance, or pretending to, and now here I am drinking champagne with a Boche and listening to this stupid song.

And now the Otto is addressing me, or looking at me and singing along.

> *Leur amour était un vrai printemps, oui*
> *Aussi pur que leurs tendres vingt ans.*

Yeah, right. So their love was like the spring and as pure as their tender twenty years. Very likely, I don't think.

'Not even twenty,' he says, eyeing me. He is managing to be soppy and condescending at the same time. It's me he means. I'm not even twenty, so purer still. Obviously.

I frown at him. He is not in the least put out but nods his head and sings along a bit more. We get to the most cringeworthy bit, the bit where they head off to the woods to pick lily of the valley, and then it's boating, and then a drink at a little bar beside the river.

> *Ils partaient à la fin de la semaine*
> *Dans les bois pour cueillir le muguet*
> *Ou sur un bateau pour naviguer.*
> *Ils buvaient aussi dans les guinguettes*

I scowl and turn away and try to close my ears to this cack. I mean, from what I hear, wouldn't they just go to bed and have loads of sex?

The only thing is, now the Otto has turned away. He is directing all his attention to Maurice and they are chatting away nineteen to the dozen. Maurice has had four glasses of champagne at Otto's expense – I've been counting – and now the Boche is ordering another bottle. I still haven't finished my little half a glass.

The singing *zouz* steps up her act to a whole new level of pap. Oh God, it's only *Le premier rendez-vous*. I saw the film at the Berlitz and that was pap too. But at least she is making less of a racket over it, so I can listen in to Otto and Maurice's little causerie while pretending not to.

It seems that this Otto is some sort of censor. His job is to read new French books and decide which ones can be published – or not. He starts talking a lot about a new Algerian author, Albert something, and his weird and brilliant new book called *The Stranger*.

'I am proud,' says Otto, 'that I have been the first to read it.'

'Any good?' Maurice asks in a simpering, sucky sort of way. As far I know, Maurice has zero interest in literature.

'Masterly,' the Otto says. 'Perhaps a masterpiece. It will endure.'

Maurice is craning towards the Otto. He looks like a puppy that wants to be stroked. He says,

'Oh! And… er… what do you reject, as a censor?'

The Kraut cracks a smile.

'Almost nothing. Your idiot French writers reject their own stuff. They censor themselves. Writers won't write the truth or they dress it up so you'd never know what they were talking about… like M. Sartre, that new piece of his, what's its name…?'

Maurice makes a vague gesture with his hands and screws up his eyes as though he is trying to recall. He's such an idiot. I don't think he knows Sartre from Stendhal.

The din has again become terrible. The singing lady and the band have finished with the saccharine *Rendez-vous* and are now banging out something I don't at first recognize.

'*The Flies*,' I say as loud as I can, I actually shout.

Then I realize the ditty the *meuf* is bawling out now is *Que reste-t-il de nos amours*? It's by that filthy collabo Trenet. Then the music suddenly stops and into the silence I actually hear that rat Maurice say with a stupid syrupy look on his face,

'Umm, *The Flies*, I think.'

'Oh, yes, good man' says the Otto, squaring his back against me and shutting me off one hundred percent. '*The*

Flies, that's right, of course. A play so clever it disappears up its own backside...'

What is going on? I mean, other than the usual *Ignore the dumb chick stuff*? I bet Maurice didn't even know it was a play.

I lean over really close to the Otto, I mean right up to him and I say in his ear,

'You passed it?'

He has the grace to turn his great head towards me. He says,

'No trouble at all, Anna-Elisa. You'd need to write a thesis to see that it's supposed to be against the Occupation, as M. Sartre so fondly proclaims.'

Otto laughs. Maurice laughs. I don't laugh, but obviously they don't care about me.

'Anyway,' Otto goes on, turning his full attention back to Maurice, 'the publishers know what to do and they do it. Right from the start. Within months of the Occupation they pulled more than 2,000 titles. Jewish stuff mostly, Freud and Einstein, and also other undesirables like DH Lawrence, that kind of muck.'

Otto has a sardonic style. He doesn't give much away. He says 'muck' in that way people have when they want you to think that is not what they are really thinking.

But what *is* he really thinking?

'The only book we actually banned in France,' he says, 'was *Mein Kampf*, the *chef d'oeuvre* of our great *Reichskanzler*.'

Maurice does a quizzical look. At least he's heard of that one.

'Oh, my dear,' Otto says, 'we had to ban it because we don't want you sensitive Frenchies to know what the dear leader really thinks of you.'

Otto pours Maurice yet another drink (but not me) and

then he leans back and moves a little closer to Maurice.

'So you see, Maurice,' he says, 'I have the best job in the world. Reading high literature in French all day, and swanning about Paris by night with beautiful people.'

5

The next day, it's a big let-down. I am no longer the *risquée* girl of the night. I am back at school, a schoolgirl in my staid old *tablier*, plain little Anna-Elisa Schneider. But I can't wait to tell Maddie and Verónica all about my evening.

But I don't see them before school and they're not in the first lesson which is Greek verses. I haven't done last night's prep and I am praying that dried up old Georgie will not call on me. We are reading Euripides' *Trojan Women* which is all about after the Fall of Troy and the fate of the Trojans. The Greeks take Troy by superior technology, slaughter all the men and enslave all the women. It flashes through my mind that just maybe Georgie has chosen this play as a sort of parable of our own present problems. But I reject this as soon as I think of it. Of course not, she doesn't have the imagination. Anyway, it's been on the Bacc syllabus for centuries.

But Otto should take a look. I think it should be censored!

All through the lesson I am in a dream and a sort of panic. In the dream I go out and do stuff and have fun and drink champagne and watch pretty *café au lait métisses* seducing stiff soldiers and listen to grown-up talk about art and books. And a beautiful young man kisses me on the lips and does that thing with his tongue, which is fine, even if he was a worm later with Otto.

The panic of course is *Where on earth is Maddie today? Where, oh where is Verónica?*

My mind wanders. I am thinking about Maurice. I sat on

his lap again when Otto drove us home and it was very snug. Maurice's hand was on my thigh which was exciting enough and while Otto was talking about Emile Zola, the hand was making sort of caressing motions. Probably more absent-mindedness than anything but it was a thrill anyway.

They dropped me off at mine. Maurice didn't get out of the car or kiss me goodbye. He just gave me a little pat on the bottom as I hauled myself out. I mumbled something in Otto's direction like *Thanks for a nice time*, then stood on the pavement thinking what a stupid thing to say and doing a little farewell wave but they were chatting away and the car moved off throatily. They didn't once look back.

Then it only remained to creep in past the Old Bat's horrid lair and up the stairs and into our flat. Pauli was already in my bed, snoozing away wrapped in my old cardigan, his sopping pyjamas on the floor. I was so tired I didn't bother going into his room to haul off his wringing wet sheets. I just flopped down and…

Whack!

Georgie has rapped me on the back of the hand, the cow.

'Black mark for you, Schneider,' she says. But I'm in luck as she doesn't bother asking me to translate.

In break, I dash out the first into the corridor to see if Maddie or Verónica are somewhere around. Perhaps they were late and put into detention. Straightway I run into the scowling plump figure of Mlle de Beauvoir. She is standing in the corridor almost outside the classroom. She has got on a shapeless brown pullover that comes down almost to her knees. She darts forward as soon as she sees me, as if she were waiting for me. She takes me firmly by the arm. Why? She doesn't even know me.

'Come,' she says, peering into my face. This close, her eyes are like lapis, startling and hard. 'Come and walk with me a minute.' It is not an invitation, it is an instruction.

She leads me out of the building into the street. For me this is hundred percent *interdit* but old Chupin lets us go. I'm with a teacher, even if she is a bit of a dodgy one. The air is warm. Spring is hotting up and today it feels close and damp. Under my gabardine tunic I feel my blouse sticking to me. Mlle steers me down into the street and starts talking about lessons, some little facts about Spinoza. Why is she chattering like this?

But after a minute, when we are some way down the street and passing the *Tabac*, she stops talking about philosophy and says abruptly,

'So what have you and Madeleine and the other girl, the Spanish one – what have you been up to?'

'Umm... what do you mean?'

'What were you up to last night?'

'But you don't know me or anything about it.'

She presses my arm harshly, digging in her fingers.

'I heard. I heard about your little escapade.'

I try to hang back but she is pulling me along.

'You know,' she says, and she sounds angry, 'we had a group, a resistance group, right at the start. *Socialism and Liberty* we called it. We were going to do something big, really big.'

I try to hang back but she drags me on.

'Really big,' she says again.

'Like what? Kill people?'

'Yes. Kill that swine Déat, for example. He was going to be the first.'

'What?'

'Yes, Déat. He's a filthy fascist. Then we were going to

blow up the German bookshop, you know the old...'

'*What?*' I mean, is *everybody* blowing up the German bookshop?

For a minute she is silent. She steers me on with a firm grip. At last we get to the corner and she stops and turns and grasps me by the elbows, pulling me to confront her.

'But then,' she says, 'then everything changed. Our thinking changed...'

I say nothing. She stares into my face with the harsh lapis eyes.

She goes *Pouf!* And pulls me round and pushes her arm through mine and starts to march me further down the road. Now she is silent, she seems angry. At last I ask her,

'Were you afraid?'

'Of course! Who wouldn't be? But it wasn't that. It was not right to resist at the expense of others.'

'Like the fifty hostages?'

'Yes. Precisely. The fifty hostages. We thought, resist, yes, if we could just find some *pure* way of resisting...'

We stop and she looks up and down the road. It is almost empty. A hundred yards off there is a sad old nag dragging a rag and bone cart behind it. The guy is sitting like the *roi des cons* on the top of a heap of old clothes and iron, calling out his incomprehensible appeal. Opposite, a small queue is forming outside a haberdashers. There must be an *arrivage* – wool, perhaps.

Mlle now marches me across the dusty road. The cobbles are harsh and a few are loose and poking up. Once over, she relaxes her grip a little and guides me more gently. We go past the shut-up Jewish tailor's shop. It was here in the early days that the gangs of youths paid by Déat used to stand in the doorway and ogle us as we trooped to school. Sometimes, though, they were too busy to do their stupid wolf whistles, too busy roughing up the people who were trying to go into the Jew's shop. Now, of course, the shop is long deserted. It's all boarded up. There are the official notices about expropriation and recently they've started using it as a billboard for the lists of *suehnepersonen*, the *Expiators*. There's a new one today, in red with black borders. It's a long list, another fifty men shot for someone else's crime. We don't linger.

'Any least little action you do, Anna, will come back like fate and be visited on someone else fifty times over, a hundred times over. Not on you but on your neighbour. On your family, your friends, on complete strangers. *Expiators* to be shot in a filthy cellar in the Vincennes fortress.'

I am walking more and more slowly.

'Whatever little good Resistance might do will cost the blood of others.'

Again, again, this blood of others!

'But Maddie...' I burst out at last. 'Do you know where she is?'

'Not on the list at least,' Mlle says.

'But where is she?'

'She's at home. She was picked up by the gendarmes last night along with the other girl, Verónica is it? It seems they had been tearing down posters. Silly girls. What good would that do? How would that help?'

'We... they... meant well.'

'Meant well? *Meant well*? That is such criminal innocence. *Meant well* is nothing at all. What was the result? That's the question. Not what did they intend but what was the result. We are responsible for the consequences of our actions.'

'But Maddie...?'

Mlle gives a little scornful laugh.

'Oh, she's alright.'

'Really?'

'Yes, really. As soon as they heard her name down at the gendarmerie they telephoned her daddy. He went round and got her right away, just like that. It seems that her daddy is right in with the Old Mummy down in Vichy. Whereas the other girl...'

'Verónica?'

Mlle looks at me hard and nods her head up and down, pursing her lips.

'The other girl... they seemed to think she was an unregistered alien or something. They got the father in and after some... err... exchanges, they finally let her go...'

'Exchanges?'

'Yes.'

Mlle does not enlarge but I suppose she means money changed hands. Who cares? At least they're both out. And apparently cooling their heels at home whilst la Bazin considers whether they can come back to school.

'I thought you should know all this,' says the Beaver. 'Mlle Bazin told us this morning. I think you should be very careful indeed. For yourself and for others.'

At lunch I run to the *Tabac* and telephone to Maddie's house. Whoever answers – it sounds like her mother – says she is not available. And not to call again. I ring a number for Verónica that she once gave me but the telephonist says there is no such number. Before school starts again I just have time to nip to the post office and scribble a *pneu* to Maddie which I send off.

I run back to school and arrive panting and dishevelled. And there parked in the South Door entrance is Natalie Tardieu. She spots me and quickly comes up. She gives me her signature sly smile, her lopsided mouth sagging further to the left. Her eyes are swivelling from side to side, not looking at me but alongside me as though there were some faintly humorous aura nearby.

Will a boy one day, I am wondering, find this strange assembly compelling? Will it drive him to passion, will it propel him to spend the rest of his life admiring such a woman? I don't know. I have no idea how such things work.

Today, for the purposes of this confrontation – for such it seems to be – she is flanked by Gilberte, her chief lieutenant. There are in attendance also a couple of her smirking acolytes from the *deuxième*. They are hanging back in the doorway, but are definitely in the offing.

'So,' says Natalie.

Her gang are not exactly obstructing me, but they've made it so it would be a definite detour to get through the doorway. I stay mum. Natalie's head drops down and she gives a little *tsk*, feigning disappointment.

'Come on, Schneider, give us the dirt. What did the Beaver haul you out for this morning?'

I suddenly feel a completely irrational urge to please la Tardieu. God knows why. Am I fragile without Maddie? Can I not stand on my own two feet when I am confronted by the witless guiles of Natalie Tardieu? There are always so many explanations of why I do the wrong thing.

Actually, I am thinking it would be such a luxury not to have to fight just now.

Whatever. There is no good reason why I suddenly blurt out,

'*Meant well? Meant well? Meant well is nothing at all. We are all responsible for the consequences of our actions.*'

I get the Beaver to a T. I'm such a brilliant mimic. The intonation, the rapid-fire talk, the husky voice (even without benefit of cigarettes). I even round my shoulders and stoop a little.

Natalie does not laugh, nor do her coterie. But what did I expect? What I didn't expect is the sudden expression of delight that flits across her face. Her eyes are staring straight ahead, but not at me. All of the gang are looking just past me. So what is this? What is the source of this wicked joy?

It is then that I sense there is somebody right behind me and I turn.

And of course, there is the Beaver.

An electric flush of shame sweeps through me. It takes away my ability to speak. My mouth is open, but nothing is coming out.

The Beaver walks past me and Natalie's gang parts to let her through.

Mmm, says Natalie, turning to follow. She is, I think, very happy indeed.

Darts of shame pierce me all afternoon. St Sebastian was not more punctured.

It's Latin, Livy on the founding of Rome. Who cares? Mlle Duval proses on about her hopes that the lost books of Livy will be rediscovered in some ancient library, like the Song of Roland she says was found in Oxford last century. But I hope the exact opposite. I hope that even the found books of Livy will be lost.

All along, my inflamed mind is running on a bigger question. What sort of character flaw is it that leads me to betray the Beaver's confidence, and to do it to Natalie Tardieu and her insidious little crew? How can I have let down Maddie and my little Mouse Verónica like that, my brave sisters? To turn Beaver's news and her trust in me into a shabby pantomime for a girl I despise in my heart.

Such a betrayal. It eats at me. I wish the cock would crow

and somehow end it.

And this stupid self-lacerating pain stops me from thinking of the Main Idea, the big question that the Beaver left with me.

What is the pure way of resisting?

That evening I am still writhing with shame. I decide I will write a letter.

> Dear Mademoiselle de Beauvoir,
> I want to apologise for my rude behaviour today. ~~I can only think I was upset about Magdalena and that made me~~ There is no excuse for ~~such a trivialising trivial your confidence my behaviour~~ what I did ~~of which~~ I am thoroughly ashamed, and I am very sorry.
> Yours truly.

I gaze at this letter, amazed by its sheer feebleness. What good would it do, anyway? The Beaver surely wouldn't care and she wouldn't believe I am sorry. She would probably say *It was your own action, and you are responsible for the consequences.* Quite right too.

Anyway, what *are* the consequences? The Beaver obviously doesn't give a damn about a silly schoolgirl. Natalie Tardieu has scored big time, so she's quids in.

And consequences for me? I am punished anyway. The hot shame surges up in me every minute of the day. And better still, a bigger punishment still – *it doesn't get any less.*

I tear the letter into fragments, and then tear the fragments again and chuck them in the bin.

The only purpose of this stupid letter was to lance my shame and pander to my disgusting vanity. What is the use of such an apology except to inflate my weedy ego? To restore me in my own eyes. First, as the *girl who owns up and says sorry*, and then as a fit friend for Maddie. To reassure my fragile self-view that I am not really that fearful creature that wanted to suck up to the loathsome Tardieu.

Bin the letter! Bin the pride! Take the hit, feel the shame, lick the scar.

Worthless Annie.

I hear nothing from Maddie. Nor from Maurice. But a letter has come from Franck, slipped under our door by an unknown hand. From time to time, the Germans release a few PoWs, top bods, artists, musicians, that kind of mec, and these guys, probably feeling a bit shame-faced, smuggle out letters for their mates.

Letter from Franck

Dearest meine Schwester
Here a sort of life continues. It is supposed to be spring but very cold and I have no warm clothes apart from my army greatcoat. Last night it was minus twenty degrees. If you can send me my old Arran sweater that Aunt Marjory knitted, this would be a lifesaver and very kind of you.

And the food gets worse and worse, and less and less. We're lucky to get a thin gruel. Everybody is incredibly hungry all the time. We spent a whole evening recently discussing recipes for *caneton à l'orange*. It was excruciating. The next day there was a young Pole executed because he had stolen three potatoes – *three potatoes*!

Please send me a little something of yours. I cannot hug you or pull your hair or make music with you, it will be a little symbol that will be *you*.

The worst thing here is that there is never any privacy, never that time of quiet when one can think and try to make sense of anything. Messiaen has taken to composing in the lats. He is doing something tremendous, I think. It is called *A Quartet for the End of Time*, which sounds about right.

I went out of the hut the other night and bribed the guard with a packet of cigarettes to let me walk for a while. It was a bright night crammed with stars and lit by a brilliant moon but the cold was intense and soon entered my bones. I felt for a moment, just a moment, that old exaltation that we used to know when we escaped to the hills, that time at the Cirque de Gavarnie, for example – remember? Or when we were at Evreux in the thrall of Beethoven, in the andante of the eighth quartet.

And then it all crashed down and I realized for the first time that all our efforts really counted for nothing. All Mama's blundering tries to organize international peace, all that frail League of hers that just melted down into a heap before our eyes. And all Papa's 'bind us together with cords that cannot be broken' – well, the Nazis not only cut the cords, *they took a bloody great pair of shears to them* (this in English).

And all our music and our fine arts and fine thinking – they're not on the back burner. They're on the pyre, and they're thrown there by the very people who created the most and the best. From this day forward, only licenced art that conforms to the norms of the tyrants set over us will be permitted.

So, Annushka, my little Anschli, you ask what it is that has come between Papa and me. I weep in my heart every minute. But I must not tell you.

Believe me, believe in me, beloved *meine Schwester*.

Je t'embrasse.

Franck

PS They have offered me the job of crane operator at a factory. All their men are at the Eastern Front. I need activity. But I will not do this, which is after all pure *collaboration*.

6

The monkey bites of shame wake me several times in the night but at last tomorrow comes. And of course it has to be a Wednesday, big day for Philo. A double lesson with the Beaver to look forward to.

I get up, do my chores, make a meagre breakfast, get Pauli ready for school and take him there, go to the *lycée* where I am in a daze. But the big excitement is that Verónica is back. She spends a long time in la Bazin's lair before she is released to us in class. She sits at the front and everybody stares at her. Of course, they've heard all about her escapade. She might as well be wearing a scarlet letter.

In break I run to her desk and give her a hug. She feels thin as a wafer and she looks wan. Her eyes are huge and dark. I breathe in her ear *Are you alright, darling?* She doesn't reply.

'Have you seen Maddie?'

But she doesn't say a word, just mouths *Uh-huh*.

And then it's time for Double Philo with the Beaver. I am quaking. Mlle de Beauvoir comes in late as usual and hoists herself up on her desk and swings her feet and swirls her bead necklace round and round. She doesn't look at me, or indeed at anyone in particular. She behaves absolutely as normal. She starts banging on about Spinoza who she says was a Jew who renounced all religion.

My fear subsides a little. Maybe she didn't hear. Maybe she doesn't care.

And then, just as we hear the courtyard clock start to strike midday, Verónica finally stirs from her interior mood.

She puts up her hand. The Beaver recognizes her and she stands up and says *Shall we observe?*

The Beaver looks pretty surprised but soon recovers. She says nothing but just stops talking and for five minutes nobody says a word.

And so we Resist! It is the five minutes silence by which we honour the fifty hostages the Boches shot the other day in the cellars of Vincennes. It was their reprisal for some trivial Resistance act, a brick through the window of the Kommandantur, was it?

Is this a pure way of resisting?

Although what good does it do? Probably it is just like Diogenes rolling his barrel. We all feel huge merit afterwards, there is a definite air of self-satisfaction in the classroom. But what good does it do?

Verónica continues to look sad and when the Beaver asks her some trivial question, she just shakes her head very slowly indeed.

The rest of the day I plod on. I do Greek, I do Latin, I do English, all in a dream.

In afternoon break I try again to talk to Verónica but she stays sulky and silent and then goes off to the lavatories. Natalie Tardieu sweeps by with her gang. She is cock-a-hoop.

After school, Verónica just pikes off, I don't know where, so I go and fetch Pauli from school, drop him at home, take Paco for his walk, then line up with grumbling beldames at the grocery shop for an hour. It is, however, worth it, sort of, because M. Macron the grocer takes pity on me and slips me an extra kilo of flour, off the ration.

I think how much we expected of our lives and now all we ask is a second kilo of flour off the ration.

We eat a listless supper *en famille*.

I keep expecting something from Maddie, another *pneu*, but nothing comes. And as for that worm Maurice, I've given up hope. Not a whisper.

So I plod on. I do homework (prep Herodotus about a mec who spent his life avoiding notice – how do you become famous in world history for *that*?). I put Pauli down, go to bed myself, get up at two to tell Pauli to *faire pipi* but too late, change his sheets and pyjamas, go back to bed and try to sleep but can't, then Pauli comes in and wants to snuggle up and why not, then up at six to finally wring out the blankets in the kitchen which have begun to smell not so good but I sprinkle some lavender water on them, make spartan breakfast, take Paco for his *matinale* promenade etc. etc. and… begin again!

Annie to Franck

I write to Franck in his awful Stalag. Purposely, I don't mention our escapade or Maddie's absence.

Mein bester Bruder,
I embrace you too, but I cannot comprehend you. What have you done to Papa? He is so low and out of spirits and will not bear the mention of your name. There surely is nothing in the world that could separate you from him, you his well-loved first-born son, you his hope for the future (for the girl will never do, and Pauli is just his little late lamb!). I write this in jest, but also in all seriousness. You must tell me and let me make it right.

In the meantime I send you my St Jude. As you know, he is the saint for the hopeless and the despaired. Maddie gave him to me years ago. He is silver and the chain is silver and you must wear him around your neck at all times. Maddie blessed him with a Catholic kiss, so he is an *empowered* symbol. Take him off *for whatever reason*, he will lose all his power – and I will wither to a heap of ash.

Here life goes on after its fashion, my half-life. Mostly I do for Papa, I care for Pauli, I go to school, I go to bed. I queued three hours yesterday for potatoes and then that crook Lebras said my coupons were forged and I had to give him a whole four sous on top if he was to turn a blind eye. I didn't believe him, the coupons were never forged. I got them from the commissariat myself. Yet he wouldn't budge. The people in the queue behind me didn't care, they didn't back me up. They are so used to this kind of petty spivvery. They were all calling out *Oh get on with it!. We've been waiting hours!* So I gave him the price and the four sous on top and left the shop shaking with indignation.

Maddie sends *bises*. She is my only spark of life. Verónica just sulks all the time, she is hopeless and v. bad company. Nothing from Eric. Officially, *il est porté disparu*, but I have my own thoughts, as does Maddie. Oh, and I have met Maddie's so handsome cousin Maurice. He kissed me (sorry, but he is not a pimply youth so I felt you wouldn't mind). I am a little bit in love with him already.

So not always such a half-life. Sorry for that too!

Embrasses and *mille bises*, Annie

Pity that I lie about Maddie. And that I have written so little that is true in this letter. But truth telling is on the ration. Consolation is the thing these days.

7

The good weather pauses. Thursday is grey and there is a chill breeze scouring the courtyard of the lycée, blowing up dust. In Maddie's absence, Natalie Tardieu bangs the big drum for assembly and she makes a fine old mess of it.

Afterwards, la Bazin keeps us seniors back. It turns out that she wants to discuss the hymn for the Old Gaffer next week.

But has anyone learned the words? Apparently not, because there is a shuffling and jockeying as we all try to get to the back of the group. Verónica is left standing at the front but as always she evidently doesn't give a damn.

There are now some black clouds edging in, so I cross my fingers and hope for drizzle to break up the meeting.

La Bazin advances. On her face is an expression that might in a lesser woman have been mistaken for a smile. She stands before us holding a paper. Does she want a run through?

But it turns out to be not that at all. She announces that we are now *not* to sing the hymn. She waves the paper. It is, she says in her most important voice, a communication she has just received from the Government Press Office.

'Let me read it to you, girls. You are old enough to begin to learn the workings of our government. It is from a M. Artuby, Chef de service, who writes as follows:

'In referring to the Head of State, the expression "The Old Gentleman" must be avoided even when preceded by a well-disposed adjective such as "illustrious" or "valiant".

On the other hand, frequent mention should be made of the Marshall's moral and physical vigour, shown in action. For example, "The Marshall came forward with a quick and decisive step. He showed the liveliest interest in the explanations given to him."

'There follows a list of texts which are not considered appropriate, and sadly our hymn is amongst them. We shall, therefore, simply welcome our Head of State with our usual sprightly rendering of *Je suis là…*'

As we go in, I catch up with Verónica and link my arm through hers. Her arm is as thin as a stick. She gives me a sideways look of endless dolour.

'But we're still on for shooting the mec, aren't we?' she breathes.

Oh God, not that again!

Not me, I demur. But quietly, and to myself alone.

At big break a huge polemic starts up. It concerns the posters that have gone up all over Paris about the pets. It's an instruction from the Kommandantur saying there are two million dogs and cats living in Paris and they are eating too much. The Kommandantur is ordering the round-up of all strays and they are offering 'free disposal' of pets that are given up voluntarily.

Is this curtains for Paco?

The girls in *première* are divided on this one. Some say the Boche are going to use our dogs for target practice. Others say they will make a handy off-ration supplement to the meat allowance. Clemence's old granny who was a toddler in the siege of Paris in '70 is apparently claiming they ate 40,000 horses plus all the dogs and cats. She says the price of a plump rat, no doubt gorged on human flesh, was completely unaffordable and that 'a well-cooked rat tasted rather like chicken on the palate'.

Well, gourmet appreciations apart, the general feeling is that No, we won't give up our pets. Clemence says her own cat ran off when it heard the news and they haven't seen it since. Verónica mutters *Bet they ate it.*

And Clemence admits her Daddy already ran their dog down to the pound and I am sure she is secretly OK with that. It was an old spaniel, a frightful greasy old thing anyway, she never stopped complaining about it. *Daddy insisted*, she now claims, pouting and pretending to cry but I'm sure she's already worked out how much more of her 75 grammes of J3 (Adolescent female) meat allowance she will be getting now they don't have to give a share to her poor old pooch.

I say to Clemence 'How can you weigh love against meat like that?' and she replies 'Bloody Occupation!'

Which seems a fair answer to a really stupid question.

But what about Paco?

As it's Thursday, it's our half day, so I have the luxury of queuing at the greengrocers for the two hours it takes to discover they are out of everything except carrots.

When I get in with my slim pickings, the Old Bat darts out at a velocity that belies her famous gammy leg. She thrusts a little blue envelope into my hands. I ferret in my purse and manage to find 10 sous for her. She accepts this with her usual grace and skips off.

But it's worth my ten sous. The *pneu* is from the girl herself. Finally.

All well. Gated by Pater. Lots to talk about. Come round tonight. Cailloux. xxx

Cailloux is code. She means chuck a pebble at her window, then she'll nip out without the fearsome Pater being any the wiser.

Of course, just on the very night that I want to get Pauli to bed early and sneak out round to Maddie's, the dog *auto-da-fé* topic is the issue of the hour.

It's not that Pa is going to stop me going out. This is actually one advantage of having an absent and neglectful father. He really won't notice if I'm not there. But Pauli on the other hand is the big risk. I'll have to get him to sleep before I go and then be back before he has one of his stupid nightmares or pees the bed earlier than his usual two in the morning slot and tries to come into mine and finds me not there and starts creating as only he knows how.

It starts badly. The minute we sit down to dinner Pauli broaches the interesting topic of Paco's outlook. Some kid at his school was apparently blubbing all day because his flea-bitten old mongrel was popped down to the pound.

So Pauli launches the polemic and the conversation goes like this.

Pauli: 'We'll never let Paco go! Will we? Will we, Papa?'

Moi: 'He's awfully rheumaticky. Maybe it would be the kindest thing.'

Pauli: 'Papa!'

Papa: 'What?'

Pauli: 'No! He's Mummy's dog.'

Moi: 'But there's already nothing for him to eat. And his rheumatism really is terrible. He's limping about all the time.'

Pauli: 'Papa!'

Papa: 'What?'

Pauli: 'Annie wants to kill Paco!'

Papa: 'What?'
Pauli: 'Annie wants to eat Paco!'
Papa: 'Oh, sometimes we must just let go, my boy.'
Pauli: 'No! He's Mummy's dog. He's *my* dog!'
Moi: 'But he's hungry all the time. He ate all those bones yesterday and was up all night vomiting blood.'
Pauli: 'You're mean. You don't feed him!'
Moi: 'Pauli dearest, there isn't even anything for us to eat. Paco's wasting away. Remember how M. Dupont at the vet's said he had a "pendulous belly" because there was nothing in it. And today I caught him chewing Mama's old pigskin suitcase.'

All this time, Paco is keeping a keen eye on proceedings, sitting beside each of us in turn with his horribly liquid pleading eyes and shoving his doleful muzzle against our legs. Papa pays no attention to this pantomime and it doesn't impress me much either, but it is deeply moving for Pauli who falls down on his knees and shoves his face into Paco's greasy fur.

Moi: 'Pauli, sit up to the table please! I didn't say you could get down.'
Pauli: 'You're just mean. Mean, mean, mean! I'm giving him my plate.'
Moi: 'Pauli, *arrête!*'

Here Pauli grabs his plate of offal from the table and puts it down on the floor. Paco leaps on it with the speed of a yearling and polishes off Pauli's supper in seconds.

Moi: 'Pauli, sit up to the table please!'

Pauli climbs back onto his chair, grinning. Paco sits beside him, pushing his grey muzzle and wet nose into Pauli's thigh and breathing out foetid vapours from his insides. Pauli pats his head magisterially.

Moi (to Pauli): 'You look a bit hungry. Would you like

the rest of mine?'
Papa (noticing for once): 'Can't you eat it, my dear?'
Moi: 'I'm just not that hungry.'
Pauli (accepting everything I am tipping onto his plate): 'Yum!' (in English).
Will this starvation make me skinnier and sexier? Will Maurice notice?

By nine I am standing in the street opposite Maddie's. I'm cold, blowing steam from my lungs in the pale moonlight. There's a sharp spring scent from a garden nearby, lilac, I think.

It took an age to get here, stuck for an hour in the metro tunnel between stops, amongst the sad old men keeping warm.

Maddie's house is ablaze as always. The treizième squanders half the electricity of France on a nightly basis. A maid is going round closing the shutters, working from the ground floor up. Before she reaches the windows of what I know is the children's sitting room I have seen Maddie. She comes to the window and looks out. Is she looking for me? I wave but I don't dare call out. She doesn't see me and turns away. Maybe she wasn't looking for me after all.

I cross the road. In front of Maddie's house is a small garden with parterres planted with roses which at this season are bare and pruned right down. I lean over the low wall and scrabble up a handful of gravel which I hurl at Maddie's window. After a minute she appears and opens the window.

'Hallo, you,' she says.
'Can I come in?'
'Nope.'
'Can you come out?'

'Give me a tick. I'll meet you round the back.'

The café Maddie takes me to is wonderfully dim and smoky. A complex smell rises to meet us as we go in. It's made up, I think, of tobacco and *anise* and the lees of ten thousand barrels of wine. The smoke smarts my eyes.

'Good Lord!' I say.

The place is pretty crammed, there must easily be a hundred men and women, shabby, Left Bank types in corduroy jackets and roll-neck pullovers, long greasy hair. It's a down-market arty bunch. The atmos is super exhilarating.

'Who are all these people?' I say into Maddie's ear.

'Antis,' she says. 'Antis like us. Sort of *faux*-Resistance types, lots of cinema people, actors, writers, what not.'

A plump little *maître d'* with an Auvergnois accent shows us to an empty table near the door. There's a bunch of Spanish guys at the next table talking in undertones. Their heads are conspiratorially close together.

'Probably POUM' Maddie says under her breath. 'They're plotting their return against Franco.'

Although the place is really full, it's not all that noisy. People are doing their plotting pretty quietly. There doesn't even seem to be a lot of drinking going on. There are beer and cognac glasses on the tables, but they're mostly empty.

'Nobody here has a bean,' Maddie explains.

'Oh, look who it is!' Maddie says and gives a little wave towards a couple sitting together at a table at the far end of the café next to some stairs. The table is piled high with books and the couple have *cahiers* in front of them and pens in their hands. They are busy writing. The woman looks up and I see that it is Mlle de Beauvoir. She clearly sees us but does not return Maddie's wave. She just nudges the mec next to her and he glances up briefly, an ugly little creature, he looks like a frog. He is wearing a dirty mackintosh over a black roll neck sweater.

'Sartre,' Maddie mutters. 'That's Jean-Paul Sartre.'

Can that ugly little man really be my hero, the author of *La Nausée*?

'You know I've left school?' Maddie says.

'No!'

'Father was in such a bate after our Resistance night out... Verónica and I were collared red-handed...'

'I know that.'

'I suppose Verónica spilled the beans.'

'She's barely spoken to me. I think she's going through a bad patch. No, actually it was our friend over there who told me.' I motion with my hand towards the Beaver.

'Ah! That's...err...indiscreet.'

'She was sort of alright about it...'

'Really?'

'...apart from thinking it was utterly futile and dangerous and we were complete imbeciles.'

'Hmm. Daddy took the same view. When he got me back from the gendarmerie he thundered away for a good hour. This morning he decided to take me out of school and put me to work. He's got me a job at *Les Nouveaux Temps*.'

'Oi oi, aren't they a load of fascists?'

'Big time. And anti-English. And anti-Semites.'

'So?'

'That's the whole point, don't you see. Re-education, Daddy calls it, straightening me out. The fascists there are good mates of my father. The editor, Brasillach, is an especial chum. He's agreed to keep a close eye on me.'

'Ghastly.'

'Actually...'

'What?'

'Actually, funnily enough, they're not a bad bunch. I went round this pip emma. They're mostly into big lunches at Maxim's and getting up snazzy parties for *le tout Paris* in aid of our poor PoWs. There's precious little politics in the office.'

'But what they write!'

'Oh, I don't think they believe a word of what they write. And nobody who reads it believes a word of what they read.'

'So... you're getting into bed with a load of filthy collabos.'

Maddie reaches across the table and takes my chubby paw into her slim, long hand. I am in thrall to this girl.

'Look, sweetheart, first I haven't got any choice, short of running away from home. Second, what I do is hardly aiding the enemy. '

'It's still collabo.'

'Don't worry, darling, I'm going to be a one woman fifth column. But actually, there is one thing...'

'Which is?'

'I won't be able to shoot the Old Gaffer now, so you're going to have to do it.'

'Yeah, right.'

Maddie laughs her big laugh.

'Other thing, though' she says, 'there is the other thing...'

She pauses. The Auvergnois has come to ask if we are actually going to order anything and Maddie asks for two brandies.

'The other thing is Eric. We had news today...'

Eric, Maddie's brother. He's the true wild child, Eric, even more so than Maddie. He just took off into the blue yonder the day the Old Gaffer signed up with the Boches at Compiègne and hasn't been heard of since.

But I don't get to hear the news right away because there is a rush of cold air as the door opens and in a moment there is a shadow at our table and a voice breaks in.

'So, what about that young scallywag, Cousin Eric?'

It is Maurice! He is standing over us, grinning. He's wearing a light overcoat in a soft, heathery weave. His brilliant white shirt is open at the neck.

I check my feelings. He's such a cunt, the way he went on the other evening. And yet something in me thrills towards him.

Maddie stands up, turning to him and he embraces his cousin with a triple *bise*, left cheek, right cheek, left cheek. Then he squeezes round the table to where I am. I put on my most neutral look and turn my face up. He leans toward me, I smell tobacco and spirits. He darts in and deftly dabs a *bise* on either cheek.

He says 'Budge up' and plumps down next to me on the fake leather bench. There's plenty of room for him, the Spaniards are leaving but he squeezes right up against me.

Noting this, Maddie's eyes narrow. I shake my head a fraction and she gives me back a simpering look. 'Yeah, right,' she means.

Maurice waves at the Auvergnois and orders himself brandy, a large one.

'So, what about our young scapegrace?'

'Ouf,' says Maddie. 'How can you? It might be terrible news.'

'About our young Icarus? Nah, I know him too well. Did you really think that his taking off without orders and disappearing the very day the truce was signed was just by chance?'

Maddie laughs.

'No, I didn't. And you're dead right. He's in England. He's joined the RAF.'

She keeps on staring at Maurice and me unnecessarily squeezed together. Her face has taken on a look of infinite tolerance.

'What will they do with that crate he went over in? It looked like a death trap to me, that one. I hope they give him a nice new Spitfire.'

Maddie laughs.

The brandies come, our two small ones and a big one for Maurice. Maurice raises his in mock toast.

'To Icarus.'

'That's not very good news for an airman,' Maddie says. She knows her Ovid. Daedalus the Dad watching his son plummeting to earth because his wings came unstuck.

'And actually,' she goes on, 'it's not exactly all good news anyway. The Old Gaffer's condemned Eric to death as a deserter.'

Maddie's father has, she tells us, got the news via the Vichy authorities. Their spies in London have informed them that Eric is in a squadron in some makeshift aerodrome in the Home Counties.

'Well done, Eric!' says Maurice. He takes my brandy and drinks it off.

'Hoi,' I say, and he waves to the Auvergnois to bring more.

'Who knows?' he says, 'Eric may be flying a sortie over our heads right now.'

We look up at the tar-stained ceiling of the café.

'But it's a risk,' Maddie says. 'I mean, if he gets shot down or something. Even my parents' fawning on the Old Gaffer wouldn't protect him then.'

Maurice takes Maddie's hand and mine too and says,

'Don't worry your pretty heads, Eric is going to live forever. Now tell me, Magdalena, how is your plot to do away with the Old Gaffer coming on?'

'Shhh!'

The old Auvergnois is pegging his way over to our table bearing our fresh brandies.

But Maurice is no longer paying attention to us. He is looking at the door. And there is a tall blonde fellow coming in. He is wearing a beautiful grey suit and a soft white collar and a sky blue tie. He looks handsome, he looks immaculate. He looks Boche.

It is Otto.

Maurice gets up.

'So long, girls,' he says.

I get the last metro back. My eyes are red with smoke and tears and in this I am not alone amongst the trainload of sad and hungry creatures who are my fellow travellers. We are all nursing our sorrows, both particular ones and the sorrows of the age.

As for me, I worry about Maddie. My dear blood sister is completely insane. She said I have to do it now that she's got the sack from the school, and when I said no she said 'Alright, you just get the gun and I'll come round on the day. Blam blam.'

I mean, what sort of a plan is that?

And. And what is going on with Maurice and the Otto? I mean.

But the oddest thing is that the very next day I come to know where I can get a gun.

8

About the gun. It happens in the least expected way. At home. We are just sitting down to our frugal supper, when there is a ring at the door and it is Ye Olde Batte, wheezing sterterously and holding out a handbill.

'Get that dog out of my house' she says affably. She thrusts the handbill at me and breezes off.

I go back to the table. Papa has stopped eating and is scribbling thoughts with a pencil into his notebook. Pauli has disappeared and I discover him in his room where he is lining up his lead soldiers on the top of a box and throwing them in one by one. I dread to think what that is all about.

'Back to the table,' I shout. He pipes the eye but I am adamant.

At last I manage to get both of them sitting up to the table and paying attention and then I read out the handbill. All dogs are to be delivered to the pound to be destroyed unless they can be trained for military or police purposes.

'And Prune Face is on the case,' I say. Papa looks quizzical. I doubt he has ever noticed our concierge's variations on a dried fruit.

As we have never been able to train Paco for anything whatsoever, let alone 'military or police purposes', and as his only (self-taught) life skill is to sit on his backside and beg pathetically for scraps from the table, his case looks hopeless. Pauli starts blubbing right away. His face quickly becomes sodden with tears.

But then Papa has one of his rare lucid intervals where

he behaves like a normal sentient human being. He puts his foot down over this Paco business.

'I will not take that dog to be used for target practice,' he says.

Pauli claps his hands together.

'So what can we do, Papa?' I ask.

'I will shoot the creature myself.'

Pauli lets out a cry. His face, glistening as it is with tears, shows both amazement and terror. He throws his hands up and stares at Papa with his mouth wide open as though he has never properly seen him before.

'How?' he manages to ask.

Papa looks at Pauli and shakes his head in interrogation.

'How what, my boy?'

'How are you going to shoot Paco, Daddy?'

'With my gun,' Papa replies. When brought down from Helicon, Papa is not above a bit of amateur dramatics.

'You have a gun!'

Without a word, Papa gets up from the table and disappears towards his study. Pauli sits transfixed. In a couple of minutes Papa returns carrying a huge black revolver.

'Gosh! Papa, can I hold it?'

Papa gives the revolving bit a professional sort of whirl. I suppose he is checking there are no bullets in it. I've seen Tom Mix do it like that, before he loads his six-shooter and guns down seven baddies on Main Street. Then Papa puts the gun on the table in front of Pauli who looks at it in wonder. After a bit he picks it up in both hands as if it were a monstrance and gazes at it reverently.

'Gosh and double golly gosh!' he says in English. 'Where did you get it?'

Papa explains with a definite hint of bravado that this was his pistol when he was commissioned in the Imperial

Austrian Army in '18, right at the end of the Great War.

'How many enemy men did you kill, Papa?'

I watch this unusual Papa closely as he works out how to field the question. Pauli is watching too, in his guileless child's way. He just wants a number. He lays the pistol down solemnly between the cruet and the empty flower vase and stares at Papa. As for me, I am also quite interested to know the truth of this but I suspect that we are not going to get it, at least not during this piece of theatre.

'Hmm,' Papa says. 'Hard to say. A dozen? A hundred? In the heat of the battle, of course...'

Yes, right! I am interested but I am not deceived. I know my father could never kill anyone.

It remains to be seen whether he can even kill a dog.

How Papa squares his bluster with the pacific principles in which Mama schooled us from the cradle onwards is another, deeper question. Right now he has declared himself an accredited killer, so he had better get on with it.

The struggle is now all with Pauli. He is torn, right down the middle. I can almost read on his brow the conflict. All his early education in the Boys' Own makes him long for a father who is, well, a killer, or at least able to kill, prepared to kill. And yes, here is a fully equipped father, a bragging revolver-carrying Papa. And there, on the other hand, is old Paco, who even now is pushing his damp black nose up against Pauli's bare thigh and pleading with milky eyes in which the misty image of Mama is somehow contained. Although for Paco of course the question is not yet about life and death but about what remains on Pauli's plate.

Pauli's struggle has a natural upshot. He starts to sob uncontrollably. I take him on my lap and hug his thin little body. He puts his arms round my neck and clings as tight as can be. Meanwhile Papa, who is by now looking a little nervy, goes off to his study and comes back with a small cardboard box. He sits down at the table and reaches out and takes the gun from between the cruet and the empty flower vase. With the gun in front of him, he opens the box and begins to take from it some surprisingly big bullets which he puts into the chambers of the gun. Each time he inserts a bullet, he gives the chamber a twirl and it spins round with a nasty clicking sound.

Pauli wriggles round in my arms to watch. His eyes widen to the size of golf balls. As for me, I am wondering, is this a warrior preparing for the trial of battle? Or is it a sad old widower trying to screw up the courage to blow out the brains of his dead wife's dog.

Papa evidently makes up his mind, because he goes out and comes back with his coat and Paco's lead. Paco, who started jumping up and down in glee when he heard the sound of his lead in the hall, seems to have second thoughts when he sees Papa picking up the revolver. He backs away. Is it some sixth sense or is it just confusion, because Papa has never ever in living memory taken Paco out for a walk?

Whatever is going on in Paco's dim loving brain, he keeps backing away as Papa advances towards him. It looks like a stand-off. But then all of a sudden Pauli slithers from my arms and dashes up to Papa. He takes the lead from Papa's hands and goes up to Paco who waits eagerly for him, wagging his tail with great whooshing strokes from side to side. Pauli collars Paco and snaps on the lead. It goes on with a decisive *click*.

Papa meanwhile pockets the revolver. Pauli then takes Papa by the hand and the three of them head for the door of the dining room. A minute later I hear the thud of the front door closing to.

And I am left in the crepuscule of twilight that filters in

to the messy dining room. Dutifully and full of thoughts and feelings, I get up and gather the dishes. I put the cruet back on the sideboard and shove the empty flower vase back into the middle of the table. But actually, really, I am – as Mama would say – *bloody fed up*.

For years now I have cared for that dog like a little mother. I have walked the old fellow day in day out, come rain and shine. I have washed the greasy creature's coat and brushed him sedulously. I have de-wormed and de-flea'd him. I have wiped his daggy bottom when he's had an accident. I have grown practically emaciated feeding him up with all the best bits from my plate. I have nursed him and hugged him and loved him, not just for Mama's sake but for his own. And now the men have piked off to shoot him dead – *and they never even asked me for my views*!

Did they think about the morality of the thing – should you kill your dog so you can eat better? Did they consider the ethics – should you obey a wicked order of the powers that be just because they are the powers that be? Did they even stop to think what you are doing when you kill your dead wife or mother's pet? No, they bloody well didn't! It was just posturing, bravado, just *I've got a gun*.

I read once in Papa's Freud that a gun is a 'penis extension'. Maybe that has something to do with the case.

I dump the dishes in the kitchen sink. I write a note and leave it on Papa's desk. Then I put on my coat and head out. I'm going round to Maddie's.

I am such a fool. Almost as soon as Maddie comes down and we are huddled on a bench in the little rose garden across from her place, I blurt out to Maddie about the gun. Why, oh why do I do this? It is the most stupid thing imaginable. Papa's gun is a secret to be kept whatever the cost, and above all from Maddie.

I know exactly why I blurt it out. It is because I am an immature child. Because I have a massive inferiority complex. Because I'm just like that other immature, weak character – my father, of course – I'm vain, I'm shy and vain and blurt stuff out to big myself up.

Maddie knows this, of course. She knows me through and through, every weakness, just as I know hers. But she has her higher purpose and she will not relent. The words are out of me, she will not let me take them back.

She bangs on and on. I want to talk about Paco, even about Maurice, anything but the stupid gun, but she will not let go. *When can I get it? How much ammunition is there? Can it be traced back?*

Feebly, I prevaricate. I tell her it's only a rusty old thing, a relic of the Great War that probably doesn't even work.

But she keeps on and on about it. I begin to regret our blood pact.

At one point, I manage to get her off the topic. I tell her that on my way over in the metro I saw my first yellow star. It was a mec of about ninety in a filthy long overcoat, huddled up like a sad animal crawling off to die. He had the crude thing stitched haphazardly onto his lapel. The conductor came round and told him to move. But the mec just got off at the next station.

'He's too early!' Maddie said at once. 'The Old Gaffer's decree about the yellow stars doesn't come in until Wednesday next.'

Of course she knows all about it. She says everybody was talking about it at *Les Nouveaux Temps* today. Big yellow stars, dimensions 3 cm by 4 cm, five points not six, washable cloth, to be worn on the left breast…

'There's a Jewish girl, one of the typists,' Maddie says,

'She was really upset about it. She kept shouting *Three coupons! Three fucking coupons to get the material!* Brasillach came out to see what the fuss was about.'

'That old fascist? And?'

'He told her it was the proud badge of the Chosen People. He said she should wear it with her head high, like the *Légion d'Honneur*.'

'What did she say to that?'

'Unrepeatable. She says she's not going to wear it anyway.'

Then Maddie says,

'Now about that gun...'

It is in dread that I get the last metro back. When our old cat died, Mama lined an orange crate with some red velvet curtain material and put Florence into it. The poor creature lay in state on the kitchen table for three days with stuff oozing from her every orifice.

It is past eleven when I open the door of our flat and there is Pauli, still up, way past his allotted hour. And he is beaming. He runs to me and hugs me round the legs. And there, behind him is scruffy old Paco, his tail wagging like one of the Redeemed.

'Good Lord!' I say, and Pauli hugs me tighter.

'He's hungry,' Pauli murmurs. I prise the boy's thin little arms from about my legs and we go together, hand in hand, to the kitchen. Paco follows, his entire rear end swaying from side to side, so ecstatic is his wagging.

I give Paco the whole piece of cheese I have been keeping for Pauli's lunch the next day. He wolfs it down in a trice and then sits there thumping the kitchen tiles with his tail. He bears the air of the reprived being he is with unusual dignity.

I put Pauli to bed and then go in to Papa with his warm milk. He looks up at me from his writing. The gun is on his desk.

'Papa,' I say, 'what happened?' My eyes are on the gun.

He looks blankly at me for a moment and then, seeing where my eyes are fixed, he seems to twig. He explains that they dragged Paco to the railway embankment, with Paco resisting all the way.

'We thought,' he says, 'or at least I did, that the rattle of the trains would mask the sound of the shot. We even thought, well, I did, that we could bury Paco there once the... erm... deed was done, so to speak. I doubt anyone ever goes on that dirty embankment. But the creature was clearly sensing that... errr... that the outing might not end well, as it were. You know he's lost a lot of weight and he took advantage of being rather skinny and slipped out of his collar. He just ran off. The boy scampered after him, of course, and eventually rounded him up, but...'

Papa stops. He seems confused by what he is recounting. I wait.

'Well, frankly, my dear, I think the heat had gone out of the whole business by then. So... we came back home, all three of us.'

So it has ended well with Paco still extant and some good old father–son male bonding. And if their machismo has drained away and been replaced by a decent measure of sheepishness, so much the better, say I.

The only challenge now is what to do with Paco.

9

I do my racing dive. It's a long one and I am almost halfway down the pool before I come up and start to power forward. I'm doing the new Australian crawl that I learned at Scout Camp, the last one before the Catastrophe.

Without my goggles it's all a blur but when I turn my head to draw breath the German isn't there where I thought he'd be, alongside me, in the left-hand lane. But at the turn, I do see him. He's behind, but close. He'll turn a second after me.

On the back length, because I am breathing to the left, my head is turned away from him, so I have no real idea about where he is. I put on extra power to keep my lead.

At the turn again I don't at first see him. Surely he can't have got ahead. I take my first breath on the outward length and then I see him. He's now a good two strokes behind.

I'm beating him! I'm winning against the German! The prize is mine! It's like I'm winning a war.

I feel the smooth wash of water over my back. All my muscles are flowing in harmony. I am the perfect sleek smooth swimmer, adapted as an otter, sleek as a seal. I shoot through the unresisting blue waters, I'm hard and soft at once, silk and steel. Ahead, I shoot straight ahead.

I come to the turn again and look back. By now he's fully three strokes behind. He'll never catch me now! I take a risk and try my new turn. I touch the bar and duck down, going for a perfect somersault. My head plunges down and my body follows, down and round and then I glide smoothly on the up, back to the surface. It's a bit long, a bit slow but then I am striking out again.

Now once again I take my breaths, my head away from him, so I can't keep track of him. True, I muffed the new turn just that little bit but still it was really fast, fast enough. Totally. He cannot catch me now. I am strong. I am winning. I am definitely going to win.

My body shoots forward like an arrow. My arms scoop and cleave in long circles, my legs bat rhythmically, I am one smooth harmonious creature. A winning creature, girl beating boy, French beating Boche. I am young. I am me.

The sandwich is in the bag!

He showed it to me, a perfect crusty brown baguette, thick with butter and inside, a slice of ham two centimetres thick. It's my prize. I'm winning it.

I power on, my limbs in perfect harmony. My body cannot tire. It insists on the sandwich. I up the pace. I am thrusting to the line. I shoot like an arrow. It is perfect. I am perfect. Victory is mine!

I touch the rail and surface and look back for him. And there he is, great grinning face, stuck right up next to me, stupid fuzzy copper knob. He has finished before me! Somehow. And now he is pushing his great red jowly face towards me and laughing.

'*Du schwimmst gut!*' He is grinning like a gargoyle. '*Aber nicht gut genug! Ha ha!*' And he laughs and he laughs. He has a tooth missing at the front.

I cannot speak. I am panting. I am in shock.

'*Und jetzt, der Kuss!*' He sticks his great stupid face towards me. '*Und jetzt, der Kuss!*'

It was the bargain. I win, I get the sandwich. He wins, he gets a kiss. I did it because I knew I'd beat such a flabby lout. And I so much had to have that sandwich.

I still desire it with all my heart. I am soooo hungry. Ham!

But this stupid Fritz is now dead set on getting his prize. 'Getting out,' he says, in a kind of French. 'Then *Küssen in den Büschen, ja.*' This makes him laugh like a drain and he says it again, 'Then *Küssen in den Büschen, ja.*' His face is bright red and covered with freckles. His hair is a horrid ginger bristle. And why is he saying everything twice?

I swim to the ladder and clamber out. He grabs my ankle but I kick free. '*Foutes le camp,*' I shout. A couple of French ladies sitting nearby look up and make little *moues* of disapproval. Their bodies stiffen a fraction and they turn their heads away. *Swimming with The Enemy*, they're thinking. They don't understand about the ham. Up at the end of the pool, the German's mates are laughing and gesticulating and going *Ra ra ra*.

I dash to my deckchair and grab my towel, wrapping it round me. I plump down into the deckchair. The German follows and stands there over me, white and fleshy. He already has a tummy and little sagging breasts.

'*Vas te faire foutre,*' I say, waving him away but he stands his ground, grinning idiotically.

'*Foutre, ja,*' he says sniggering. '*Küssen* then *foutre, ja.*'

He seizes my arm and tries to drag me out of my deck chair.

'*Komm mit, Fräulein. Küssen in den Büschen.*' He keeps making smacking sounds with his chubby lips.

I give up and say to him in German,
'Give me the sandwich. Then I'll think about it.'

He looks surprised. His eyes narrow when he hears me speaking in his own language.

'*Nein,*' he says and tugs at my arm again.

'What's going on?'

It's Maddie. She's finally come. She's in a fabulous costume, all colours and stripes. She's holding a ball. She looks like the pale nymph Nausicaa.

I explain the bargain and she laughs. The German gapes at her.

'It is an immoral contract,' she says, 'food for sex. Unenforceable in law.' She turns to the German. He is still admiring her. His pudgy body is slick with water and there is a drop hanging from his right nipple.

'*Wie heissen Sie?* What's your name?'

Maddie has learned a little German at the lycée. The man's name is Walter something. He's actually an officer of sorts, or so he says, something in the Transport Corps, not high up but not so loutish after all.

'*Sehr effreut!*' Maddie says. 'But I'm afraid, Walter, that you cannot claim such a prize.'

Walter looks from Maddie to me and back again.

'Such lovely girls,' he says, in German, '*Die schönen Mädchen.* Such beauties in your bathing costumes.'

I feel coy at this and pull the towel tighter across my front. My bathing costume is one of my mother's. It's faded red like old curtains and it's got a little pleated skirt. That's probably why I lost the stupid race, the stupid skirt. Maddie's costume, though, is the *dernier cri*, it's got to be from Jacques Lauque's last collection, the one that came out just before the Catastrophe. It's got broad stripes in red, green and yellow running on the bias, and there are tiny thin straps with snazzy bows tied at her shoulders. She looks a million francs in it.

'Such lovely girls,' the Walter repeats. His eyes are now all for Maddie. I think she's more his type, taller, more slender, not all brown like me. She motions to him and they take

a step away. She whispers in his ear and off he goes.
'How did you do that?'
'Just wait, dear one.'

In a minute plump Walter comes back

He has wrapped a towel around his shoulders, clutching it across his boobs with one hand. In the other hand he has the ham sandwich, wrapped in greaseproof paper.

'*Hier, Fräulein, bitte schön,*' he says, holding out the sandwich to me. I grab it and off he scoots as quick as he can to rejoin his friends who are all watching from the far end of the pool. They greet him with what looks from here like extreme scorn.

Maddie waves her arm and summons the pool attendant who brings her a deckchair, and a plate and a knife. She cuts Walter's sandwich into two. We eat it in silence. It is much too good to waste in chatter. It's an entire baguette, so a half is a huge share. It is more than one whole year since I tasted ham. And butter in such quantity is like a birthday treat from a distant childhood dream. My whole body and every sense I have seizes on this sandwich. I eat it very, very slowly. I want to remember every mouthful forever.

Maddie calls the pool boy again to bring drinks and we sit sipping Banania. I feel the sun on my arms and legs. I even feel the workings of my tummy. It is as though health and strength are flowing into me from the rich ham and the unctuous butter. I start to feel slightly sick and quaff the Banania as quick as I can to line my stomach. God! Surely my body's not going to reject this precious food!

I lie back in my deckchair in a haze of ham and love.

'So,' says Maddie, 'now that we've got rid of *ton flirt*...'

'But how did you do that?' Maddie puts her finger to her lips and lies back in her deckchair too.

'Ah, the sun, the sun. It's brilliant to be out, after a week in that bloody office.'

'Your collabo office.'

'Oh, darling, trust me, what we actually do is hardly evil. Yesterday, for instance, Luchaire sent me to that posh florist on the Place de la Madeleine to buy a huge bouquet for Coco Chanel who was visiting the offices with her German lover. And then I typed out place cards for some big dinner at l'Aiglon that they were putting on for a visiting Vichy bigwig. So you see, it's all very harmless.'

'It's still collabo. That Chanel's a collabo. Vichy is archi-collabo.'

'Shush! As I said, I'm going to be a one-woman fifth column. I even asked Luchaire if I could try writing something. He said fine… and I suggested I could interview your Dad about his views on trade and peace and whatnot.'

'Oh, God, that! I'm not sure that's a good idea at all.'

'But it's the talk of the town. France in the New Europe! And your Dad's the brains behind it.'

'Oh my God.'

'So, dear one, when can I interview him?'

'I don't know. Can I trust you?'

I say this sort of flippantly but she takes it seriously.

'I promise.'

'You won't make him look silly or anything? He's not very good at interviews and things.'

'Lord, no. I wouldn't do that. Anyway *Les Nouveaux Temps* is, well, *Les Nouveaux Temps*. They're not going to let me criticize one of the Old Gaffer's big policies.'

'So why do you want to do it?'

'Just to set down the facts, let people judge for themselves. And…'

I waited.

'...and to give it just the tiniest bit of a spin, just as much as will get past Luchaire and the censor...'

'But not to harm Papa?'

'No, darling, no, never. Promise, promise, promise.'

So I agree to try and wangle an interview with Papa, although he's certain to refuse. He doesn't trust journalists.

'By the way,' Maddie says, 'when are you going to get me that gun. The Old Gaffer will be here in a week or so and I need to practice a bit first.'

I stare at her. I had thought, just for a few minutes, that Maddie might have regained her sanity and begun to see things a bit more like a normal person. But it seems not.

'Never,' I say. 'Never ever.'

'Oh, go on,' she says, but drops the subject. We talk about Verónica. Maddie says she asked her to the pool but she said no.

'She's moping. I'm worried about her, she's still losing weight, she's as thin as a stick. Thinner, actually.'

After this we sunbathe for a while which is alright at first for me with my dark skin but Maddie quickly reddens and retreats under an umbrella. It's so warm I doze off and dream of ham. When I come to, the afternoon is already drawing in. The air is chill. I stir and stretch and yawn. I want to leave, but Maddie isn't there. I can't spot her anywhere around the pool, so I heave myself out of the deckchair and go to hunt amongst the bushes and trees at the end of the park. And soon I come across her. She is under a big lime tree. And I am amazed to see she is playing ball with that podgy Walter! He now has his uniform on, except for his jacket which is lying on the grass. I see on the sleeve the insignia of an *oberleutnant*

Beside the jacket sits a large German shepherd dog. The

dog is watching the play with an attentive eye. Beside the dog, on its other side, is a little pile of rare things, an orange, a packet of biscuits, a large brioche. Plainly Walter's little pile.

I am completely astonished. The pudgy German throws a high ball to Maddie, who is still in her bathing suit. She raises her long slim arms and tries to catch it but it's too high for her. The ball sails over her and lands on the ground next to the trunk of the lime tree. The dog bounds over, picks up the ball and brings it to Maddie. By this time she is dropping decorously to one knee.

She has never looked lovelier. She's like a Cranach virgin. So what is with this game, this to and fro?

I suddenly think that this must have been the deal. Maddie said yes to ball with this flabby creature to get me off the hook.

Well, now it's my turn to get *her* off the hook.

I call out to her.

'Erm… time to go home Maddie.' But to my amazement she calls back,

'You get on darling. Don't worry about me.'

I don't want to leave her. I coupie down next to the dog which regards me sardonically. Its eyes are red. Maddie goes on playing. Walter sends her any easy one, a dolly. She catches it and gets up from her one knee down. I can see the muscle in her perfect thigh tighten as she raises herself up. She shakes her flaming hair from side to side. The declining sun catches her. She is a vision of white and gold. She throws the ball like an athlete. It's not a pootsy little girl toss but the throw of a Spartiate.

My lovely blood sister! My noble, beautiful sister. Maddie! Now stop this nonsense with this flabby Boche farm boy!

But she plays on. I watch in amazement and terror. Surely she has paid the flaccid Walter back for the sandwich by now.

'*Arrête*, Maddie!' I can't stop myself from calling out. And she turns her lovely head to me and passes her white hand through her streaming, glowing locks. She says,

'Just go, darling. Just go.'

10

Next day, I am still pondering Maddie's madness. I think I will go round to hers if I can. In break I send a *pneu* to her office. After school I pick up Pauli and take him home. I give him his tea and he settles down in his room to read his *Boy's Own Annual*. Nothing from Maddie. I really should go round tonight.

In the meantime, I nip out to collect Papa's shoes from the cobblers. The guy is doing a roaring trade patching up anything and everything. He can charge what he likes – and he does. He asks twenty francs for Papa's new soles. It's daylight robbery. Before, you could get new shoes for half that. Not that you can get new ones these days for love nor money. You need a chitty and a million coupons. They're changing hands for a small fortune.

I am clacking back along the Boul' Mich in my *sabots*, pondering on Maddie, my wonderful, strange Maddie and on her weird goings on yesterday when a big black Mercedes draws up beside me and there is Maurice beckoning to me from the front seat. He calls out,

'Hop in, darling. We're off to the Breker *vernissage*.'

I bend down and peer into the car. At the wheel in full Boche fig, dress uniform with a bunch of ribbons and tin stars on his left breast, is Otto.

How weird is this! I mean, what on earth is going on? First Maddie flirting with that Boche and now Maurice all chummed up with the Otto.

Maurice seems quite serene about it. He looks so eager and charming. I feel that tug towards him again.

Otto is gesturing to me to get in.

'I can't,' I say. 'I have to take Papa's shoes home. Anyway, I'm in my school uniform.'

This is true. I am still in my schoolgirl's outfit. Am I seriously going out with Maurice to a *vernissage* in my slip with my name stitched across the front? How stupid would that look! Hallo, this is schoolgirl ANNA-ELISA SCHNEIDER, indeed!

'Oh, just get in, Annie,' Otto says and he slips the car into gear. He leans across and opens the back door of the big car for me. He grasps me firmly by the wrist. This I should seriously not be doing. I wriggle but Otto holds really tight and yanks. At that moment two sullen-faced old biddies heave up beside me. One of them bumps into me accidentally on purpose and mutters *collabo horizontale* just loud enough for me to hear.

That does it. I throw Papa's shoes on the floor of the car and jump in.

'Bravo,' Maurice says. I settle back in the cool leather seat, trying not to think too much.

Otto drives very fast and ignores all the traffic signs. I suppose he has an *ausweis* or something that lets him do it. Anyway, the streets are almost empty of cars. There are only a few of those bicycle rickshaws carrying some BCBG types, ladies in flamboyant print frocks and cloche hats. It is, of course, the working-class girls with thick calves who are pedalling these rickshaws and who have to swerve as Otto careers through red lights and ignores the *priorité à droite* signs.

All the time, Otto and Maurice are chatting in German which Maurice seems to know pretty well. They're talking in lowish voices so I can't really hear, but the tone is definitely friendly. They seem as thick as thieves.

* * *

The Orangerie is decorated with the hideous spider flags and a new banner:

ARNO BREKER, SCULPTOR – HIS RETURN TO PARIS

Otto parks his car right in front and there is some low-ranking Fritz NCO or something in a rather rumpled and ill-fitting grey field uniform saluting away. Otto says a word to the soldier and apparently we are allowed to leave our car right there, half on and half off the pavement.

Maurice opens my door and offers me his hand and while Otto is conducting some official biz about our visit, showing cards and *ausweis* and gesturing at Maurice and me, we walk into the hall, hand in hand, like lovers. Or, sadly, more like brother and sister as I am clearly such a child in my stupid school uniform.

Straightaway, the minute we are inside, I feel even more out of it. Because the Orangerie is cram-packed with gigantic male nudes. Really gigantic, like 20 feet high and everything in proportion.

'Gorgeous,' Maurice says at once.

Not! Really not!

I mean, how can Maurice think such a thing, let alone say it? These nudie statues are truly grotesque with their bulging thigh muscles and the great torsos like steel drums and the jutting Germanic jaws. They are like caricatures of men, like marble dolls on a gigantesque scale.

And the huge pendant willies!

Maurice is gazing at these stony titans.

Otto now catches up with us and says that Arno Breker is the Fuehrer's favourite artist. I catch the hint of an ironic tone in his voice. Perhaps I am beginning to appreciate Otto.

'*Et le tout Paris est présent,*' Otto goes on, clearly pleased by the big turnout. 'Oh my God, Bonnard's going to make a speech. He shouldn't do that.' Maurice looks quizzical and Otto explains. 'It's not that he's a filthy collabo, although he is. It's just they say he's rotten at speeches.' Filthy collabo? Hang on a moment, Otto is supposed to be a Boche officer. Whatever. Otto turns out to be quite right, Pierre Bonnard's speech is in fact pretty rotten, just platitudes and some *lèche-cul* about Breker but as Otto now says, *Somebody has to do it.*

The speech is over. Otto plucks at Maurice's sleeve and off they slope to meet some personage. I am apparently not required. 'Have a wander,' Maurice says breezily, so I mosey round amongst these megaliths. They are all up on huge plinths. I reach up to touch the feet on one of them. The stone is freezing cold. I look up, really I can't help it, and ten feet above me is this huge *zizi*. It's three feet long. I think of the *phalloi* in the illustrations in the Aristophanes book, the one that Georgie keeps hidden at the back of her desk drawer.

'Really, it is just crazy!'

It is a woman, at my elbow. Actually, she is more a girl than a woman, she can't be more than a year or two older than I am. She is big built, not tall. She has a beautiful face, round like the moon, and almond shaped eyes. Her skin is the colour of the palest terra cotta. She looks like what I imagine a Turcoman woman looks like.

'What?' I ask.

'Such blustering. Blustering males.'

I laugh, pretending that I understand her. She looks up

with perfect composure. She has a sort of triumphant femininity about her that makes me feel quite shy.

'Imagine,' she says, 'imagine if they really were that big.' She laughs and I laugh. There is something nicely elemental about her. She looks away amongst the crowd, as if searching for someone. It turns out to be this incredibly old man in a beret and an artist's smock with his beard ravelling halfway down his chest. The old man beckons to her and she nips off, waving her hand at me behind her back.

'Aristide's got himself a new muse then,' says Maurice who has materialized beside me. Otto is with him. Maurice gestures at where my girlfriend and the geriatric old artist type are now conversing, huddled against a wall. He gives an appreciative murmur.

'Just look at those hips and those thighs. My God. And the full high breasts. No need to sculpt her. She's a walking Maillol bronze. But I'm surprised he's come to this collabo bean feast.'

'But it could be an opportunity, no?' says Otto mysteryously. 'Maillol, *il est spécial, non?*'

Maurice nods and grins and says to me,

"Come on, chicken, let us meet the Grand Old Man.'

It turns out that Maurice sort of knows Maillol, or at least he says he does, as he has interviewed this old National Treasure before the war for a radio programme. So over we go and the girl looks up and smiles at me what I take to be a complicit feminine smile. I feel both shy and grown up at the same time.

Maurice does some introducing business whilst the old man looks him up and down with a sceptical air. It is obvious that Maillol has no recollection whatever of Maurice but this doesn't seem to bother Maurice, who presents Otto and says he is a lover of French art, and of Maillol's art in particular etc. etc.

The old man's face is stupendously wrinkled and although I peer at all those corrugations, it is very hard to tell what he is thinking. He just stares at Maurice and at Otto. The girl, the muse, puts her arm comfortably through the old man's and they just stand there looking at us and saying nothing. This, however, does not deter Maurice who now embarks on a conversation in which he has all the lines. He babbles on, questioning Maillol about why he has come, and whether he was abandoning the rounded ladies for the erect male, although the girl at Maillol's side seems to suggest otherwise etc. etc. Or could it be that he was there for Bonnard's sake as they were both disciples of Gauguin in their salad days.

I feel somehow ashamed at Maurice going on at this old French monument and I give him a discreet kick. But finally Maillol does speak, and in a dignified sort of voice, not at all old man quavery.

'*En effet*, I am here to ask for Arno's help.' He means Breker. He pauses, then goes on.

'He was my friend. I helped him when he was in Paris before. Now I want him to help me. I presume that such courtesies still exist in the world in which we are now compelled to live.'

With this, Maillol turns to Otto, looking up at him as he is a foot shorter than the German.

'You like this *caca*?'

Otto answers with elaborate sincerity which he is probably putting on.

'I was told that he once was very good, that he was our Michelangelo.'

'Hmm.' Maillol says nothing, just stares at Otto. The old

man's eyes are blue and filmy. The girl at his side hugs his arm tighter and then she looks at me and rolls her eyes. Men and their talk, I read into that, but I am much too shy to say anything.

'It is clear,' Maillol says at last, 'that Arno got Nazi religion and that this has ruined him. I think, poor Arno, has it come to this? Have you really come to believe that art is an 'expression of the essence of the Volk', as your despicable little *fuehrer* pontificates?'

Otto now gets a whimsical smile on his face and says, 'And your art, Master? An expression of your Volk...'

'I have no Volk.'

'...Germany represented by a dirty great phallus and France by the lovely curves of a Maillol bronze. Male and Female. Destined to be joined, perhaps?'

This sounds clever to me but Maillol stares at Otto without expression, then he says *Vas te faire foutre* and turns and walks away.

The girl hangs back. I think she wants to talk to me. I hope she wants to talk to me.

Maurice and Otto both put on judicious faces, pursing their lips and nodding their heads slightly up and down.

'Hmmm, that went well,' says Maurice, and Otto laughs.

'Oh, look, there's Jean with Sacha Guitry.'

The two speed off to talk to 'Jean', who looks to me like the pictures we see in the papers of the aesthete Jean Cocteau.

So I am left with Maillol's girl. She tells me her name is Dina and takes me by the arm. I have no need to tell her my name, she has clearly already read it off my chest. She says 'Ah, Anouchka'. We follow Maillol.

'Intolerable, intolerable,' the old man is muttering. We

stand beside him and he takes my hand.

'Feel!' he says and he pushes my hand inside Dina's wrap. There is something, a piece of cloth, stuck on her blouse. I realize it's one of the new stars, the yellow stars.

Maillol leans over and whispers in my ear,

'Dina's a Bessarabian Jewess. And so, obedient to the orders, she is wearing the badge of her race. Only she is marked, she has been marked, because she's a *passeur*, she gets people out over the mountains. They are going to arrest her soon. My local gendarmerie have had the courtesy to inform me in advance. So I am going to ask Arno for his help. For old times' sake. Despite this pile of shit.'

He starts to walk away, then turns slowly back.'

'Your friend, your French friend, what does he want?'

'No idea,' I say.

'He wants something, I can see that.'

Maillol turns and walks off slowly, leaning on his stick.

Dina is now lolling back against the wall, perfectly composed. She gives me the sweetest smile. I am awkward with her but I want to like her. And I want her to like me.

'Ah, *les garçons*,' she says. 'But really, what do you think. For me, they are not so bad, whatever Aristide says. Look at that Prometheus.'

The thing is twenty feet high, like a Titan, strangling in his own muscles. The puzzling *zizi* hangs down like a gigantic vegetable marrow.

'Are you really a *passeur*?'

'A bit. A few runs. They come to Banyuls where we live, Aristide and me, up in the Pyrenees. Aristide tells me which path to take them to go into Spain. It's very easy.'

'But dangerous?'

'Just ordinary danger. And you get some good ones. I ran

a son of Thomas Mann last week. He was so polite and thankful. And poor Walter Benjamin.'

I have no idea who this is.

'But now they're on to you?'

'That's why we came. He hates Paris these days. He is afraid of the traffic. He hates this Occupation. He's only come for my sake, to beg his chum Arno to help get me out when they arrest me.'

'And what will you do then, I mean if… when you get out?'

'Oh, I don't know. Maybe Spain, maybe Switzerland.'

A waiter comes with champagne. I wave it away but Dina says,

'Take it.' She gives me one and takes one herself.

'These days,' she says, 'you never know when it might be your last.'

She drinks her glass off greedily and takes mine from my hand.

'But why do you do it? I'd be so afraid.'

Dina smiles.

'You get used to it. I was six when we got out of Russia. We came here without a kopek. After that, everything is good. I want to help the good people. Anyway, Aristide insists. He says, if I won't do it, he will. And of course that is impossible.'

She looks around and inclines her head towards me.

'And you, little Anouchka,' she says in a low tone, 'perhaps you'd like to try.'

Before I can reply, there is Maillol pegging back towards us. Dina looks hard at me. She takes my hand and squeezes it.

'Think about it,' she says quickly as the old man comes up. 'Think about it, Mlle Anna-Elisa Schneider.'

'It's alright,' Maillol says. He is breathing hard. 'Arno says it's alright, he'll put in a word. And he knows the right lawyer.'

Dina laughs and throws her arms around the old man's neck.

The *vernissage* is fading at its own pace. People are drifting away. I find myself alone with Otto. Although he is so official, and a Hun, there is a gentleness about him. That German face is not so chiselled after all. He looks down at me and gives me a beatific smile. I feel negligible and very young.

'You must not be so hard on Maurice,' he says.

Who, me? As if Maurice cared a fig for my opinion. I want to say that I really like him, that I have a pash on him, but my mouth won't open. Anyway, Otto surprises me further by saying,

'You see, he wants to do the right thing.'

'Whatever that is,' I say. Otto gives me a sterner look.

'Between you and me,' he says and touches my arm with his hand, 'between you and me, there is much to do and I count on Maurice.'

This is very mysterious. I say nothing. Otto glances around him, then goes on.

'You see, *ma petite*, M. Abetz, our so Francophile ambassador, has employed his huge knowledge of the very best houses of Paris to have them emptied of all their works of art. It is a special mission he has been given by Reichsminister Hermann Goering whose love of art, especially second-rate art, is boundless. Our embassy has amassed 450 crates of the stuff, ancient and modern.'

'So, dear Annie, you will ask,' he says kindly, although I am too nonplussed at his confidence in me to dare to say a word, 'what has this to do with Maurice?'

Yes, Otto, I suppose this is the question.

'Well, now, Annie, these works are to be submitted to a thorough triage by the Rosenberg process. This will sort the sheep from the goats. There will be a big pile of accepted works, these will be despatched to Germany. And there will be a big pile that are refused. These will go to the bonfire.'

'And Maurice...?'

It turns out that all this is just preamble, just *mise en scène*. There is, it seems, a brave lady in the Jeu de Paumes who is already working to save what she can from the pyre. Maurice's role is quite different.

He will go round the artists' studios and the private collections that still exist and buy what he can of what remains, of what is worthwhile. He will then find safe homes for this art.

'Is that... I mean, what you were doing with M. Maillol?'

'It was our first attempt. A start. Sadly, it did not go well. Sometimes I think that Maurice may seem a little... flamboyant? Even a little shallow?'

Otto smiles and shows his perfect teeth.

I want to ask Otto why he is involved in this. Isn't it some kind of treason, working against his own side? But then perhaps there are several 'sides'. Perhaps even the angels have sides.

I don't have time to complete this thought, let alone quiz Otto about it because he is turning to greet Maurice who is bounding up.

'I think I saw Braque,' he says. 'Let's go and try him.'

11

After this, after Breker and Maillol and Dina and so on, I need to breathe and think a bit. I can't face Papa and Pauli and all that *quotidien* just yet.

I turn down Otto's offer of a lift and I walk back towards home but the long way round. A pale sun is out for the moment and the late afternoon air is still warmish. From the Orangerie, I walk along the Quai des Tuileries and past the Louvre.

I walk very slowly and run my fingers along the stone of the parapet. It's rough and cool but it feels somehow alive, not like Breker's monsters. It's alive like Paris is alive. I feel a rush of warmth for this my city. It is all somehow so full of a familiar power.

I turn over the bridge. On the corner, there is a hideous Boche pill box in grey concrete. From inside a stupid voice calls out Mam'selle, mam'selle. *Quel con*!

As I head over the Seine towards the Ile de la Cité the sun goes in. Two barges move slowly downstream, not under power, but at the speed the current bears them. One gives off a melancholy hoot as it comes to the bridge. The alien sound startles me. I look down. There is a bargeman leaning on the tiller, and another mec hanging out his smalls on a line that runs the length of the barge. I dawdle there for a moment, still grasping Papa's shoes, swinging them back and forth in my right hand.

I pass beneath Notre Dame. The fugitive sun returns for a moment and sheds a pale light over the apse and on the linden trees beneath it. The sap is thrusting up and the raw new leaves are opening, remembering and yet also forgetful of all the endless seasons that have gone before.

My mind is this salad. I turn over the fragments of the afternoon, I mean for instance about the Dina. She can be little more than my age and yet already she is a great man's muse. And so incredibly self-possessed! I wonder, is she, for example, a heroine or a traitor? Or just a fool? Or a tart? What exactly is a muse anyway? Does she just simper and take off her kit when that old mec wants a free model? Will he be right now fondling her young body? How creepy is that! Doesn't she need a boyfriend her own age?

Boys like my Maurice. My love, my perfect boy, my smooth and comely boy, my thrilling, honeyed boy.

And those huge willies hanging down! Of course, I know about these things. After all, during our school outings to the Louvre I've made my close study of the Dying Slave where he hoiks up his vest and shows everything. And I've seen Franck when he skips from bathroom to bedroom without a towel, grinning when he sees me and making no effort to cover up his thick dark forest and the *zizi* springing out like a big carrot.

But these Breker ones, these stupendous, hard cold stone ones, a metre long. God in Heaven!

So my mind is running on to the related question, for the question remains, how *exactly* does it all work? Love, I mean.

As I head down the Boul' Mich, it is suddenly chilly in the shade so I take the short cut through to the Cinquième. I come out just opposite the Lycée St Louis and turn into the Place de la Sorbonne, and that's where I spot her. She's standing by the black iron gates of the university, looking up.

***

It is just as I round the corner that I see her. First, I see Auguste Comte, pondering beneath the plane trees. Mercifully, he's a human size and reliably still there (the Boches are destatue-ing Paris, trying to put out the eyes of our beloved city).

And, by the gates, looking up at Comte, also perhaps pondering but looking less reliable, is the small plump figure of my philo teacher.

Mlle de Beauvoir is clothed in a mud-coloured woollen frock which is super-ugly. She looks a fright, dumpy, and no waist at all.

She doesn't see me, her face is turned away, looking up at Auguste. I think, I will slip by. Hot shame revisits me, that stupid gaffe in front of Natalie Tardieu.

I walk quickly behind her a dozen paces off, heading for the little passage that will take me into the rue Cufas. But it's as though she has some sixth sense. She whips round and sees me. She calls out 'Anna-Elisa Schneider, *viens*', although whether she has so well remembered my entire name or just read it off the bib of my school uniform which I am of course still shamefully wearing is another, deeper question.

So over I go, still clutching Papa's old shoes. As I approach, she keeps her pale oval face towards me and as I come up to her I see her big blue eyes and her pretty little nose. She is, of course, a fright, dumpy and plain and extremely old, but also of course there is a sort of scent of life about her which is probably from her shining intelligence or something. Even as I come and stand awkwardly before her, I am struck by this. It is compelling, this vitality.

She takes my hand and presses it.

'Annie,' she says. It is almost as though she was expecting me. It makes me feel special, singled out.

'I... I...' I mutter. I am completely stupid and abashed.

'Whence?' she says. 'Whence, whither?'

'Whence, from the Breker. Whither, home I suppose.'

'Ah, home, *place of last resort, open all night*. And with Daddy's shoes, I see.'

She smiles the sweetest smile and gestures at old Comte and then at the Sorbonne behind her, at the huge clock which says five o'clock and I give a start as I have dawdled away so much time. I should have been home an hour ago. Papa and Pauli will be fretting and Paco will no doubt be pooing in the hall again as Papa and Pauli never ever take him down for his *moment sanitaire*. But la Beauvoir links her arm through mine, detaining me with a firm grip and waving her plump hand at the Sorbonne façade where there are the niches with a bunch of gods and goddesses.

'When I was a Sorbonnarde,' she says, 'and working on Spinoza, I thought that I would be a god like them and live forever.' Her voice is strangely deep, almost masculine. I always thought this was just her voice for class or for that time when she was ticking me off, but now when she is all friendly it is just the same, rough and a bit harsh. 'I thought then I would be a woman with a unique life, that every minute I would be writing my own life story and then... then I would tear it up and start all over again.'

She looks at me intently with those piercing blue eyes. She is smiling the way a cat can seem to smile.

'So, Annie, what do you think? Shall I just be a *bas bleu*, a humble *agrégée* teaching in a lycée – or shall I be a woman with that unique and interesting life?'

Her face is alive and she speaks in poetry. Now, strangely, she looks quite beautiful, transformed by thought.

'And will you be a god and live forever?' I want to know.

'Of course, my dear, of course. I already am. You too. You see, *if we live in the moment, we live forever*. And eternal life is at least one attribute of a god.'

'But then,' she goes on, 'I wonder if you are interested, really interested, in *philo*...'

'Do you think it would help?' I say, and she laughs, a big laugh.

We do a round of the courtyard in silence, and then she says,

'I remember your friend, what was her name? That fiercely moral girl who did silly things with fishing rods.'

'Maddie. Madeleine Grandidier.'

'Yes, Madeleine, now *she* was interested in *philo*.'

She pauses, breaks her step,

'What's she up to now? Another school? I can't imagine her idling at home.'

'Oh, no, she's working for *Les Nouveaux Temps*.' And I blurt out without thinking, 'And playing ball with Germans...'

'Is she now?'

A hot flush of shame surges up my back and into my neck. I don't enlarge. I have already betrayed Maddie quite enough. Why oh why did I say such a thing?

Fortunately, Mme changes the subject.

'But you, Annie, if you are not interested in *philo*, then why choose it? You might have done Letters instead.'

'Oh, you know, Papa...'

'Oh, yes, of course, the father. The father is always a problem. And what says Maman?'

'She died.'

'Aha, yes, the mother died. Yes, of course. And you, Annie, what do you really really want to do?'

'I want to study English literature and write a great

novel. Like *La Nausée*...'

'Oh, indeed!'

Her arm squeezes mine and she says 'Let's walk. What's your direction?'

I tell her I am going home.

Her grip on my arm tightens a little and we scuff companionably across the cobbles, kicking at last autumn's leaves which the threadbare municipality has neglected. The pigeons scatter into the trees.

Down the rue Soufflot she steers me, and on into the Place Corneille. And there before us lies the Pantheon.

'Oh, do let's go in,' she says, almost like a child. 'Let's go in and touch Marianne, touch *l'Esprit de la Révolution*. It will be like the King's Touch. It will heal you of all those monstrous German bodies you saw at Breker's.'

She marches me to the door and wrenches on the great brass handle. It is locked which is not really surprising. It is, after all, an Occupation.

'They locked up Marianne,' she says, screwing up her nose which gives her a humorous, truculent look.

But no, I spot an old fellow skulking behind a buttress. He watches us and looks around and then nips out and comes lurching our way with a lop-sided walk. He has the tin badge of a *mutilé* from the last war.

'Ah,' Madame breathes, 'here is *M. le gardie*n.'

'*Veux voir?*' he says, '*vaut voir.*' He pulls from the pocket of his dirty tweed coat a big iron key and he unlocks the door with the flourish of the professional. Simone takes my hand and I feel the sure thrill of being the favourite, if only for an hour. Inside by the pale daylight which falls from the dome we see Marianne, battling spirit of our battered old Republic.

She is a tall girl with a fierce look on her rather square face. Her full breasts are bare like those in the famous Delacroix. Her frock is awkwardly pushed down and her whole body surges forward. She is the very image of battling womanhood. At her feet, on the plinth are those old words of Mirabeau *vivre libre ou mourir* – Live free or die.

Someone has put a posy in her hand. Probably violets but they're old and long since withered. I reach up and touch them and they shiver into dry brown fragments and flutter to the floor.

'Madame...' I say but she grasps my hand and says,

'Call me Simone, dear.' In that moment, some arrow seeks my heart. I dare to stammer out 'Simone'.

She smiles and turns to Marianne.

'And what,' she says, looking up 'what in Heaven's name were you doing at Breker's?'

'A... a friend took me... Maillol was there.'

'Was he now?'

'And his muse. A girl called Dina.'

'Tell me about it. About her. About the images.'

So I tell her the whole story. She listens, looking all the time at Marianne. When I have finished, she says,

'So! The giant Boche male is rampant in the Orangerie, while our poor slip of a Marianne is locked up in the Panthéon and in need of a good dusting.'

She laughs to herself and says under her breath '*Quelle métaphore!*'

She puts her arm around my shoulder. It's thrilling. I smell something, it is, I think, a camphorated rub.

'So, ma petite, *vivre libre ou mourir!*'

'But...' I want to say *But the blood of others* but I can't get it out and anyhow at that moment the old guardian heaves up wheezing, an oil lantern in his hand and he mutters *Veux voir?* again. He waves towards the darkened staircase that goes down to the crypt.

She removes her arm from my shoulder and takes my hand. We go down. The oldster holds the lamp up and we admire first Rousseau, then Voltaire. I ask her, *Simone... do you... um, admire Voltaire?* Not that I really want to know. I want just to utter her name. She has given me this gift of herself. I have to utter it one more time – *Simone*. So I say her name a second time by the guttering lamplight with the creased and bent old man peering and hawking. The arrow has stuck, somewhere.

She waves her plump hand towards Voltaire.

'He first showed us that God is dead and that we are alone. And responsible.'

She falls silent. I so much want to prolong the moment which is full of obscure meaning. I want her to ask me again *vivre libre ou mourir?* – and to tell me the answer. And I want to ask about Maurice and those gigantic *zizis* and everything that is on my mind. But sadly she begins shuddering, she says *It's so cold down here*, and she shudders again or pretends to. It's enough, it seems, she's had enough of me and she wants to end it. She gives the old mec five sous and we scamper out of there. In the sunlight, blinking, she briefly embraces me and it's over. She hurries off, still a dumpy figure but now, I don't know, somehow transfigured in my eyes. At the corner she stops and turns. She gives a faint wave and calls 'I'll introduce you to the author of *La Nausée*. I'll send you a *pneu*'.

Oi, oi, Mamselle, the old guardian says behind me and he holds out Pa's shoes which I had set down on Marianne's plinth and quite forgotten.

Franck to Annie

Dearest Anschli,
I am sick to my stomach. This incarceration has gone on for such centuries and my chances of being young enough when it is finished and to start all over again, to relearn the piano or something quite new, are dwindling away to nothing.

Anyway, I shall probably die of typhus like half the fellows here, or else the Boche will shoot me out of hand like the dog I am becoming.

I have so abandoned hope it is almost soothing. I have no plans, no expectations, almost no curiosity about what may happen next, because it will be the same or worse.

But when I see Messiaen I am ashamed. He looks like a scarecrow these days, he has lost his hair and his teeth and his fingers are swollen with chilblains. And yet he is so very Catholic. He is on his knees and praying all the time. All day Sunday he prays in the Chapel.

And he is still at work on his big project, the *Quartet for the End of Time*. Did I mention it? It is, he says, about the end of the notion of past and future. It is about the beginning of Eternity. He sits there in the lats, day after day, composing this piece. He says it is Catholic doctrine and colours and bird song altogether. The colours he sees in dreams, he says the physical deprivations here give him these intense, coloured dreams and his quartet is the music of these colours. You hear him explaining his quartet in words like *The first transition of mode two is blue-violet, speckled with grey, cobalt blue, deep Prussian blue. Second transition is gold and*

silver spirals...
  And the birds! In the quartet the violin plays the song of the Nightingale and the clarinet, the Blackbird. Birds, he says, symbolise our longing for light, and also our desire for freedom. *Above the horror of the abyss, the bird flies in freedom, in joyous freedom.*
  Soon we are to hear it. I shall write to you and tell you all about it.
  But for me, sadly, I cannot even think straight. I have no end of time to kill, but I am always in company, always in discomfort, always cold. So I never can think. It is a low life, a vegetable life. I think a root vegetable, what is that one – mangle wurzel. I am a derided low-life root vegetable.
  Oh darling, remind me that it is not all winter and darkness and death. Remind me that love still exists in the world, quick and warm.
  With my love and kisses,
  Franck

12

Papa says,
'You look so thin and beautiful, *ma belle.*'
This is so unusual, a compliment from Papa. I almost look around to see if he is not actually talking to someone else, Verónica, for example, that starveling beauty. But it is me he is addressing and I push my bosom out in pride. But it's not much compensation for my perpetual state of near-starvation. It's completely worn away my natural chubbiness. I can count all my ribs now. Clothes hang off me. I think about food *all the time.*

And the ration is down again this week. Last night I divvied up my J3 (*adolescent female*) meat ration between Papa and Pauli. Then Paco stared me down with liquid eyes. His grey muzzle quivered, he yawned and licked his lips, his tail thumped on the parquet, so of course I give him half my bread too, with a dab of gravy.

Paco! After his surprise reprieve, he has been surviving largely on huge quantities of bones, big animal bones the butcher chops up for him. For hours he licks out the jelly, concentrating with the professionalism of a *pointilliste* artist. When I can get chicken bones, he eats them out of my hand, crunching them up and swallowing them down whole. I watch him, terrified he's going to get one stuck in his throat. Yesterday he sicked up blood again. Yet for all that, he's adapting well to the Occupation. The worst is getting him out for his *moments sanitaires*, past the Old Bat who darts out and waves the circular about dogs in my face and has to be bought off with a five-sou piece every time.

Anyway... if I'm skinny as a rake, is my sex appeal growing? Certainly I'm getting thin in all the right places anyway, not just wasting all over. My hips and boobs are still nice and round. *So will Maurice notice?*
Another thing. *Mes règles se sont toujours arrêtés.* I haven't had a period for ages. What this means I have no idea. I'm going to ask Maddie. Or maybe not. That flirting with the Boche thing still sticks in my throat. What was my blood sister thinking of?
Anyway, tonight she's coming round to interview Papa. Maybe I'll have it out with her.

Our feast tonight is going to be – potatoes. Like a Peruvian, I worship the potato these days. After all, they're practically the only thing I can get. The old Incas apparently had more than 4,000 species. They would just put them in icy water and they would keep for years.
So, in honour of Maddie's visit tonight I have prepared a gala spud dinner. I slipped round the back of old Rioust's shop and got from him two kilograms of bumpy golden Prince de Bretagne potatoes. I paid him dearly but it is so worth it. We are out of olive oil but I have raided Papa's iron reserve that he keeps to put on his hair. We are going to have a huge blow-out of *frites*.
I have put out Ma's Spode and the silver flatware that came from Papa's grand house on the Ringstrasse. There are crystal glasses, heavy as lead. I filter the muddy tap water through muslin. It takes out the bits although the water still has that dull used up look like it's already been through somebody else's digestive system more than once.
Even Papa is alert to the celebratory character of the evening. He has decanted a '19 Nuits and a '21 too. I just manage to stop him putting in a sprinkling of iodine crystals

which he thinks will stop us getting cretinous and developing pendulous goitres.

'Chips!' cries Pauli, rushing in and grabbing one. He completely ignores Maddie who arrived just now and who is leaning against the sideboard. She is wearing one of the prettiest frocks I have ever seen. It's a startling white with a pattern of brilliant red hibiscus flowers. Agh, these old families! I think of the mound of sopping grey-tinged sheets I have just shoved into the darkest corner of the kitchen. The Grandidiers probably have some specialized domestic serf dedicated to whitening Maddie's frocks.

Of course, the scarlet flowers don't quite go with her flame-red hair, but her lips do, they are also scarlet with lipstick. This fabulous look, and her pale face and the deep set of her eyes above her high cheek bones deeply impress Papa who gazes at her as if she were some goddess popped down for the evening. He treats her to his best old Vienna courtesies.

'What a lovely girl you are,' he says, almost to himself. 'So lovely, so tall and slim. And your flaming hair.' He starts to reach his great hand towards her locks but then drops it down at his side.

'Oh my, what a crown you wear!' he says.

I know what he means. I dread to say that, unlike me, unlike us, Maddie is a fine breed.

And yet her take on this is so fiercely different. *Not fine*, she would say. *Worn out, the fag end of too long a line.* She would say, *From Charlemagne to now, Good God! Stretched sooooo thin.* She would pat her narrow hips as if to say *nature rebels, etiolated, no more heirs! Time for us to disappear.*'

Eric, she always says, *will die in a dogfight, heroic and childless. And I* – and here she would pat her hips again – *I shall conceive giant twins and die in childbirth.*

I have no idea why she talks such rubbish. Fiery spirit and *élan vital* fill this girl. She will have many children. Countless generations will succeed her and she will live forever.

Anyway, this is all beside the point. Tonight she charms Papa effortlessly, simply by *being*. She stands there radiant and lovely beyond words – which is as well, because later she is to interview him and this is sure to make him cross. But right now she piles on the charm. She says she has read his book and she lobs him some trivial question, about free trade it is. Papa nods and says, 'Later. We will talk later, my dear.' In old Vienna, I know, you would never talk business at dinner.

Maddie falls on the *frites* and devours them with gusto. 'Ah, Prince de Bretagne!' she says with playful reverence, 'lovely and nutty.' This girl manages to give a stately character to a humble dish of chips. She also charms Pauli by letting him pinch some from her plate. She says,

'When I was in England, they told me you must never eat with your fingers and never take food from someone else's plate. With one exception – *the chip!*' *The chip* she says in English and Pauli laughs. Now that he has had some of her chips, he is completely enchanted with her and he spends the rest of the dinner gazing at her whilst he expertly navigates his own chips and a lot of hers towards his yawning mouth.

'*Down the red lane with you,*' Maddie says in English as Pauli feeds in an especially long one. Pauli loves this, it's Mama and nursery talk again.

All this time Paco is sitting beside Maddie, pushing up his grizzled muzzle. Like Pauli, he has fallen for her charm.

'How old is your dog?' Maddie asks Pauli.

'Thirteen. He's Mummy's dog.'

Maddie counts the *frites* left on her plate. Then she puts six onto Pauli's empty plate, pops two into her own mouth and puts the plate with the rest, which number thirteen, onto the floor. Paco wolfs them down in a trice and sits there beaming up at her.

So the dinner is a success and Maddie is a success. We drink our wine, Maddie and I in moderation, just a couple of glasses, Pauli three drops in a tumbler of water. Papa polishes off the '19 and makes inroads into the '21. It is the nearest thing to a dinner party we have had since Mama died and he is exhilarated by it.

After dinner, Papa invites Maddie into his study. She goes into the hall where she has left her smart bag, it's a briefcase in polished Morocco leather, super chic, and she follows Pa into to his lair. I get on with the tasks of Minerva, washing out the pan and scrubbing the plates and cleaning the silverware and putting the Spode away in the glass-fronted cupboard where Mama kept her heirloom china. Pauli sits at the kitchen table reading his *Boy's Own Annual* for the umpteenth time. He only agrees to get ready for bed when I say he may come out in his pyjamas and say goodbye to Maddie when she goes.

'She's like a lady,' he says. This boy clearly needs some Republican training.

I sit in the kitchen composing my Latin verses, iambics in the style of Catullus. When I have finished I start on my Herodotus. I can hear Maddie's voice, quite high, and Papa's answering rumble. At one point there is a long silence, and then my father speaking in a raised voice, not quite angry but loud and forceful.

* * *

At length the door opens and Maddie comes out. Papa is there in the doorway. His face is quite flushed. Maddie turns and kisses him on either cheek. Papa glows at her in a dulled kind of way and then goes back into his study and shuts the door.

'VSOP?'

Maddie nods. 'Yes, we finished off the *Nuits* and got into the cognac.'

'But you got what you needed?'

She hesitates.

'Yes,' she says at last. Her violet eyes are searching mine, and then out runs Pauli in his old English pyjamas. When Mama first bought them, they were much too large for him. Now they're much too small and his bare calves show, thin little sticks. He throws his arms around Maddie's legs and buries his face in her skirt. She strokes his fuzzy head.

'His ideas are... well, honestly, they are beautiful. It's all lovely, perfect, a wonderful, humane... story. It could have been the future of us all. It should be the future of us all...'

'But?'

She wags her pretty head from side to side and adjusts her swirl of hair from shoulder to shoulder. I know these gestures all too well. She is going to contradict.

'Such optimism is not for now. Now we need to see the world clearly as it is.'

I say nothing. Maddie's hand drops down to where Pauli is still nuzzling in her skirt. She strokes his hair again.

'Oh,' she exclaims. She sounds exasperated. 'He just doesn't realize what a plot it all is. He's putting his head into the mouth of the lion. You should stop him. We should stop him.'

'Don't go, Maddie!' Pauli says in a muffled way, his head still in Maddie's skirt. She pats his head.

'But you won't... I mean, you won't write against him, will you?'

'I should, Annie, somebody should. It would be better for him.'

She hesitates, running a nervous hand through her hair and switching it again from shoulder to shoulder.

'Your father is a great man, you know that. One of the two or three top economic minds we have. But he is, well, unworldly. He has no idea how these people will use him and exploit him and then...'

I wait.

'They're sharks. It's *collaboration à outrance*, collaboration pure and simple, and he just doesn't see it. He sees it all through a mist of good intentions. He simply doesn't get what they are up to.'

'Which is?'

'They are going to use him. They want him to give a veil of legitimacy to their dirty New Europe project, and then when he's squeezed dry, they'll toss him aside.'

'Erm... did you say that to him?'

'Not in so many words, but yes. I told him that if he gets up on that platform next week with Goebbels...'

'With Goebbels?'

'Yes, didn't you know?'

'I had no idea.'

'This is the huge buzz all around the office. At Montoire, the Old Gaffer promised Hitler *collaboration* and Goebbels is coming to Paris next Tuesday to spell it out. He's going to offer economic integration, export markets, investment opportunities in the new eastern territories, an economic mission to the Ukraine... And your Dad is being put up there to make it look all pretty with his fine visions and his grand reputation.'

'But… is it all really such a bad idea?'

'Oh, Christ, Annie. Don't tell me you've got the same damned innocence as your Daddy!'

Maddie is almost shouting now. I have never seen my cool sister so worked up about something. Her pale cheeks are hot and pink. Pauli reaches out and tries to pull me towards Maddie and get his arms around my legs too. He hates arguments. I let him pull us in and I come right up close to Maddie. I can smell her scent but why is she so angry? What's suddenly so wrong with Papa's ideas? He's been saying the same thing for years, hasn't he?

Maddie turns her face away and goes 'Pfoof.' She pats Pauli on his little head and strokes his cheek.

'Oh, darling, this is so hard. You know…' – and here she whispers in my ear – 'you know they're going to name your Daddy on the BBC?'

I jerk away and say 'How do you know that?'

This is horrible. Name Papa on the nightly lists of *collabos*, the ones the Free French are going to 'settle with' at some stage!

Maddie's face is an inch from mine. Her violet eyes are bright and lovely and full of tears. Down below, Pauli starts piping the eye, of course. Suddenly Maddie throws her arms around me and embraces me and then we are all sobbing away. Bloody stupid. Pauli is clinging to us both, with his thin little arms around our legs.

So now I don't want Maddie to go. I make us a weak cup of ersatz and we sit in the kitchen, side by side. Pauli climbs onto Maddie's lap.

'*Mon Dieu*,' she murmurs. 'I can't wait for all this to be over.'

'That's all we can do, though.'

She leans in and kisses my hair and shoots me a dangerous look.

'No, my chicken, no, never. We resist. We have to. It's not a choice.'

'Uh uh.' I'm shaking my head like mad. 'No!'

Her violet eyes pierce my soul.

'Not me, I mean.'

'Then who?'

'Just not me, Maddie.' I try to stare her out but I am not very successful. Instead she stares me out and I look down, burning.

'Come,' she says to Pauli, 'give me a big *bise*.' He turns an unusually angelic face up to her and she gives him six kisses. He laughs and tries to pull her nose. She gets up to leave, heaving him up expertly and angling him in her right arm. With her left she draws me in and gives me half a hug and a serious look and says we will meet tomorrow, she'll send a *pneu*.

I pick up her leather *serviette* to give to her. It is heavy and bulging, much fatter than when she came.

'What did Papa give you?' It's as heavy as gold bars.'

'Ouf,' she's says, craning Pauli down and plonking him on the parquet. 'You're as heavy as gold bars, Pauli.'

'No, you're as heavy as gold bars!'

'No, you are.'

Paco wriggles up arthritically and she gives him a pat. With this she takes the *serviette* from me and scoots out of the door with a backward wave at Pauli.

It is only when she is gone that I realize I didn't ask about her playing Nausicaa with that podgy Boche. But on the scale, what's that compared to Papa and his speech and Goebbels?

Papa

So the girl has gone and I am plunged into thinking about the start of it all. More and more it preoccupies me, the *noble project*.

Keynes looked me first in the eyes, and you understand that he was very tall and so was looking down on me, looking on my heavy lids, and then he looked at my hands which in my anxiety I was clasping damply together, sliding the fingers of either hand in and out.

After, long after, I learned that this was his way with a new man, to study the hands. What he saw in my nervous clammy movements I have no idea. He just put his hand, which was large like a giant's, on my forearm as though to still me.

It was the moment when our people had begun to starve. I was in London to show lantern slides of the children. The pictures, the *Manchester Guardian* said, showed 'rickety bodies, horribly distended, shrunken limbs, bent and twisted, wizened, old, questioning baby faces.' Gracious English ladies came and saw and then set up the Save the Children Fund and raised thousands.

But all the time the *Daily Mail* was ranting, and the Blind Four – Clemenceau, Orlando, Lloyd George and Wilson – they blundered on with their scheme to seize the maximum of booty from the dying beast of defeated Mitteleuropa. The starvation question was in the margin.

The gracious ladies aside – and the right-minded readers of the *Manchester Guardian* – it was only this big, ugly man with the wet, fleshy lips, only Keynes, who seemed to care about the wretchedness of our people. He swore about the cynical militarist newspapermen, the ignoble lords who owned *The Times* and the *Daily Mail*. He said never would God, any god, ever forgive that speech of the hog Lloyd George: '*The war is a road paved with gold and cemented with blood.*' I am filled, he said, with perpetual contempt of the government and of the press.

But this was not then his concern with me. He was asking me *Where are the intellectuals? Where are the economists?* They, he said, just ply their feeble pen and feel sorry for themselves.

We economists must, he said, *inflame the minds of everyone we meet.*

So what then must we do to be saved? I asked and he laughed out loud.

'Ah, you have caught me out,' he said. For he knew he was proselytizing like the Apostle he was.

'We must bind Europe together with bonds that cannot be broken,' he said.

And then he seized me, body and soul, and bound me to his noble project.

'You must understand, Schneider,' he said – and he stooped down to me and gripped my lapels, he was so much in earnest – 'understand that in any age only a handful of men can do things well. You have talent. You must sacrifice everything to make that talent flourish and to help with the noble task of rebuilding Europe justly and fairly.'

So now, here I am, decades later and charmed by a carrot-top slip of a girl and recalling that project. And asking Can I carry the project forward – *or am I about to ruin everything?*

13

Now begins a beguiling, terrifying time for me. Maddie doesn't send a *pneu* and we don't meet. I thought at least a *pneu* to thank me for the other night. I suppose she is busy with her Fifth Column at *Les Nouveaux Temps*. I lead my mechanical life, from day to tedious day. I am the perfect *attentiste*. I put up with every privation. I queue up endlessly for stuff, I minister to Papa's every whim, I clean up after Paco and wipe his soiled bottom, I lift Pauli twice each night and wring out his pee-sodden sheets, I go to school, I fill my *cahier des notes*.

A law comes out of Vichy annulling all acts of naturalization made since 1931. So technically Papa and Franck and Pauli and I are aliens and no longer French citizens. However, Papa reassures me over and over that we are safe in the protection of the Old Gentleman and of his lustre and apparatus, and so I believe that we are lucky and still somehow French despite the law.

Now that Maddie has left school and Verónica is so duff, the only light is lessons with the Beaver. I hug my new pash on her tight to me. I don't tell a soul. I hang on her words although I don't understand so very much. I just watch her move and see the kingfisher flash of her startling eyes, and I wonder just how it is that she corrupts the young. Which of us is it that she is corrupting? Is it just me? Or is it all of us with her free thinking and her talk of free love?

As for her, she completely ignores me.

The strangest thing, though, is Maurice. I sort of hate

him, because he does not take me seriously. Yet he is often there, hailing me on the street or sending a *pneu* or telephoning the school to say my great aunt is dying and I must go home at once when what he wants is to take me on some escapade, but it is ridiculous and impossible. I've got a household to run and two big babies to care for and doesn't he know there's an Occupation on and it takes two hours now to queue for a cabbage?

Yet he is still the man I dream of. When I see him, tall and slim with his beautiful hair and his broad shoulders and taut body, his big hands and his supple musicians' fingers, his perfect grooming – well, I yearn, in a completely physical way.

Anyway, these outings he proposes, they are not like dates. There is always Otto.

In fact, there they are now, just as I am getting out of the lycée gates and heading to Lafarge's where there is a rumour of a major *arrivage* of off-ration sprouts and I mean to nab a kilo if I can get there in time.

But Maurice is standing up in a red sporting car, and at the wheel, there is Otto. Where there's Maurice there's always Otto too, they're like the Cisco Kid and his sidekick, Pancho.

Otto is in full uniform today, very smart, very Boche. I recognize the car of the day, it's a red Panhard open top, super sexy. As I come out of the gates there are already a dozen girls clustering around this sports job and Maurice is chatting them up. They're from the *quatrième* and *troisième*, old enough to be interested in boys and their red car, not old enough to have an ounce of sense.

Anyway, it's big envy from these kids when Maurice turns away from them and calls to me. I shake my head and run off down the street as fast as my stupid sabots will let me but of course the red Panhard comes cruising after me and all the silly girls are shrieking with laughter and running after us, trying to keep up. I kick off the laming clogs and gather them up, flying like Atalanta barefoot after apples. I round the corner into the rue Quercy and put on a burst of speed. Fleet as I am, I soon throw off the girls but I can hear the throat rattle of the Panhard which whizzes past me and stops twenty yards ahead. Maurice leaps out onto the pavement and spreads his arms wide in a stupid herding gesture to bar my way. I feint to the left of him and try to duck past on his right but he grabs my arm and whirls me round into a tight embrace.

I struggle but it's not much of a struggle as I can feel the warmth of his body and the beating of his heart and like a fool I relax because I do actually want it to go on. He says,
'Annie, *arrête*! We've got a special treat for you today.'
I put my face up towards him and push out my lips a fraction, so he kisses me, but just the lightest touch.
'Come on you two lovebirds, hop in,' Otto calls out. His voice is impatient. Maurice slips his hand under my bottom and lifts me up in his arms. The car has no actual doors but just a scalloped bit that Maurice steps over and he slides down in the seat with me still in his arms.
This is when I decide my Descartes homework can wait.
'Where are we going?'
But it's to be a surprise. First, we have to go via Maurice's apartment but when we pull up outside a building in the Avenue Iéna I say,
'I thought you lived in ----'
'I moved, little one,' he says without explaining. So I get off his lap and climb out of the car, and then he leaps out and runs into the building.

***

I am left with Otto. I realize suddenly that it is the first time I have been alone with him and I don't know what to say. I sit down in Maurice's seat and fiddle with the cigarette lighter in the beautiful mahogany dashboard.

'Ah, yes.'

Otto slips his hand inside his jacket and pulls out a flash cigarette case. He offers me one and I say I will never ever smoke. He reaches across and pushes in the cigarette lighter, waits a moment, then draws it out and lights his cigarette.

'You know that my sister is coming to Paris. You must meet her.'

I want to say I don't know why I should meet this sister but he turns a friendly face to me and I just say lamely,

'Gosh. She's coming to visit you?'

'No, of course not. There's a war on. That sort of visiting is not encouraged. My sister is coming as a Noble Typist.'

This means nothing to me, but I think it would be impolite to ask what a Noble Typist is. So I wait but then he changes the subject. He turns in his seat and leans toward me in a very confidential manner. This close up his face looks very big. I can see the little dots on his chin where his beard is already pushing out, although it is only afternoon.

'Anna-Elisa,' he says, quite solemn, 'I hear that your Papa is going to make a speech next week and that he is to share the platform with our Mr Goebbels.'

I nod cautiously.

'I know your father's work, of course. Everybody does. Such a brilliant economic case for European integration.'

Otto wags his big head from side to side, keeping his eyes on mine. So close, all his good features are distorted. The nose is much too big. His skin is rough and slightly pitted on his cheeks. I can smell breath which is faintly sour.

'He is,' Otto continues, 'one of the finest minds of our generation. A continental Mr. Keynes.'

'Oh, I wish he could hear you say that. Mr Keynes is such a hero to him.'

However, I know there's going to be a 'but' to all this. And so it turns out as after a pause Otto says,

'But your Daddy should beware of that *parvenu* Herr Goebbels. You will find that his notions of European integration are quite different from your Daddy's...'

Otto pauses. He turns away and puts his hands on the steering wheel which looks like it is made of tortoiseshell. He taps his fingers against the wheel.

'In '32,' he says, *à propos* of nothing as far as I can see, 'I was at Heidelberg, writing my thesis. It was a good time and also a terrible time. We were young and gay, it was a long summer, very hot. Every day we swam naked in the river. We picnicked on the banks beneath the willow trees, all our clothes off. So much wine, so much love-making. And then each evening we were at the cafés in the gardens beneath the ruined old schloss. We sat and drank the beer and talked and talked of poetry, above all of the beloved Heine, my thesis, you see, was on that shooting star...'

Pute!

A ragged boy going by has spat at the car, perhaps at me, but his spittle is on the bonnet. He stops a yard ahead and looks at me and says it again. *Putain.*

'*Foutes le camp,*' says Otto, heaving himself up in his seat to get out. The kid looks on. He must be twelve or thirteen, he is too big for his scruffy coat.

'No, you fuck off,' he says.

By now Otto is out of the car and he makes a flicking gesture at the kid who turns and saunters off. Otto pulls out a very white handkerchief and wipes the bonnet clean.

'Ah, see that,' he says, clambering in and coiling himself back into the tight little seat. He nods towards the wall over the road where is written in newly painted letters two metres high:

Défense de cracher
Article 74 du décret du 22 mars 1941

We sit for a minute in silence and then he goes on.

'We lived of course in our own little world, a world of foolish innocence. We were so happy that we never saw that others were angry in a measure we could not have comprehended. We never understood until it was too late.

'My landlady, for instance, she was forever angry and yet we never listened, although she talked all the time, about her husband lost in *der grosse Krieg*, all three sons dead in the Great War too, about her life after the loss of her entire family. She worked at the local hospital in Wiesbaden where they brought amputation cases back from the Front, her job all day long to throw severed limbs into the hospital furnace.

'And after, came our brave Weimar Republic, a so good time for us. A time of freedom and abandon and forgetting, but for her, my landlady, just crippling taxes to pay our Reparations to the French, and inflation that in a week wiped out her savings and her small pensions. She would show me the billion-mark banknote she had received in change in a grocery shop in '23. And then the day when the French Occupier paraded their troops through the street, coal black Senegalese marching through the centre of her town holding over their faces masks that were caricatures of the dirty Hun.

'It was done to cow and humiliate us. Instead, it created an anger that could not be quenched. My landlady would say *My life is over, and there is no one after me. But I will not be humiliated.*

'And then one day she was brighter, almost cheerful. She said to us, *When Herr Hitler comes, all will be well.*'

Otto continues his nervy drumming on the steering wheel. Today he is a bundle of nerves. He trembles when he speaks.

'*When Hitler comes, all will be well.* And of course he came. And to us in Heidelberg came your Herr Goebbels, Herr Hitler's intellectual emissary. He came for the burning.

'Dutifully we marched in our corps, in the regalia of our duelling clubs, in our red caps and our blue tunics, our perfect white breeches and our polished high boots and our sparkling spurs. We marched through the streets singing our songs, our songs of love and wine and eternal friendship, songs of the joyous years of student life, *From High Olympus*, even *Gaudeamus igitur*. And we sang their songs too, we were obliged to.

Es schau'n aufs Hakenkreuz voll Hoffnung schon Millionen.
Der Tag für Freiheit und für Brot bricht an!

Millions are looking upon the swastika full of hope,
The day of freedom and of bread dawns!

'In the square below the castle we had built a grand bonfire, like a Homeric funeral pyre. And there was your Mr Goebbels, a small, dark, common little man, standing with his arms straight at his side. He was dressed like a comic opera character in the full fig of Nazi fancy dress, but the darting eyes were watching everything, watching us as we began our shame. Our hands lit the pyre and each in turn we threw on our books.

'It was planned that each man threw on some book of his own, some text he had studied, even treasured. So our corps captain, he was a medic specializing in psychiatry, he must throw on *The Psychopathology of Everyday Life* and then he must cry out in a great voice "There, there... that is for falsifying our history and degrading its great figures." As Freud's great work fell into the flames, Goebbels nodded. He was approving our shame.

'Then each of us burned the books he loved. There went Thomas Mann, there went poor Helen Keller, there even Jack London...'

He stopped.

'You did this?' I had to ask.

'Yes, me too. I stepped up and the captain gave me Heine... Oh where, oh where, is Maurice...?'

Otto's great face is pale. Now he grasps the steering wheel hard, turning away from me, peering into the building, after Maurice. But Maurice does not emerge and so he at last goes on,

'I threw on Heine. I should have thrust my hand into the flames before I did such a thing. And yet I threw on Heine's *Almansoor*. But I did not shout. I said, but very softly, *Das war ein Vorspiel nur* (That was but a prelude).

'Our captain looked at me, a warning look, although not surprised. He just made a small gesture with his hand, unseen by your Mr Goebbels, to tell me to step aside. Goebbels was right there above us, perched like a hawk, but I believe he did not hear, or maybe Hitler's intellectual did not know how it goes on.'

'*Vorspiel*?' I had to ask. Otto clearly expected me to ask. 'How does it go on?'

'*Dort, wo man Bücher verbrennt,*
Verbrennt man am Ende auch Menschen

> So when they burn the books
> They end up burning men

'And then that little shit got up on the rostrum and began to scream "Jewish intellectualism is dead, the German soul can again express itself." And...'

'And?'

'Oh, how we cheered! Ach, here is that damned Maurice at last.'

Sure enough, just then Maurice appears in the doorway of his building looking so debonair and carefree. My heart is low, very low, and yet the sight of Maurice lounging his way towards us still thrills me.

Otto says in a low voice,

'Anna-Elisa, you tell your Daddy no good will come of it. He will be the loser. Your country will be the loser.'

Then Maurice is gesturing to me to get out of his seat. He jumps in and pulls me in on top of him and we are off on this spree. We are all laughing like crazy although I don't know why and I still have no idea where we are heading.

'You are brave to stay,' Otto says. He has recovered his composure during our drive. The wrinkled little man with the big chest does not reply. He's got his top off. The big chest is very hairy and looks too large for him.

'Brave to stay when you don't have to.'

Otto sounds unctuous, too insistent, too keenly acting the 'good German'.

Pablo Picasso is clearly irritated and will have none of it. I can easily see how much he is regretting having let us in, he is already waiting for us to leave. He stands quite still, his arms folded across the big chest, looking at us each in turn.

I look away, embarrassed.

At last Picasso says something.

'Where would I go?' His French is heavily Spanish-accented. 'Vermin have now infested all of Europe.'

'America?'

'Hah!' Picasso shrugs. He looks disdainful.

'I thought that for you people America is the one big free place left in the world.'

'We people? Freedom loving people? Oppression haters? Ordinary people wanting just to get on with their lives in peace and security?'

Otto stays silent.

'America! A Philistine and mechanized hell.' Picasso sounds quite vehement. 'More exploiters. More exploitation. And worse than exploitation. Hypocrisy. Less cruel than you, maybe, but hypocrites. Fair seeming, talking freedom and then acting like the rest.'

Picasso warms to his theme.

'...a country where size and speed and money are the gods. Where doing down your neighbour is a virtue. Everything mere activity. An automatic life.'

Maurice all this time has been sidling around the studio. Now he has come up to a canvas still on an easel standing in the centre of the studio. Some of the paint is glistening and looks like it is still wet. I look past Maurice at the painting. It shows a seated woman dressed in blue and yellow and wearing a white apron. Her nose and eyes are off to one side. She is wearing a hat shaped like a fish, or perhaps it is just a fish she is wearing on her head.

Picasso is staring hard at Otto. I understand he is trying to see what the man is worth. Something in Otto seems to persuade him that, despite Otto being a German officer, he may yet be worth talking to.

'I didn't stay,' he says at length. 'I just didn't leave. It isn't virtue. It's inertia. So I stayed and I work and I close my eyes to the catastrophe around me.'

At that moment, Picasso seems to notice Maurice for the first time. He calls out to him,
'By the way, there were some other critic friends of yours here the other day. Very incisive, they were. Not at all afraid to express their opinions frankly. Actually, with this.'
He seizes a knife from a nearby table. He holds it up, the point towards Maurice.
'I use this knife to sharpen my pencils. They used it to destroy my degenerate works......' – here he makes some downward stabbing motions with the knife – 'Like your masters. The ones who held that great bonfire last year. Four thousand paintings in one great bonfire! Some of them mine, by the way. And now you come here and pretend that you are not one of them! Well done, my friend!'
Picasso thrusts the knife in Maurice's direction.
'Here. Take your pick. Spare not the knife.'
Maurice steps back, waving his hands in front of him, but Picasso is already bounding across the room. He throws the knife down at Maurice's feet.
'Here,' he says, wrestling a canvas from a lot that are against the wall, 'here!'
But Maurice takes another step back and turns half away.

This visit is not going too well. Maurice, however, makes an effort and rallies. He turns and faces Picasso who is still standing before him.
'Do you wish to sell?'
'Sell what? My soul?'
Alright, so now I understand. This is the Project, Maur-

ice's Project *to save art*.

'Your art. I mean, I can buy, well, all of this or some of this.'

'And then?'

'And then, well, after the Occupation, I will sell it back to you at cost. Or give it to the Jeu de Paumes if you wish...'

Maurice's Project! It seems wafer thin before the iron will of the painter.

Maurice limps on. He tries to explain how it works. The story is he buys up degenerate art, keeps it safe for the duration.

'Keep it from the pyre, or from Herr Goering's grasping hands.'

The problem is that although this is exactly the project Otto has explained to me, Picasso plainly does not believe it. Maurice talks in his usual ironical way and Picasso watches him closely for a minute and I can see contempt spreading on his face. Maurice is coming across as a lightweight, a bit of a shyster. Even before Maurice has finished, Picasso spits on the floor and picks up a postcard from a pile on the table.

'Take it, take it!' He thrusts the card into Maurice's hand. 'Souvenir of your visit. And now... *foutes le camp*.'

I can see the postcard is Guernica. He hands them out to all his visiting Germans.

Maurice takes a step towards him, but Picasso turns his back.

'*Vete a la mierda, pedazzo de mierd*. Fuck off, you piece of shit.'

We get ready to leave. Otto picks up his cap and cane and we head for the door. Then Picasso calls to me, just to me 'Anna-Elisa Schneider, come here please.'

Of course he knows my name. He's read it off the front of my stupid schoolgirl's smock.

He is standing by his huge deal work table, fiddling irritably with his paintbrushes.

I am already at the door with the other two. Otto says to me *Go* but I want to leave with them. Otto insists, however. He puts his hand on my shoulder and turns me round and gives me a little shove Picasso-ward.

'Go,' he says. 'When the Master calls, you go. We shall wait on the landing for you. Or maybe in the bistro.'

I feel utterly ashamed of our visit and I'm completely wishing we had never come. But between Picasso's summons and Otto's little shove I find myself walking over to the table. Picasso pulls out a chair and says 'Anna-Elisa, please sit down here.'

He sits down opposite me.

'There is nothing brave about staying on,' he says. 'It is just sloth. And anyway, where else would I go? Not to Spain for sure.' Here he makes a gesture with his thumb across his throat. Then he says,

'Do you drink wine, my pretty child?'

I say I do, why not? He gets up and fetches two tumblers, both of which are filthy. He pours out red *vin ordinaire* from a large bottle.

'Here you are, *ma belle*.' He puts one tumbler in front of me. He grasps the other and sits down again, this time right next to me. I can smell the linseed on his smock and hands.

'Yes, I am quite passive. But then where should I move? How should I act?'

I have no idea what to say, so I say nothing.

'Yet,' he goes on after a moment's pause, 'in a passive sort of way I will not yield. Either to force or to terror. Or to the enticements of the "good collector", like your French friend who wants to buy my pictures on the cheap.'

'I don't think….'

'You are young, my dear, you don't know. But after all, whilst we are oppressed by the Nazi tyrants and exploited by spivs like your friend, what can we degenerates do? Nothing, nothing but work and struggle for food, see our friends quietly – and look forward to the day of freedom.

'And *ma petite*, even the "good German", ones like your other friend, do you know what he thinks deep down inside. He comes to us artists and he so admires our work and he eats at our best restaurants and drinks our best vintages and he fucks our prettiest girls' – here Picasso touches my hand and breathes *'Not you, I trust, my dear?'* – I shake my head – *'No? Well, that at least is good* – and he expresses so much admiration for *la vie de douceur*, for our lovely France. And all along deep down you know what – he despises us! He despises us because we are soft. He despises us because we value beauty and truth above his hard and supreme value. And what is that supreme value of his? Why, the mastery of the world. Mastery of the Herrenvolk!'

This last Picasso calls out towards the doorway where the shadows of the lurking Otto and Maurice can be detected.

'Remember Nietzsche,' Picasso calls out again, 'remember your comforting philosopher. *Fear nothing more, because your soul will be dead even sooner than your body.* So now, my master, please go, and do not trouble to visit me again.'

I get up. Picasso kisses me, a double *bise*. His stubble rasps against my cheeks like wire wool.

'You know what to do, *ma belle*,' he says softly. 'So do it.'

I join the other two who are still in the doorway. As we go down the stairs, Otto mutters *We shall not do such a thing again*. Maurice says nothing, but I can see that he too is quite deflated.

And me? Well, I have drunk wine with Picasso. I have been kissed by Picasso!

In the car, Maurice bounces back. He gives me the postcard of Guernica and then starts chatting with Otto.

'I picked up yesterday for a song,' he says, 'a Cézanne of woods and a ruined cottage beneath Mt Saint Victoire. It has an atmosphere so clear and pure that it delights my eye and sings to my heart.'

Maurice is such a puzzle to me. He seems sometimes almost like a crook. Certainly that's how Maillol – and now Picasso – take him. Yet he has a joy in beauty that astonishes me. I sit on his lap, puzzling and yearning.

The next day at school I boast to Verónica about the visit and offer to give her the postcard.

But she has a different take on this. She spits. She asks me if Picasso told the story of the Boche visitor who sees that big photo of Guernica and says (thick Hun accent) Mein Gott, did you do that? And Picasso says 'No, *you* did.'

'Cinema!' she says. 'Just cinema. What did he ever really do for the Spanish people?'

When I get home that evening, the Old Bat darts out holding a little blue envelope.

'A *pneu* for you, Mam'selle,' she says with unctuous menace.

I scrabble in my purse and buy her off with my last five sous. The *pneu* is from Maddie.

Meet me at the office tomorrow 1 p.m. sharp. I will show you something that will change your mind about doing in the Old Dotard. Bises, M

14

First thing the next morning I dash to the post office on my way to school to *pneu* Maddie back. It had better be worth it as I'll have to bunk off school. But I mean, when my life might be completely over in days or weeks, why not skip Herodotus Book VI, just for once.

Maddie is waiting for me outside her office.

'Well?' I say, but she isn't letting on. She just says, 'Don't worry, darling, it is so worth it. It will change your mind about M. le Maréchal and his grim cohorts forever. Trust me.'

So off we set. It is now half past one and we are clumping up out of the metro at Richelieu-Drouot and we just stop and gape. Bad-tempered office workers rushing back from lunch push past us muttering but we stop right there near the top of the grubby steps.

What have they done to the Palais Berlitz?

Maddie grasps my hand and presses it. Her hand is dry and long. Her touch feels lovely. She stands a little closer to me and I can smell her lavandery scent.

Everybody knows the Palais Berlitz, the great ocean-going liner, the sleek slim art deco wedge. Its prow glides between the Boulevard des Italiens and the rue du Hanovre, in a sort of V. I love this building. We used to always go to the flicks there, I mean *before*. We saw all the cowboy pictures and all the Garbo ones and the ones with Merle Oberon and poor Jean Harlow whom we loved although they always called her a slut, and Dorothy Lamour. The Palais was *the* big cinema.

It is also where people used to study English in the far-off days when we thought that would do some good. Mama was even a teacher there for a spell, teaching business English. Now English is not taught, they're only teaching Boche-speak. All the *collabos* are learning Boche.

But today the Palais Berlitz has been desecrated.

All down the front of this beautiful building is a gigantic poster – oh why this perpetual gigantism, this hugeness in our faces all the time, huge blood red flags with huge spiders crawling across them, huge posters that shriek such horrid things at us? This poster is truly monstrous in every way possible. It reads

LE JUIF ET LA FRANCE

This motto is written in a scary script, all wavy. I suppose it's meant to be Hebrew-looking. And there is some hideous old titanic-sized Abrahamic *type*, and I mean a mec ten metres tall, who is lowering over the globe with menace. His skanky oily beard is flowing over the Western Hemisphere and his huge gnarled tentacle of a hand is grasping at Europe and Africa. His thumb is on France, which is the only bit coloured in, with a *tricolor*.

Which is weird. Isn't the *tricolor* banned?

'You've seen nothing yet,' Maddie says, linking her arm through mine and guiding me forward.

Weird and monstrous and repulsive though this is, *le tout Paris* is streaming in. It is the Official Opening, Maddie tells me. In the crowd I get my bottom pinched twice but I don't bother looking round, I just get my own back by jabbing randomly with my elbow. There is a satisfying Ouf! from whatever mec it is. I mention this to Maddie who says that nobody is pinching her bottom but then she is looking round fiercely all the time and in general these craven pervert types are pretty scared of her.

Maddie shows some tickets to the specky youth on the door.

'Press,' she says grandly.

'You don't need those,' he says with a snigger. 'We're trying to get as many people as possible anyway.'

'And why would that be?' Maddie asks but the kid clearly doesn't do irony as he says nothing. He starts fumbling with a pile of programmes he has squeezed between his left elbow and his skinny torso. His bulgy eyes flick nervously from me to Maddie and back again. He obviously has some hopeless flirtatious intent but the only result is that he manages to drop his entire stock of these pathetic programmes onto the floor, which is satisfyingly filthy from all the dirty footwear that is treading in.

'Get on with it,' Maddie says, nudging her slender foot among the mess on the floor. The specky youth drops to his knees and scrabbles in the dirt, collecting up the scattered programmes. Maddie puts her hand on her hip and angles her body slightly. It's her self-assurance that makes her such a star, even if she's not necessarily all that pretty.

The specky youth jumps up with the programmes awry in his arms. His face is scarlet and a pimple on his left cheek is pulsing. Maddie puts out her hand and tugs out two programmes from the heap.

'Read the Introduction,' he manages to say. 'It...it's brilliant.'

'Very likely, I don't think,' Maddie says, turning away and carefully treading on the kid's foot.

'Collabo bastard,' she says in an undertone.

I glance back at the kid. His pimple pulses brighter.

'I'll report you,' he says.

'Go on then,' Maddie calls back over her shoulder.

We get seats right near the front of the huge hall. Maddie leafs through the programme, flipping the pages irritably.

'Listen,' she says, and she starts to read out.

The general theme of this seminal and remarkable exhibition is the corrupting grip of the Jew on our country – on the army, on the economy, on literature. Sexual inversion and the destruction of our traditions are the foremost subjects of the Jewish author... bla bla bla.

'Who thinks this cack?' I ask. It's a whatsit, a rhetorical question.

'Who writes this cack?' she says.

'Who reads this cack?'

She tosses the programme on the floor and puts her foot on it, screwing it around a bit. We look about us. The walls are plastered with more samples of the New Gigantism, enormous five-metre-high pictures of weird-looking so-say Jewish folk and there is a helpful commentary in letters a metre high. We gaze at these for a while and learn:

The HOOKED NOSE is 'their' most characteristic feature
And the EYES THAT CONTINUALLY BLINK
Not to mention the BUNCHED-TOGETHER TEETH
And PROTRUDING EARS
And SQUARE-SHAPED NAILS
Together with the TOO-LONG TORSO...
...the FLAT FEET...
...and the ROUNDED KNEES

'Oh for those,' Maddie says, meaning rounded knees.

I am shocked at her flippancy. Me, I am not exactly laughing, more like crying, but actually it's hard to know what to do with these huge grotesque images staring down at us. I mean, how can the French, we French, produce this murderous tosh? And how can the thousand French men and women who've crammed in here bear to look at it, bear to be in the room with this filth.

'You see,' says Maddie, looking at me in her most irritating told-you-so kind of way, 'you see, there is no other way. We must cut off the head of this horrid thing.'

I say that actually I would prefer to go home but Maddie grips my hand very tight and says 'Hang on, dear.' So I go on looking and learn about ankles that are EXTRAORDINARILY TURNED OUT. And the killer sign of the Jew – VERY OFTEN THEY WILL HAVE ONE ARM SHORTER THAN THE OTHER.

The guy behind leans forward and touches me on the shoulder.

'Don't worry, love,' he says, 'you can actually tell the Yid nowadays by his Yellow Star.' He gives a little snort and wrinkles his flat nose.

'*Vas te faire foutre,*' Maddie says.

Dignitaries are filtering in and assembling on the stage.

They are a motley lot, all men, all in poorly pressed suits. Is there a tiny hope that maybe, just maybe their wives don't agree with them? *That the wives say If you want to be a peddler of rags and bones, then you can look like one too.*

Most of these run-down mecs are also balding and all of them have very bad posture. One is limping, although maybe this is a get-out, his credential to hold extreme and vile opinions as a *gueule cassée* (*a broken face,* used of those maimed in the Great War).

Above the dais is more gigantism, it could even be titanism, an enormous picture, that covers the entire back wall of the room. It shows a great big hairy black spider straddling *la patrie*.

JEWS WEAVE THEIR WEB WITH THE BLOOD OF OUR FRANCE

Next to the rostrum is a tantalising Mystery Item, like our childhood conjurors would bring on. It's a big bulky thing covered by a large black cloth.

After some discussion over rankings and protocol and consequent shuffling and reshuffling and scraping back and forth of chairs, the dignitaries get themselves ranged along the dais behind the big table. This is covered in a not quite clean white cloth like a sacramental altar where the wine has spilled. Actually it's more like a soiled tablecloth in a redneck cafeteria.

They begin their cinema. Sadly, the tone does not rise to that of the exhibits.

The movie actor Jacques de Féraudy is there! He's a heartthrob of mine – at least up until now. He stands up and reads out a dreary poem called *Jews Get Out*, which is by some eminent old Jew-hater called Drumont who apparently, according to Féraudy's speech, has never got the recognition he richly deserves. Sadly he won't get it on the strength of this poem as it is really really badly written. Even Jacques de Féraudy looks slightly sceptical at some of the prosody, not that I care about *him* anymore.

Jacques ends his reading by saying,

'Drumont foresaw the disease from which France nearly died!'

He declaims this line like it was Shakespeare or something instead of the nasty pile of *caca* it actually is. The *préfet* is there, and a bloke called Sézille who has surprisingly bunched together teeth and protruding ears. Maddie and I crane to look for further evidence. We spot that he has a nice pair of meaty-looking hands but he keeps them bunched up so we cannot see whether his nails are the (bad) square ones or the (good) almond-shaped ones.

When it is Sézille's turn to speak he lays his text on the lectern with his beefy paws. Maddie nudges me and points to the side wall next to the lectern where there is yet another big educational placard. It says,

THEY HAVE THE SOFT FLESHY HANDS OF HYPOCRITES AND TRAITORS

Despite its arresting theme – *The Yid and World Conspiracy* – Sézille's actual speech is a real bore. He kicks off with some familiar stuff about Jewish conspiracy and *inversion sexuelle* but he never gives any detail on the sex topic which is the one I'm really interested in. I mean, what actually *is* sexual inversion? I ask Maddie in a whisper.

'Search me,' she says, too loudly, so that some of the mecs in front turn round. 'Maybe woman on top?'

At the end of all this tosh, Sézille tries to redeem himself with a *coup de théâtre*. He steps over to the big bulky thing beside the rostrum and pulls at the large black cloth. With a bit of a tug the cloth slides off. A gigantic black head is revealed.

The whole room gasps. The sound is like a zeppelin farting. We all gaze in astonishment at the huge head. It is the height of two men.

'There!' Sézille declaims, 'There!'

We stare.

'Look and learn, my friends,' Sézille cries. He is suddenly more confident of his audience. 'There you have the characteristic signs of our born enemy, carefully and scientifically reproduced.'

He approaches the great head. Excited, he waves his arms about.

'Look! Study! See the crinkly hair... the slanting eyes... the out-sized ears... the thick descending nose... the loose and fleshy lips constantly agape...'

For sure, the head does show these features. They are all strangely vast. It's a fantastic mannerist monster. It's like a Picasso restyled by El Greco and modelled by Arno Breker high on dope and in his most transcendent mood.

There turns out to be a scattering of decent people in the audience. You can tell because they laugh out loud. This human sound interrupts Sézille's rapture for a moment. He pauses. He looks crestfallen. There are furrows on his shiny brow.

But he's a pro. He gets a grip on himself and carries on.

'The purpose of the exhibition,' he says – and here he emphasizes the high seriousness of this purpose by waving motions of his beefy mitts – 'is to instruct the French public on a subject about which it knows little...'

He pauses.

'... the Jew...' he says, and then another drama school lull, a dotted minim long...

'...the Jew *in all his manifestations*.'

Sézille drops this and it falls like a wet fish on a slab. I look around. Heavy men in suits, sad-looking women in thick, shabby, disappointed outfits, tradesmen catching an hour out of the shop, a few grubby *gamins* and *gamines* who have sloped in, hardly for politics, more likely for anything they can scrounge to eat. Apart from the *gamins* and the *gamines* who are pointing and laughing, no one looks much moved.

Sézille ploughs on regardless. He is now clearly approaching his peroration.

'...and that is why our native artisans have laboured night and day to construct this...' – here a theatrical flourish of the hams at the gigantic head – '...so that we may know the Jewboy and thus defend ourselves against his influences.'

He winds up, reading fast now from his script.

'The exhibition is now open,' he says. 'Educate yourselves quickly, my fellow citizens. Hasten to the Morphological Section where Professor Montandon has put on a wonderful display of outsize plaster casts of Jewish noses, eyes, ears and mouths.'

'We, the organizers, wish you a fruitful visit. And if the exhibition inspires feelings of horror, disgust and disdain in you while at the same time giving you renewed hope in a France rid at last of its Jews, then we shall have succeeded in our bold and noble enterprise.'

There is some scattered applause, largely from the grey men on the rostrum. Sézille looks a little put out by this wan reception and takes on the look of a man much put upon and subject to troubles nobly borne. He walks towards the steps down from the dais. As he comes out from behind the table, I see that his trousers are wrinkled and sagging at the knee. He steps carefully down and comes over towards us. Erk! Has he somehow spotted us as delinquents?

But no, he stops before an old biddy who is sitting in the front row. She stands to greet him, turning a little so that we see how incredibly wrinkled and antique she is.

Sézille gallantly attempts an embrace but is prevented by

the hat this old gammer is sporting, a broad-brimmed affair topped with a great variety of (I hope) artificial fruits and flowers. He clutches at her, wags his head from side to side sizing up his approach, and then darts under the brim and gives her a peck on either of her cheeks. As he draws back from under the hat, I can see the rouge has come off the little red roundels on the gammer's cheeks and smudged his lips which gives him a shabby vaudeville look.

He talks in a loud voice to the old biddy. Presumably she is deaf, or perhaps he has forgotten that his speech has ended and he can talk normally now. We can hear him saying that 'we' should name a street in honour of her *époux pionnier*.

Who is this 'pioneering husband'? And *we*? What *we* are we in here? No *we* that includes me, that's for sure.

'Rue Drumont,' he says, so the 'we' must be his lot, all the run-down panto stars who have put up this whole farrago. And the rouged beldame must be the relict of the Drumont mec who wrote that dreadful poem.

I say to Maddie *Let's go*, and she says *Yeah, enough of this cack*.

We start pushing out through the throng, heading for the exit. At once, a couple of guys come up to us. Or rather they come up to Maddie. I think they spot that she's posh totty, BCBG. They glance at me, brown and doubtful-looking me. Do I perhaps have some of the pictured characteristics of the Yid? Whatever. Anyway, both these mecs start talking to Maddie. This I don't mind at all. Why would I want to talk to two middle-aged creepos on the *drague*?

Although these guys are slightly better dressed and a deal younger than the *moyen* here, they both have lardy faces and they reek of tobacco. Both are wearing wedding rings. Really, why would I want to talk to them? Thank God I'm small and brown.

It turns out that Maddie shares my views.

One of the guys, the fatter, clean-shaven one in a brown suit says,

'What's a nice girl like you doing in a place like this?'

The other taller one, green suit and a sandy moustache says,

'What do you think of all this, my dear?'

Maddie stares at them, looking from one to the other, as if deciding which guy to answer. Eventually she looks at green suit and says,

'Well, monsieur, it makes me feel *horror, disgust and disdain.*'

The guys are not so witless that they don't scent danger in her reply. They both look slightly confused. Brown suit looks up and green suit looks down. Maddie continues without mercy.

'Actually,' she says, and here she lowers her voice in a confiding way and touches green suit lightly on the cuff, 'actually, my Dad's crinkly hair and slanting eyes are a bit of a give-away. And his out-sized ears... his thick descending nose... his loose and fleshy lips constantly agape...'

Metaphorically at least their jaws drop. Their heads give a little involuntary start that betrays some level of shock. Their eyes shoot to her face and then drop down towards her breast. You can see they are wondering why she isn't sporting her Star of David.

'In fact,' Maddie goes on and waving towards me, 'Annie's Dad's got one arm shorter than the other... oh, and he's a *gros bonnet* (big wheel) in the Maréchal's government.'

Brown suit starts fiddling with his face, green suit looks at his watch. The exiting crowd is bearing us along and they filter off.

'And my brother's in London with de Gaulle,' Maddie almost shouts after them as they scurry away. She is such a fearless creature. I love her forever.

And outside in the street, breathing a fresher air, she looks at me craftily and says,

'So you see, darling, we must rise up. We must cut off the head of the hydra. There is no other way.'

I say nothing, just breathe to myself 'Alright, maybe, but why does it have to be me?'

Letter from Annie to Franck

I write to Franck but in a state of flat dejection. Try as I may, I really struggle to summon up the optimism my poor brother so clearly wants.

After today I do wonder really whether we do not belong to an accursed generation. Why are we condemned to witness such horrors and such banality?

But I write. I have to write.

> Dearest mein Bruder Franck,
>
> I got yours and embrace you. We talk of you all the time, Pauli and Maddie and I. And of Eric, too, our two brave warriors. We long for your return. What duets we'll play. What trios, what quartets!
>
> I think of that last time at Evreux, all four of us together. We played the Beethoven last quartet. Do you remember how we got half sick on not so ripe strawberries and on far too much of Blanchard's *douze degrés*? It was the one last perfect day before the Catastrophe, the last day when we were ecstatically alive.
>
> I fight every day to keep this memory and all the others from dimming into insignificance.
>
> You ask about Papa. Well, you should know that he doesn't mention you and he grows angry if we do. I said your name last night, I said I had had your letter, and he scowled and turned away. Your little Pauli blubbed, he misses you so much. Like me, he cannot bear that you be simply *effaced* from our family.
>
> What is this, Franck, that should so explode our *petite*

famille? With Mama gone we need more than ever to be together. And yet you are not just far away somewhere in Germany. You have quite gone away from us altogether. What is it? What did you do? What was your argument with Papa that last night?

Write me the truth, because I love you, and if you love me.

A

15

At three, Mlle de B – Simone – rings the bell. I run and answer the door. She is wearing a man's shirt, brilliant white, without a collar. It shows all of her neck which is rather thick and short. Her lips are bright red with lipstick but she wears no other make-up. Her hair is hidden under a turban of a startling emerald green. Her skin is shiny from the heat and her cheeks have lost their usual pallor. She looks sportive and healthy and not at all philosophical.

I don't expect it but when I open the door to her and am standing in the doorway to greet her, she darts forward and busses me expertly on either cheek. She then draws back and laughs. She fishes in the pocket of her shirt and comes up with a tiny handkerchief. She wets a corner with her tongue and rubs away the lipstick from my cheeks.

'My sturdy brown smiling girl,' she says.

It appears that we are going out. Fortunately, I have parked Pauli with his chum and he will stay for a sleepover, so we have all day.

I quickly change into my best blouse, it's a pale blue cotton, and I pull on my white summer shorts and dash down, ignoring Prune Face who is sweeping the common hall with ostentatiously laboured strokes of her broom. As I go past her she turns to stare at my bare legs and in a flash she selects from her ample repertoire of disapproval her snakelike hiss, *Tssss*.

Mlle is waiting in the street, leaning against the railings in the sunshine. She looks so neat and somehow oddly pretty. She has a basket over her arm. I ask if I may carry it for her but she says no and off we set, walking quite fast up the rue Dangle. In a very few minutes we come to a gate. Mlle opens it and pulls me inside. There is a small, cobbled courtyard and behind it a low two storey building. At the side is a wooden shed. She opens the door of the shed. Inside are two beautiful ladies' bicycles, English bicycles, Raleigh. One is red and the other one is blue. They look almost new.

'But how...?'

She puts her finger to her lips and leans towards me. She breathes,

'My friend is a bicycle thief. These are ours for the day.'

Mlle pulls up her skirts and hitches them in her belt and I see her bare legs with her plump white thighs and strong calves. She hops on the red bike and pedals expertly round the courtyard. The muscles in her calves shimmer and ripple. I get on the blue bike and do a similar, more wobbly practice round. Mlle dismounts and expertly straps the basket to the little carrier behind her saddle. Then she remounts and we cycle out into the street.

Mlle goes ahead and I pedal after her, watching her neat behind. She is pedalling as fast as she can and I have to press really hard on the pedals to keep up. We bump over the cobbles through the faubourg and out into the banlieu.

These English bikes are very good and strong but solid and heavy and really hard work. In the sunshine we soon become hot and Mlle's face grows red. There is little traffic, just the occasional *vapeur* and a few elderly workers on bicycles. I pedal up beside her and call out to her that her face matches her lipstick and she laughs and puts on a spurt, pedalling for all she is worth. I stand up on my pedals and catch up to her, then settle in my saddle, pedalling and pumping away, my knees rising, brown and strong and then pushing down, straight and hard as steel rods.

As we leave the built-up area we settle into a new rhythm, pedalling side by side at a good but slower pace. For half an hour we pedal like that, glancing at each other from time to time and wiping the sweat from our brows with our handkerchiefs.

'Your legs are so brown and strong,' she says. I look at her plump white thighs. I want to say something nice but they look so much like hams with the fat on them that I just smile at her.

At last we turn off the *goudron* onto a dusty track which leads right into the woods. We pedal more slowly now, enjoying the shade cast by the tall oaks and the glinting sunshine that filters down through the dense canopy of leaves. At one point the trees fall away and there is an open swathe of rough grass where the light is blinding and the air scorching. The dusty track is white in the withering sunshine. Then ahead of us through the trees, I see the blue and silver river. We pedal on. The track turns to run alongside the water a few yards from the bank.

After some minutes we come to a glade where there are patches of sunlit grass and shade right down to the river bank. We prop our bicycles against the trees and run down to the water. Mlle tugs off her shoes and so do I and we bathe our boiling feet and calves in the cool water. I slap water all up my legs and Mlle lifts up her skirt and does the same.

She unstraps the basket from her bicycle and brings it to where a willow tree overhangs the water. I stretch out in the shade of the willow while she spreads a red and white chequered tablecloth on the grass and sets out black bread and a small flask of olive oil, thin slices of rosette which she says she has bought 'under the counter' – and the real treat, a bottle of white wine.

We stuff ourselves greedily and swig the wine straight from the bottle, passing it between us. It is warm and tastes like nectar. Mlle asks me about my life and I tell her stuff. She asks if I feel like a little brown metic girl and I cry No! A French girl! She says Ah, my little brown French girl, and starts to tickle my bare thighs with a grass.

What's strange is that I don't breathe a word about the things I had meant to ask her.

Because it was me who invited her, at least to come round, I didn't have a lovely picnic by the Seine in mind. It is just that I am so confused, I had to talk to someone. I literally have no idea what I should do. Maddie keeps on and on pressing me to do something which could possibly be the right thing but which is also plainly the wrong thing, and I could never do it anyway. And then Otto and Maddie keep telling me to stop Papa from giving his speech. How could I ever do that? And… well, my life is just so hideous. It's like all my girlhood, all my young womanhood, have been cancelled off. All that love and trust and hope that I used to have are gone, and in their place is nothing, just a void that I refuse, completely refuse, to fill with hate.

So my idea was to ask Mlle, to ask Simone. She is the philosopher. Surely, she could tell me what is the right thing to do.

Yet here is Mlle, Simone, all mine for a day – and I don't breathe a word of any of this.

And the reason is, I want to be happy. In the haze of the wine and the heat and lying on the soft grass alongside Mlle, I forget about Papa, and about Maddie, and Goebbels, and all my rubbish life. I just feel utterly happy in a way that is completely new to me. I say so.

'This is a perfect moment.'

And Mlle murmurs,

'Yes, and this one too.'

Then she kisses me on the lips, deftly darting her lips to mine, and it's not a *bise* but a kiss full on my lips. She keeps her lips on mine and I feel her tongue pass softly across. I am not shocked at all. It is still a perfect moment. Her lips feel very soft and they are scented with the wine. On her tongue I taste a little savoury, fatty tang of the rosette. It is all quite perfect.

At last she stops kissing me. Slowly she raises her lips from mine and shifts until she is lying stretched out beside me, her head resting on her outstretched arm, her face turned to me. She brushes my cheek with the back of her hand.

'Perfect,' I murmur and turn my head to look at her through half closed eyes, at her queer Chinesy face and her bright lapis eyes.

'I want this moment to go on forever.'

She laughs and feels for my hand

'Dear Anna-Elisa, dear Annie, there is so much to learn.'

'About love?'

'Yes, also about that. About the authentic life, authentic love.'

I am too tired to ask her what that is. She murmurs something close to my ear, perhaps it is *The act of love is the perfect moment, the only perfect moment.* Or perhaps it is something else. My drowsiness overwhelms me. I cannot help myself. My eyelids close of their own accord and I fall fast asleep.

* * *

When I awake, dusk is already gathering. The river has grown black. Far off, in the middle of the stream, a skiff is passing, one man pulling rhythmically, shooting back and forth, back and forth in his seat. Mlle is not beside me and for a moment I panic that she has gone off and left me. But I spot our bicycles still there, leant against the tree, and there is the basket with the remains of our picnic cleared away and packed into it under the red gingham cloth. Then I see her through the trees. She is paddling in the water at a little sandy beach a few yards off. At that moment she turns and sees me.

'So my dear brown girl, you have woken up at last.'

We pedal back in silence. My limbs are aching now. We must have ridden a hundred miles. The ride back is a good two hours and very hard for me. Mlle seems unaffected, her plump legs go round and round at an even pace. Once I fall back, I need to stop and rest a minute. She looks back and sees me, then she stops and pedals back to wait with me. On a hill, at the entrance to the city, I have to dismount. She gets off too and we push our bikes wearily up the slope, side by side.

By now it is dark. The night is still warm with a light breeze gusting from the south. We pedal through the silent blacked out streets by the light of the half-moon. A solitary *traction avant* passes, its muffled headlights showing an obscure blue light.

It is past nine o'clock when we arrive back at the little low building where we got the bikes. Mlle opens the door of the wooden shed and wheels her bicycle in. I start to follow her but she holds up her hand. *No*, she says, *this bicycle is yours.*

'But how...?'

She puts her finger to her lips and shushes me.

'Don't even ask,' she says.

So we separate. Mlle lives the other way. She shakes my hand and I pedal home through the dark streets. I am very happy.

16

It is three days later when our neighbour on the landing knocks at the door and says there are cabbages at Raoul's and only about a hundred people already queuing up. I throw on my coat and dash down. The *tricoteuse*, old Prune Face, hears me clattering down in my sabots and pokes her head out of her *guichet* to watch me sourly and silently. I think her constipation is spreading through her body.

I pull back the heavy lever that releases the street door catch and I yank the thing open. As I step out a girl comes running barefoot towards me. It is Verónica. She is in a white frock with a red sash. She looks extravagant and pre-war and very pretty and very panicked.

'Quick, let me in,' she says and pushes past me through the doorway. She pulls me back inside and slams the door.

'Annie,' she says throwing her back against the door as if there were an enemy pushing at it from the other side.

I shush her, holding my finger to my lips and nodding towards the Old Bag's lair. Verónica gets the idea. She gasps and clutches my hand. Her breast is rising and falling rapidly. She bends over and touches her toes and her mass of long black hair tumbles down and sweeps the floor.

When she comes upright again, she is still panting hard. I take off my sabots and grasp her hand. We creep past the *guichet* and take the stairs at a run. On the landing we stop to catch our breath.

She grasps my hand again. Her little face is sharp, her eyes are swivelling.

'Is anyone else in?'

Little Pauli is at school. Papa is at the Collège. I open the door of the flat and Verónica dashes in.

I bring some soothing vervain tea for the poor kid but when I go to open the door of my bedroom, it is locked. She calls out,
'Give the secret knock.'
'Don't be ridiculous. It's my room. Just open the door. I'm spilling the tea.'
We sit on the bed and she tells me the story.
'*C'était une rafle,*' she says.
So it is happening. They have started rounding up the *métèques*, the newly non-French aliens, starting with the tough nuts like Verónica's communist father.

'They came this morning,' Verónica says. She sips her tea and pulls a face and gives way to her agitation. She puts her arm around my neck and sobs.

'It's alright,' I say, soothing, meaningless.

She is so lovely. Her skin is smooth like satin, I want to reach out and stroke it. Her face is narrow and it tapers to a pointed chin. Her eyes are big and brown, they look too big for her face and they shine. She stares hard at me, and it strikes me suddenly that she must be short-sighted, a vain girl who needs specs and won't wear them. All the time she is touching me, putting her hand on my forearm as though she is trying to bind me in.

'Can I get into your bed?'
'Why not.'

She clambers in fully clothed, smoothing down the skirt of her white frock, then pulls the cover up to her chin. Her soft black hair lies thick on the pillow. I want to apologize that the linen is not so clean. I want to explain to this gazelle that I'm the skivvy and we are just surviving. Laundry is not my current priority. But I don't bother. The girl has escaped the *rafle*, she's on the run, running for her life. *Sod the sheets*, as Ma used to say.

'They came this morning,' she says again. 'At four in the morning, *les connasses*.'

'Who, the Boche?'

She shakes her head.

'Uh-uh. Collabo bastards, *putes de français. Les bleus* doing the Krauts' shitwork for them. They blammed on the door until Papa let them in and they grabbed him and told him to pack a bag. I heard Papa ask why. *Because you're off on your holidays, Monsieur*. Papa protested, of course, but he didn't have to pack. He'd been ready for ages, he's always been ready. So the *bleus* barged around all the rooms and looked in all the cupboards and then the head guy said, *OK where's the girl, where's she hiding*. And *Papito* said, *My daughter? She ran away last week with her lover*. I could have hugged him. There was some noise then, I think they roughed him up a bit but there was nothing they could do. So off they went.'

'And you? Where were you?'

'In the piano.'

'How could you do that?'

'Papa took the works out right at the beginning. He knew it would come to this one day. He made me promise that whenever they came, I would clamber inside.'

'But how did you know?'

'That it was the *rafle*? Easy. Blam blam on the door at four in the morning? You know it's not the postman.'

'And the piano?'

'An upright. A bit of a squeeze but I managed. *Papito* made me practice so often.'

She stops and has a little cry. I ask her what next. She shrugs.

'Dunno. We have a cousin in Nice. Perhaps I can get there and take my chances with the Eyeties. They're a softer touch they say than the Boche or those *bleus cons*.'

'But getting there?'

'Yup. That's a good question, Annie.'

Ever since the Vichy law came in that cancelled our French nationality and once again made us foreigners, it was going to start some day.

We saw it coming, but then we didn't. We stuck our heads under the pillow and hoped for better dreams.

I suppose I must help the Mouse. Is this the start of my Resistance career?

END OF PART TWO

PART THREE: RESISTANCE

17

"Well, 'it's an old trick but it might just work.' Not. Really not. Maurice's idea sounds completely loony to me. But then I have no idea myself at all and I am desperate for someone else just to take this on. Take control, any control. All this is way beyond me. And Maurice is such a plausible guy, so cocksure, so quick and witty, and he's ready to take any number of risks. So what can I do? I go along with his plan and when I explain it to Verónica she has the exact same reaction. 'Yeah, *putain d'idée, faut pas merder*. What else can I do?'

So this is Maurice's plan. He's going to get Otto to drive us to some village in the countryside on the pretext that we are going to buy meat. That's illegal, of course, but it's not all that illegal. Loads of people are doing it. Maurice thinks that buying black market meat is the sort of peccadillo that Otto would think is an amusing jape and be happy to go along with. The idea is to choose some dorp which is known for illicit meat and also close enough to the Line for there to be *passeurs* who can take Verónica over into Vichyland. Then, Maurice says, she can make her own way to the Italian Zone.

'Côte d'Azur,' Verónica says appreciatively.

'It'll cost,' Maurice says, but this turns out not to be a problem at all.

Verónica has serious wads of cash that she says she had in the piano with her. This is a surprise, given the penury of their life but this cunning little minx had her mother's jewellery. She pawned some to get the cash and kept it well away from her Daddy's clutches. Of course he would have spent it on printing pamphlets about the workers' revolution and the lost Spanish Republic – or on drink.

She also has a little canvas bag with the jewellery that's left, gold brooches and necklaces with diamonds and rubies and so on. She proposes stuffing all the jewellery up her backside and she wants me to do it for her but I really can't. Maurice says he's happy to do it but she then has second thoughts. Instead she knocks the stones out of their settings and sews them into her underwear. The gold she puts in her suitcase.

'And what about the meat business?' I ask Maurice.

'You'll see,' he says with irritating assurance.

He goes off to see Otto. Meanwhile Verónica makes herself at home *chez nous* as easy as a cat. I tell Papa that she is a school friend sleeping over, and he nods and smiles. I have no idea whether he buys the story. Any ordinary person would be aware of Verónica's distressed arrival and even he can't fail to hear her occasional wailing from my bedroom. But Verónica mostly does her sobbing on my pillow with the door locked. When she's out and about in the flat, she is a plausible little actress, very calm and super-nice to Pauli. Actually she charms the kid with her pretty ways. She plays with him for hours on end and makes him clever toys from old bits of paper and cardboard.

As for Papa, it's only days to his big speech and he is eyes down, drafting and redrafting morning, noon and night.

Maurice comes to the flat on the second evening and says that Otto's up for it. His sister has now arrived in Paris as one of the Noble Typists who grace the Kommandantur. Because they are posh and there is a dearth of high-class German totty around, they are both invited for a Friday to Monday at the château where the Boche top brass hold court.

'And the meat?'

'He finds it most amusing. Germans understand meat.'

Verónica is to be my cousin. The biggest hitch is that we will need an *ausweis* for the road. Maurice's papers are all in order, and so are mine but Verónica is on the run. No problem, Maurice says. Verónica gives him some pieces of gold, earrings and a pendant from which she has gouged out the stones and the next evening he returns with an identity card and ration cards for her in the name of Isabelle Dufroy, and an *ausweis* for each of us to travel to a dorp called Sully. This apparently is Meat Central.

We hug Maurice. He says we will set off on Friday, after lunch with Otto and his sister.

'Can we skip the lunch?' I ask. It doesn't seem a good idea to expose Verónica like that.

'Skip lunch at the Tour d'Argent?'

'Oh God, really? But we can skip it, can't we?'

But Otto insists on us coming to the lunch. It's part of the deal. Maurice says Otto particularly wants to introduce his sister to two elegant young Parisian girls of her own age. And he wants to show her that he has pretty girl friends. I am pleased I qualify.

Maurice takes risks like a tight-rope walker without a net. He insists on the lunch. Glumly I tell Verónica.

She claps her little hands together and lets out a stupid squeal.

'The Tour d'Argent!'

I can only conclude that after what she has been through, her nerves are dead.

'It's a bit risky.'

'Sod that. I don't give a damn any more.'

Me, I am absolutely terrified. But then I must trust Maurice, dodgy, sexy Maurice.

18

Alexandra, Gräfin von Sternberg is a girl of about nineteen. She has clear grey eyes, and features that are completely regular and proportionate. Her skin is perfectly soft and smooth and pink. Her shining golden hair is plaited into a little crown around her head. She is a collectible, beautiful in a hard perfect German style. Otto calls her Alex, and she says we must too.

She talks a lot in excellent French in a light, frothy way. She talks about life in their big family house in Munich. She talks about Otto who is her beloved big brother, her *Big Bear*. We learn that Otto has had a stellar academic career, he has studied at umpteen universities. After a first blooding at the Stiftung Maximilianeum in Munich, it was on to Bonn, Würzburg, Freiburg, Heidelberg. She babbles on about his 'masterly' doctoral thesis. Clearly Otto has said nothing to her about his travails at Heidelberg and the *auto-da-fé* of Heine's works.

In any case, before anyone else has got a word in edgeways, she moves rapidly on to talk about her mother's ancestral roots in the aristocracy of East Prussia and her father's brilliant career in the diplomatic. And she talks about Paris and how there is so much in the shops and all so cheap and how she is hoping to have the time of her life in the City of Light.

'Never could I have imagined being so happy,' she says.

Alex's stunning level of self-absorption is a big relief to us. We cannot even mind her airhead ignorance of how the conquered might just be experiencing the conditions of wartime Paris slightly differently from the conqueror, because with all her artless prattle, Verónica and I barely have to say a word. We don't have to make up stories about ourselves. We just feign shared delight in everything that delights Alex. And we can't begrudge her this happiness she enjoys. She comes across as a good-natured creature with no more malice in her simple soul than she has self-awareness. I don't even mind that she is having such a good time even if it is at our expense. Who cares? At least someone is enjoying the war. And if it comes to the test, she may even turn out to be a good person too.

So there we are, Verónica and I, in our best frocks and being super-polite and smiley so that Alex will like us, and she does. Perhaps she is not quite so taken with my brown and sturdy look but I make up for it in smiles and charming interjections in her prattle, and Verónica, who says absolutely nothing at all but does extremely well on the wines, is the very picture of a slim and elegant young Parisienne. And we have the amazing luxury of a table right in the window of the Tour d'Argent. I can look down and see the silvery Seine and there straight in front of us is the Ile de la Cité and the towers of Notre Dame.

And all those things that preoccupy our poor minds and souls – tainted blood or the status of aliens or the fine lines that distinguish collaboration from just getting by – none of this crops up in Alex's world view and none of us is required to know her thoughts on the subject or to reveal our own. Instead, we fly across fashion and perfume and elegant night spots and the thrill she has had meeting Coco Chanel and her handsome German lover.

While Alex fashionably toys with her lunch, pushing her food around her plate, Verónica and I eat like horses. We eat and eat and eat. First we eat *foie gras d'oie des Trois Empereurs*, and then Otto insists we all have some famous signature dish called *caneton Challandais à la Royale*, and just when we are bulging he goes on and orders not one but two puddings for us all, a Guanaja opera cake and a *baba champagne*. Verónica puts away her share of the food and also does rather well on the drinks side. She quaffs most of the bottle of the good Chablis with which we start and has several glasses of the St Emilion. It is Maurice who keeps her glass full. Otto perhaps notices but he says nothing and Alex is too busy gushing and when she is not gushing she is looking around the Tour d'Argent and exclaiming *Oh, that's a pretty girl!* and *My goodness, what a type!*

Worn out by eating, I can only pick at the *baba champagne*. Alex nibbles at both puddings. Verónica pushes hers away and, unwisely in my view, orders a large Armagnac which she drinks off in one go.

At long last the lunch ends. Not too soon for me. I have serious bloat. I also feel a little queasy. The toady *maître d'* who has been giving Verónica and me sardonic, hostile looks all through the lunch, probably taking us for prostitutes, brings the bill and Otto signs it and leaves an unimaginably large tip, large enough to keep a family in rations for a week.

Verónica now turns out to be a problem. She is completely smashed. I am not sure whether Otto and Alex have noticed this. They say nothing, just get up together from the table and head for the door. I help Verónica up and take her to the *toilettes* for a pee. She goes and goes, and then we powder our noses and teeter out.

A long black Merc appears as if by magic at the kerb at the exact moment that we come out of the restaurant. Maurice brings two very large leather suitcases which he has left with the porter. Otto picks them up and humorously puts on an effortful pantomime, pretending the bags are enormously heavy, although there is precious little in them. He stows them in the vast boot of the Merc alongside his and Alex's small suitcases that they have packed for their Friday to Monday.

'I do so long to see the château,' Alex says. 'All the Noble Typists are mad to get an invitation. I am such a lucky girl.'

Otto sends away his chauffeur and takes the wheel. His sister sits beside him. We three Frenchies cram into the back together, and off we go.

Otto and Alex chat companionably to each other in the front. Otto tells his sister about the people she will meet at the chateau. From what I can make out, these long weekends combine R&R for the Boche top brass with a dating agency for the Noble Typists to meet all the equally noble *grafen* and *freiherren* who have managed to wangle a Paris posting. How far exactly they take these boy-girl encounters is a question I want to ask but don't.

I look out of the window at my Paris. We pass the Arc de Triomphe which is hung with scarlet flags and crawling spiders. All down the Champs Elysées, these huge swastika banners hang from every lamppost. Every street corner is cluttered with signage and imperatives in Gothic script. In the road almost the only cars are Boche ones, with just an occasional *gazogène* taxi and a scattering of bicycle rickshaws for the French bourgeoisie. Meanwhile, most French are hoofing it on the pavements. In the centre of town they are gay enough, well-dressed even. The BCBG life goes on, only a little reduced. The women are in fashionable, pretty frocks, the men look well-groomed in suits.

All this changes as we bump over the *pavé* through the Deuxième and the Bois. There we begin to see the working people, the shabby men and women trudging along, the endless queues at the butcher, the baker and the candlestick maker. I spot a furtive old man in an overcoat which bears the yellow star. He has not yet been picked up by a *rafle*. Yet he is still respecting the law of his country that says he must wear the badge of his own doom.

We head out on the N7 through Evry towards Fontainebleau. I turn away from the window and look past Maurice, who is between us, to Verónica. She is fast asleep with her mouth wide open. I hear a little snore. I nudge Maurice and he turns to her and breathes *Mouth closed, ma petite*. But she just snores on, so he leans over and deftly eases up her pretty chin.

I look up and in the mirror catch Otto's eyes on me and then on Maurice. His eyes narrow slightly and little creases appear in the corner and I know that when he is looking at Maurice he is smiling.

And then our comfortable ride ends.

'Ah, no!' I cry out suddenly. 'Otto, please, stop the car...'

It is too late. The motion of the car, my looking at the scenery, the richness of the lunch, the vast injection of fat after the two long lean years, it is all too much. Even as I cry out to Otto it's already too late and I hurl up everything, over my frock, over Maurice's trousers, over Otto's car. It is such a massive hurl that it almost reaches the front. In fact some flecks appear on the back of Alex's perfect dress and on her coiffure.

'Ach, so,' Otto says, pulling into the side of the road. Alex laughs uncertainly.

I tumble out and, kneeling on the grassy verge, I sick up everything I have ever eaten in my entire life. I sick up more and worse than ever Paco did when he ate the pig bones. I sick up everything and it lies there steaming on the scanty grass.

I stay there on my hands and knees for an age. When I have sicked up everything I have ever eaten I have a go at sicking up all my internal organs too. I go on like this for half an age, voiding and retching and choking and dying of shame.

Then there is Alex kneeling beside me and saying, *Sorry, dear Annie, so sorry*! She helps me up and there is a demonstration of just why the Germans are a master race. She walks me into a little café which is conveniently just there beside the road. We pass through the greasy café itself where the patrons stare idiotically. A woman comes from behind the bar and Alex murmurs to her and we are shown into the filthy lats which stink of stale pee. There Alex helps me to take off my dress and my underwear and everything until I am quite naked. She gives me an efficient, appraising look. Then she sponges me down proficiently and dries me with a cleanish towel which she has commandeered from the bar lady.

All this she does in a friendly but not too personal way. She tells me to wait in there and she goes out and come back a minute later with – a silk slip! And the prettiest frock I have ever seen which bears the label Balmain.

'It fits not so bad,' she says. 'You can take it up a little if you wish, as you are perhaps a little short.'

I protest at all this but she won't accept any protest. She says, What else can we do? And I am to keep everything. She will get another, the same or better. And I look so pretty in it.

She starts dabbing me with some costly perfume and while she is doing this she suddenly asks, very earnest and in a low voice

'Are you Maurice's girlfriend?'

Her look is serious and she pauses in the dabbing, waiting for me to answer. It seems to be an important question for her. I murmur *Mmm* which could mean anything but I mean her to take it for a yes and she does as she smiles and says 'Gut. *Ausgezeichnet*'. You are a pretty girlfriend for handsome Maurice.' Then she kisses me on my cheek and we leave the toilets.

Outside there is Maurice. We see that he has taken off his soiled trousers and is now wearing some leather shorts which are presumably Otto's, some of his national kit. The shorts show off Maurice's fine slim legs and both he and Otto are laughing over this outfit. Otto has organized a shampoo and set for the car. A couple of mecs have been mobilized from the café and they are plying scrubbing brushes. The *patronne* has appeared, a great fat granny with a massive goitre. She is drying the seats and the carpet with towels.

From time to time she pauses to pick up a stone which she chucks expertly at a pack of black and yellow mongrel dogs who are lurking in the mouth of a nearby alley and making tentative sorties towards my pile of sick.

Otto hands out shedloads of francs and a few packets of cigarettes to all involved. Alex sprays the inside of the car with Chanel Number 5 from a giant atomizer. Maurice goes into the café and brings out Verónica who has drunk three *petits cafés* and looks like *merde* but at least she's walking in a straight line.

And then we are off again. I glance back and see the pack of dogs polishing off my Tour d'Argent lunch. As the car gathers speed, we become quite gay and chatty, feeling a strange togetherness, except for Verónica who goes straight off to sleep again.

When our chat flags, I let my eyes rest on Maurice's thighs, which are bare in the hilarious leather shorts. These downy limbs of his are lean and strong-looking and very pale in colour. I want to reach out and touch them, pass my hand lightly over the soft dark hairs and feel the strong sinew.

But I don't. Maybe later. Who knows what may happen on this strange outing?

After an hour in which we have passed only German military vehicles and some peasant carts drawn by big spavined nags that have been saved from the knacker's yard only by the war, we reach the dorp of Sully, our goal.

19

Sully turns out to be an ugly village of low houses set in a hollow by the river. The only large building is the church, which is like an oversized barn with a squat, peasanty tower. But we're not here for sightseeing. We have only chosen this verminous dorp because there is a railway station from which Verónica can pick up a slow local train that will take her close to the Line, and also because it is the number one destination for illicit meat. Its brutal and licentious peasantry are coining their fortune from slaughtering everything in sight, probably including dogs and cats and even rats, to sell to black market crooks like us.

Otto and Alex drop us at the railway station, which lies half a mile from the village. This station is only a short wooden platform with a single stone building serving as ticket office, waiting room and station master's house.

We tumble out. The brother and sister stay in the car. Their thoughts are clearly already on the night, on the château and the noble *grafen* and the *freiherren*. Alex has heard that after dinner the General plays Chopin on the pianoforte and that then there will be dancing to the gramophone.

The Mercedes whirls away and we wave them off.

The station is deserted. The station master's flat is shuttered up. He is no doubt taking his siesta, for the day is very hot. Verónica and I sit down on a bench in the waiting room. Verónica is pale as death but by now a bit less comatose. Maurice consults the timetable. In a little over an hour there is a train that will take Verónica close to the line, to the place where her *passeur* will meet her. It is a slow stopping train, ideal as such a train will not be inspected.

Maurice says we must all change our clothes. In his case, this is a total imperative as, for all his handsome limbs, he looks just too Grand Guignol in those lederhosen. He produces from one of the two giant suitcases the outfits we are to wear. Verónica is a war widow travelling to stay with an aunt. She takes on a lower middle-class self which requires scrubbing off all her make-up and perfume and changing into some shabby kit that Maurice gives her. She goes dutifully into the toilet in her pretty frock and comes out in a shapeless woollen suit and gabardine mac. Her lovely hair is concealed beneath a frumpy cloche hat knitted in dark brown wool. Maurice takes her elegant strappy shoes from her and gives her a pair of clogs.

She accepts all this in a passive leaden way which in fact makes the impression intended – of a depressed and down-at-heel war widow. When she blotches her cheeks with tears, Maurice pronounces the effect perfect and she hits him on the arm and goes off and sits on the bench and sulks.

Now it's our turn. Maurice gives me a bundle and I go off to the Ladies, while he heads for the Gents. Sadly I unbutton my beautiful Balmain frock and take it off. I fold it carefully and then pull the silk slip up over my head. I roll the two up together and slip them into my knapsack. I pull on the course blue chemise Maurice gave me, and the plaid skirt. Filthy woollen stockings and a flat cap along with my old clogs that I brought from home complete the outfit.

In five minutes we come out in our rough new togs and admire each other. We are a working-class couple which is fine for me as I am brown and strong and can easily pass in this kit for a young woman worker. For Maurice, who is such a refined fellow, it is harder. His height and beauty and slim tapering build make him stand out.

'But look…' he says. He pulls on a dirty cloth cap and picks up a cheap walking stick and goes up and down the waiting room with a limp and a stoop. It is passable, more than passable.

Verónica has now curled up on the bench. Maurice goes to sit beside her. She pulls away but he starts to go over the arrangements with her, so she has to sit up and listen. The stopping train will reach Choisy, a mile from the Line, just before 8 o'clock this evening. Her *passeur* will meet her there. He will be wearing a green beret and carrying a copy of *La Révolution Nationale*. She will pay him in advance 5,000 francs for expenses. At midnight she will cross over and from there the Network will pick her up and take her onwards. If all goes well, she will be in Nice within two days.

'But if it all goes wrong…?' Her pointed face is grey like alabaster and her eyes look dull behind the cheap spectacles that Maurice now puts on her to complete his effect.

'Nothing can go wrong,' he says and Verónica smiles wanly.

Now the train can be heard, far off. The station master appears and opens the *guichet*. He eyes us with circumspection and when Verónica asks for a third-class ticket to Choisy he looks suspicious and asks for her papers. *Veuve d'un ancien combatant* makes him change his attitude and he becomes solicitous and asks civilly if there have been any children, any orphans. She shakes her head. He wants to help, though, and gives her advice to sit in the Ladies Only compartment. Sometimes, he says, there may be rough types, unemployed labourers and scroungers, low types, spivs, black marketeers travelling for meat. Even folk making for the Line in clear violation of the law.

Verónica acknowledges all this demurely with her head

bowed. She pays for the ticket and here there is a tricky moment as she hasn't separated out a small float from the great wodge of her money stash. She has to fiddle in her bag. At last she comes up with some grubby notes of small denominations, and she counts out some coins too as though they were her last.

We take our leave of her before the train comes in. She kisses Maurice and gives me a lingering, tearful hug.

'*Vas bien. On se reverra après...*'

'And now,' says Maurice, pulling his cloth cap down further over his eyes, 'and now for meat.'

20

We trudge through a sunken muddy lane mired in animal shit until we come into the village proper. By the barn of a church, there is an ancient sitting on a stone bench. Maurice greets him and he regards us with the customary insolent silence of the peasant. His face is lined and pitted like parched earth. With his beaky nose he resembles a fierce old moulting bird of prey.

'Grandpa,' Maurice says, pressing the price of a drink into the dotard's hand, which the fellow trousers without comment, 'Grandpa, put us on the road to Percheron's place, will you?'

The old mec ponders a minute and then gives Maurice a crafty look.

'Percheron's place?'

'Aye,' says Maurice, who evidently feels he is getting the hang of this.

'Mmm. Percheron's, eh? Don't want to go there. Dirty old place, that is.'

Maurice decides to up the ante and gives the fellow five francs. The mec looks at the coin, spits on it and then points out a road that runs behind the church.

'Half a league,' he says.

We head out. On either side of the track lie open fields extending to the horizon. Not a single tree breaks the monotony of the plain as it stretches into the distance, only a hamlet or two, standing out in the folds of the landscape like islands of stone. Telegraph poles line the track. We tramp through heavy mud which stains our clothes red.

We are each carrying two huge suitcases, as Maurice had put one slightly smaller suitcase inside the other, so we only had two in Otto's car. Over our shoulders we carry canvas bags with our other clothes in. Mine has my Balmain gown in it. Maurice said to dump it, but I'm hardly going to do that. Dump my first ever designer dress a couple of hours after I've been given it!

We trudge along for what seems like an hour, arguing over how far half a league might actually be. Maurice says it's about a kilometre, I say it's how far you can walk in an hour. Maurice then says it's the distance you have to travel before you need to ask again. We are still squabbling about it when we come to a farm. There is a big square farmyard which is surrounded on three sides by a ragged assembly of cow sheds, piggeries, sheep pens and a large stone barn. On the fourth side is the farmhouse. The buildings are low, slumping under a thick hedge of ancient thatch on which there is a field of green moss. A bunch of black crows are perched on the roof, tearing at the thatch, in which they have already gouged out big holes.

'I suppose this is Percheron's,' Maurice says.

No-one is around to confirm this theory. Maurice pokes his head in through the open door of the farmhouse and there is a loud shriek and shouting from inside. Maurice ducks out again.

'Erk,' he says. When I question him, he shudders in abbreviated phrases.

'A stoutly built young wench at her toilette. Standing in a zinc bathtub quite in the nude. A horrid sight. She referred me to her father around the back.'

We pick our way through a litter of straw and the shit of a whole menagerie of farm animals mixed with rusting tractor parts. Beside the cow shed we spot a male figure bent double, trousers down, evacuating massively into the manure pit. He stares at us obstinately and we turn away and hurry on into the stone barn. There a red-haired youth in a filthy smock is in the act of wringing the neck of a protesting chicken. Around the barn are the carcases of numerous farmyard animals suspended on giant hooks. There is an entire pig, half a cow, a pair of sheep, a string of ducks and geese. The cobbled floor is red with blood.

'Maurice,' I say, 'I think this is more a man's thing. Here, take my suitcases. I'll wait in the road. Give me your clothes bag.'

He looks at me sadly. I know he was on the point of asking me the same thing.

I wait an age in the lane. At last Maurice comes out and beckons to me.

In the farmyard is a handcart and on it the four suitcases.

'They weigh a ton,' he says. 'I bought the handcart too. I've invested my entire fortune in this little lot.'

We struggle back along the lane to the village, taking it in turns to push and pull the cart. When we get there, it is already dusk. We carry on, very slowly, heaving the cart along and by the time we reach the station, night has fallen. It turns out the last train back to the capital has just gone.

We flounder back. The moon is high and full enough to light our way. When we reach the village, the street is completely deserted, although there are dim lights in several of the cottages. Maurice parks me by the church with the meat cart and sets off to search for lodgings. After what seems like hours, he looms up out of the dark and says that there is a sort of inn at the far end of the village. We head down, dragging the cart.

The old beldame who keeps the inn does agree to take us in but she is as tough as gristle and the price of the room she quotes is huge. Maurice haggles but the beldame has the peasant's skill at bargaining and he gets nowhere. I know that she is reasoning that we are a man and a girl clearly not married so there is a big surcharge for that, and then she points to the four bulging suitcases cram-packed with meat which are also needing lodging for the night. And also, she is concerned about 'what was we up to at the station with that other woman'.

All in all, five hundred francs for the night begins to look quite a bargain. We hump the suitcases up the narrow stairs. Our hostess stands at the foot watching.

'What did you get, by the way?' I ask Maurice.

'Don't even ask,' he says. 'Actually, I'm none too sure. He just sort of stuffed it all in.'

After a brief glum inspection of the room and its amenities we go down to the bar of the inn to see about a supper. We find a bunch of depressed residents who regard us with suspicion, avarice and contempt in roughly equal parts. Maurice negotiates with our hostess for some bread and cheese and a bottle of *douze degrés*.

We take our supper back upstairs and stretch out on the bed on the filthy sheets. The suitcases are all around the room. One is on the end of the bed, there is so little room. We gnaw at the bread and break off big pieces of cheese, cramming them into our mouths and gulping down the wine straight from the bottle.

That is the moment that Maurice asks me to marry him.

21

In that squalid room on the low bed, lolling on the filthy sheets, Maurice with his feet resting on a suitcase bulging with 20 kg of raw meat, by the sparse light of the 30 watt bulb which hangs without a shade by a wire from the ceiling casting a doubtful light which makes the dirty walls look black and our suitcases like the last effects of some old dead pauper, that is the moment that Maurice chooses to propose.

I am completely shocked. I am afraid that I laugh, just from surprise. Maurice joins in, leaning forward and laughing. After an interval I pat his hand and ask him *But why*?

'Because I love you.'

'I... no...' I start to laugh again from sheer nerves this time. This time he doesn't laugh. He sits watching me. All the same I can see he isn't offended at all.

'We should think about it,' he says, 'definitely.' He takes my hand. 'Your old Papa and Pauli will come and live with us. We'll live *la vie de bohème*. We'll be as happy as larks.'

'What do you mean, you love me?'

'I love you. I love you. I want to spend my life with you.'

It is all very strange, in that gloomy desperate room in that cretinous village full of *vieux tarés*, with a ton of packed meat set on the floor around the bed, even on the bed.

'I can't even begin to think about it.'

We talk for a while, getting nowhere. Plainly it is impossible but Maurice keeps pressing me. In the end he says,

'Shall we do it anyway?'

'It?'

He looks at me in his silly way and pulls my hair.

'Yes, It.' He spells it out. 'What you do when you're married.'

I laugh again but he goes on looking at me like that. He starts to stroke my hair and pat my hand. I try looking away but the only other thing in the room is meat so I look back at him and wonder what it would be like.

The Beaver said, what was it? *The act of love is the only perfect moment.* Authentic love. What is that? Here is Maurice with his slim strong body and his elf-like wit, loving me, apparently, so he says, and making silly propositions, suggesting something I really really want anyway which is to make love to him, and also just to stop being a stupid virgin.

So after I have thought about it and Maurice has sat in docile quiet for a few minutes I say *Alright* and he laughs and asks me why, which is an odd question but in the circumstances perhaps quite fair.

'The perfect moment,' I say.

'*Tiens*, little one! So it's a yes then?'

He begins to take off his clothes. His body is strong and thin. I can see the muscles in his broad shoulders like shallow ripples as he throws his clothes in a heap in the corner. When he has taken off his top and his shoes and socks, he has a thought and gets up and heaves the suitcase off the bed onto the floor. I watch the muscles tighten across his back and in his shoulders and arms. Then he turns away from me and takes off the rest of his things, tossing them on top of the heap.

He sits on the edge of the bed and slides under the grimy sheet.

'*Et toi, chérie.*'

So I take off all my things too and throw them in the

corner, on top of his.

I lie down next to him. The sheet feels greasy under my bottom. After a minute we turn to each other and begin to cuddle, like children. It isn't much different from cuddling Pauli when I get him out hot from the bath. We cuddle on one side and then on the other and he says he always likes to be on the left of the bed so we change places, me on the right and him on the left. I can feel the wrinkles in the grubby sheets and the buttons in the lumpy mattress underneath.

After we have rolled about like that for quite a time he takes my hand and puts it on his hair down there which is thick and a little bit damp. Then he puts my hand on his *zizi* which is longer than I expected. I fondle it for quite a time but nothing much happens.

'Hmm,' he says. Then he puts his hand on me and does some things and I think of when we went with Ma and Pa to the Château de Chinon and the way the sunlight shone through the leaves on the dark water of the pool there, and then of that time at Deauville in the last summer before the Débacle, the sparkling sea flowing slowly towards me across the yellow sand and the terns swooping over the gentle waves in the sunshine.

And then with this strange perfect man on the grubby sheets in the dingy room next to the close-packed meat I feel the most piercing ecstatic pleasure I have ever felt in my entire life up to now.

The Beaver said to me, the act of making love is the perfect moment, the only perfect moment. This with Maurice isn't love, not real love. I know that now, I can tell it straightaway, but it is still so very perfect.

So what, I wonder as sleep comes over me, *must love itself be like?*

***

I wake in the small hours. Outside it is still very dark. The electric light is burning, the shadeless bulb casts a melancholy brownish light around the room. The four huge suitcases, our clothes in a heap in the corner, the form of Maurice who is curled up like a baby, his broad shoulders and his tapering torso and his tight bottom towards me. He shows no signs of being awake.

'Maurice,' I say softly.

At once he turns towards me, putting one arm above his head and rolling his body over as neatly as a snake. His face is wet and his eyes are red.

'Darling,' I say without thinking. It's what I would say to my lover. It just comes out. In my entire life I have only ever called Franck and Pauli that. And only Mama ever called me her darling. But I have slept with Maurice. My first man. So can't he be my darling? Isn't he my darling?

'Oh, pet,' he says, sobbing like a girl. He cries so easily. I have no idea what this is about, so I just touch his hand and wait.

At last he props himself up on his elbow. He looks me up and down and says,

'You look nice.'

Which is good of him, as I know that my strong brown body may not be God's gift to men. He manages a smile but it is rather a tragic, woebegone thing. I ask him what is the matter and he says he can't marry me after all.

'Of course not,' I say. 'I know that.'

'Oh? How do you know that, Annie?'

'I just know. I mean it's pretty obvious , isn't it?'

He gives a little laugh and then looks pensive again. He closes his eyes and says,

'Anna-Elisa, let me tell you a story.'

'Alright.'

'Are you lying comfortably…?'

'Not really,' I say but he ignores this.

'…then I'll begin.'

'A boy met a boy and they fell in love. The first boy, let us call him M, was older and experienced. The younger boy did not at first know what love was but M showed him and the younger boy was in heaven and the two became lovers, bound together and faithful to each other. They went everywhere together and knew much happiness.

'Now the younger boy had a father who came to know about their love and he grew very angry with his son. The father called on M and made many threats and menaces. But M laughed at the father and tried to persuade the younger boy to leave his family and to come to live with him. M had a beautiful apartment in the Seizième and fine furniture and dined often at Pruniers.

'The younger boy said Yes, he would come. He would tell his father and he would come. But he never came. Instead came the *mobilisation générale* for the third and last time in that one year. The younger boy was called up and went to war in enmity and bitterness against his father. He did not come back. He was captured by the Boche and put into a camp.'

The whole time he is telling this story, Maurice is looking down. Tears come often into his eyes and he keeps dabbing at his face with the tattered edge of the bolster cover.

'Maurice, darling,' I say, pulling the sheet over my breasts, because I suddenly feel the shame of Eve, 'Maurice, are you M?'

He doesn't answer but goes on.

'Listen, *ma belle*. So, M tried to forget his love. He went back into the world and sought out other lovers. But all the time he knew this was just pleasure and that the love he had known with the younger boy he could never find again.

'Until one day he saw a girl who was so like his lover that she could have been his twin. And so it turned out, nearly. She was the younger sister of his one great love, and he loved her for that.'

Maurice stops and fiddles with the bolster. I pull the sheet over my head. I can smell the dirt of others on it.

'And then?' I ask. I am suffocating beneath the filthy sheet.

'And then. What do you think, Annie?'

'And then M asked the girl to marry him.'

'And then M asked the girl to marry him.'

My mouth opens and no sound comes out. I throw off the filthy sheet and squirm up onto my knees and I begin hitting Maurice on his chest with the side of my fist as hard as I can and he lies there unresisting. I make so much noise hitting him that eventually the landlady comes and bangs on the door. Then Maurice stirs and rouses himself and wrestles with me. We kneel there on the bed, quite naked, and I only stop wrestling and hitting him when I am completely worn out.

I sleep for an hour. When I wake up it is still dark outside. Maurice is dressed and sitting on the very edge of the bed. Rain is slanting in against the window and sheets of water are cascading down and leaking in. A puddle has formed on the floor next to one of the suitcases. Maurice lifts the suitcase carefully onto his side of the bed. It is between me and the window.

I see my clothes at the end of the bed, neatly folded. Rather than stare at a suitcase packed with raw meat, I ask Maurice to pass me my things and I put them on. He looks the other way, out of the window.

'Let's go,' he says. 'We can catch the milk train.'

I help him heave the suitcases out of the room. The last one we take is the one that he put on the bed. As we shunt this last case out of the room, I glance back and see that it has left a scarlet patch where the meat has bled from the suitcase onto the filthy sheets.

22

After a century during which I have crushed myself into a corner and pressed my nose to the grimy window of our hard class compartment, the sun nudges above the bleak landscape of abandoned industry and shabby marshalling yards that we are passing through. Maurice says from the far corner of the compartment that it is *time to get cracking*.

By this he means, heave the meat suitcases down from the luggage rack. And think about how to get them out of the station and away home.

Neither question interests me. Actually, nothing interests me this grey dawn. I just sit there turned away from him while he clambers onto the seat and starts to yank the cases down. One tumbles onto the floor. I can see out of the corner of my eye the blood oozing from it and trickling in my direction. I pick up my knapsack from the floor, saving my precious frock, and curl my feet up beneath me on the hard wooden seat.

Maurice says *Can you help?* but I don't stir.

When at last we clack into the Gare de Lyon, Maurice heaves all four suitcases onto the platform and then says *Come on!* to me but I don't move or even look his way. So, after a minute in which I suppose he must be standing there he says *Ah, merde!* and I hear him above the station clamour effortfully picking up cases and huffing off.

He cannot have taken more than two of the bags, so I expect him to return. Nothing happens for a while and I stay curled up on the wooden seat. At length a voice calls out

'*Come on, Miss, 'op it.*' It is an elderly mec in a station porter's uniform.

I stand up and he says to '*get out and get the clobber off the platform.*'

Something is apparently contravening regs and it turns out to be two bulging suitcases that Maurice has left.

'Will you help me, please?' I ask the mec, as there is no way I can carry these two great suitcases myself and he is in a porter's unform. However, he just goes 'Pah!' and plods off.

I sling my knapsack over my shoulder and get out of the train. I try to pick up one case and then the other but both weigh a ton. I try shoving the less heavy one along with my foot but it won't budge.

Anyway, I am sick of the whole thing. There is so much that was disgusting about these last two days. I think I will just walk off and go home.

I have only gone a few steps when a gang of young German soldiers who cannot be any older than me come clattering up and surround me.

'*Nous aidez,*' one says. '*Können wir dir helfen bitte, schönes Fräulein?*'

They almost fight each other for the privilege. One, who says his name is Herman, hoists the heavier suitcase up on his head.

'*Wie ein Neger,*' he says and makes a sort of ape noise. They all laugh. A second boy picks the other suitcase up by the handle and begins to carry it.

'*Verdammt,*' Herman says as he wobbles along, '*quoi dans valise, Mam'selle? Was zum Teufel hast du hier drin, Fräulein?* What the hell have you got in here, Miss?'

'*Fleisch,*' I say and they all laugh like crazy.

I trail along beside them, happy to be so unattractive in

my drab workwoman's clothes. They still keep peering at me though.

And, oh God, there is Maurice at the end of the platform, signalling to me.

Herman says,

'Oh, boyfriend, *ja*?' I want to say no, absolutely not, but prudence holds my tongue.

Maurice comes up. He looks unusually sheepish and subdued. To me he says *Sorry, sorry, sorry* but I look away. Then, more usefully, he says he has found a *gazogène* taxi and persuaded the cabbie to take us and the meat. Herman and the other boy stow my two cases in the dickey. The inside is already crammed with Maurice's two, so that there is scarcely room for the two of us to squeeze in.

'*Also Liebling, wie wär's mit 'nem Rendezvous?* So darling, what about a date?' says Herman, pushing his face in through the window. '*Wie wär's, wenn du mir 'n schönes Steak kochst?* What about you cook me a nice steak?'

I give him Maurice's phone number.

23

I've had it with sex. I've had it with Maurice. I've had it with philosophy. I've had it with shooting the Old Gaffer.

I have formed my own Resistance!

I get up with the lark. I check on Pauli and tell him to get up and get ready for school. I tell him I'm off on important Resistance work. He bleats but accepts. Then I am out of the house and sneaking round the back to the empty coal shed where I have hidden my lovely blue bicycle and soon I am pedalling like a mad thing through the empty streets.

The swimming pool at Butte-aux-Cailles opens at seven but I am there by five to. There is a new notice on the gate which says the pool is forbidden to dogs and to people of the Jewish race. The pool guy is never there on time. I just clamber over the turnstile anyway.

The water is freezing. Pauli's *Boy's Own Annual* makes out this is good for you. The English are a strange race.

First, I swim breaststroke like a girl, with my head out of the water, so I am doing only pootsy little strokes, and then I take the plunge and duck my head right under the icy water. I go on with the breaststroke but now I swim four strokes before I come up for air. It takes me ten strokes to swim a length, so I have to come up twice. This is annoying. I am working to make my strokes more powerful and to glide through the water more smoothly. I'm working on the leg kick, making my thighs like steel, powering away, pressing out the water and propelling my body like a torpedo up the pool. I dream of the day when my shoulders and thighs will be so strong and my lungs so big that I can do an entire length on one breath and never come up at all.

As I swim I think *I am young and I am brown and I am strong.*

And so I resist. I thrust away all those things I am so sick of. I am swimming for me and me alone. I grow in strength. I lift my arms and feel my shoulders which are as brown and hard as teak. My legs are like smooth rods. I am growing ever stronger and more lithe. My body is taut like the string of a bow.

I will get stronger still until the longed-for perfection appears.

Stronger and cleaner. Swimming cleanses me.

I kidded myself that he could love me but all along it was my brother that he loved. When he was holding me, when he kissed me or when we were lying in that mucky bed, it was not me but my brother. And he couldn't even do it.

And then Franck's lies, his whole life a lie, and Papa's anger, and stupid Maman dying, our whole family *foutu, pourri.*

I am in a sort of shock.

I haven't even told Maddie. I haven't even seen her. She is so busy at her stupid office. I sent her a *pneu* in schoolgirl code to tell her Verónica got off alright, and another to say I need to see her, could she come for a meat supper because I have got a scrag end of neck (part of my share of the contraband meat)?

Apart from everything else, I have to tell her that the Old Gaffer isn't even coming to Paris anymore!

Mlle Bazin made this shock horror announcement at Assembly yesterday. No reason was given. Maybe the Old Mummy realized that running after Napoleonic body parts tossed to him courtesy of the Fuehrer is not all that noble a mission.

Or maybe he was afraid someone might take a pot shot at him.

But Maddie just replies to say *later, I'm quite tied up just now.*

And so I swim and swim, becoming strong. Or do I only mimic strength? How weak I really am! I pretend to be a Résistante because my life is such a mess. There's the outer mess, and the worse mess within.

And I just know the mess is about to get worse.

I get bored of doing breaststroke. It's such a girl thing. I switch to my brilliant Australian crawl. I've got it almost perfect now. I've done twelve lengths on my front. It is splashy and exhausting, so I have a rest, sculling, doing an indolent back crawl.

This is when I see the most extraordinary thing, the prohibited thing.

I see Maddie coming in through the turnstile and paying her two sous to the mec who has just turned up. She has her towel rolled neatly under her left arm. She is in the nice white top and baggy white shorts that only a house with servants could keep clean. She glances into the pool to see who it is who is splashing about so artlessly and she sees me and gives a start of surprise. She knows it's me because it is me and she knows me so well, and anyway I am wearing that old faded pink effort with the skirt that I got out of Mama's things. I mean, how many small strong brown girls in faded rose costumes with a skirt does Maddie know?

But it's not so much seeing Maddie that is extraordinary,

although it is hard to imagine anyone less *matinale* than she is. It's more that she's not alone because behind her at the turnstile is a boy who is close enough to her to be surely with her. I can't straightaway make out who this boy is. He is wearing khaki shorts and an open necked white shirt. His outline looks vaguely familiar though.

I touch the rail at the far end and turn and start on a front crawl. Now I am swimming towards Maddie so I will meet her in the time it takes to swim back the length of the pool. I'm now on my front, my head in the water, turning to the side, so I won't see her until I come up at the end. I put on a spurt, measuring my strokes, eight, nine, ten, and I touch and come up.

There is Maddie, waiting for me. She is by herself, crouching down. I pull myself up and she leans over and gives me the *bises*.

'*Où est ton flirt?*'

She puts on a puzzled look but she's a poor fibber. She is so clearly shamming.

'The boy you were with. Where is he?'

'Oh!' she says, acting all surprised, 'you mean the kid behind me at the turnstile. He was following me all the way from the metro. I told him to get lost.'

Sorry, Maddie, but I think I can tell when a boy and a girl are together. Maddie and that boy were definitely together.

I clamber out of the pool.

'I'm going to change,' I say.

Maddie walks alongside me and we stand in the changing room looking at each other. Maddie says *About that meat supper*.

But it is false. It's sad.

'But I can come, can't I?' she says. 'I mean, to your Daddy's speech.'

She gives me a sharp, shy look. She knows that I know she has lied to me.

'Maddie, Maddie!'

'What, darling?'

'I can't stand this.' I go towards her and throw my arms around her. 'Maddie dearest, who was that boy just now?'

'I told you, darling. Just a kid bothering me. I told him to buzz off.'

'Maddie, don't do this.' I breathe in her ear and hug her tighter.

'What? Do what?'

'Lie to me,' I whisper.

Her face is next to mine, her cheek against my cheek. A small shudder passes through her. I know that I should stop. I should trust her but I can't. How can I, when she is lying to me? Especially because I did actually recognize the boy. In a tiny voice I say,

'Maddie, Maddie, I saw the boy. I know who he is.'

She pulls away from me and I see that her front is all wet from my bathing costume. She stands and looks me in the face.

'Stop it, Annie, just stop. Stop asking me. Just trust me. Please.'

'Why? Why trust you when you lie to me?'

She gives me a fierce look, shaking her head, then turns away from me. I grab my stuff and run outside. I am in tears as I stand there pulling my stupid frock over my head and ramming on my stupid clogs. I grab my bike and pedal back home as fast as I can, standing on the pedals all the way.

Because the boy was that young German she was playing Nausicaa with the other week.

**

The next day a letter comes from Maddie. It is on her family notepaper with the arms and all.

19 rue Boniface
Paris 16

My dearest little one,

Tout comprendre est tout pardonner. Please please please can we meet? And may I come with you to your father's speech?

Bises from always your, Magdalena

This seems no atonement for her lie, especially as she is persisting in it. I don't accept.

But I must give her a chance, because she is my blood sister and my love. Anyway, I so long to spill out all the *merde* that has fallen on me, about Maurice and the meat and the sex, and all about Franck and Papa, the whole *putain* mess. Not to mention the Old Mummy's not coming any more.

I send her a *pneu*, neutral and adequate, and I go round to Les Nouveaux Temps.

She comes out and we embrace, a bit awkwardly. We just do the two *bises*, not our usual three.

It's her *pause café* and we set off towards the Luxembourg Gardens. She links her arm through mine in her old way but it is not the same as before and we separate as we cross the Boulevard Raspail. Somehow I cannot walk arm in arm with her right now, not until she explains herself. She knows I want her to explain, but she just mutters *Tout comprendre* again.

We walk through the Gardens. I can't share anything with her right now, I don't understand what's going on, so I let her chatter on nervily about Les Nouveaux Temps and other stupid guff and I am all silent. Perhaps it is fortunate that there is some cinema going on to distract us. There is a big Citroën truck backing on to the lawn. The ground is wet from yesterday's rain and the truck sinks in. The wheels spin and score ugly tracks in the grass.

The truck backs up towards a statue that I've never noticed before. It's a huge nudie figure of a woman. She's got barely a stitch on, just a completely see-through robe which conceals strictly nothing. This busty creature is striding forward, clasping a baton firmly in her hands.

'What is that?' Maddie asks.

'I dunno.'

Workmen in blue overalls are wrestling with this titan. It certainly is a struggle. The thing is really gigantic, it must weigh tons. The mecs are tugging and hauling. They have the lorry backed up against it now and they have got ropes around the neck and waist of the statue. We watch as the guys manage to get her to rock back on the plinth. She falls with a huge crash into the back of the truck which goes right down on its springs. The workmen pick up two objects lying on the ground. I see that these are the woman's arms which have broken off.

A German lieutenant is standing by. He has a hammer and chisel in his hands and when the statue is in the truck he clambers up and places the chisel on each of her eyes in turn and hammers hard.

'Chipping out the eyes,' Maddie mutters.

And then all at once there is Maurice. *Ugh.*

He appears as if from nowhere. He just materializes around the side of the truck. It seems, though, that he is expected because the gang foreman goes up to him and they have some chat. The foreman mec wags his head from side to side and then Maurice reaches into the pocket of his jacket and pulls out a brown envelope and gives it to the mec. The mec trousers it and the two shake hands.

By now the German lieutenant has finished his work. He jumps down from the truck, nods to Maurice and goes off. Maurice looks about and notices us. He makes towards us across the ruined lawn.

'Hallo, girls,' he says breezily. He embraces Maddie, *three bises*. I hang back, scowling.

'What was all that about?' It's Maddie who asks. I am not going to speak to Maurice.

'It's *Paris pendant la guerre*.'

'Which is?'

'It's the rather bad statue they put up after the last war to honour the defence of Paris against the Hun. Not surprisingly, now that Fritz is on top, he wanted it down.'

'So what's that to do with you?'

'Oh, you know…it's just for my collection, really,' he says and saunters off.

Maddie starts to laugh. It's an edgy laugh. I stare at her. Then I bend down and pull off my stupid *sabots* and start to run and I don't stop until I turn the corner and I know that she is out of my sight.

I haven't even told her about the Old Mummy not coming.

24

The only person happy about Papa sharing a platform with Dr Goebbels is Pauli. It gives him an opportunity to sing the new song which he has picked up God knows where.

> *Hitler, he only has one ball*
> *Goering, his are very small*
> *Himmler's are very similar*
> *But poor old Goebbels*
> *Has no balls at all*

He runs it on by singing it to some old marching tune so that the last line runs back to the first

> *...But poor old Goebbels*
> *Has no balls at all – all – all – all...*
> **Hitler**, *he only has one ball...*

***

It *is* his life's work. Since my eyes first opened on the world, and long before that, Papa has been studying and working for this thing, the *economic integration of Europe*. We all trade together and this makes everybody rich and happy and peace-loving. Well, that's noble, isn't it? And Papa's won prize after prize for it. He got his chair at the Collège de France for it. He got a chestful of medals from Blum's Socialist government for it, he's been made a *Chevalier de la Légion d'Honneur* for it. He won the Prix Goncourt for it, for that Big Book of his. He even got nominated for the Nobel Peace Prize for it. He would have been only the second Frenchman ever to win, after his big hero Aristide Briand...

And now he believes that it is his big chance to realize his dream, the New European Order, all the nations of Europe coming together to trade without customs in one big single market and with one currency. And the Old Gaffer and his crowd are all in favour, and Papa is their big hero right now.

This Big Meeting is supposed to decide it. Papa will speak and then Goebbels will speak and then it will be decided once and for all.

At the last minute, someone plonks down in the empty seat next to me. It is Maddie. I give her a hard shove but she pushes back. I shove her again but she holds on and I give up. She leans in to me. I smell her perfume, violets. She whispers in my ear,

'Last night your Dad was named on the BBC. A "prominent collaborator", they said.'

I pull away from her. I look out of the window, across the *quai* to the Pont Royal. An open truck crammed with men in uniform is chugging over the bridge towards the Left Bank.

We sit there, stiff and silent. At one point Maddie gets up and goes back in the hall. I glance behind me and she's having a pow-pow with some mec, probably collabo scum from *Les Nouveaux Temps*. She comes back and plumps back down. I can't be bothered to spat with her anymore, so we sit there like spiteful gargoyles and wait and wait.

At last I mutter 'He's not coming of course, the Old Mummy.'

She shows not the least surprise, or even interest. She just murmurs, 'Mmm. Yes, I know.'

What on earth is going on with her?

But things are hotting up at last. A mec fiddles with the microphone, saying *Testing testing*. Papa shuffles onto the dais alongside some Boche mec in a snappy suit. They sit down at the big desk up on the dais.

'Abetz,' Maddie says. She sees me looking. 'Abel Abetz. He's the Boche ambassador to the Court of Philippe le Gaga.'

I say nothing. It's broken, Maddie. It's so broken, so why don't you just push off and leave me alone?

But she will go on. Now she is saying,

'He's the worst type, Abetz. *Francisant*. Fair-seeming, French-loving guy. He did History of Art or something at the Sorbonne and ever since then he's been schmoozing around saying how much he loves us.'

Maddie, just shut up, please! I turn and look out of the window again. The truck has stopped at the end of the bridge. Two Boche soldiers jump out of the cab and open the back of the truck. A dozen or so *bleus* pile out. It's another *rafle* in the quartier Latin I suppose, mandated by the Boche, carried out by their willing French *collabos*.

Maddie is ploughing on. She's very nervy. She babbles on about how at heart they, the Boche, all despise us. The worst are those like this Abetz who pretend they don't.

But then all falls quiet. *Here comes power*, says Maddie, and a smallish fellow in an immaculate black uniform steps out onto the stage. He is limping slightly, his right leg drags as he moves toward the dais. His face is thin and gaunt. He is *nothing much of it*, Mama would have said. Yet power sits visibly on his shoulders. Creepy, creepy power.

'Street urchin mentality,' Maddie mutters.

Everyone gets up and starts to applaud. Everyone that is

except stupid Maddie. Like a good schoolgirl, I go to stand but she pulls me back down. *Don't be a Bochophile,* she says.

Bochophile yourself! I say under my breath.

This is the Goebbels mec then. He does a Nazi salute. People are taking time over sitting down, which largely relieves them of the question of whether they have to salute back. Goebbels takes off his military cap. His black hair is slicked down. He removes his gloves slowly and carefully. They seem very tight-fitting. He takes great care to pull them off finger by finger. He nods to the Abetz, glances at Papa, and sits down.

At this point Abetz stands up and tells us what an honour it is to have the Reichsminister of Public Enlightenment here to talk to us today. The minister has apparently so many other better and more important things to do than to talk to half the government of France and all the great and the good of our country. But he has accepted the invitation with his customary magnanimity and we should record this as a Red Letter Day in the history of our two nations etc. etc.

'Hitler calls him his *faithful, unshakeable shield-bearer,*' Maddie is whispering in my ear. 'He sees himself as John the Baptist to Hitler's Jesus.'

I literally couldn't care less about this, about the Goebbels or even Maddie for that matter. I am watching Papa. He's madly scribbling things on his text and striking things out. All the while he is shaking his head about. Frankly he looks a bit loony. Suddenly Abetz is saying,

'...and to represent the Government of France today we have the very distinguished economist, Chief Economic Adviser to the Head of State Maréchal Pétain, Chevalier de la Légion d'Honneur, Professor of the Collège de France... so please welcome Professor Schneider, who is to talk to us today about the New European Order...'

The gulf yawns. Here we go.

Papa is on his feet, kind of, but he's bowed over and still shuffling his papers. He taps the microphone and clears his throat, and then he begins.

In a mumbling way, with his head down, he says he is going to talk about whether the New European Order is 'Keynesian'. Abetz looks surprised at this. He glares at Papa and brushes his hand through his hair in an irritated gesture. The Reichsminister simply looks bored. He is staring into the middle distance.

Papa now proceeds to give what must be the most tedious speech I have ever heard in my entire life. He says that Keynes is all about 'counter-cyclical deficit spending', which equals governments spending money they don't have. Papa says that this is how Germany went from one third unemployment and half of industrial capacity idle in 1933 to full employment and the wheels of industry whirring round apace by 1936. In this sense, German economic policy can be called Keynesian.

'So that's all right then,' Maddie mutters. But if she has followed what Papa has been saying she is in a very small minority as this first part of his speech has been almost inaudible. Only we in the front few rows can possibly have heard Papa's shrunken, hoarse voice, especially when he bends over to read from his notes which is practically all the time.

Ambassador Abetz looks irritable. He leans over and whispers something in Goebbels' ear and the Reichsminister smiles.

'But there is a difference,' Papa is now saying, 'and that is the role of the state. For Keynes, government should control the money supply and public spending but leave everything else free – trade, prices, wages, private investment. But Germany does the opposite – they regulate everything.'

'Not Germany,' Maddie mutters, 'the Nazis.'

Papa drones on. His speech is really not being delivered in a very coherent way. In fact it's ninety-nine percent unintelligible. Even to me, and I sort of know what it's supposed to be about. He keeps pausing and shuffling his papers, and the whole thing is given with his head bowed down, like he is talking to the desk rather than the audience. During all this, Abetz looks super-irritated. His body language is all negative and hostile towards Papa. By contrast, Goebbels' face is inscrutable, his eyes look like they are fixed on some distant vision. I doubt he is even listening. Abetz scowls and again whispers something in Goebbels' ear, and then he leans towards the microphone and says loudly,

'Professor, I think you had better wind up now.'

Papa turns slowly to look at Abetz and nods.

'Ah… ah… yes, wind up. Just so.' He picks up his papers and leafs through them, tosses down the greater part and then holds one single sheet up to his eyes. He looks totally like a mad professor and completely unworldly. Still mumbling, he reads out,

'So, my views may bear a superficial resemblance to the New European Order proposed by the Nazis but the differences are stark. The Nazi project is one of compulsion, of the domination of one people by another, of service to the higher end of the *volk*, of a Europe purged of its mongrel elements.'

'*Mon Dieu!*' says Maddie.

Startled, I look around. No-one else seems to have registered these subversive thoughts. On the dais, Goebbels continues to stare straight ahead of him. Abetz yawns.

'But the real difference between the two...'

– here it seems to me that this is a fragment of some longer part of the speech or maybe some other speech altogether –

'...the real difference between the two is that for Keynes, economics is just a means to an end, and that end is social good. When we have solved the economic problem, Keynes writes, then we shall move on to solve the real problem, the relation of man to man. How shall we men and women live together in a free world on a basis of mutual respect and love? And in the end, when we have solved that question, then we shall sing madrigals in the Garden of Eden.'

Papa sits down. Abetz smirks. Goebbels sits motionless. There is no applause, in fact there is almost complete silence in the room. A couple of people titter. Clearly no one can work out what to make of this speech. Is it an attack on German economic policy? Or just the musings of a demented professor?

Abetz stands up. He starts ticking Papa off in an oily fashion. First, he thanks him in a kind of back-handed, thanks-for-nothing way. He says he wonders if this distinguished audience really needed to be reminded that economic policy is only a means to an end. He says,

'Let me read to you what the Reichskanzler, our Fuehrer, says. He says that economics is only "a necessary servant in the life of a people and their nationhood."'

He pauses and raises his hand for effect.

'And the Fuehrer goes on to say that "it is the privilege of the victorious race in the ceaseless struggle amongst peoples to use that necessary servant, economics, to show a way of life for the next hundred years."'

'So that's alright then,' Maddie mutters again.

***

'And so,' Abetz is now turning towards Goebbels, who has sat without moving and without the slightest sign of emotion through all this, 'and so now we have the most extraordinary privilege of hearing from one of the very architects of this "way of life for the next hundred years". Dr Goebbels, Minister of Public Enlightenment, will now talk to us about the New European Order, the Europe of the future, and about the high place which France may occupy in that New Order.'

Maddie pats my arm. I pull away from her but I still hear her whisper, 'Now for the great manipulator. He boasts *I play upon the national psyche as on a piano.*'

Goebbels stands up and moves to the end of the table where we can see all of him. He motions to the attendant and the mec comes and brings the microphone on its stand. Goebbels waves a hand, meaning *Raise it, raise it*, and the mec fiddles with the fitting and brings the microphone up to the level of Goebbels' shoulders. There is a pause, the hall falls quiet. And then he begins. He speaks clearly in quite good French, as follows:

> Today there are more people in Europe than there used to be, and their numbers have created quite new problems for European society – problems of food supplies and economic policy as well as those of finance and defence.
>
> At the moment when British power is collapsing, we have the opportunity to reorganize Europe on principles corresponding to the social, economic and technical possibilities of the twentieth century.
>
> What it means for you is that you are already members of a great New Europe which is preparing

> to reorganize our continent, tearing down the barriers that still separate the European peoples and making it easier for them to come together. Germany intends to put an end to a situation which quite clearly cannot satisfy mankind for long. We are performing here a work of reform which I am convinced will one day be recorded in large letters in the book of European history. Can you imagine what the New Europe will actually be like after the war?

No-one volunteers any answer to this. But this doesn't matter to Goebbels. He simply ploughs on.

> Let me tell you, because we are already preparing the organization of this New European Order.
>
> The most important precondition is to do away with the economic Balkanization of Europe. A large new economic area will come into being, in which the economy can develop with only basic direction from the state. Europe must be unified in the same fashion as other continental areas like the USA.
>
> This creation of an economic area on a European scale was arbitrarily prevented after the Great War by the dictated peace of Versailles which set up 35 independent European states, 16 of which had less than 10 million inhabitants, and created 7,000 kilometres of new customs frontiers. Attempts at unification such as the Anschluss of the former state of Austria to Germany were frustrated, and the regime of small economic units was artificially encouraged.
>
> Our project is thus the large-scale economic unification of Europe. Such a European economic community under German leadership will require

that European currencies must be placed on a uniform basis by establishing a fixed rate of exchange between those of the other countries and the Reichsmark. Customs barriers in Europe must be abolished.

Such a European union would give a powerful impetus to the European economy. As far as numbers are concerned, a European economic bloc would comprise a much larger population than the 130 million people of the United States.

And so, gentlemen – and I am speaking now quite realistically, without any appeal to sentiment – it would be foolish not to profit by the formation of the New European Order. I appeal to you today to claim the advantages it offers.

This whole speech is delivered without notes. It is a compelling performance. Masterly, really. And it is given with movements of his body that perfectly match his message. Most of the time he has his arms loosely akimbo, his hands placed easily at the top of his thighs. He looks like a slim, predatory fish. Only once, when he talked about Balkanization, did his right arm go up, raising a twisted fist into the air, the thumb crooked over and the finger pointing. It is a gesture of menace.

He sits down and Abetz leads off the applause, clapping his hands vigorously. The audience is obliged to follow, whatever their thoughts.

I look at Papa. He is slumped, shoulders down and his head hanging, almost touching the table.

Abetz now asks for questions. Nobody moves, they clearly don't know which way to jump. Maddie looks around behind her and then stands up. Abetz seems taken aback, but for lack of any other volunteers he has no choice but to recognize her.

'Very well, young lady. But first, please introduce yourself.'

Maddie says,

'Magdalena Grandidier de Vernay, *Les Nouveaux Temps*...'

Abetz nods, apparently approving the organ.

'So, Mlle, ask your question. Please keep it brief.'

'Could the Minister please tell us what role compulsion will play in forming this New European Order?'

Abetz immediately says,

'Please, Mademoiselle, the question is impertinent...'

However, Goebbels is already on his feet, his arms again caressing his upper thighs in calm assurance.

'It has never been our intention,' he says, 'that this new order or reorganization of Europe should be brought about by force. We with our Greater German outlook have no interest in infringing the economic, social or cultural individuality of the French people.'

'But you invaded our country!' Maddie exclaims and a palpable ripple of fear runs through the hall. Abetz starts to rise to his feet but Goebbels calmly waves him down. He approaches the microphone again and, after a significant pause, he says

'Young woman, you must know that, unprovoked, France declared war on Germany. We had to defend ourselves. We have always sought to bring about this reorganization of Europe by negotiation. However, those efforts were refuted by historical developments – and history, I don't need to remind the more experienced and thoughtful amongst our audience, history generally operates with harsher laws than those that prevail around the

Dear member of Hennock book club

Thank you so much for reading my book. I would really welcome your views. Here are some possible questions:

- Was it gripping? Did it hold your interest all through?
- Were you transported to the world the novel is set in? Did anything jar?
- Did you believe in the characters? Could you empathize with them? Did they sometimes act out of character?
- Was it easy to read? Was the style appropriate to this type of book?
- Was the political and economic subtext well integrated (Goebbels, Keynes, Annie's father's plans)? And did the brother's letters fit in?
- Was the ethical question of 'how to resist an unjust occupation' well woven in?
- Was the opening with the three young men out of step with the rest of the book?
- Was the ending too abrupt? Or was the unresolved business a good lead in to the proposed sequel?

<u>If you have views and the interest, it would be great if you would review the book on Amazon (if you have an account)</u>.
If you aren't familiar with that, here's how:

- Open your Amazon account and call up the book
- Go to the bottom of the page (after all the ads) to where the other reviews are
- In the left-hand column, click on *Write a customer review*

conference table.'

Goebbels smiles slightly and steps back. Maddie jumps up again. Abetz makes a furious gesture at her to sit down but Goebbels again waves the ambassador away. He stands easily, clearly steady under light fire.

'Yes, my dear. Let us have the benefit of what more is in your pretty head.'

'You mean reorganization by conquest and compulsion of the defeated nations.'

'Well, my dear...'

I'm not your dear, Maddie mutters. Goebbels must have excellent hearing because he smirks and says quietly but audibly *Perhaps not*. Then he goes on.

'...you see, a clear basis of mutual understanding must be created between our two nations. We must approach each other either as friends or as enemies. And I think your parents at least know well enough from the past experience that the Germans can be terrible enemies, but also very good friends. We reach out our hand to a friend and cooperate with him in a truly loyal spirit, but we can also fight an enemy until he is destroyed...'

Maddie is on her feet again.

'And if France refuses?'

'France will not refuse. Either France will adapt to this reorganization with genuine good will and sincerity, or France will inwardly resist it. Whichever stance France may choose will make no difference to the facts.'

'You mean...'

'Please, Mademoiselle, please, let others have their say,' Abetz calls out, but Goebbels wants to complete his thought.

'France may take it as certain that once England is overthrown, the Axis powers will not permit any change in the power or political situation of a Europe reorganized in accordance with these great political, economic and social ideas. If Britain can do nothing to prevent this, certainly the French people cannot. If you have learnt anything from recent history you will know that nothing can or will be changed in the power-political situation as it exists today.

'So, gentlemen' – and here Goebbels raises his voice to make it clear that he is no longer answering a mere slip of a girl but addressing Maddie's elders and betters and probably the French nation beyond. He raises his fist above his head with that peculiar arrangement of the thumb crooked over and the forefinger pointing up – 'and so, *gentlemen*' (with a nasty emphasis on gentlemen, which clearly sidelines Maddie again) – 'and I am speaking now quite realistically, without any appeal to sentiment, it makes no difference at all whether you approve this state of things or not. Whether or not you welcome it from your hearts, you cannot do anything to alter the facts. You have seen the Reich in wartime, and you will have formed some idea of what it can be in peace. Our great nation with its large population, together with Italy, will in practice take over the leadership of Europe. There are no two ways about that.

'Now it is my opinion that when you can do nothing to alter a state of affairs and have to put up with the disadvantages it may no doubt present, it would be foolish not to profit by its advantages as well. I do not see why the French people should adopt an attitude of inward opposition to the New European Order. I appeal to you today to claim the advantages it offers.'

Goebbels steps back again, and again he smirks. There is complete silence in the hall. I look back and see even the delegation from Vichy more or less sitting on their hands. Goebbels is not fazed by this. He simply stands quite still.

He does iron hand with the same verve and self-assurance as he does velvet glove.

'There's nothing more to be said, really,' Maddie whispers to me. 'Is there?'

But Goebbels is not quite finished. He returns to the microphone.

'I would like in closing to say something about Mr Keynes who enjoys very high respect in Germany because of his thoughtful and annihilating critique of the consequences of Versailles. And also for his wicked pen portraits of the foolish men who imposed that pernicious peace on Germany. But I have to differ with him about the ends of economic policy.

'The National Socialist and Fascist revolutions are not only national solutions but parts of the general European revolution. It follows that they have not only national but also European objectives. Their providential leaders, Adolf Hitler and Benito Mussolini, are therefore not only the greatest men of Germany and Italy, but also the greatest Europeans. They are not only the leaders of their national revolutions but also of the European revolution. They are leaders of the reorganization of the European continent on a basis of race and territory.

'This reorganization will provide a better economic order in place of the dying British world economic system. And it will provide more noble, more manly objectives than – what was it, Professor Schneider? – *singing madrigals in the Garden of Eden*! Wagner at Bayreuth perhaps – but not madrigals!'

There is some scattered nervous laughter.

'Because we proclaim a new European morality: that just as the individual cannot with impunity transgress the higher law of the racial community into which he is born, so a people cannot with impunity transgress the higher law of the community to which it belongs by race or violate the political, economic and cultural interest, rights and duties which arise organically from it. The European community of peoples, the common *Lebensraum* of the white race, demands from each of its people the same discipline that the national community imposes on every one of its citizens. In this way the peoples of Europe must again be Europeanized, so that they once more become citizens of their continent and, thereafter, of the world. Europe for the Europeans!'

Goebbels stops and sits down and Abetz immediately springs up, clapping his hands. A few toadies in the audience clap with him and then Abetz holds up his hands for silence. He clearly wants to close the meeting.

However, Maddie is on her feet again, shouting out.

'One more question.'

'Mlle, I think that Dr Goebbels has already answered you.'

'But my question is for Professor Schneider.'

Maddie's cheeks are burning red. I tug at her skirt to make her sit down. She slaps me off.

'Don't!' I hiss at her, but Abetz is already saying,

'If Professor Schneider feels up to it. So fire away, young lady.'

Papa has been resting his head on his arms which are folded on the table but he looks up when Abetz says his name. I pull at Maddie's arm.

'Stop it! Papa's had enough…'

But there isn't any stopping her. She shouts out her question.

'Professor Schneider, does the Vichy government which you represent agree with everything that Dr Goebbels just said? If not, what part does it not agree with?'

'Come off it!' someone shouts from the back and there is a confused hubbub in the hall. Goebbels sits quite still, staring into the mid-distance with a thin smile on his wolfish face.

Papa is looking vaguely from side to side. He seems to be losing it.

Abetz leans over and prods Papa.

'Well, Professor,' he says, 'any answer?'

Papa stands up. His face is perfectly white. He opens his mouth. He says,

'I...'

Now there is not one sound in the hall. A thousand people are listening. Seconds go by, like hours they seem. Everybody leans forward, straining to hear Papa's answer.

I get up and start to push past Maddie. She doesn't stop me.

'I...'

I am past Maddie now and running up towards the dais. Abetz is leering at Papa. Goebbels has turned away and is pulling on his tight-fitting gloves.

'I...'

I run up the steps of the dais. Pa's mouth is gaping and his head nodding. His face is like ash. He puts his hand to his chest and leans forward. I make him sit down, I push him down and he collapses onto his chair. He puts his head on the table.

By now there is uproar. Abetz shouts out that the meeting is over and he and Goebbels walk off the dais and leave the room. As Goebbels goes out, a woman's voice shouts

'*Merde, tu es le roi des cons!*'

It's Maddie, I know it's that bitch. Her voice is lost in the hubbub, the scraping of chairs and the murmur and clamour of frightened men.

I put my arms around Papa and say 'Come, Papa, come home now.' Then, just next to me, I hear Maddie's voice. She must have just run up onto the dais. Beside her is Maurice.

'Let us help,' she says. I hit her with the back of my hand as hard as I can, smacking her on the mouth. I feel her teeth against my finger bones and there is blood, either mine or hers but I don't care.

'*Foutes le camp*,' I shout at her. '*And you*,' I shout at Maurice.

I throw my arms around Papa again. He is rocking backwards and forwards. His mouth is open. Maurice, who has not gone away, wipes Papa's mouth with a big white handkerchief.

Papa goes on rocking. He opens his mouth again.

'I…' he says.

'Yes, dear papa,' I say, and hug him tight.

'I… I… can't…'

His mouth hangs open. His body shakes. It goes limp and his head falls forward on his chest.

'Maurice, help me to lift him.' Papa turns his great head and looks at me. Does he even recognize me? His eyes look empty. But then he turns to Maurice and stares at him and says quite distinctly,

'You.'

'Yes, it is me, Sir.'

Maurice manages to get Papa's right arm over my shoulder, and then he stoops and gets under Papa's left arm. Like this we lift him up until he is more or less standing. His head is hanging down. We start half-dragging him across the dais. His body sags, it is a dead weight between us. Somehow we manhandle him down the steps and get him to the door of the now nearly empty hall. A few random mecs are still sitting around. They watch us without emotion, watch this last act of the charade.

And there is horrid Maddie again, waiting at the door. She is holding a handkerchief to her mouth.

'Please let me help,' she asks again.

'*Foutes le camp,*' I say.

We settle Papa in a chair by the door and Maurice goes out to look for transport. The last stragglers are leaving. They walk by us, staring. I have no idea what might be in their heads, or in their hearts for that matter. All I know is that not one of them offers us any word, neither of consolation nor of dissent. I guess they are all Yes-Men now, all *collabos* now.

I stand by Pa with my arm around him. He's sagging badly but I hold him up as best I can.

Maurice is back in a minute and he says that Otto's car is outside and can take us home.

'Really? After all this?'

'Otto says. He had to go with Goebbels but he left the car.'

So we struggle out with Papa and an NCO, a *Stabsgefreiter*, leaps out of Otto's Merc and helps us get Pa into the rear seat. I squeeze in beside him. Maurice asks if he should come but Papa is glaring so fiercely at him that he retreats.

Maddie appears at the car window.

'Take me,' she cries, 'take me! I can help. I am so sorry.'

But I turn away from her and ask the lance-corporal to head for home. I am cradling Papa in my arms, like he is a baby.

That bitch Maddie is not so easily put off. She dashes round the car and as the driver puts the car into first she throws open the car door on the other side from me and jumps in. She squeezes herself into the seat next to Pa.

'*Connasse*!' I shout at her, '*merdeuse*!'

I want to hit her very hard but my arms are around Papa. I want to scream at her but Papa is grunting and screwing up his face.

She says quietly,

'I can help get your dad up the stairs.'

She has a point, and her bloody mouth gives me some satisfaction.

'You promised!' I shout at her. 'You fucking promised!'

Maddie puts up her arms in front of her face to ward off my slaps.

'You shit! You cunt!'

I go on slapping at her and shouting foul words until I spot young Pauli in the doorway, all agog, so I have to stop. Anyway, my father may be able to hear me from next door, from his bedroom where after a fantastic struggle we finally hoisted him up from the car. It was only Otto's driver really who managed it. He held Papa under the arms and Maddie and I took his legs. We went up backwards with the Old Bat looking on from her little booth and not lifting a finger, only scowling and going *Tsk! Tsk!*

'Oh, Annie, Annie, don't!' Maddie lowers her arms. She is daring me to hit her again. Blood is still oozing from her lip where I clocked her.

I still want to hurt her, I really do and I could do it because although she is taller, I am tougher. She just stands her ground, two feet from me, her arms at her side, pale as death, her lips bloody. She says,

'Don't, Annie, don't, please. I had to do it.'

'No you fucking didn't! You promised. Now you've killed him.'

She moves a fraction closer to me. Now I am seriously going to hit her.

'Don't you see?' she says. 'Don't you see? I had to stop him siding with that shit Goebbels.'

'What? He wasn't siding with him.'

'Saying nothing is siding with the enemy. You heard Goebbels. You heard the whole thing. We'll be slaves. I couldn't let your father say nothing.'

'But he didn't say anything, anyway, *toi, chatte stupide.*'

'Annie, Annie… I hope that you will see that in a way I've saved him.'

'*Saved him*? Destroyed him, more like.'

Maddie takes a step away again. She looks at me very earnestly. She says,

'Oh darling…'

'I am not your darling.'

'Annie, I had to do it. They asked me to do it.'

'They?'

'Yes, they. The patriots.'

'So ruining my father is patriotic? Killing my father is patriotic?'

I can only think of Papa. At this moment I hate Maddie. I want to hurt her more, I want to kill her.

'And do the patriots know you're dating the enemy?'

'What?'

'I saw you.'

'Saw what?'

'I saw you with that disgusting sandwich boy. At the pool. You lied to me.'

Maddie lets out a small sigh.

'At least my father's not a hypocrite.'

Maddie seems completely deflated. She says,

'Look, Annie, I can explain…'

I put my arms on my hips and wait.

'…but not yet. Not now.'

I stare at the girl. My former friend. My former blood sister. I say,

'You'd better go. Thanks for your help.'

'Shall I stay until the doctor comes?'

'No, just go.'

She turns and leaves the room. After a minute I hear the front door closing. I go to Papa. In the hallway is Pauli, crouched down against the wall. Of course he's in tears. Who isn't?

END OF PART THREE

PART FOUR: WORSE AND WORSE

25

The next day Papa will not get up. I prop him up with a hundred pillows and then I take him a cup of ersatz coffee. He waves it away with a vague gesture but he does not speak. He will accept only a glass of water and he immediately drinks all of it. His eyes flicker in my direction for a moment and then he stares ahead. I touch his hand, which is very cold. I put my hand in his, but he does not respond.

Pauli comes rushing in and clambers on the bed, crying *Papa Papa* in his little piping voice but Papa does not hug him or even seem to notice him. He just stares straight ahead with dead eyes. Pauli starts to boo-hoo and I take him out.

A *pneu* comes from Maddie. It just says *Sorry sorry sorry. Can I come round?* I screw it up and throw it in the bin.

At eleven Dr Mercier comes. He has been our doctor for ever. He was at the birth of Pauli, and he did his best for Mama at the end. He is a small, pedantic, correct man. He spends quite a short time in the bedroom with Papa. When he comes out he says that it is not a medical case. In his view there is nothing physically wrong with Papa at all. It is perhaps the effect of shock, for he has heard about the debacle yesterday. He says it is all over town. Papa must stay quiet, he says. If need be, we may call in an eminent psychiatrist whom he names and who he says takes on such cases.

'He is,' the doctor says, 'apparently expert in the techniques of Dr Freud and, like Freud, is one of yours…'

For a moment I wonder what he means by this but then

I grasp it. He means 'foreigner', Austrian. Have we suddenly become aliens in our own country?

'...so he may understand better than I the workings of your father's mind.'

I stare at Mercier. For the first time I notice that his front teeth protrude slightly.

I show him out quite quickly. I won't pay his bill and I shan't call on him again.

It is a long dull day in which I make what little things I can in order to tempt Papa's appetite, snacks of chicken, a little *gâteau quatre-quarts* that I rub up with flour, butter, sugar and eggs that I have to buy under the counter for a small fortune from that crook Lafarge. But it is no use. Papa pays no attention to these treats and I end up giving the snacks and the cake to Pauli and a dog-end of chicken, the *bout de chien*, to Paco.

I try to keep Pauli busy but he is mopey and tearful the entire day. All afternoon we sit together in Papa's room and I read to him. We read the book his English cousin gave him – *Biggles Gets It Right*. We read it from end to end. Papa pays absolutely no attention whatever.

At dusk I go next door to ask our neighbour, the kindly Mme Bolduc, if she knows of a nurse who can care for Papa in this state. She says Yes! She has a niece who may well do. The girl is out but in the evening she presents herself at the door of the apartment. She is called Amélie, a neat slim girl with a simple country sort of air about her. She is from Brittany, staying with her aunt and in want of work.

She asks to see Papa and I take her in. Papa is awake but staring blankly toward the wall. He shows no sign of recognition as we come in.

Amélie looks at him for a minute and then nods. Yes, she would be able to care for Papa. We agree her fee, which is not very great, twenty-five francs a day. She will continue to stay with her aunt and she will start tomorrow.

Later, towards the end of the evening I receive another *pneu* from Maddie. This one too I don't read but throw straight in the bin.

When the boy asks *Any reply?* I say no but ask him for a form. I scribble a *pneu* to the Beaver.

> Dear Mlle, You will have heard about my father's illness. May I see you? I need your advice.
> Cordially, Anna-Elisa Schneider

I spend the night in Papa's room. I drag to his bedside the high-backed comfortable winged armchair with the worn chenille covering and sit on its edge, leaning forward with my knees against the hard wooden frame of the bed.

I take hold of Papa's right hand. I have never really noticed before how fine and delicate this hand is. I stroke it, it is soft to my touch. Why did I not know that my father has soft hands?

I see that the little finger bends over at the top, above the joint. Below this bend, there is a scar that bands the finger, a scar from an ancient accident. It was not Papa but Mama who told me of this accident that befell him when he was a child, about five years old. A servant was chopping salt, Papa put his hand on the block, and *thwack*! Off flew the tip of his little finger. The doctor sewed it back on, only a fraction crooked at the time. Over the years it has grown a little more crooked

It is a small affliction. But why did Papa never tell us about this?

I lift his hand and put my lips to the little finger. I can feel the angle in the bone beneath the skin, and the hard fingernail, pared down. A multitude of lines like little creases run up the length of this small finger, over the banded joints to the smooth pad towards the tip where the creases lose themselves in a random scribble.

This finger, its origins, its history, is, like almost everything about my father, unknown to me. And yet he fathered me. Everything that is in this insignificant digit is in my bones and in my brain.

I know nothing of it. I know nothing of my father.

A knocking at the front door wakes me. I find I have curled up in the winged armchair and slept all night long.

Papa is lying on his back, his great lion's head turned away from me, immobile against the piled-up cushions. His mouth is open. I uncoil myself. God, how stiff I am! I lean over and close his mouth. His eyes stay shut but he lets out a little groan and his torso moves a fraction.

Again the knock comes and I run to the door. It is Amélie. She is wearing a blouse and a nurse's *tablier*, white and stiff with starch. She looks just the thing.

I start to apologize. My hair is in a tousle and I have slept in my clothes, which feel filthy. I haven't done anything for Papa, his needs or anything. She says Fine, fine, no need, she is here to take care of him. I should go and have some breakfast, get the little boy up, get off to school myself.

School!

Anyway, Amélie sets to work without ado. I peek in and see her washing Papa expertly and preparing to handle his other *besoins*. I ask Amélie should I make some breakfast for him but she says no, she is sure he will eat nothing for now, perhaps just sip at water.

I take Pauli to school, just to get him out of the house. I haven't changed my outfit, I'm still in the frock I wore yesterday. Under the arms it's stiff with stale sweat. Of course Pauli blubs the whole way until we reach the corner of avenue Bousquet. Here he starts hopping between the paving stones, avoiding the lines. Then, as we turn into rue St Dominique, we meet his chum André who is with his mum. André's mum says she will take Pauli the rest of the way. I kiss him goodbye.

I don't go to school, but I don't go home either. I am not needed there now. And actually I can't bear the thought of my angry horrid Papa now so blank and emptied. I need fresh air and to think. It is the most beautiful spring day. Sunshine is marking out sharp shadows. The morning is still and fresh and sweet, not yet mixed with the sickly odour of the drains. I move between the sunlit pavements which are already warming up and the cool dark shade where the early sun has not yet reached.

I head past the Invalides into boulevard Raspail and turn into the Luxembourg Gardens. In the park the roses are already budding and the air is full of the scent of jasmine. I treat myself to a lemonade at the little café and sit in the sunshine. I am without any stockings. My legs drink in the sunshine.

All the time I am thinking and thinking about Papa. About that demanding Papa who always asked too much of us, the Papa who somehow out of love or lack of it drove away my dear dear Franck. And about Laureate Papa, the leading economist of our time.

Before, he was our rock – and our scourge. Now for the Résistance he's a *collabo* – and for his former friends, his *faux amis* in Vichy, he's just a broken reed, or maybe something worse.

I cannot believe that this great mind should become a useless old *débile*. One of the great minds of the age, they called him. Will he now be abused and shamed for just the same thoughts that have won him all those honours?

And then Maddie, bloody Maddie, bitch Maddie. How I hate her! Bleating on about Resistance and gulling us to take part in that ridiculous painting of the letter V which had already been appropriated by the Hun, and then getting off with a Boche, probably sleeping with him like a common slut, *collabo horizontale*, and saying off a half dozen Hail Marys after. And then that cruel question she asked Papa. He was down, she could see he was down and then she killed him, just for the sake of her own cleverness. *Pute*! No sister of mine. No friend of mine. I hate her and hate her.

Although. Although what was it that she said about that cruel question? *They asked me to do it. The patriots.*

26

I walk back the long way, along the Bd St-Germain. The *pavé* has really heated up under the burning sun. The heat rises from the stones and I start to perspire. My feet hurt in my *sabots*. When I get nearer the river there is a little breeze and it is a bit cooler but when I clack off to the left along the rue Saint-Dominique, it heats up again. The buildings are like canyon walls, reflecting heat. The sweat pours off me. Under the arms my dress is soaking again and it stinks. The drains of Paris are stirring. I can smell their sweet foul odour.

All the time I am thinking and thinking in a random, confused way. What to do? What can I do? It seems I am also walking in a random, confused way as I find I am wandering down past the Invalides. But I have an idea and quickly make up my mind. I will get a cake at *A la Petite Marquise*!

There before me is the Champ-de-Mars parade ground. A squad of Boche soldiers is exercising. They have their tops off. They are all fine, strong, muscled young men. They are doing press-ups. I can see the muscles in their flanks gleaming as they sweat in the afternoon sun. An NCO is calling out the moves. *Eins, zwei, eins, zwei*. The men are grunting like animals.

I think, or perhaps not, perhaps I just feel *What if one of these beautiful young men got up now and came to me and put his bare strong glistening chest against my breast and the muscles in his arms flexed tight around me and he held me until he drove the breath from my body. And then he took me up some alley – that alley, there – and he fucked me and fucked me until I cried out with it.*

Quickly I turn my head away. My whole body is pulsing, I can't bear it. I stumble on across the Champs and into the avenue de la Motte-Picquet and suddenly I am at *A la Petite Marquise*. And of course, the bloody place is closed. What was I thinking of? Cake, indeed!

When I get back to the flat, I am filthy and exhausted. My mind is in no better state.

I let myself in. A feeling of further dread seizes me. Why?

Amélie is at the door as soon as I open it and she says 'Oh dear, oh dear', so I know something new is wrong. Then Pauli comes running from his room and throws his arms around my waist and begins to cry. Paco lumbers arthritically from the kitchen and starts up barking. He makes a feeble attempt at jumping up at me.

'Paws off, Pompey,' I say to him, like Mama used to. I push him down. But he goes on sniffing at my dress. It's just the sweat and dirt of the street. I know that. But somehow it's still like I fucked a Boche. Like the dog knows what was in my heart at that moment.

'What is it?' I ask Amélie. 'Is it Papa? Is he worse?'

'No, no, it isn't that. Your father is sleeping. There's no change. I gave him a sleeping draft I got from the pharmacy. He drank it, with warm milk and a dash of brandy.'

'So what is it?'

'It's… a letter. It came for the Professor by Special. You weren't here. I… I'm afraid I decided I'd better open it…'

I see the letter at once, it is right there on Mama's old half-moon table in the hall. The envelope is typewritten, from the Collège de France. I see Papa's name typed out but there aren't the usual flourishes, the *Professeur Docteur bla bla bla*. Today he is just plain Monsieur. *M. Julius Schneider.*

The envelope is open, the silver letter opener is on the table.

'I thought, you see...' Amélie says.

In the envelope is a single thin typewritten sheet. I glance at it and sharp spines thrust into my chest. I hold the sheet away and turn my head. Pauli keeps clinging to me and crying 'What, Anschli, what?' I rub his fuzzy head and pull him into my skirt. He hugs my legs, like a small dumb creature.

At last I read the letter, diagonally at first – *Government Decree – Certificat – null – not fulfilled – voided...* Then I read it all through. My chest is tight like my heart will burst out.

M. Schneider

By Government Decree of March 15th, 1941, you were required to submit to the Collège de France a *Certificat de nationalité française*. Up until the present date, the Collège has received no such certificate from you.

We hold on file a *'certificat de naturalisation'* in your name dated 13th September 1936. You will be aware that such certificates are null and void under the terms of the aforementioned decree.

As such, you have not fulfilled the nationality qualifycation for the tenure of a post at the Collège. Your tenure has therefore been voided from the date on which you failed to respect the requirements of the law, that is March 15th, 1941.

All emoluments paid to you during this period in which you have occupied the post in illegality must be reimbursed to the Collège forthwith.

All property belonging to the Collège which is in your possession must be returned to us. All personal property belonging to you which is on Collège premises must be removed promptly or it will be destroyed.

In the name of the Director, I am requested to thank you for your services up to the date of the termination of your employment.

Yours truly

Jacques Dupont,

Directeur Administratif et Financier

All the while I am reading this missive, Pauli is still clinging to me, not exactly sobbing but hanging on in a really clingy way. His arms go right round my thighs and he holds on for all his worth. Dazed, I rub his head again and run my fingers through his hair.

'What is it, little one?' I ask. Of course he won't know what's in the letter. He just feels the wretched atmosphere. He shakes his head and buries his face in my skirt, then pulls it smartly out again.

Suddenly he springs away and looks up at me mischievously.

'Ooh, you stink,' he says.

Later, as the day fades and evening draws in, I remember to ask Amélie if a *pneu* has come for me. I need to see Simone. I need her advice badly. Amélie shakes her head.

I go to talk to Papa. It is truly with dread that I go to him. I knock on the door of his bedroom.

Of course he doesn't answer. Our angry active father doesn't answer. Perhaps he never will answer again. But I am certainly going to talk to him.

And with that thought comes another. Which is that, just now, I am in charge. In some weird way it is now me the parent and him the child. I am the aware awake acting deciding one, and he is senseless.

I am the parent, he is the child. I am free and generous

and full of love. I forgive my father.

I go to the bed and I kiss him. He opens his eyes. They swivel a little and then fix on me. But I don't think he sees me. I think he is gazing somewhere into that gap between me and eternity.

He closes his eyes. He is asleep again.

I settle down in the high-backed chair, burying myself in the worn chenille covering.

I watch over my father.

It's an hour or two and then he grunts.

'Papa,' I say. I get up and go to him. I kneel beside him and take his hands in mine. His hands are very cold. He gestures. I think he wants water.

I go to the kitchen and draw a pitcher of water. As I pass Pauli's door, I can hear him inside singing to himself,

Himmler's were very sim'lar

It is a struggle but I manage to get Papa to sit up. He weighs a ton.

I fill the glass with water from the pitcher and I try to give it to him. I take his hand and close it around the glass. There is no tension, no pick up, so I hold his hand tight to the glass and raise it to his lips. He sips at the water.

The evening is darkening but not in a good way. The spiritless light barely illuminates the room. Papa gestures towards the window. I think he is calling for more light.

'There is a power cut. I will light a candle.'

I find a stub of candle and light it. I put it on the mantelpiece where it flickers. Against the mirror the light is amplified. It is enough for me to study Papa's face, which is grey and dull. Does he see that I am looking at him?

I used to think of him as 'the absent father'. But only now do I understand what absence is. I understand that all his pedantry and his constant struggle to overpower my will have been a form of love. His struggle with me was his way of loving me. Now I am struggling, but he is not struggling back.

Papa, come back to me.

For a while I keep quiet and then I decide to start.

'They fired you,' I say. 'They fired you summarily. You are discarded. You, Chevalier de la Légion d'Honneur, adviser to the Maréchal. You who are exempted from everything, for your merit – they fired you, Papa.'

He sits quite still. But now his head moves. He is shaking it slowly from side to side. Is this a gesture of resignation?

Myself, I am thinking something quite different from resignation. I think *Damn you, France*. I think, we trusted you, France. M. Briand, *Aristides the Just*, he took us in and we trusted you. We gave you our lives. We gave you our brother Franck. We trusted you with our hopes. *Et maintenant tu nous fous.*

'This is so unfair!' I cry. 'We must tell the Maréchal. He will never let this happen.'

Tears begin to stream from Papa's unseeing eyes. It is the worst sight I have ever seen. My lion, my bullying heart, my antagonist, my strong defender, my father, just lying in his bed weeping. I put my arms around him and hold him. His shoulders seem already thinner, his body less substantial.

'We must fight!' I say. 'It is so unfair.'

His hand moves a fraction. I grasp it. It is quite cold. It keeps moving inside mine. I realize that he wants to write.

I fetch a paper and a pencil, and a book to lean on – the book, I notice, is du Gard's *Summer 1914*. I put the pencil in his hand and very slowly his fingers grasp it and his hand begins to move. He traces great loops across the paper. It takes an age and then it is quite indecipherable until at last

I realize that it is not French but German.

He has written (I think),

```
Man kämpft nicht gegen seine Mutter,
wenn sie ungerecht ist.
```

One does not fight one's mother when she is unfair.

'Oh no!' I cry, 'One bloody well does!'

Amélie is suddenly at the door, peering round. I realize I have just shouted. I quieten down.

'It's alright, Amélie, please go back and rest.'

I press Papa's hand and kiss his brow. I say,

'But you are adviser to the Maréchal. You have exemption.'

Papa moves his head very slightly from side to side.

'So what to do?' I ask him. His face is blank and his eyelids are almost closed. He moves his hand again and I fetch fresh paper. His hand gets a weak grip on the pencil and he writes again, this time a little faster. The result is clear. Again it is in German. It is an answer to my question *So what to do?*

He has written,

```
Man beugt den Kopf und wartet.
```

One bows one's head and waits.

Well, sorry Papa, but that cannot be the way.

The evening has darkened further. Sullen clouds shroud the last remaining light of the day. The candle is burning down. It is so dark I can barely see my father's face. A tremor like a sob passes through his body.

His hand moves a fraction and I close the pencil within it and guide it to the page. His hand writes again.

Das Entsetzliche geschieht jetzt sofort.
The Dreadful is happening right now.

He means that he has already lost a life, a life in his own country. And now the dreadful thing has followed us, and again he is losing a life.

'Papa,' I say. I have more to say to him. 'Papa.'

We cannot go on living in untruth. We are at the bottom. If we are to rise again, we have to speak the truth to each other.

'Papa, I know about Franck.'

The candle gutters. For a long, long moment we sit in silence. In the mirror I can see our dark reflections, huddled close together like two mourners, our miseries entwined. I can hear the breath sighing in my lungs. I can hear Papa's breath rasping like a smoker's. It is a long electric moment, of anticipation and foreboding.

He speaks. One word.

'*Was?*' (I think it is.)

With dread, I go on.

'Before your speech I went to Sully with Maurice. We went to get some meat. I spent the night with him. Nothing happened. He told me about him and Franck. He told me that he tried to be my friend because of Franck. Because I looked like Franck, I reminded him of Franck. He even asked me to marry him but I told him that was such rubbish.'

My father lies against the pillows, still like a stone. Do I really believe in truth, in truth telling? Do I think that in our misery, truth will heal us and set us free? Can we really learn to know each other again, if we are only honest and truthful with each other? I say,

'He told me about him and Franck. He asked me to

marry him because I look like Franck. I said no. But, Papa, now I know about Franck and him. And about Franck and you, why you quarrelled.'

I say all that. It seems right to say it. I say it and I feel free. I felt free because I said it and because I was honest with my father. I could not go on any longer in the old way, the old muddle, the old lies.

We are outcasts, aliens, failed *collabos*, failed *résistants*, failed French. Franck is an invert. I am a stupid little girl in love with... what? Ideas, the idea of love? Maybe with Maurice still?

Papa has lost his job, we are losing our life, our lives.

We are touching the bottom. It is a very long way down. We shan't rise again on a bed of lies.

'Papa,' I say, 'I love you so so much. Pauli loves you so so much. Franck is your first-born son. He loves you with all his being. And Franck loves Maurice. He really really loves him.'

This is the bottom. This is the bedrock. We are at the bottom. Can that be the firm foundation of our love? Of love for each other. France, whom we loved like a mother, like life itself, is deserting us and spurning us. We are at the bottom. Is that a foundation for love? Can we rise again from there?

Papa is still like a stone.

I touch his hand. It's very cold. The candle gutters and dies. I call Amélie.

27

Next day I get up with the lark. There is still no word from Mlle, from Simone. I go in and kiss my father. Amélie is hovering. I tell her that I shall be going out for a while. I go and change into my new best outfit, my Balmain frock that Alex gave me. I put my head round Pauli's door. He is happy playing with his lead soldiers and takes no notice of what I say.

I tell Amélie that Pauli can have *congé* today. I step out past the Old Bat and head for the metro. As I queue for my ticket, Germans in uniform push past. One feels my bottom and strides off through the barrier. He scarcely bothers to show his free pass to the ticket guy, who is a derelict old *mutilé de guerre* which is the only male specimen left to us French.

Us French? I have a nasty moment when I think that to myself. Us or them?

I dash onto the platform just as the train is pulling out. It is packed with Germans, laughing monstrously. One of them leers out at me, it's the mec who felt me up. He puckers his lips into a kiss. He looks like a monkey. I make a continental gesture at him and he laughs.

I wander up and down the platform, looking at the latest posters the Boche have put up. Most of them are photographs of *francs-tireurs* who have recently been shot. From their pictures, they all look about twelve years old, but then all the grown-ups are PoWs. These kids are too young to have fought the war, so they are fighting the Occupation instead. Desperate!

Then there's a totally huge poster edged in black and crammed with Gothic lettering and copious Heil Hitlering. It is an official announcement of a decree of the *Kommandantur* that the male kin of saboteurs will be shot, their houses razed to the ground, and their women and children deported to forced labour in the East.

Nothing, but nothing, has changed since the Trojan War. Except the efficiency of the apparatus that carries out these crimes.

The platform is filling up. A gendarme is standing two yards off, watching me. Does he think I look like an alien? Or a saboteur?

I am thinking about Papa, about his trust in France. He always said, always says, France is our great *mamelle*. She took us in and nourished us, gave us work and hope, gave us life. So we trusted in France.

I look again at the posters. I know who arrested these boys. It was not the Nazis, not the handful of Gestapo officers in their comfortable billet at place de Saussaies, in fact not the Boche at all. It was our police, the French police, the *collabo* police. Maybe even this gendarme who is standing close by me, still watching me.

The platform is full and at long last the train comes. The first four carriages are reserved for the Boche. Some are already inside, lounging on the banquettes, smoking and laughing. Two get off, laughing, one gets on and throws himself down on one of the many vacant seats. We French race down the platform to the back of the train and cram into the other two carriages which are already full, standing room only. It is incredibly hot and the air stinks of our sweat and dirt.

Suddenly I feel utter despair at the meaninglessness of all this. I have no love, and no purpose, and no hope. The mec crammed in next to me is wearing filthy dungarees. I can feel his dirt seeping into my beautiful frock.

France, the great *mamelle*. Well, I think, *Damn you, France.* We trusted you, France, the Great Teat. You gave us suck and we trusted in you and had hope in you. And then you turned on us, you took away the teat, you cancelled off our Republic, you cancelled our liberties. We gave you our brother Franck. We gave you our hopes. And now you turn your face away from us.

Really, when I think like this I actually feel like shooting that old fart Pétain!

But then France, you have one last chance to redeem yourself. Right now. One chance, heading your way on this very metro train.

I feel a sharp jab in my ribs. Some guy is jabbing me with his elbow.

'*Ouch*! What?'

It is an old mec in a black suit who reeks of tobacco from every pore. He says in a low voice,

'Keep quiet, Mademoiselle.'

I have been raving out loud, it seems. I give the old mec a grimace of a smile and he looks back at me, sort of sad and kindly.

It seems everybody is looking at me. What have I been saying?

'Fuck you, bloody foreigner,' one guy says.

'Probably a Yid,' another says. 'Where's your pretty star, Miss?'

But anyway here is Cluny-la-Sorbonne, my stop, so I mutter *Thank you* to the old fellow and fight my way out. People are already pushing in. There is no decency in public any more.

***

I fall out onto the platform in a frenzy and run up the steps to the street. Up there, I gasp for air. I go at a run down the rue St Jacques and into the rue des Ecoles. And here it is, the noble Collège de France. Here is the very nipple of that great *mamelle*. *Docet omnia*, the inscription reads. Teaches all things. Yes? Human decency?

I calm myself. I walk up the steps as slowly as I can and into the embrace of this great college, past Ronsard and into the cool high chamber that is the entrance hall.

There is a tiny desk in this great vestibule, right next to the marble statue of Margaret of Navarre. She is dictating the founding charter of the Collège to her brother, Francis I – the last time a woman had any role to play in this college by the way, but no time for that thought now as the receptionist, whom I know quite well and who knows me back, is peering at me through his pebble lenses as I approach.

'Yes?' he says, without really acknowledging me. 'Yes?'

'Well, hallo, M. Henri.' Years ago, Henri used sometimes to keep an eye on Franck and me while Papa was upstairs on his business. He even played *Bataille* at cards with us, shouting out *Bataille, bataille tous les deux* when we turned up cards of the same value.

Now he closes his eyes and opens them again. Word is clearly out, I am not welcomed, not *persona grata*.

But, *merde*, he's just the receptionist, and my father is a tenured Professor of this most mighty of colleges.

'So I wish to see the Administrator, if you please. Professor Deschenes.'

Professor Deschenes has dined at our house several times, while Mama was alive of course, not since, and Papa has always been on good terms with him, as a friend as much as a colleague. I've even baby-sat his pimply kids.

M. Henri's nostrils dilate sharply but he says he will

telephone to Deschenes' office, if I will wait in the little waiting room.

I sit there for a few minutes looking at the wall and thinking dark thoughts. A gendarme appears. He has a certain amount of braid on his uniform, so I guess that he is not just the usual *bleu*. And indeed he introduces himself as Captain Falloux.

He sits beside me and says in a low voice that I would do well to make myself scarce as he is aware that my father is an 'unregistered alien'. As the daughter of an alien, I must myself have registered. Would I care to show him my identity card? Of course, it may be the case that I have *not* registered. If so, it would seem that I am breaking the law. But he, Captain Falloux, can temporarily turn a blind eye to such an infraction if I just leave right now and don't come back.

'But we have an exemption,' I say. 'From the Maréchal.'

'No,' he says, 'you have no exemption.'

So I bow my head and leave.

28

Blam blam blam!

It is two days later. Like Papa, I have spent my time in a vegetable state. Pauli sits in his room reading the *Boy's Own Annual* or dishing out some strict discipline to his lead soldiers. I lie in bed all day. Amélie cares for Papa and makes us snacks from whatever she can scavenge. I have heard nothing at all from Mlle.

It is six in the morning and there is a great hammering on the front door of the flat. Before I can get out of bed to go to see what it is, I hear the door being opened from the outside. I run into the hall. Pauli is already there, by Ma's half-moon table, holding on to it. He runs to me and clutches at my nightie.

In the doorway stands the Old Bat, our dear concierge. She is flourishing her big ring of keys, one to every door in the building. Behind her, on the landing, are two gendarmes, two *bleus*.

'Residence of Schneider?'

I say this is where we live, yes.

'We have orders to search the flat.'

They come into the hall. Unkindly, they close the door in the Old Bat's eager face.

One of the guys is short and lean and grey-haired. He hangs back behind the other bigger one who seems to be in charge. At any rate this bulkier mec steps up close to me, too close. I can smell the sour breath on him. He is a sizable guy with a red face and a big, ruined nose.

'My father isn't very well. He can't receive you.'

Pauli clutches harder at my nightie. I rub his hair and murmur *Never mind*. He is a bit green-looking. He makes a little grizzling sound, like a small soft animal.

'Well, Miss, it's us that decides about that,' says the big guy looking me up and down. His nose is glowing. I feel awkward and exposed in my nightie and take a step back. I feel the curve of the half-moon table against my bottom and I put my hands back against the rim. I wish Ma were here.

'So where might he be right now?' His tone is rude. He's a bully.

I tell them to wait, please. I whisper to Pauli to go to his room. He throws his arms around my legs. I say to him in English *Go, Simpson, go, Dark Horse* and off he runs. I go to my own room and throw on my dressing gown. I didn't like the way the ruined-nose mec was looking at me. Then I go back into the hall and beckon to the two of them. I open the door to Papa's bedroom, just enough for them to see in. Papa is lying against his big pillow with his eyes closed. Amélie is bathing his face with a sponge. He really does look as sick as a dog. I hope the *bleus* get the point.

But they don't seem to want to. They push past me and into the bedroom. Amélie looks up in surprise. She stands up and starts to protest but they just stride up to the bed.

'What's up with him then?' This is the big, ruined-nose guy. His tone is rough.

'He had a stroke,' Amélie replies, sweet enough but super-defensive.

The leader guy, the one with the broken hooter, starts shaking Papa by the shoulder. Amélie jumps up and tries to grab the mec's arm.

'*Arrête*! Can't you see this man is ill?'

As Papa hasn't stirred or opened an eyelid, the guy stops shaking him. He gives a grunt and motions to his little chum and they leave the room.

'Now we're going to search your flat,' they say to me as they come into the hall. I pull my dressing gown tighter and fold my arms. It helps to control my shaking.

'Whatever for?' I manage to say.

'Well, we won't know till we find it, will we? Where's his, umm, whatnot, study or whatever…?'

'Errr, don't you need some warrant thing? Some authority?'

The big one pats his holster. There's no gun in it, of course, the Boche have taken away all their firearms, but he makes his point.

'Look, just show us his study, Miss.'

But there's Papa's gun in there, that's where he keeps it. When they find it, that will be the end of us. I can't think what to do. I don't even know where exactly the gun is.

I show them in. The little ferrety mec immediately clambers up Papa's library steps and starts pulling down books at random and riffling through their pages. Does he expect some secret cipher or counterfeit banknotes or something to drop out? The other mec, the one with the big, ruined nose starts looking through Papa's desk, also pulling everything out, glancing at it, then tossing it on the floor.

'Let me leave you to it,' I say. Big Nose flips his hand at me and I go out and run to Pauli's room.

'Darling, where's that gun?'

He stares at me, wide eyed and stupid.

'Papa's gun?'

How on earth many other guns are there?

'Yes, darling, Papa's gun. Where does he keep it?'

'It's in his big cupboard. On the top shelf. In the biscuit tin.'

'Oh, God!'

I run back to the study. The *bleus* are making a fine mess. The little guy is still up the library steps, pulling out books. There's already a whole shelf-full chucked on the floor. I see there are some holy texts there, Keynes' *General Theory*, *The Economic Consequences of the Peace*.

'Aha!' he cries but he's only found the little pages of notes Papa makes and leaves in the books. He glances at these and then chucks them and the books onto the floor. The big fellow is still rummaging through Papa's drawers, chucking stuff everywhere. He already has a small pile of papers under Papa's old paper weight.

I just stand in the doorway and watch. What else can I do?

'Well sod this,' the big guy says, getting up. 'Now for the cupboard.'

I can't watch this any more. I go out and close the door and head back to Pauli's room. He's now got his soldiers out and is giving them some strict punishment. One by one he condemns them to death and lines them up in front of a firing squad. I throw myself on the bed and pull Pauli's pillows over my head. I can smell the old pee coming from his mattress. I must turn it...

Amazingly, I fall asleep and I have one of those dreams you have when you are only so very lightly asleep. It is a dream of disorder and of death.

In a minute or an hour or some passage of time anyway, there's shouting and I throw the pillow off and sit up. Pauli is up against me, curved in a little S, his arm across my tummy. He's fast asleep and sucking his thumb. So it could have been an hour.

'Aha!' It is the pint-sized ferret who is shouting at me. He's in the doorway. 'Aha!'

'What?'

'You're snookered, Miss,' he says. 'You're for it now.'

I take Pauli's little arm very carefully off my tummy and slide off the bed. He doesn't wake, thank goodness.

The little *bleu* jerks his head. He means that I am to follow him.

Papa's study is a complete tip. They've thrown everything out of the bookcase onto the floor, and everything from the cupboard too. They've slashed all the cushions on Papa's old sofa and there's a sea of feathers. They've opened the window seat and hurled all Papa's old letters and papers around. And there on the desk is the biscuit tin and a nearly full bottle of VSOP brandy.

'So what have you got to say about this?' says Broken Nose, gesturing extravagantly at his finds.

'Nothing.' What else can I say?

'I thought all this stuff went to the Boche these days,' he says, giving the brandy bottle a little pat. 'So I wonder how your Pa got his hands on this little monkey.'

'Black market, I should say,' the little one chips in, looking at me.

'Yes, I think so. So it's looking pretty bad for your Pop, young Missie.'

But the gun! What about the gun?

But they say nothing about the gun. Why are they not talking about the gun?

The biscuit tin sits there like a huge ticking bomb. It's called *Chiltonian Biscuits*. I remember Ma's parents, my English grandparents, sent it for Christmas. It was our first Christmas in Paris, when I was six and Franck was eight. Franck and I ate all the biscuits at one go, when Mama and Papa were out. We ate and ate until we were sick. Franck actually was sick into the empty tin. *Chiltonian Biscuits Limited, Lewisham, London SE 12* it says on the side. A strange talisman from a world we could then barely apprehend. Maman cleaned Franck's sick off it and Papa took it to his study 'to keep things in'. It was always on the top shelf of his cupboard, sometimes glimpsed when he opened the big doors to look out something. Only just now did I get to know from my little brother what he was actually keeping in it.

The big mec's hand is resting on the lid of the tin. Desperately I say.

'Fancy a nip?'

They give a little start and then they both look at me for a longish moment. Big Mec's nose glows brighter.

'Well, that's certainly an idea, Miss.'

He looks down at the little one and some lad telepathy crackles between them. Then he says,

'If you insist.'

'Well, please take a seat and I'll get a couple of glasses.'

'Make that three, Miss.'

Matey! A matey booze up with two gendarmes who have just trashed our flat!

'Right,' I say.

The big guy takes his hand off the tin, picks up the bottle and heads for the ruined sofa. The little one follows him and they sit down on the very edge, amongst the drift of feathers.

I rush out to the kitchen. I grab two glasses from the dresser. I have to wash a third. My hand shakes wildly as I run it under the cold tap. I dry it on my nightie. I put all three glasses on a tray and draw a carafe of water. The water is slightly brown. Do you put water in brandy? I have no idea. But if you do, it being brown won't show in the brandy. I run back in.

The *bleus* are still perching amid the sea of feathers, not making themselves too comfortable. Actually they look a bit conflicted. This is all too weird.

I go to roll Papa's chair out from behind his desk. The big guy jumps up and says,

'Let me help, Miss.'

We sit there, the three of us, really awkward. I sway a little on Papa's rotating chair. Now that the worst is bound to happen, I am suddenly not so afraid. Sideways, I look at the two guys. *What are you worth?* I think. *What are you worth as men? Well, Big Nose? Well, Ferret Face?*

I hold out my hand and say,

'Anna.'

'Gaston,' says Broken Nose. He looks suddenly sheepish. 'Gaston Buteau. Sergeant.'

'René,' says the Ferret. They both get up and shake my hand. They ask if they may take off their coats and, *grande dame*-like, I say *For sure*.

'May I?' says Gaston Broken-Nose with old-fashioned courtesy. He is holding out the bottle.

'Oh, goodness yes, please do.' Yes, quite the hostess.

Gaston pours out three stiff tots, a good inch for each of us.

'Say when,' he says, proffering the carafe of water. I let him fill my glass almost to the brim. They take theirs neat and drink it off all at once.

I glug mine too. I am shaking again. I need to stop.

'Atta girl,' says Gaston, watching me.

'Have some more,' I say.

So he replenishes us all, again a big two fingers. Papa's brandy is going down fast. I can feel the heat in my legs. My arms are still quivering, though.

Gaston fills my glass up with water. Now they drink more slowly. They don't say anything. They are still on the edge of the sofa. The mood is becoming fuzzier and less unkind. And again, quite soon, it comes to topping up once again.

'More?' Gaston says to me, a little bit fatherly now. He even looks at his watch. After all, it is not yet eight in the morning.

I nod and he pours another two fingers for each of us. They toss their képis on the table and loosen their collars.

There is a knock at the door and Amélie puts her head round. Below her the little face of Pauli appears.

'Shall I take Pauli to school?' she asks.

'Would you?'

It seems a good idea to get Pauli out of the house. I have no idea where this is heading, but it can't be upwards. It's safer for Pauli to be at school, if our two friends will let him go.

The two *bleus* say nothing but settle back amongst the feathers on the sofa and sip at their cognac. Amélie withdraws her head and so does Pauli and the door closes on our symposium.

The two guys start to chat about their families. Broken Nose, Gaston, his wife has left him, gone back to her mother and taken their two little girls. I gather drink was in the frame, and in fact Gaston's glass is already empty again. I reach out for the bottle to give him a refill but he takes the bottle from me, quite gently, even with a certain delicacy, and he says,

'No, Miss, it's gents that pour the drinks, not the ladies. Now let me replenish you.'

'I'm fine, thanks.' By this point, three stiff drinks have made me nerveless. I think more would make me witless, which is probably not a good idea right now.

The little runt, René, talks about his family too. He has a

wife who clearly dominates him, and probably unfairly I imagine a large lady with a rolling pin, and there are five children, the eldest boy a PoW. So I tell them about Franck and while I am doing that they pour themselves the last of the bottle.

At last I dare to ask them,

'So what is this all about?'

They glance at each other and have the grace to look ashamed.

'Dunno, Miss, we're never told. We get the order every so often, you know, nip round to so-and-so's and rough them up a bit. Don't ever really know why. It's just orders, and we never really hurt them much.'

'But you must know who my father is!'

'Search me,' Gaston says. 'Just another guy who lost his protection.'

'I mean, what exactly were you looking for?'

'Search me,' Gaston says. 'It's really just to put the frighteners on folk, that's all.'

I want to keep their attention from the Chiltonian tin, so I get up and head for Papa's desk, keeping my body between them and the sight of the tin. I am going to fetch the papers Gaston has piled up, so that he doesn't have to go back and rummage on the desk. I glance back and I see they are not looking at me. I nudge the biscuit tin towards the back of the desk, so it won't be quite so obvious from where they are sitting.

I take the papers over to them and we sit and pass them round and study them. There are some letters from the Collège about admin and stuff, and there are a couple of tax bills. There is a prescription for Paco's skin problem, and a letter in German about the preparations for the Goebbels conference.

'Not very incriminating, this stuff,' I say.

Gaston mumbles that they have to have something to show for the visit, so I gather up all the pages and thrust them at him. My gesture is a little cross and this makes for an awkward moment but then Gaston takes the papers and holds them in his big hand.

They finish their drinks and gaze with a slightly surprised air at the empty glasses before they put them down very carefully indeed on the table. Gaston gives the empty bottle a little pat.

'Not a bad drop,' he says.

'Some problems are soluble in water and some are soluble in alcohol,' René says affably. He is clearly the philosopher. But Gaston wants to say something more. He leans towards me and talks in a lower voice.

'You see, Miss' – and he is a little blurry by now, which is not surprising seeing that he has taken half a bottle of brandy on board in about twenty minutes – 'you see, we don't like this any more than you do. Like the *rafle* the other week, that was terrible, with the little kids and all. We refused, me and him' – here he jerks his thumb at René who nods vigorously – 'but they threaten you like, and when you got the wife and maybe kiddies to support... And in the end, orders is orders.'

'And there's our pensions and that,' chips in René who in fact looks old enough to be nearing retirement.

'No sense rocking the boat unless the beach is in sight, I always say.'

'And you can swim.'

'And there aren't any sharks.'

They seem happy to wrap it up with these platitudes. They get up and start to take their leave. Gaston makes a sort of lurch towards me. I think he wants to give me a slobbery goodbye kiss to say sorry and thanks, but I quickly stick out my hand so he has to shake it instead. Then he says,

'Oh, Miss, just give me that old tin to stick these papers in, would you?'

Oh God!

'Let me give you a folder, that would be better, wouldn't it?'

'No, never mind about that, love. Just give me that tin.' He points at it. It's in plain sight.

There's nothing for it. I go to Papa's desk and I let my dressing gown hang open, like a screen so that they can't see what I am doing. I'm going to see if I can't get the gun out and slide it away under something on the desk without them spotting it. Then I whip the lid off the tin – and it is quite empty.

There is a very faint scent of sick, though.

Quickly I close the tin and turn around. Gaston is looking at me in a different way. It's a moment before I realize that, with my gown open, he is looking at me in my nightie like he did when he first came in.

I thrust the tin at him and make for the hall. There is a short interval, presumably while they shove the papers into the Chiltionian tin. I open the door of the flat and who should be there but the Old Bat. She stands in the open doorway, her arms folded across her chest.

I'm sure she has been lurking there the whole time, straining with her ear trumpet to hear what's been going on. We stare at each other for a moment, both of us really on the wrong foot, so postponing any moral tussles for later.

Gaston and René come out. They nod to me with a kind of mock-severe look which presumably is more consistent with their mission than boozing away all Papa's cognac. And off they go. Gaston turns on the stairs and calls *We'll be back!* but he does this in a not very threatening voice and clearly only for the benefit of the Old Bat who does indeed tighten her prune face into a grimace of self-satisfaction.

It is then that it dawns on me how it all works. It isn't philosophy or politics or morality or patriotism or racial hatred or loyalty to the Maréchal or even duty or conscience that make these people do what they do. It's just this family man thing, the wife and kiddies thing, the pension thing, that makes them do it.

They do all this stuff because they're scared for their pathetic little livelihoods.

But then, there is the bigger, deeper question. *Where on earth is Papa's gun?*

29

I need help! Automatically I think of Maddie first but then I quickly don't. And where oh where is Mlle? I slip out and send her another *pneu*.

And then, on the spur of the moment I scribble one to Maurice, to his address in the Avenue Iéna. While I wait for his reply, I have a little lie down as I am frankly pretty drunk. I get back into bed in my nightie and immediately fall fast asleep. Hours go by. I surface from time to time and hear Amélie moving about the apartment. I know she is tidying. I know I should be helping clean up the mess the *bleus* made but, well, frankly I'm worn out.

It must be afternoon already when Amélie comes in with a cup of tea and a note from the post office returning my *pneu* to Maurice, GONE AWAY. NO FORWARDING ADDRESS. And still nothing from Mlle.

I get up and wash. I scrub out my stinking mouth with salt and water. I brush my hair a hundred times, really hard, and feel my scalp pricking. When I go out of my room, there is Amélie carrying two cushions. She has stuffed the feathers back in and sewn them up. It's like one of those labours the gods used to put on people, or Cinderella's stupid tasks that she could only accomplish with her animal helpers. I try to thank her but she hushes me.

'Why don't you collect Pauli?' she says. 'You could probably do with a breath of fresh air.'

Pauli's teacher, the willowy and harassed Fleurette, waves me over and says he is doing alright now, not speaking much but at least not speaking English.

As though I cared about that. Just now Pauli could completely lose the power of speech – or speak in tongues – for all I care.

'And you?' I say to Fleurette in a flurry of feminine solidarity. She looks so bedraggled. Sadly she immediately bursts into tears and I regret the inquiry. My empathy is at rock bottom these days. Anyway, I give her a hug and she says *Thank you* blearily and steps away towards her desk.

Pauli and I trail out. 'What's up with Mlle Fleurette?' I ask him. I scarcely expect him to know but he says,

'She's sad because she's lost her job. M. Dupuy (*this is the archbeak*) says she's a Communist.'

I hold Pauli's hand very tight all the way home.

30

I wouldn't have called Gaston and René's visit feelgood but it turns out that it was a picnic compared to what happens after.

What happens after starts the very next morning when the Old Bat once again opens our door with her big key. I am in the hall at the time, on my way to the kitchen to prepare a meagre soup.

'Madame, kindly do not open our door like that,' I say stiffly, pushing her out, but she pushes back with surprising strength for such an old biddy, and one with a famous gammy leg. I imagine it's the black bile that lends her power.

'It's my apartment,' she says. She's lying, she's just the concierge. I manage to get her out onto the landing but she inserts her big black boot into the doorway and then I can't get the door closed.

'Here,' she says, and thrusts a buff envelope at me. 'It's government business, so I brought it up meself.'

She takes her foot out and I slam the door.

The envelope is not very thick and it is indeed 'government business', addressed to M. SCHNEIDER Julius, no Prof or Dr or anything. Printed in the top left-hand corner is the name of the department

Commissariat Général aux Questions Métèques

I go into Papa's study. Amélie has done a famous job tidying up after the gendarmes' visit. She has even put Papa's notes back in the books where they belonged and reshelved everything in the right places. Only Kurtner's *Nazi Economics* has taken any damage. The cover has come away from the spine. Fair enough, I think and chuck it in the bin.

I settle down at Papa's desk and put the envelope in front of me. As a child I used to love this desk, the smell of beeswax polish, the shine that Mama got on the mahogany and the smooth cool feel of the green leather top. There would be Papa, august, severe, puffing on his pipe and writing writing writing.

Now Papa is dreaming or maybe something lower, more vegetable. Will he ever sit at this desk again? I am not so sure.

And now it is me, only me. I must open this letter from the *Commissariat Général aux Questions Métèques*.

I reach for Papa's letter opener. It is a silver sword. It bears the arms of the University of Vienna and along the blade the legend *Honour to our Beloved Teacher Professor Julius Schneider from his Grateful Students 1928*.

All this was before, before. Before the Fall.

The blade is sharp and slides easily. The cut is perfect, invisible. I push my fingers in and draw out a single sheet of paper, rough wartime paper, like blotting paper. I unfold the sheet, it is a letter signed in a flourishing hand by a M. Chaboeuf, Noel, *Per Pro Le Commissaire Général aux Questions Métèques*.

The letter reads:

Monsieur:

Given the abrogation of the Constitution by vote of the National Assembly

Given the vesting of supreme plenipotentiary powers in the Head of State and President Marshall Pétain by the National Assembly

Given the dissolution of the National Assembly by its own decision

Government Decree of March 15th, 1941 has been issued rescinding all acts of naturalization made subsequent to March 29th, 1931.

Therefore, the act of naturalization of 13th September 1936 which intended the naturalization of Julius Schneider, Austrian Citizen, as a French citizen is ipso facto henceforth voided and all actions, powers and privileges exercised by you in the status of French citizen are considered null.

You are required to report immediately to the Gendarmerie of the 13th Arrondissement to register your correct status as a non-resident alien. You must surrender any passports, identity cards or other documents issued to you or held by you which may purport to show a French nationality.

Pauli is at school. Papa is sleeping. Amélie too, she had a wakeful night with Papa and she is exhausted. I leave her a note and slip out.

It is a crisis. I decide to swallow my anger and go to my blood sister. I go to her office. The collabos are having some sort of party and the place is in an uproar. Everybody is already tight even though it's only eleven o'clock in the morning. And Maddie is quite right. Despite being really nasty people, the collabos turn out to be very bonhomous and welcoming. They try to get me to join in their party but I just ask for Maddie and they say she is not there, she is out on some cub reporter trail they think. They don't actually seem to care. They are having far too good a time.

It will have to be Maurice. I race round to the place in the Avenue d'Iéna where he used to live. I hope that someone there has a forwarding address for him. But a very hostile lady answers the door and says that Maurice does not live there anymore and no, he has not left any forwarding address. And if I do run him to earth and get his new address, she would like very much to be informed as she has some unfinished business with him. In particular she would like her carpets and her furniture returned.

What to do? Stumped, I make a last try for Simone. She still hasn't answered my *pneus*. It's Thursday, so she won't be at school. I head for the Café Flore to see if she is there – and actually there she is, sitting in state at the table at the far end beside the staircase. And beside her is ugly little Sartre. A massive pile of books almost hides them both.

Simone is writing furiously and does not look up.

'Mam'selle,' I cry, 'Mam'selle!'

She becomes aware of me. She puts down her pen and looks up.

I show her the letter and she glances at it.

'What shall I do? What can I do? Can you help me, please? Tell me what to do?'

She rolls her eyes.

'Oh darling,' she says, 'we all have our own wailing wall these days.'

She passes the letter to Sartre who reads it more carefully and then fixes his extra power binocular vision on me. I cringe at the dreadful spots that have erupted on his cheeks but force myself to hold his gaze.

'You are asking, what should you do? Is that the question?'

I nod. His leering look is scary.

'Then, my dear, only you can answer it.'

'Pah!' It just comes out, Pah. My body says Pah to this crap. I think of what Papa used to say, 'If a son ask his father for bread, will he give him a stone?' But Jean-Paul Sartre does not notice Pah, does not deign to notice it. He says,

'Because you are free to choose. Or can be free. Because we can always choose. And because we can choose, we are always responsible for who we are. And we are responsible for the consequences.'

Pah. I look to the Beaver, I want to appeal to her. But she is getting up from the table. I turn to her again but Sartre grabs my wrist and holds me tight.

'Listen, Missie,' he says, 'listen! At times like this you must seek authenticity above all else. The authentic choices of the free spontaneous selfness, of *ipséité*. Do you understand? Tell me, do you understand?'

I burst into tears and I smack his hand as hard as I can to make him let go. I snatch up the letter from in front of him and turn and run.

From the door I look back. There is the Beaver heading for the filthy Flore *cabinet*. Sartre has already picked up his fountain pen and is writing, quite unperturbed.

I stop outside the Flore on the pavement and put my head down between my legs. There is a sharp little wind blowing down the Boul' Mich'. It tugs at my skirt and I grab the hem and hold it down. When I straighten up, there is this mec standing right in front of me, he is so close he is practically on top of me. I jump back in surprise.

The guy is tall, broad-fronted, with close-combed hair, clean shaven. A good-looking man. And well dressed, in a chalk grey suit.

Does this beautiful man know me? Do I, somehow, know him? The guy is looking so hard at me I think I must.

I decide to get in first.

'No, is the answer,' I say.

He gives a short laugh.

'No what?'

'No, I do not want to be in films. No, I do not want to sleep with you for money.'

'That's got that straightened out then,' he says.

'Look, just push off, will you?'

But he doesn't, so I turn and start to walk very fast, practically running, towards the metro. He keeps up with me, evidently a fit bloke.

As we race along like this, he tilts his head towards me and he says distinctly, in English, there is no mistaking it,

'It's about the Networks. Dina said you might be interested.'

Dina? Dina? By now I am really running, and so is he, but I am out of breath and he isn't. We get to the metro and he is still alongside me, so I slap him in the face and say,

'Just push off, will you?'

And he does.

On the metro I forget the mec straight away. I have other stuff to think about. I have decided what to do. What did Papa use to say? *We must all come over the high road, there is no other way.*

31

The gendarmerie is a disaster area, crammed with dregs and derelicts. It is a maze and everyone is lost.

At length I get into the waiting room where there is just a handful of other suppliants. There is the prettiest young girl, about my age. She has lovely blonde hair and a complexion so smooth it is like milk. She has a baby and she asks me if the kid's head looks a bit square as it's German. She says she works in the German officers-only brothel on rue Maximilian but she's having trouble with her health certificate.

Sitting opposite, there is a young artisan who is eyeing this girl with a mixture of scorn and desire. He says he's been called up for work in Germany but he got his hand mangled in a machine tool accident. The gendarmes have brought him in because they think he did it on purpose, to get out of going to Germany. There are a couple of grannies brought in for begging, and a pile of drunks who are chained to the wall and howling.

At last Gaston comes. He looks smartened up, less seedy than the last time I saw him. When he sees it is me he looks a bit guilty and takes me aside. I show him Papa's letter and he says it looks bad. He ums and ahs for a spell and then makes up his mind.

'Best thing,' he says, 'is to open a file. Things always go better when there's a file.'

I look puzzled and he explains.

'When there's a file, people think it's being dealt with, something's happening like. And you know how long a file can take once it's in the works.'

He takes the letter from me and puts it in a manila folder. Then, in a laborious longhand, he fills in a staggering amount of information on the front cover of the file. On a spare sheet he writes a couple of lines and files the paper in the folder.

'What did you write?' I ask, and he shows me.

> *Subject's daughter, Anna-Elisa Schneider, reports subject is unwell and unable to attend in person. Will attend in due course.*

'I'll keep that under my elbow for a day or two, and then I'll send it upstairs to Admin for processing. Knowing Admin, that should be the end of it, for a while at least.'

He closes the folder with his great meaty hands and smiles at me.

'Good luck then, Miss. Should be alright. I'll keep an eye on it.'

I walk back to the apartment feeling pretty hopeless and oppressed. I frankly don't put much faith in Gaston.

And then I remember Dina. *Dina said you might be interested.*

Dina! Dear brave Dina, Maillol's muse. Not only keeping France's greatest sculptor going as a national treasure but running celebrities through the Pyrenees. So what was that mec on about?

32

It doesn't work. Of course, it doesn't work. It doesn't fucking work.

When I get back to the apartment, it is late in the afternoon. Amélie is seeing to Papa's needs which are pretty disgusting and stinky. Then Pauli comes running out and throws his arms around my legs boo-hooing and he won't let go until I promise him a meat supper.

In the kitchen, the meat safe looks like it's turned blue. The reason is that it's covered with a quantity of chunky looking flies. I bat at them and they disperse to the corners of the room, biding their time and I open the safe and pull out a great packet of some slimy dark red flesh. It is the last of my share of the meat raid with Maurice. The stuff is a week old and has not done well in the heat. There are grey bits and it does not smell too good. I pare away the worst of it and chop up the better bits very small indeed. I have a few drops of oil left, so I sauté the meat, put it in a baguette and stick it on the table.

Then of course, Pauli won't eat it, he doesn't like it, he doesn't like me, in fact he says that when he grows up he's going to be an army man and kill everyone, which is actually not such a bad idea. Anyway, all this has the advantage that Pauli stops clinging to me and runs off crying to his room. I cut the sandwich in half and eat one half. It is truly disgusting. Then I go in and offer the other half to Amélie who has finished dealing with Papa's needs and is just opening the window to freshen the air a bit.

'Is it beef or pork?' she asks and then says the old joke,

'Waiter, if this is pork I'll have the beef, and if it's beef I'll have the pork.' We sort of grin at this and then she wolfs the sandwich down faster than you can say Robinson Crusoe.

After this I rest in my room, fighting to keep my lunch down. Pauli is quiet and Amélie and Papa doze.

Later, as it is getting dark there is a faint knock at the door of the flat. Amélie puts her head round my door.

'Do you know who it is?' I ask.

'At least it's not the *bleus*,' she says. 'Not their kind of knock, is it?'

I rouse myself and go to open the front door. And there is Maddie! I quickly slam the door in her face but she taps again and again. At last, I remember that I need her badly, so I open the door again.

She stays on the doorstep, looking at me. It really is Maddie but she looks like *merde*. Her face is blotched, her eyes are red with tears. For a fragment of a second I think *Merde is as merde does* and in that moment I am going to slam the door on her again shouting *Fuck off, bitch*.

But this does not happen. Instead I spot Prune Face emerging from her lair and peering about. I pull Maddie into the flat before the old cow can get a bead on her. I close the door – and then I embrace her. She is my blood sister. If she is in the *merde*, we are in the *merde* together. Whatever she has done, whatever this now is, is nothing when faced with the great foul thing that sits on our lives.

I hug my sister for all I am worth. Of course, she starts sobbing. We're all sobbing these days, inside or out. Even, it seems, Maddie, tough flinty virtuous beloved Maddie. I let her sob. I say nothing, just hug her tighter.

Pauli comes running out. He sees that it is his Maddie, so he runs up and clasps her round the legs and starts wailing too.

After a bit Amélie looks out and wags her head which means don't wake Papa, so I realize the group grief is getting too much. I prise Pauli's hands apart and shush him. I tell him to go back to his room. His little face puckers but for once he obeys and he goes.

'What is it, my darling?' I say. She is wearing a raincoat, belted up and she's shivering. I draw her through to the kitchen, my arm around her, then run and get a blanket off my bed. Maddie sits on the old kitchen chair and I put the blanket around her shoulders.

'Milk is all I've got. The *bleus* were here the other day and finished Papa's cognac.'

I have half an inch of milk left. I let it down with water and warm it in a pan. There is a little honey left in the jar, so I pour the milk into the jar to mix in the last of the honey, then pour it into a mug. Maddie takes the mug and nurses it. She is rocking herself back and forth like an old street sleeper. She mutters,

'Can I stay here? I know, I mean…'

'You can.'

'Are you sure?'

'You are my beloved,' I say. 'I love you like myself.'

But what is this mystery that has so reduced my self-assured princess, the girl who never suffered a moment's uncertainty in her life? I draw up a chair opposite her and we sit with our knees touching while she sips at the milk and honey, poor comfort though this must be.

We sit like that for a spell. Maddie goes on sipping at her mug of milk and we look at each other. Her eyes are big and dark above the mug, quite tragic. There is some mascara which has flowed with her tears and streaked her cheek. I gaze at her and she gazes at me and her eyes narrow and look black in her face which has no colour. Her eyes narrow more until she is looking at me through eyelids that are only slits. I lean my face towards her until our brows are almost touching. She bows and now her forehead is on mine and we both burst out laughing and crying all at once. I throw my arms around her and she lays her head on my shoulder and cries like a baby. I hug her tight and we go on like this for a while until she pulls away and runs to the bathroom.

I hear her retching in there and I think uh-oh.

I wait a minute in the kitchen, washing up the mug, then go to wait for her in the hall. She comes out of the bathroom with a clean face. Her hair is still wild, flaming Maenad snakes. I take her into my room and sit her on my bed.

'Can you believe Maman actually pulled my hair?'

'Well, yes I can. I mean if this thing is what I think it is.'

'She threw me out.'

'Christ! Drastic. But I thought Catholics welcomed new souls.'

She gives a start, and then she laughs.

'How did you know, anyway? Was it the barfing?'

'Lord, Maddie,' I say.

'What's that supposed to mean?'

'God knows.'

Her eyes are closing. I say, 'Lie down, darling'. I start to undress her. Of course, I can't help looking at her tummy but she's a tall girl. I honestly can't see a thing. She knows I'm looking and says 'Silly! Nothing to see here yet.'

I put her in my spare nightie, which is miles too small for her. On me it comes to my ankles. On her to her knees. I pull the covers back and she slips into my bed.

'Come in with me,' she says, wriggling over.

'Budge up then,' I say and she gets right over. I clamber in with all my clothes on and she puts her arms around me.

'I am so *foutue*,' she says. Now that really makes me

laugh, my BCBG princess, doyenne of the proprieties, saying she was fucked-up just like everyone else.

She reaches for the covers and pulls them over our heads. We lie in the dark. It's stifling. She puts her arms around me again. She is breathing in my face. She smells vaguely of sick.

'Is it your Boche?'

'Mmm.'

'Jesus Christ, Maddie!'

'And Mary the Mother of God and St Joseph and all the saints!'

'I mean,' I say, 'you are seriously screwed now.'

'Ha!'

'You're laughing!'

I mean this *foutue* girl is actually laughing.

'Are you sure?'

'About what? That it was the Boche? Why, do you think it might have been one of my other lovers?'

'No, I mean about the…'

'I am.'

I hug her tight and kiss her all over her face and arms. She pushes her long thigh up under my dress and we wind our legs together. We start laughing together and for a while we can't stop.

'Ouf!' she says at last and pulls the covers down. Then she wriggles herself up the bed and sits with her back against the chevet.

'Hairbrush, darling,' she says, and I get my brush and hand mirror. She tugs the brush through her flaming mane but it resists and she lets the brush fall on the covers.

'Turn around,' I say, grabbing the brush. Obediently she shifts round and I brush her hair.

'Like Nanny. Hey, are you still cross with me?'

'Very,' I say and brush harder.

'Just like Nanny,' she says.

Little by little I get the tangles out of her gold-red hair. The brushing soothes her and after a while she says in her normal BCBG drawl,

'Would you like to hear about it.'

'If I must.'

'Then I'll begin.'

'It was Maman who told me,' she says. 'She was staring at me all morning and then suddenly she shrieked at me, "Magdalena, you are pregnant!" I said No, that's just not possible but Maman grabbed me and marched me down to Dr Duvalier. We went straight in, in front of a waiting room full of panel patients and I had to lie down and submit to Duvalier poking about inside. Then the old pervert took Mama aside and whispered and Mama burst into tears, so I knew the worst. She just pulled me out of there and on the way home she said such bitter dreadful things, asking how is it possible? And who is the boy, you will have to marry him at once? Back home it grew worse, she called me a *putain* and tried to beat me. I hit her back and I called her a "cow", so there was this big eruption, and she came after me with some old cudgel thingy that Father got as a gift when he was in Madagascar and she was screaming *I'm going to kill you*. So I ran out of there. I walked around a bit. Then I came here.'

For some reason telling this story puts Maddie in a fine mood. I go on brushing and brushing. When she has finished her tale and I have done with the brushing and her blazing mane is smooth and glossy from head to waist, I hug her round the middle. She gets under the covers again. I get into my nightie and we wriggle back down the bed.

'What will you do now, darling?'

'Stay here. I'm going to live with you and Pauli forever.'
'Not forever.'
'Oh, well, just until the English get here.'
'Well, actually we're hanging by a thread ourselves.'
'How so?'
'We've had letters. First Papa got the sack. Now his citizenship has been cancelled.'
'Jesus and Mary and all the saints!'

We lie in silence for the longest while, contemplating impossibilities. Actually, I can't help Maddie, and she can't help me, so we're equal. Then we just lie there comfortably, thinking of our fates.

'It's a blessing, isn't it?' she asks at last.
'Yeah, right. A Boche baby. Just what we need.'
At last she says,
'Bags of hybrid energy. Boche oomph and Gallic soul.'
She goes quiet again and then she mutters, as though to herself,
'Actually, Annie dearest, it didn't work out quite right.'
'You can say that again!'
'No, I mean, seriously…'

I turn over towards her and wait. She says in a low voice,
'I mean I was just supposed to get the information. Not make love to him. Go just as far as you need to, they said…'

She turns over and I twine my body with hers, perfect spoons we make, my arms around her breasts, my fanny against her bum, my thighs against her thighs. She is all cool lean flesh against my hot brown body.

I wait.

'It's called TA,' she says at last. '*Le Travail Allemand*. They tell you which German boy you are to go with and what they want to know. You wangle a meeting with him at the pool or somewhere and then you let him take you out and kiss you, and you go on until you have some information...'

She was quiet. I breathed in her ear,

'It was that Walter character, wasn't it, the chubby-faced mec with the boobs and the brilliant sandwich.'

She kicks me.

'They're not chosen for their looks. They have to be useful.'

I fumble for her hand but she wriggles her body round so that she is facing me again. She props her head up on her elbow.

'Walter is a train despatcher at the Gare de l'Est. He's actually frightfully important. He makes up all the trains that carry *matériel* for Germany. My job is to learn what is going where and when.'

'And he tells you that? That's unbelievable.'

'No, of course not, not at all. He is very discreet and correct. But I've told him the only time I can see him is in my lunch hour. I tell him my parents are very strict and don't let me out at night. So every day at noon I go round to his office which is this brilliant sort of glass cage high above the Gare, above that big main concourse, you know...'

'Mmm.'

'From there he can see all the platforms and check the trains. He has this gigantic board there too where he chalks up what each train is carrying and where it's heading. It's a doddle getting the info. We snog and I look at the board and try and remember as much as possible. Then I pass it on.'

'Gosh! Who to?'

'My runner. It's super exciting.'

'And they let you in there? The Germans, I mean.'

'No, of course not. But he's the officer. He sends everyone off to lunch and I sneak in.'

'And...'

'What?'

'That's where you…?'

'Annie!'

I give her my piercing look and she laughs.

'Well, if you must know, yes, that is where we did it…'

'Did it? You mean…'

'I mean we only did it once. I told myself it was needed. The information was so good and my runner was so pleased with me. The network were passing everything on to London and London wanted more. I told myself it was the only way… Walter was pressing me, you know, like boys do. We went on kissing and petting and so on and so forth but he was getting sort of frustrated and then one day…'

She is silent for a moment.

'…and, well, the thing is when it came to it, you see, I didn't really mind all that much…'

'You mean you *wanted* it?'

She gave my hand a little slap.

'No, but I didn't really mind. And that was the problem. Because I thought if I didn't enjoy it, it wouldn't be a sin… and there wouldn't be a baby…'

'Good grief! Is that the way you people think?'

'Sadly yes.'

I feel her body start to shake and then we both burst out laughing.

'Gosh! What was it like? Was it worth it?'

She wriggles away from me to the edge of the bed.

'Almost.'

33

Maddie and I agree she must go to Maurice's. This is a bit of a mission as neither of us know where Maurice's actually is. Maddie says vaguely that he sort of shifts about and has a weird variety of living arrangements and they seem to change every week or two.

I think of Otto, but I have no idea how to contact him either. In the end I pedal off to the Abteilung and send up my name to the offices of the Noble Typists and after a few minutes Alex comes down. She is in a smart blue uniform with some stars and a ribbon on her chest. She looks a bit cross but she kisses me nonetheless and takes my hand. We go round the corner to a little café, which is full of German officers and super-smart *mädchen* in the same uniform as Alex, so these are presumably Alex's fellow Noble Typists. The officers and the well born girls are taking *la pause*, chatting and flirting. Some touch each other's hands. I get the idea.

Alex sees me looking. She still looks cross but she gives me a faint smile, which shows her perfect teeth.

'You see our role, Annie, pretty girls for the officers. Shameful really, but I suppose it would be no different back home. It is a sort of *coming out*, ja?'

She relaxes a bit and gives me a better smile.

'Alex, I'm in a spot of trouble.'

She gives me a wide-eyed look, more guarded now, which is fair enough.

'Uh huh.'

'I need to get in touch with Maurice. Do you know where

he is, or does Otto know?'

'Humph. Maurice, hmmm.'

I gather that Maurice is not in her best books.

'Annie, you told me that you were Maurice's girlfriend.'

'Did I? Well, I was sort of. At least I thought I was.' Alex looks doubtful.

'We went to bed. He asked me to marry him.'

Alex gives a short, mirthless laugh.

'Did he now? Pfoo.'

There is nowhere to sit, so we stand at the counter. She orders coffee for us. This is good coffee, real coffee. This café is actually reserved for German officers, off limits to us natives. But I am Alex's guest, so it seems to be OK.

'You know why I'm here, Annie?' she says, 'Why I am really here?'

I shake my head. I thought she was having the time of her life in Paris, so the question hasn't really come up.

'No,' she says, 'I am not here for the good time, not at all. I am here because my father asked me to come. He wangled the posting. It wasn't easy.'

She pauses, probably weighing up how much she can trust me, and whether I really need to know this stuff.

'Father sent me here to keep an eye on Otto.'

'Wow!'

Alex looks quite nervous now. The café has emptied out and she draws me to the corner. We put our coffee cups on the counter. She lights a cigarette and puffs away a bit.

'You see, Annie, there was a boy at Heidelberg, well, a young man. Very nice. Very correct. A *gnädiger junge*. He was a good student friend of Otto's. It was hiking, duets on the piano, swimming in the Wandersee, visits to Vienna and Bayreuth, student clubs, all the ridiculous dressing up and horsing around. But there was a closeness, too much closeness. Mother found a letter. Father blew up. It ended badly.'

'Christ! And since?'

Alex hesitates, drains her coffee cup and looks into it for a moment.

'Since then he has sort of gone to ground. Sometimes we meet some nice girl, very suitable, she comes for a lunch or a tennis match, but it never comes to anything. It always seems like he is somehow acting, if you can understand that. And always there are rumours, one hears things, as though he has quite another life. My parents are very afraid that he is… well, you know…'

I wonder randomly for a moment if Otto's parents would have thought of me as a 'nice girl'. But this is not about me. I say,

'Gosh! And you think Maurice…'

'No, Annie, I don't think, I know. I have seen them together. Otto is in love.'

I watch her face. She is saddened by this somehow but also I know how she loves her brother and wants him to be happy.

And me? I love my brother and want him to be happy. I think Otto loves Maurice but Maurice loves Franck. And Franck loves Maurice.

But this is so irrelevant. Franck won't be here for years and years and we shall all be dead by then.

'What do you think about it, Alex?'

She looks surprised by the question.

'What? What do I think about what?'

'I mean about Otto and Maurice in love.'

'Oh Annie, Annie, that is not the point, love or not love. Love I suppose is always good, even that love. But that is not the point.'

Alex is talking very low and very fast.

'The point is that there is such danger. You see them everywhere, Otto and Maurice, holding hands, flaunting. Questions are being asked. I *know*. Questions even at the highest level, in the Abteilung even.'

'Have you talked to him?'

'Of course. But you know him, he is very strong. Even as a child he always had his own way.'

Alex looks at her watch. It is, I see, a beautiful little Cartier. She sees me looking and I catch a glimmer of a naughty smile. I do like this girl. In some other world I would like to be her friend.

'Annie,' she says, 'I must go. Even Noble Typists have duties. And if you want to find Maurice, he is at 79 rue Montmorency. I know because Otto went there last night.'

34

I hotfoot round to rue Montmorency on my bike. Number 79 is a grand building of posh apartments, each of which takes up an entire floor. I am getting to know the type of apartment Maurice favours.

The concierge is built on the usual lines and gets full marks for the face she pulls when I ask for Maurice. Her lips practically disappear into a tight little lozenge and her scornful hiss *deuxième étage* is another triumph of professional *conciergerie*.

I go up the broad staircase which is lit by daylight from a huge lantern in a cupola far above me. I look up and see the pure chalk blue of the sky. On the *deuxième etage* the door is open, on the jar. I knock and call out *C'est moi!* and Maurice's voice comes back to me from somewhere deep inside.

I go in. There is a big dark vestibule with large black and white tiles on the floor and nothing else, not a stick of furniture. I walk through into what looks like a drawing room, with elaborate mouldings on the high ceiling from which a complicated crystal chandelier is suspended. The room is lit by three full length windows that give onto the rue Montmorency. The noon sunshine casts a bright light on the scuffed parquet. The only furniture is a rough deal table with a few old chairs around it. The next room must be the dining room, but it is quite empty. I wander down a long corridor – there are five bedrooms but only one has a bed, a huge Empire four poster with embroidered hangings, but not another stick of furniture. There are no chests of drawers or armoires at all. As I walk from room to room, the whole place echoes as there are no carpets anywhere.

I finally run Maurice to earth in the kitchen where he is sitting at a long rough country table, writing in what looks like an account book. He is wearing glasses. Never have I seen him in glasses and I almost laugh. But when he looks up, my unruly heart leaps towards him. I cannot hate him. I cannot love him. But still my whole being embraces him.

And I need him, so badly, so very much.

'Pop some wood in the stove, will you darling,' Maurice says without looking up.

On the floor is a pile of wood which I see is in fact the legs and seats and backs of wooden kitchen chairs which have been chopped up.

'In this heat?'

'Otto wants a bath when he comes over.'

'Maurice, where is all your furniture?'

'Actually, it wasn't mine, it came with the apartment. Sadly, I had to let it go.'

'You mean you sold it? Sold your landlady's furniture?'

'Hush, child. Although actually I got 60,000 francs from an Armenian for the carpets. And there was a nice chiffonier, Louis Quinze I think, but I could only get 10,000 francs for that as the bloke thought it might be repro.'

Against the wall a large number of paintings are stacked, all turned inwards so that I cannot see what they are. Maurice sees me looking.

'Rescue art,' he says. 'I got them from the Jeu de Paumes, they were going to put them on their bonfire of the vanities.'

I shake my head, not understanding.

'They're all condemned, decadent art, decadent artists. They were all going to be burnt, so I bought them for a song. So they won't have burned them, but they'll say they did.'

'And what will you do with them?'

'Mind your own business, little one.'

As Maurice's shady life is not what I came to discuss, I let this pass.

'Maurice,' I say, 'I need your help. Maddie needs your help.'

He looks up at me from above his glasses. Then he gets up and comes to me and takes my hand. I tell part of Maddie's story, just that her parents have kicked her out and that she needs a place to stay, a secure place. At once he agrees.

'Stiff-necked lot, the Grandidiers de Vernay, both the aged parents, *mère et père*. Just tell Maddie not to bring too much stuff though. The landlord is promising to come round any day, so we may have to move on quite sharpish.'

I say that Maddie is travelling light.

I pedal home as quickly as I can. Maddie is in the kitchen, sitting in the old high backed wooden chair that came from Papa's grandparents' house in another country.

'Maman always sat in that chair,' I say and feel a rush of love for Maddie.

'Oh God!' she says, jumping up. 'I bet it was a family nursing chair.'

She is in high spirits. She is wearing my blue dressing gown. It suits her red-gold locks which she has brushed over her shoulder in a swathe.

'I found an egg,' she says. 'I boiled it and ate it for my breakfast.'

I pretend to be shocked. It was supposed to be for Pauli's tea.

'Pauli told me to have it. He wanted me to have it.'

I tell her that she is to stay with Maurice. She is very pleased.

'Will he take me to lunch at the Tour d'Argent?' she asks.

It seems that, for all her woes, Maddie is *back*.

Letter from Franck

Dearest child,
I am so far from you, yet you are always on my mind and in my heart. I think of you in the freezing dawn when we have the distribution of cold *ersatz* coffee, and during my morning's labour when I am breaking rocks in the quarry, and at noon when we have a watery bowl lyingly called cabbage soup, and in the afternoon when I am back in the quarries, and at dusk when we have the soup again with the joy of a fifth of a loaf of black bread and a cup of lukewarm *ersatz*.

And I thought of you all day yesterday when we finally had the performance of Messiaen's *Quartet for the End of Time*. Honestly it is more mystical intention than music but in the darkness in which we live it was a bright beacon. Everybody crowded into barrack 27 which was done up as a rude theatre, and we were all sorts – farmers, factory workers, lawyers, doctors, intellectuals, street sweepers, priests. They even brought the wounded and the sick from the hospital block and set them out on their stretchers in front of the dais. It was as though they were to receive a healing blessing.

Old Messiaen shambled on to the rough wood stage. He was virtually in rags, clothed in a tattered bottle green suit that hung off him in shreds and tatters. On his feet were enormous clogs. Straightaway he launched into an obscure and moving speech, made more obscure by the whistling sounds that came from the gaps where his teeth have rotted away. But some of what he said was clear. There was a long quotation from Revelation about a mighty angel wrapped in a cloud with a rainbow on his head, standing on the sea and on the land. He even did some theatricals, lifting his arm over his head as he cried out *And he raised his hand toward Heaven and swore by He who lives forever, saying And there will be no more time.*

The music, it seems, was to carry us to those high realms in which Messiaen himself appears to dwell. He said that his piece would *realize melodically and harmonically a sort of tonal ubiquity that brings us closer to infinity, closer to eternity in space.*

Well, we listened in religious silence. And definitely it was an experience. It transformed the banality of the Stalag, transcending place and class and nationality. Even those who were musically ignorant sensed that this was something exceptional. I think that most people were quite bewildered both by the unusual musical language and by the intense mysticism. And yet there was a lot of lyricism in it, some fanciful and noble dances.

Frankly, we are all at our wits' end, starving hungry, emaciated, worn down by work and privation and the cold and the mud. If ever there was an audience that could approach the mystical plane of this work and have some comprehension of the music and the spiritual intentions of the composer, it was us.

At the end there was an awkward silence. Quite honestly, nobody knew it had ended. But then applause began, very hesitantly, and then uproar. Whatever Messiaen intended, whatever he had achieved, it was a supreme act of revenge against the misery of the Stalag. We all suffer from endless anxiety and bewilderment, but for that one hour we were all free, all lifted above this abominable earth to something that approached, for some, religious awe.

And so I embrace you, dearest little one. Be yourself for me.

Franck

This letter stays for some time in my inert hand. I read it without seeing it. I stare at the words without understanding them.

Oh, Franck, you and the mystical sublime! I get it, I really do, your endless anxiety and bewilderment, and to be lifted above this abominable earth.

But your daddy and your little brother and your petted *Schwester* are in dissolution. Come to us, my dearest one, just come.

35

Maddie has left for Maurice's. Amélie comes in to look after Papa and I go back to bed and have a sleep. Pauli comes and gets into bed with me and has a nap which is fair enough as the little kid isn't having much of a time. Except that while he is napping he pees the bed massively and I have to get him up. He is still drugged with sleep, lucky thing, so I put him down in his own bed. Then I spend half an hour at the big sink in the kitchen wringing out my sheets and hanging them up to dry on the kitchen rack. When I struggle through these slopping sheets to the kitchen door, they flap against my face like jelly fish.

I look in on Papa. Both he and Amélie are dozing and I leave them be. Sleep seems to be the best posture these days. I go back into my room and lie on my mattress, keeping well away from Pauli's disgusting big wet patch but I cannot sleep. At five I wrench myself up and wrestle my way through the damp sheets in the kitchen to make Pauli his tea. Pauli however, refuses to eat in the kitchen, and it is certainly very nasty, festooned with the still sogging sheets and incredibly humid, so I take the tray through to the dining room and we sit in there, up to the table on the old Louis Treize chairs. Pauli then starts bleating about there being no egg but when I remind him Maddie ate his egg, that he gave it to her, he says *Fine* in an adult sort of way. He loves Maddie of course, much more than he loves me, old Dobbin.

After the kid has munched his way through his bread and cheese, I read to him one of the stories in his *Boy's Own*

Annual. It is actually a brilliant adventure story where the boy hero Edward is being pursued by dogs. He is blameless, of course, but the dogs don't know that. They have been set upon him by some criminal master mind. At first Edward throws stones at the pursuing hounds but this doesn't put them off one bit, in fact it only enrages them and they bare their fangs and snarl and foam. Then Edward scatters aniseed balls along false trails. Apparently this works as the dogs become crazy going after the aniseed and forget all about Edward. Pauli pays special attention to this bit, presumably in case he is ever pursued by snarling dogs and has aniseed balls in his pocket.

'But what is an aniseed ball?' he asks.

I have no clear idea but I reply just to shut him up,

'It's like a ball made of Pernod.'

'But what is Pernod?'

'*Oh, vas dodo!*' I say and he makes a rude gesture at me.

'For Heaven's sake! Climb the wooden hill,' I say in English and off he trots.

Going from Pauli's room back to the kitchen to do the washing up I notice an envelope that has been pushed under the door. It bears no address and it is not sealed. I open it. Inside is a slip of paper that says,

> Je crois que le vautour est doux à Prométhée et que les Ixions se plaisent en Enfer

Ugh! De Nerval!

This can only be for Maddie. I fight my way through the wet sheets which are still flapping in the kitchen and rinse out the dishes, then I look in on Amélie and ask her if she can stay and she smiles sweetly and nods without speaking so as not to disturb Papa. I grab my coat and dash out and pedal fast round to Maurice's. The concierge's performance remains top notch. She tries to bar the door against me. However, she proves a venal soul. I give her two sous and she lets me in, and for an extra two sous she even lets me park my bike in the hallway.

36

I race up the stairs to the second floor. The door to Maurice's apartment is wide open. As I approach, a shifty looking mec comes out and shoves past me without raising his head. He is dressed in a grubby trench coat. Under his arm is a rectangular, picture-shaped parcel wrapped up in hessian.

I wander through the empty flat. In one of the bedrooms I see there is now a mattress, although the rest of the room is still bare. Maddie's raincoat is thrown down on the mattress.

In the kitchen I find Maurice, Otto, Maddie and Alex. They are sitting at the table eating lobster. Several bottles of wine stand open.

'Come and eat, Annie,' says Otto, springing up and drawing out the one remaining chair for me.

So we eat the lobster. There is a good mayonnaise that Alex says she made and Maurice ferrets in the kitchen drawers and finds a hammer with which he cracks the claws for all of us. We drink a lot of wine, it is a lovely cool Montrachet, and we talk about Goethe in Italy, the *Good German* Otto calls him, laughing.

'He said that until you have seen the Sistine Chapel, you have no idea of what man can accomplish.'

The evening sun slants in and lights everything with gold.

'It seems so normal,' I say. They all laugh.

'Remind me again, what the hell is that, *normal*?' Otto asks.

'I mean, so like what life should be like.'

'Oh, *ja*, eating together with friends, drinking, chatting about books with nice, cultured people. No threats, no cares…'

'I remember that!' Alex says. 'No Germans, no French, no English, just friends.'

The Montrachet has gone to my untutored head. I lift my glass and cry out,

'To life! To life as it should be!' We all drink deep to that, except Maurice who shakes his head at my childishness and says *Pouf*.

Later Otto and Alex sing folk songs in German and Maurice brings out a bottle of cognac. He says he swapped a Matisse for it but nobody believes him. We drink expansive and elaborate toasts to each other.

It is like there is no Occupation and the War never happened. Just us five, laughing, talking, drinking and singing. Like we are all in love with life and with each other.

Somehow this is the happiest night of my life so far.

It grows dark and of course there is no electricity. Maurice finds some candle stubs and we sit in their flickering light, smelling the sizzling wax which is like honey, and talking and laughing, talking and laughing.

Otto says,

'And why, you ask, did we not cry out?'

'I think we learned, didn't we?' says Alex.

'Of course, we had to learn. When we found that telling the truth was a one-way passport to Dachau, it became impossible to speak the truth. In some indefinable way, we moved to a different place and we learned how to live there. We learned English irony, we learned codes, we learned how to say one thing when we meant quite the opposite.'

Otto pours more wine.

'But you young girls, he says, 'you, Annie and Magdalena, and you my darling Alex, you are too young for irony. The attitude of the young must be hope and sincerity. You must speak truly about what you see and what you think. But without illusion, seeing the world for what it is and not for what you would like it to be.'

'But how...?' I start to ask.

'Just see right, *liebchen*. Vision is before action. You need to see the world right to act right.'

He pauses. His eyes are clear, they look beyond me to something that is not quite there. He leans in to me. He smells of wine and tobacco and brandy. He breathes,

'And that is the secret of loving, dear Annushka... Seeing well, losing yourself, setting aside that great fat self. True love is seeing people properly, realizing that something other than yourself is real.'

The others are talking. Otto's great chiselled face is right next to mine.

'I can't picture it,' I mumble.

'No!' he says, low and urgent. 'Annie, promise me no pictures. Man creates pictures of himself and then comes to resemble the pictures. You cannot see others clearly – and you can never truly love – if your mind is clouded by such fantasies. Recognize yourself and see others clearly. And so, so you will find love and goodness.'

He draws back. I am confused and he sees this. He takes my hand in his. His grasp feels huge and dry. He closes his hand on mine and squeezes it.

'Of course, this is not for today, Annie, please, not today. Write it down, no don't do that, hide it in your heart. Remember well, so that when all this is over...'

'But I might be old.'

'Yes, *une vieille dame accroupie*... There are worse fates, perhaps.'

'Or dead.'

'No, Annie, don't be dead. Please. Love yourself too much for that. Unless... Unless there is one big thing that only you can do.'

Otto turns and crosses his right leg on his left. He puts his elbow on the coarse deal table and rests his big chin on his palm.

There is a pause, like a touch and the long moment before you feel the pleasure or the pain. What is it that is coming?

'What do you think?' I ask. I am suddenly shy despite the heady wines. 'I mean what one big thing?'

He sighs and says,

'Annie, dearest, you will know, when the time comes. If it comes. But do that one big thing not for what you love. Do it for who you love.'

Pa and Franck and Pauli? Maddie?

He stares at me. His whole hard, wise being seems to concentrate on me.

'*Lieben, leben*. Life, love. It is all one. They annihilate the one, they annihilate the other. Hold on to both, Annie dearest. Hold on with both hands. Never give up love. And when you act, I mean the one big act, do it out of love.'

'And...'

He pours the last of the wine into our glasses and raises his glass to me.

'And so, Annie, take your time, love yourself, be yourself, look and see clearly. And then in the end you may just do the right thing.'

I am quite drunk. I say, I think I say, that there is too vast a gulf between me and the girl who existed before.

And Otto says something such as 'we have no props, no faith, no ideology, no politics. All we have is our self and the people we know and perhaps love.'

He raises his glass, or perhaps it's me, do I raise mine? Anyway, he says,

'This is all we have to defend ourselves against this great blackness which crouches over us and makes us no more than a thing.'

I think Alex is more drunk than I am even. She declaims,

'And we cry out only that beauty and truth should return.'

Schiller, maybe? Schiller, Schmiller.

And Maurice: 'Is there no chance of rescuing anything good, no wisp of truth or hope? Do we have any means to mould the future? Or are we just things before Juggernaut?'

'But what is that act, that one big thing?' I have to ask Otto. He shakes his head and smiles at me. He is too drunk to answer me, I think.

'I mean, I met a girl,' I say, indiscreet after wine, 'who said she took Walter Benjamin over the Pyrenees…'

But Otto is not too drunk. He says 'Alas, poor Walter,' and we all look at him. He goes on, just half-coherent.

'The Fascists would not let him in. He despaired and so ended it. His dream was to grasp at all the elided memories of mankind and with that to fight the present danger. But it was too frail, just a dream. The fragments of evil were too far flung.'

It gets too late for me to go home. Amélie, I know, will hold the fort. I lie down with Maddie on her mattress and we kiss each other good night.

Just as I am about to blow out the candle I remember the

message and give it to her. She glances at it, says Uh huh, and puts her head on the pillow. I can tell from her breathing that she has gone straight to sleep and so do I.

37

Our room has no curtains. The morning sun shines cruelly on my face. It forces open my reluctant shuttered eyes.

Maddie is standing beside the mattress, pulling on her skirt. She is her tall, virginal self.

'Jeanne,' I say. 'Joan of Arc'.' She tosses her head.

'I'm going out,' she says.

I groan. My head is stuffed with cotton wool and my throat is dry like biscuit.

'Does the skirt still fit?'

She laughs and puts her hands on her tummy, which is super-flat. She looks pale though.

'I think I'm going to throw up,' I say. 'Do you think it's morning sickness?'

She laughs again and does a little twirl.

'I already did.'

'Must you really go out, though? Why not rest for a bit.'

She is buttoning her blouse up to the neck.

'No, it's time,' she says and comes over to give me a hug, kneeling on the mattress beside me.

'This is my last time.'

'Ah! Was it that message? That *vautour est doux à Prométhée*? I've always hated that poem.'

'Me too. Really creepy stuff. But it's my code.'

She is still leaning over me, crouched on the mattress. She has put on her jasmine scent. Even as she fled the spiteful tongue of old Ma Grandidier, it seems she scooped up a bottle of scent. This is my Maddie, on form, unbeatable.

'And if…' she says, and stops. She gives me a big hug and a kiss and she jumps up.

And that's it. She leaves the room. She does not look back. In a minute I hear the door of the apartment close.

My mind is in a turmoil and yet the beast takes over. I confess I do not keep watch for Maddie as I should. Instead, I fall asleep again.

When I wake I feel, impossibly, even worse than before. My head is exploding and my throat is rasping dry. The sun has moved. It is shining the length of my body and heating me to the temperature of a little hell. I guess that it is by now be mid-morning. I must get back to Pauli, I must relieve Amélie with Papa.

I have been thrashing about. I have disturbed the cardigan Maddie was using as her pillow. I go to fold it and feel something hard wrapped inside. I pull it out. It is Papa's gun. Ah, the wretch, faithless Maddie! She nicked Papa's gun. Do I care? Right now, I couldn't give a damn. I slip it into my bag. Then I go to the kitchen to get a glass of water.

Maurice is sitting there with Otto. Alex is making an omelette.

I burst into tears. Alex comes and puts her arm around me and says, 'Come, darling, have a bite to eat.'

But I pull away, saying I must go. I run out.

And that was it. As I tumble down the stairs, I feel very afraid. Shall I ever live such a night again? Shall I ever be among such friends? Shall I ever even see them again?

38

Down in the hallway of the building, the perfect concierge is standing over my bike, peering at it.

'Where's the reg number?' she asks. 'I think this bike's bin stolen.'

I give her two sous and she lets me wheel the bike out. I know she is standing watching me as I pedal away but I don't give her the satisfaction of wobbling. Instead, I stand on the pedals and whizz away.

Like that I get back home in record time, under ten minutes door to door. So is it some sixth sense that makes me fearful as I race round the corner into our street, or is it just that I am shaky after wine last night?

The morning sun is shining right on our building and the Old Bat's black and white cat is curled up on the steps, taking the rays. It looks at me with its hostile green eyes. Its pupils have shrunk to wicked little slits in the bright light. As I go up the steps, the cat turns away and rolls in the dust.

I let myself in. The Old Bat herself is nowhere to be seen. Which is a first. Any other day I would have been glad to escape the steely eye but today is just makes me more uneasy. I gallop up the stairs two at a time. When I reach our floor, I find the door of our apartment wide open. Inside, in the hall, I see Mama's half-moon table lying smashed. Beyond I can see papers and broken china on the floor.

'Annie! Annie!'

It is Amélie, hissing to me from her aunt's apartment next door. 'Come in here!'

I duck in and she closes the door behind me.

'Where have you been? Where have you been all this time?'

At that moment Pauli rushes out of their drawing room and throws himself at me. He seizes me around the legs and starts battering at me with his little fists.

'You cunt!' he cries in English, 'you cunt! You went out and left me.'

I hold his wrists to make him stop hitting me.

'*Arrête*, Pauli, stop that!' Amélie has grasped his little arms which go limp. He bursts into tears. She lets him go and he throws his arms around me again, wailing.

'What on earth is going on, Amélie?'

'They came for your Daddy.'

'They took Papa!' Pauli cries. 'They carried him out.'

I have to sit down. Amélie helps me into the drawing room. Pauli is still clinging to me. I throw myself on the sofa. Pauli sprawls next to me, hanging on to my neck.

Amélie tells me the story.

'It was your friend,' she says, 'a Sergeant Buteau, he said he was the one who came before. He came round at about ten last night to warn you. He said you should all clear out if you could as they were coming for your Daddy in the morning. You were on the list too, and Pauli.'

I sit up and take Pauli onto my lap. He buries his head in my bosom.

'We didn't know where you were so there wasn't much we could do. When they came, there were four of them. Sergeant Buteau was in charge. He said his hands were tied, he must take your Daddy. But he said to take Pauli away if I could, so I brought him in here, and your dog too. Then there was a lot of banging and crashing. I think they were trying to make it look like a proper raid. I looked out and saw them carrying your Daddy down the stairs.'

'Was he awake?'

'I don't think so. They'd put him on a stretcher.'

I jump up.

'I must go. I must see the Sergeant.'

Amélie, dear soul, is in tears, her face has a crumpled up, crushed look, but she says to leave Pauli with her while I run to the gendarmerie. 'Take your time,' she says. 'Get it sorted out.'

'Don't come back here' she says. 'It's too dangerous. Send a message.'

Pauli is clinging to me all this time, trying to twine himself round my legs. I bend down and whisper,

'Be brave, little one, be brave. Like Biggles in-----'

I can't offhand remember what book Biggles is brave in but Pauli gets the general idea and lets go and runs to Amélie, who picks him up and kisses him.

'Come, Pauli,' she says, 'let's go and see what there is for Paco to eat.'

I pedal at top speed all the way to the Gendarmerie. My head is splitting and my throat is like sandpaper and all the time I am thinking Why am I putting my head in the lion's mouth? My heart thrashes like a steam pump.

The gendarmerie is hell on wheels, just like last time, cram packed with pitiful cases. But I have no time to worry about that. I shove my way through the crowd up to the desk and gasp out that I want to speak to Sergeant Buteau please. It is a civvy mec at the counter, all the blues are no doubt out beating people up and stuff, but the guy, a small pale guy with a black moustache and spectacles that are smeared with dust and grease, just says in a bored voice that I'll have to wait my turn. However, just then Sergeant Buteau actually appears. He has a file in his hand and his back to me, he is opening a filing drawer. I call out, he turns and sees me. His eyes widen. He looks suddenly angry. He jerks his head towards the door, just a fraction. Then he turns back and gets on with his filing.

I go out and sit on the kerb by my bike, beneath the railings that surround the gendarmerie. I wait what seems like hours and hours. I almost give up. I start to think that maybe he just meant *Bugger off*. And then at last he comes out smoking a cigarette. He strolls past me, sketching a gesture to me that I take to mean to follow him. I give him a minute, he is fifty yards down the street and then I get up and wander after him. He goes into a small park and when I reach there I see him dawdling near a sort of wooden kiosk with a veranda that I suppose is a summer house. When he spots me, he steps into this cabin and in a minute I follow him in. He is standing at the wooden railings that run along the front. He gives an angry wave of his hand and hisses,

'Get to the back, get right back into the shadows there. Sit on the fucking bench.'

I sit down in the dark corner.

'Where the fuck were you last night, you stupid cunt?'

'I... I...'

'Screwing with your boyfriend, I suppose. Well, I bleedin' put myself on the line for you. Came to warn you and all, and you weren't fucking there and nobody had a clue where you were...'

Sergeant Buteau brings his fist down on the railing. I say nothing. What could I say?

'I tried to help you, you little shit. And God knows what'll happen to me when they find out.'

'Maybe they won't.'

'Oh, you know that do you, you little Miss Know-it-all? If you're so bleedin' clever, where the fuck were you last night when your Daddy needed you?'

He starts walking up and down the little hut, cursing under his breath. After a few minutes, he tramps over to the back of the hut and sits in the shadows, in the middle of the bench, a few feet from me.

'You know you are on the docket too, don't you, you cunt? And the kid.'

'I don't know anything about it, Sergeant. But please, please you've got to help me.'

At that he explodes, talking fast and low.

'I already did, you stupid stupid child. And what good did that do? Fuck all, except probably get me shot at dawn, or lose me job and me pension and ten years hard at the very least for aidin' and abettin'. Oh Christ, what a fuck up.'

He goes on like this for a while. I keep quiet and in the shadows. I am shaking and crying anyway, so I don't have anything to offer him. In the end he does seem to calm down a little.

'You see, the order was to bring in the lot of you, you and your Daddy and the little kiddy. You were all on the docket. Your citizenship has been cancelled off, you're like your Daddy, an enemy alien.

'So the orders come through from Division about nine for us to do the *rafle* in the small hours as per usual. The lads are not all that keen because they are fed up with that kind of thing, doesn't seem to them like what we should be doing. But they agree because it's overtime, and orders is orders. I wangle it so I get put in charge, knowin' the place and all and having done the previous. So I say I'm off for a bite and a kip before it's time, and I nip round to yours, and of course you're not bleedin' there and the girl you left hasn't a bloody clue. I tell her to take him out somewhere but she says no can do, got to wait for the little Miss to get back. But then it's time for me to get back to the station and I hope and hope that you've come back and she's told you, but no such luck. So we had to take your Daddy. Had to give Division *something*.'

I shrink into the corner and pull my knees up and hug them. At last I ask him if Papa is at the gendarmerie, could I see him, but he shushes me because all of a sudden there is an old biddy walking past, red hat from which her unkempt grey hair pokes out, shabby brown coat, and before her, prancing on its slim lead like a princess, a little *chien coton* as white as snow and beautifully groomed.

The old biddy moves away, she is doing a long slow turn around the little park. Buteau says quietly – he seems calmer now –

'You know what it is, don't you, girly? It's more of the bleedin' *rafle*. Your Monsieur Pétain and your Monsieur Laval says all the aliens has got to be rounded up and carted off somewhere…'

'No, that's the Boche.'

'Uh uh. It's our lot I'm afraid, Missy. And frankly you and your Dad were lucky to escape the first round, the big one, *la grande rafle* they called it. Seems you had protection then. But you must have lost it pretty sharpish because your Daddy's been put on fast track now and no mistake. Orders from Division for him and you and the kiddy, marked URGENT and PRIORITY. And I don't mind telling you, Captain Daumier was pretty pissed off when we brought in just your Dad. *Where's the bint*, he asked, *and the kid?* and we've instructions to keep obbo on the flat to pick you up when you came back.'

'But…'

'Don't worry, Miss, I put old René onto it, you remember, the old chap that we had that little party with, and I told him to not look too hard. He's quite used to looking the other way, so you're good for today. But after that I can't guarantee who it will be.'

Buteau stopped talking and we sat in the gloom for a minute. At last he says,

'Sorry, Miss, I mean I'm sorry your Daddy got taken.'

'But where is he? Is he at the gendarmerie?'

I feel like a stupid dog, hoping for the best.

'Christ no. This is much bigger than us. We had to pack him straight off. Division sent transport right away.'

'But where to?'

'Search me. Drancy probably, like the rest of them.'

'What's that?'

'It's a bunch of HLMs out to the north, just beyond St Denis.'

'But why there?'

'It's the place where people are stacked before they're sent east.'

'What do you mean?'

'I mean, they're rounding up... erm... you lot, I mean, aliens... They're all stacked up at Drancy and then they get to go east. In special trains, like.'

'What for?'

'Search me. A new life, someone said. They're saying maybe Poland. Labour camps and that.'

The old biddy with the princess doggy heaves into view again and Buteau mutters that he must get back. But I just want to know one last thing.

'Sergeant, why are you doing this? Why are you helping us?'

'Pfoo. Fat lot of help I've been.'

'But why?'

He gives a sort of snort as he moves along the bench and

takes my hand.

'Why would I help? Because I don't think it's right, all this. I'm a Socialist, I voted for Blum in '36. Pity he made such a fuck up of it. But whatever he did, or any of the others, whatever the wrongs, nothing can make all this mess right.'

He gets up and walks to the rail. The old biddy walks past on her circuit, almost out of sight behind some hawthorn bushes. He puts his foot on the step and says, 'Well, tara, Miss.'

'But Sergeant Buteau...' I wail after him.

He turns.

'What? That's it, Miss, I'm sorry.'

'But what shall I do?'

He gives a sort of snorting laugh.

'That at least is bleedin' obvious.'

'*What?*'

'If I was you, Miss, I'd scarper – and sharpish.'

39

I give Sergeant Buteau five minutes, then I go and retrieve my bike from outside the police station. I pedal like a mad thing round to Maurice's. I am hoping that Maddie is back. But even Maurice might be some use.

In fact it is just Maurice who is there. He is sitting in the kitchen amidst the litter of last night. The plates are still on the table, the glasses are lying here and there. A dozen empty wine bottles are on the dresser. All that seems a hundred years ago, though. Even my hangover is gone, although my head is still throbbing, my whole body is throbbing.

Maurice is sitting with a mec, it looks like it's another of his art dealers. This one is wearing a shabby raincoat and he has on a pink tie which adds a weird dab of gloss to his otherwise grey appearance. On the table is a small painting, shapes done in very bright blue and orange.

'Hans Arp,' Maurice says, seeing me looking. 'It was in his show at the Jeu de Paumes in '38.'

The run-down mec in the pink tie is counting out francs in very small denominations of incredibly dirty notes, tens and fives mostly, and when he has made up a wad that is semi-thick he mutters *Voilà les cinq cent francs* and he shoves the pile towards Maurice. Maurice trousers the cash and the mec gets out a gunny sack and pops the Hans Arp into it. As he slopes off I say,

'Five hundred for a Hans Arp!' I can hardly believe it.

'Who knows if it's a Hans Arp,' Maurice says casually. 'And if it is, it may belong to some mec who'll be back to claim it sometime or other. Anyway, it's decadent.'

I have no power left to be shocked by Maurice.

'Where's Maddie?'

'Not back.'

And then I break down, right there at the kitchen table. I break down and Maurice just comes and sits next to me and hugs me. He has no idea, but he is my friend. He asks nothing, he just holds me tight until I have sobbed my heart right out. Then I tell him.

'What can I do, Maurice?'

'Pfoo,' he says, but not in his usual flippant way. He says nothing for a bit and I look at him hopefully. If ever I needed a twicer on my side, it's right now. At last he says,

'You know, darling, there's no good solution to this one. I have no idea about this Drancy and trains east. But you have one thing on your side – your Papa is a pretty famous guy and however stupid and nasty the Vichy and the Nazis are, they must realize they can't just treat him like anybody.'

I shake my head. It is less than a straw Maurice is offering.

'I mean, in some less rancid corner of their souls they must still care…'

'They don't!'

'No, I don't mean that they care about right or wrong. It's too late for that. But they do just care one tiny dot what the world thinks of them…'

'So?'

'Well, for example, they never treated Bergson like this. The world wouldn't stand for it.'

'Oh, God, Maurice, Bergson got the Nobel. And he went and fucking well died anyway!'

'But I mean if we could just get a message to the BBC and they could broadcast it to the world. That would make people sit up, wouldn't it?'

'Oh, I dunno. You do it if you like.'

'Annie, darling, don't despair.'

I put my head on my arms on the table and close my eyes. I think I actually sort of doze off for a while as big ghoulish faces loom at me for a few seconds and then I sit up.

'Alright.'

'Alright what?'

'Alright. Maybe Maddie can get a message to the BBC.' But then I shut up because Maddie has sworn me to complete, total and utter secrecy about her links with the Resistance and that means even her cousin Maurice. However, Maurice says,

'Yeah, maybe some of her Resistance chummies can find a way.'

'You know?'

'Maddie is my cousin, darling. I read her like a book. I even know she's up the spout.'

'*What*?'

'Well, a chap knows, you know. But anyway, Maddie's problems are Maddie's problems. Now about yours...'

Maurice gets into his idea. We will appeal to the people that Papa was working with, the ones he helped with that stupid New Europe thing.

'Abetz, the Ambassador,' Maurice says. 'He's supposed to be a Francophile. He poses as an even-handed guy. We can call his bluff. And there's the Old Gent himself.'

I have my doubts. After all, I've seen this Abetz at work. But what else can I do? So we get pen and paper and we spend the afternoon drafting and redrafting. My tears spill and blotch the ink but what the hell, by four o'clock the table is littered with second and third drafts and the complete rubbish ones are lying crumpled up on the floor.

At last we have a possible draft for Abetz. Maurice says Abetz is keen to see an equal peace between the two nations, whatever that might look like. Of course, Maurice doesn't actually believe a word of it. As he says, Abetz is after all the enemy.

'But sometimes, you can even get the enemy to do the right thing if you show them it's in their interest.'

It is a very humble letter, but who cares about that?

Anna-Elise Schneider to SEM Otto Abetz, Ambassador of Germany in France

Sir: My father, Professor Julius Schneider, doyen of the Collège de France, Principal Economic Adviser to SEM Yves Bouthillier, Minister of National Economy and Finance in the Government of France, Adviser to the Chef d'Etat Maréchal de France Philippe Pétain, Légionnaire d'Honneur, winner of the Prix Goncourt 1937 for his chef d'oeuvre *Vers l'Intégration de l'Economie Européenne – Perspectives d'un Marché Commun*, has been taken from our home. My father is a naturalized French citizen. He has never been involved in any political activity and has always dutifully rendered service to the French state as is attested by the numerous honours he has received. Since the Armistice he has worked tirelessly to help prepare the entry of France into the New European Order of which you yourself have been the leading advocate in this country.

I beg you to intervene with the appropriate authorities in his case. Thank you in advance and yours very truly.

The letter to the Old Fucker, as Maurice is now calling him, is easier, as he is believed to be a simple old soul who will respond like a Pavlovian dog if we just mention the military. This too is a very humble letter and it goes like this:

Anna-Elise Schneider to Chef d'Etat Maréchal de France Philippe Pétain

Sir: My father, Professor Julius Schneider has been Economic Adviser to the cabinet of the Chef d'Etat and has rendered great service to your government both in the National Revolution and in the preparation for economic collaboration in the New European Order. In this he, a naturalized French citizen, has steadfastly contributed to his adopted country for which he has the deepest affection and loyalty.

Arrested by the authorities, his whereabouts and status are unknown. A widower, he has three children, all French citizens, my elder brother Lieutenant Franck Schneider who was wounded in the recent hostilities, awarded the Croix de Guerre and the Médaille Militaire and who is currently a prisoner of war in Germany, my younger brother Paul (aged 6), and myself (a schoolgirl lycéenne aged 18).

I beg you, Sir, as the father of our country and defender of true patriots, to intervene with the authorities to obtain my father's release. Thank you in advance and yours very truly.

'But what address can we put? I mean, I suppose I'm on the run or something, aren't I? Sort of homeless, a sort of non-person.'

Maurice has a think and he can only agree. Whatever address we put, somebody will be compromised as I am a hunted person.

There is a sound from the hallway and Otto now comes

in, breezily.

'*Mein Gott*, who is writing their memoirs here?' he says, looking at the screeds of paper and all the crumpled-up drafts. Maurice explains and says we are writing to the powers that be.

Otto comes and sits beside me and takes my hand very nicely. He mutters,

Wer immer strebend sich bemüht ... him we can save.

'What?' I say.

'Faust,' he says. 'Faust. He has struggled in the service of man. He has reclaimed vast lands from the sea for the benefit of man. At the last, Hell tries to seize his soul, but angels bear it away.'

'Hmph,' I say. 'Papa doesn't need poetry.'

'Well, dear Annushka, it does give at least a hint of redemption, what your father has done for humanity.'

I cry out in vexation.

'Otto, *please*. No more like that. You've got to help me.'

He considers for a minute. His fine face looks strained. We all seem in a very different place from last night.

'Alex has a post office box for her private mail. Put this for your reply address.'

'But won't that hurt Alex?'

'No, I doubt it. They will assume that you have stolen it. In any case, you are surely not expecting any replies.'

'You mean you don't think it will work?'

'No, that is not the point. They may act on the letters, I have really no idea. But I assure you that nobody is going to write to you about it.'

We accept this and now that it is settled, Otto starts pacing up and down the kitchen. Maurice too looks slightly awkward, shifting about in his chair and picking up drafts from the table, folding them in two, then folding them again. He makes a dart of one and throws it at Otto.

Eventually, Maurice says,

'Look, Annie, why don't you make a fair copy of the letters and do the envelopes. You can do that here. I've just… err… got a painting in the other room. I want to show it to Otto.'

They go off together and I settle down to write the fair copies. I finish them and write the envelopes and slip them in my pocket. I will ask Otto to send them off.

And then there is BLAM BLAM BLAM on the door and I know who that must be.

40

But it's not exactly who I thought it was.

I jump up and look around, terrified. There is a pretty big broom cupboard and I scuttle in there. It's dark and musty. I crouch down amongst God knows what, pails and brooms and what looks like a box of straw. The doors don't quite close.

After the blamming, they don't need to batter down the front door of the flat as it is already wide open. I hear what sounds like quite a hefty group barging through the flat. I try again to pull the doors to but they still won't close. There is a little slit left between the doors and through this I peer out to see what is going on.

After a couple of minutes during which these mecs are rampaging elsewhere in the flat, the kitchen door is kicked open and a couple of them parade in. My God! These are not run-down old gendarmes looking after their pension. These are *echt* Boche *soldaten*. Their uniform is super-smart and I recognize it. On their shoulders they have the Death's Head. Gestapo.

The two guys stump up to the table and look around. I am trembling, crouched down in my cupboard. I'm sure it's me they're looking for.

Just then there is some furious shouting from deeper in the flat. I hear Otto's voice. He is shouting angrily, and some other German guy is shouting back. My guys cock their heads and listen for a bit, smirking, then one says to the other,

'Looks like we found more than we came for.'

They start chucking some of the kitchen stuff about, throwing some pots down on the floor, the ones I've just washed and hung up. Then one of them spots Maurice's canvases stacked against the wall. He tugs on the sleeve of the other guy who is just chucking some crockery out of a cupboard and they both go *Ach so*! One goes to the door and calls out and pronto a youngish officer, a Lieutenant, comes in and says *Gut* and then a whole posse of the others tramp in and they start pulling out the pictures and looking at them,

'*Was ist diese Scheisse,*' says the Lieutenant. I can see he is looking at a Braque.

'*Sehr decadent*!' says the guy who spotted them, he's got sergeant's stripes. They all laugh.

'So which ones does the Reichsfuehrer want, I wonder?'

'Let's take the lot, the big ones anyway. There's still a bit of room in his special train. And we can chuck the little ones.'

'Hang on, we've still got to saw that altarpiece into bits to get it in.'

'Yeah, but we can stuff this shit in on top.'

The Lieutenant orders the men – there are five of them – to 'take everything down to the van' and they start carting the pictures away. There must be a hundred of them.

As the last of the canvases goes, the Lieutenant comes in to have a last look round. The sergeant says,

'What are you going to do about those two shirt lifters?'

'Shoot them on the spot like the dogs they are!' the Lieutenant says, and they both laugh.

'But really?'

'I don't know. The French black-market guy, we could just give him a fucking good beating and chuck him in the cloaca where he belongs. But Herr Oberst Graf Otto von

Sternberg is a more tender chicken. Man-love is *streng verboten*, and bottom-screwing a Frenchie is like treason or something.'

'*Mein Gott*. What a filthy puppy!'

'Trouble is, the boss wants this all very hush-hush. It's been OK with the regular stuff, the Raphaels and what not. Even that fucking great altar piece is OK provided we can saw it up small enough to get it in a wagon. But this stuff is on his special list, it's all decadent. There's even a couple of our own lot's crap, home-grown degenerates. That's a Franz Marc, for sure, and this bollocky one is a Kandinsky or I'm a Dutchman. We can't make too much noise about this whole op.'

'So what will you do?'

'What do you think? Kick it upstairs, of course. Let the brass decide. We'll just take the two fucking sodomites in and turn them over to the Major. Let him work out how to deal with it.'

41

God wills me one thing. It is still the little squitty one, the skinny grey-haired old *flic*, the René (was it?) who is standing guard outside our building, just like Sergeant Buteau said. Well, not exactly standing but recumbent in the doorway, fast asleep.

It was an age after the Boche had carted out the 'big ones' and trashed the 'little ones' – they stamped and peed on them – and an age after I heard the lieutenant say in a clipped, not entirely disrespectful way Heraus, Herr Oberst. Komm mit, I have my orders, and then the sound of some shoving and slapping about, probably of Maurice but not a sound from either of them, it was an age after the front door slammed to and the silence of death closed on the apartment that I crept out of that stupid cupboard and saw the filthy mess where just last night we had such joy and I felt empty of everything and the desolation of the whole thing rushed in and filled the void in me. I went to the bathroom and was sick.

The flat was darkening, evening was coming in. I felt my way to the bedroom I shared last night with Maddie and lay down on the mattress where she lay last night. It was to conjure her to come back that I did this. If only she would come back, together we would put all this right.

But she didn't come. I waited and waited. It grew truly dark and a pale moonlight slanted into the room and fell across the mattress. I prayed for Maddie to return but no god answered me. At last I got up. I blundered back to the bathroom and splashed water on my face. Then I opened the door of the apartment and slinked down the stairs. My sabots were in my hand. The stone steps were cold and gritty under my bare feet.

I eased open the front door – the resident *tricoteuse* was not at post, by the sounds of it she was having a good session in the *cabinet* – and stepped into the dark, quiet street,

And so I arrive at Number 46 and there is the René – stupidly I think 'dear René' as though he were my friend. He is curled up in the doorway like a tramp, fast asleep. I shake his shoulder. He wakes with a start and eyes me blearily. After some moments of peering in the faint light he recognizes me, without surprise.

'Oh,' he grunts, 'oh, here comes trouble.'

He struggles up and stretches.

'Three months,' he mutters under his breath. 'Three months to me bleeding retirement and now the Sarge has got me into this.'

'Hallo, M. René,' I say. 'Can you let me in?'

'Blimey, that too. I'm going to be shot at dawn for this,'

He grumbles on. I stand before him looking super-humble but of course he can't see that in the gloom. At last he says,

'*D'accord*. But do what I say young Missie or I'll tan your backside for you.'

He pushes open the door. Inside there is a pale light from a candle which stands on the shelf of the Old Bat's half-door. The Old Bat herself is dozing just inside but wakes in a flash as René steps inside.

'Ah, officer, have you caught that mucky girl yet?'

'Not yet, Madame, but we shall.'

'And that disgusting little boy. You know, I'm sure he's hiding up there somewhere. Let me come up and help you look.'

'Ah, Madame, if only. But I have me orders. Keep watch, they said, keep watch. We'll be back.'

'Well, good, and the sooner the better. Clear out all that foreign *canaille*.'

'But Madame, if you would be so kind as to fetch me just a glass of water. The night is long and I have a thirst on me.'

Charmed by uniform and by *politesse*, the Old Bat pikes off to her kitchen. The coast is clear. I creep in.

It is ten o'clock at night when I telephone from Mme Bolduc's apartment to the Grandidier de Vernay residence. The Matriarch herself answers and I ask for Maddie. The *grande dame* hangs up at once. I ring again but nobody picks up.

I phone the Abteilung where there is bound to be a *permanence*. And so there is, the Occupation is a round-the-clock business, of course. I put on my best German accent and say I am from the Sternberg family and I must speak urgently with the Gräfin Alexandra. Some brief consultation takes place at the Abteilung end and then I get a number for the hotel where the Noble Typists stay.

I telephone the number. It turns out to be The Ritz and after long delays, there is Alex's voice,

'*Ja*,' she says in a flat tone, '*ja, wer ist das?*'

'It's Annie,'

After a pause she says,

'Do you know?'

'Everything, I think. I was there. Hiding.'

She says nothing for some time. At last I ask,

'What can we do?'

'Nothing.'

'Your father…'

'He refuses. He will not help.'

Again a long pause and then she says *Tell me,* so I do. Everything.

At the end she cries, she really cries, and so do I. At last she says,

'I must go. They are calling me. But tomorrow we must talk. Come to me tomorrow.'

She wants to ring off but I have one last thing.

'My father,' I say, 'how can I find him?'

'Oh, Annie,' she says, and the line goes dead.

•

42

The next morning I go out the back way and by ten I am lurking close by the Abteilung, over the road, in a doorway.

For an hour I kick up my heels. A couple of German ORs, already tipsy at eleven in the morning, try to chat me up and I pretend I don't understand and turn away. They hang about for a minute or two, offering me cigarettes but I keep turning away from them and at last they conclude there is nothing doing and stroll on.

The café is super-busy, German officers coming and going for *la pause*, little gaggles of Noble Typists tripping along arm in arm, laughing. At last I see her, she is stepping along the other side of the road towards the café. There are two other noble-born young women with her but they are walking a little ahead, laughing with each other. Alex is a little behind them. She is nodding her head as though she were listening to their conversation, clearly not wanting to show her difference but I can see she is elsewhere.

She spots me and gives a little start. She makes the tiniest gesture with her hand. I am sure she means *Wait there*.

She follows her colleagues into the café. After five minutes the other two girls come out, still laughing. They are carefree. A minute later, Alex comes out. She tips her head sideways a fraction and sets off down the road away from the Abteilung.

I trail her. She keeps looking from side to side, trying to find a place for us to talk. After a hundred yards she looks to her right and turns in. I come up. It is an *allée*. I follow her in. It is a dead end flanked by walls on either side. There are several gates, which must let into the yards behind the shops. For now the alley is deserted.

Alex is waiting for me up at the end, where some packing cases are piled. She takes my hand and draws me in behind the cases and embraces me. Her body feels like she is sobbing but when I draw away from her, I don't see tears. She just looks wretched.

'Anna, I am learning how to cry inside,' she says. 'It is a very easy thing once you have practiced it.'

We hug again. She is soft and smells of lilies.

'It is such a mess, such a mess.'

She starts talking in a very low voice about Otto and Maurice. She has found out that they were taken to the Abteilung. Otto was taken before the General, who said he felt *persönlich beleidigt* [personally offended] because Otto had been his house guest at the château. The general it seems has a strong revulsion from *Männerliebe*. He was so angry he called for summary justice, shooting Maurice out of hand and immediate court martial for Otto. But then came a call from Goering himself. The Reichsminister was not so keen for the details about the circumstances under which Maurice and Otto were taken to become public.

'So it is being hushed up. Maurice is to "volunteer" for work service in Germany. There are vacancies, it seems, for crane drivers in Silesia.'

'Oh God! And your brother?'

'The Eastern Front...' Alex breaks down at last and cries, really cries and I hold her to me as best I can. She is like a beautiful filly that has been lamed.

'It seems,' she goes on, 'it is not going so well out there in the campaign against Russia. They need more bodies...'

We stand a minute in silence and then Alex pulls away

and asks if she looks OK. Fortunately she has a little compact in the pocket of her jacket and I help her repair her face.

'I must go, Anschli,' she says.

But I cannot contain myself. I cry out *About Papa?*

She turns away.

'Ach,' she says, 'worse and worse.'

'But please tell me. Just tell me.'

'This morning I asked to see the lists,' she says. 'There was some problem, they wanted to know why would I want to know. Especially today. Noble Typists are not supposed even to know about such things. And on such a day as this, why would I concern myself with such a thing? But I pushed them and in the end it turned out they don't actually have them.'

Her long pale face is in shadow and half turned away from me. She leans against the pile of packing cases.

'You see, all that *rafle*, it was a French affair. The only paper I saw from the French side just said *livraison clés en main*.'

'*Delivery key in hand*? What on earth do they mean by that?'

'It means you French do all the work. The gendarmes do the round up and send people to this place…'

'Drancy?'

'Yes. And then they put them on the trains to the East, special trains. The French do all this, right up to the border with Germany. And there they hand them over to the German authorities, *clés en main*. And there we do have lists.'

'What do you mean?'

'At the frontier there is a handover, a *bordereau d'envoi*, an *accusé de reception*. Very correct. The gendarmerie sign that they have delivered… the cargo… then the Gestapo sign that they have received it.'

We hear footsteps. Someone is turning into the *allée*. Alex pulls me into the shadow of the packing cases and we wait. She puts her hand behind my neck and pulls my head against her bosom, I can feel her heart pounding through her uniform. She strokes my hair.

'*Es kommt, wie es kommt.* Whatever will be, will be,' she says quietly.

Whoever it is lets themselves in by one of the gates and we hear the footsteps no more. Alex goes on stroking my hair. I murmur

'Papa?'

She nods.

'Yesterday. Train 42-017. Truck 17B.'

I open my mouth but no sound comes out. Alex hugs me tight.

'Just crying inside,' she says. 'We must all learn it.'

At last I can speak, it is just one word, it is all I can say,

'Truck?'

'Yes. Truck.'

She hugs me again. At last I ask if she knows where the train was going but she says that is not mentioned.

'Can we see each other again?'

She shakes her head.

'They have made me resign, because of Otto. I have to finish here and then I am to pack up his things. I leave tomorrow for Berlin.'

I grasp her hand.

'I so much loved knowing you, Alex. I loved our evening at Maurice's.'

She kisses me on either cheek and hugs me tight. She murmurs,

'Perhaps after all this, we will meet again.'

She walks off and I watch her go, slim, tall, noble girl.

Everything now is loss.
And me? I realize that I have literally nowhere I can go. But I must get Pauli. And where, oh where is Maddie?

43

I join the shabby throng tramping down the grubby steps to the metro. There is a hold up, someone has fainted further down, I think, or maybe dropped dead of hunger or boredom or vexation or thrown themselves on the line or something, and we move very slowly and then barely at all. I look at the posters which are plastered all the way down.

There is nothing good, only orders and prohibitions and restrictions. There are penalties for the least infraction in our shrivelled lives. If we dare to raise our heads, if we ever dare to say *Non*, our men will be shot, our women and children deported, our house razed to the ground and our name erased from memory.

And then there is Maddie's photograph.

The crowd is moving now and presses on me from behind. I stumble and almost fall. A bloke catches my arm and says, Careful, Miss, and I am carried on to the bottom of the steps by the push of the crowd. I turn and look up the black steps, over the dark crowd. My eyes are dazzled by the light.

I grasp the rail and try to go back up. It is just five steps to that photograph. I can see the fuzzy square and the white of Maddie's face from where I am. I am hemmed in, pushed against the filthy wall by people crowding down, impatient, shoving past me, muttering to themselves. But I must get back up. I start to push up, step by step, pressing upwards and there she is, my Maddie, blurry on the yellow poster, but it is her.

The photo is from her first communion. She is neat in a

white blouse, buttoned at the throat. There is a crucifix on her breast, held by a slim chain around her neck. A broad ribbon draws her hair back, showing her high forehead. Her eyes look out, confident.

Deutsches Reich

Magdalena Françoise Grandidier de Vernay, 19, journalist, shot for espionage and treating with the enemy. By order.

SD Reichsgruppenführer Weil

44

I say, I have come for my sister.
They say. Who is your sister?
I say. Maddie. Magdalena.
They say, Your father came.
I say, I have no father.
The thin sergeant says, Well, he came. *Désolé*.

The thin sergeant goes. The young gendarme lingers, looking around me but not at me. Me, I look at him. He is a child, too much of a child to have gone to the War. There is a fuzz below his fat nose. It follows the curve of his fat lip. Soon he will be trying to pass for a man. Or for what passes for a man in these days.

In the meantime he is already doing dirty work.
I say, Did he take her?
The boy says, No, he left her to us.
My heart springs towards her.
I say, Let me see her then.
He says, Fuck off.
I say, I just want to hold her.
He says, *Foutes le camp*, Fuck off, you weirdo.

His eyes are shifting from side to side, then looking down. He can't stand the brightness of my unwashed face.

He says, You're crazy, you know that.
I say, Just let me see my sister.
He says, Too late, witch. She's pushing up the daisies.

Something rushes up inside me. It starts deep down, around my bowels and rushes up to my heart and then my throat, and then to my eyes. I feel the tears spurt out. My eyes are pools that drown my sight.

I say, Just let me see.

He looks straight at me at last. His pasty face is full of indecision.

He says, It's just a patch of ground, just a *lopin de terre*.

I say, I don't believe you. Let me see.

He says, No.

I step up to him and push my bosom against his chest. He steps back, startled.

Go home, he says.

I have no home, I say.

Go somewhere. Go anywhere. Just go away.

Alright, I say, docile.

He looks surprised.

I am sorry, he says.

That's OK, I say. There is another way.

A more active way to mourn my sister.

It feels wicked to be alive without her. I have only one wish now in life and that is to do what she so wished to do, and so end it.

45

I cannot believe this mec is English. He speaks Parisian French like a native.

But why would I care? Mama always said, *Any port in a storm*.

I just ask, me *and* Pauli? He ums and ahs a bit but he doesn't really seem put off by the idea. He says coolly,

'For part of it, an *en famille* look could even help. On the trains, for example.'

He asks a couple of questions about Pauli, how big he is, does he do what he is told, is he a cry-baby, does he sneeze in the sunshine, stuff like that, which I presume is to do with whether Pauli would give us away or not. It all seems quite thorough, quite professional, although he omits to ask if Pauli is a bed-wetter.

I tell him Pauli is an Anglophile and half-English, and that he is well versed in adventure and escape. The mec, whose name it turns out is Nick, or at least he says it is, asks how that is and when I say the *Boy's Own Annual* and Biggles, mostly, he laughs out loud, so he probably is English after all.

Anyway, 'Nick' says he is up for it. This afternoon we leave, tomorrow we will be in Vichyland, which is a sort of escape although no doubt all our troubles will go with us. I say this to Nick, just to let him know my mood and he nods and grins and says

Caelum non animum mutant qui trans mare currunt
[They change the sky and not their soul, those who run across the sea]

And when I get him to repeat it and once I figure out his weird Latin accent, I get it and when I say Horace Epistles One he looks delighted, like it was his birthday or something.

And the price, because there is a price to paid for everything?

Well, nothing much. Except that we are going to kill the Old Gaffer after all.

THE END

The Author

Christopher Ward is an author who writes both fiction and non-fiction. He has written about the natural world and has published four books on the environment and the consequences of scarcity and climate change. He has written half a dozen novels that deal with themes of life and love and responsibility, including three books that take up themes about humanity and the ends of life mooted by JM Keynes. All these novels are in the press or are coming soon, including the sequel to *The Resistance of Anna and Magdalena*. He lives on Dartmoor with his beloved, Isabelle Ruth, the artist.

Printed in Great Britain
by Amazon

49470048R00219